£3

D1492698

PARA HANDY TALES

PARA HANDY TALES

BY

NEIL MUNRO
('HUGH FOULIS')

William Blackwood & Sons Ltd.
Edinburgh and London
1966

EXECUTORS OF THE LATE DR NEIL MUNRO

PARA HANDY AND OTHER TALES

First Impression	November 1931
Second Impression	January 1933
Third Impression	August 1937
Fourth Impression	January 1941
Fifth Impression	June 1942
Sixth Impression	January 1943
Seventh Impression	September 1943
Eighth Impression	November 1944
Ninth Impression	October 1945
Tenth Impression	May 1947
Eleventh Impression	October 1948
Twelfth Impression	December 1951

PARA HANDY TALES

First Impression	January 1955
Second Impression	January 1958
Third Impression	December 1960
Fourth Impression	November 1963
Fifth Impression	December 1966

PRINTED IN GREAT BRITAIN BY
WILLIAM BLACKWOOD & SONS LTD., EDINBURGH

CONTENTS

IN HIGHLAND HARBOURS
WITH PARA HANDY

HURRICANE JACK OF THE *VITAL SPARK*

FOREWORD

FIFTY years ago the 'Evening News' of Glasgow began to publish a series of light sketches by an unknown writer, "Hugh Foulis." No daily paper in Scotland had produced anything of the kind so perfect in its depiction of the shrewd and quietly ironic humour that is a part of the character of the Scots of Glasgow and the West Coast.

For many years Neil Munro, the author of these tales, concealed his identity, and it was only with the greatest reluctance that he later allowed them to be published in book form; for they were merely a hobby, by-products from the literary workshop in which he fashioned his serious novels—'The New Road,' 'Gilian the Dreamer,' 'John Splendid' and the others; and, indeed, he was not greatly interested in the popularity of these humorous tales.

After his death, in 1931, all the sketches were collected for the first time and published under the title 'Para Handy and Other Tales,' a book which went to twelve impressions.

This new volume, 'Para Handy Tales' has been completely reprinted. It is, as it were, a farewell to Erchie and Jimmy Swan: but Para Handy and the *Vital Spark* survive, and will last for as long as ships are launched in the Clyde, and puffers—the *Maggies* of this generation—continue on their independent and lawful occasions in the waters of the West Coast of Scotland.

THE *VITAL SPARK*

THE *VITAL SPARK*

I

PARA HANDY, MASTER MARINER

A SHORT, thick-set man, with a red beard, a hard round felt hat, ridiculously out of harmony with a blue pilot jacket and trousers and a seaman's jersey, his hands immersed deeply in those pockets our fathers (and the heroes of Rabelais) used to wear behind a front flap, he would have attracted my notice even if he had not, unaware of my presence so close behind him, been humming to himself the chorus of a song that used to be very popular on gabbarts, but is now gone out of date, like "The Captain with the Whiskers took a Sly Glance at Me." You may have heard it thirty years ago, before the steam puffer came in to sweep the sailing smack from all the seas that lie between Bowling and Stornoway. It runs—

> " Young Munro he took a notion
> For to sail across the sea,
> And he left his true love weeping,
> All alone on Greenock Quay,"

and by that sign, and by his red beard, and by a curious gesture he had, as if he were now and then going to scratch his ear and only determined not to do it when his hand was up, I knew he was one of the Macfarlanes. There were ten Macfarlanes, all men, except one, and he was a valet, but the family did their best to conceal the fact, and said he was away on the yachts, and making that much money he had not time to write a scrape home.

" I think I ought to know you," I said to the vocalist with the hard hat. " You are a Macfarlane: either the Beekan, or Kail, or the Nipper, or Keep Dark, or Para Handy——"

"As sure as daith," said he, "I'm chust Para Handy, and I ken your name fine, but I cannot chust mind your face." He had turned round on the pawl he sat on, without taking his hands from his pockets, and looked up at me where I stood beside him, watching a river steamer being warped into the pier.

" My goodness! " he said about ten minutes later, when he had wormed my whole history out of me; " and you'll be writing things for the papers? Cot bless me! and do you tell me you can be makin' a living off that? I'm not asking you, mind, hoo mich you'll be makin', don't tell me; not a cheep! not a cheep! But I'll wudger it's more than Maclean the munister. But och! I'm not saying: it iss not my business. The munister has two hundred in the year and a coo's gress; he iss aye the big man up yonder, but it iss me would like to show him he wass not so big a man as yourself. Eh? But not a cheep! not a cheep! A Macfarlane would never put his nose into another man's oar."

"And where have you been this long while?" I asked, having let it sink into his mind that there was no chance to-day of his learning my exact income, expenditure, and how much I had in the bank.

" Me! " said he; " I am going up and down like

yon fellow in the Scruptures—what wass his name? Sampson—seeking what I may devour. I am out of a chob. Chust that: out of a chob. You'll not be hearin' of anybody in your line that iss in want of a skipper? "

Skippers, I said, were in rare demand in my line of business. We hadn't used a skipper for years.

" Chust that! chust that! I only mentioned it in case. You are making things for newspapers, my Cot! what will they not do now for the penny? Well, that is it; I am out of a chob; chust putting bye the time. I'm not vexed for myself, so mich as for poor Dougie. Dougie wass mate, and I wass skipper. I don't know if you kent the *Fital Spark*? "

The *Vital Spark*, I confessed, was well known to me as the most uncertain puffer that ever kept the Old New-Year in Upper Lochfyne.

" That wass her! " said Macfarlane, almost weeping. " There was never the bate of her, and I have sailed in her four years over twenty with my hert in my mooth for fear of her boiler. If you never saw the *Fital Spark*, she is aal hold, with the boiler behind, four men and a derrick, and a watter-butt and a pan loaf in the fo'c'sle. Oh man! she wass the beauty! She was chust sublime! She should be carryin' nothing but gentry for passengers, or nice genteel luggage for the shooting-lodges, but there they would be spoilin' her and rubbin' all the pent off her with their coals, and sand, and whunstone, and oak bark, and timber, and trash like that."

" I understood she had one weakness at least, that her boiler was apt to prime."

" It's a —— lie," cried Macfarlane, quite furious;

" her boiler never primed more than wance a month, and that wass not with fair play. If Dougie wass here he would tell you.

" I wass ass prood of that boat ass the Duke of Argyll, ay, or Lord Breadalbane. If you would see me waalkin' aboot on her dake when we wass lyin' at the quay! There wasna the like of it in the West Hielan's. I wass chust sublime! She had a gold bead aboot her; it's no lie I am tellin' you, and I would be pentin' her oot of my own pocket every time we went to Arran for gravel. She drawed four feet forrit and nine aft, and she could go like the duvvle."

" I have heard it put at five knots," I said maliciously.

Macfarlane bounded from his seat. " Five knots! " he cried. "Show me the man that says five knots, and I will make him swallow the hatchet. Six knots, ass sure ass my name iss Macfarlane; many a time between the Skate and Otter. If Dougie wass here he would tell you. But I am not braggin' aboot her sailin'; it wass her looks. Man, she was smert, smert! Every time she wass new pented I would be puttin' on my Sunday clothes. There wass a time yonder they would be callin' me Two-flag Peter in Loch Fyne. It wass wance the Queen had a jubilee, and we had but the wan flag, but a Macfarlane never wass bate, and I put up the wan flag and a regatta shirt, and I'm telling you she looked chust sublime! "

" I forget who it was once told me she was very wet," I cooed blandly; " that with a head wind the *Vital Spark* nearly went out altogether. Of course, people will say nasty things about these hookers. They say she was very ill to trim, too."

Macfarlane jumped up again, grinding his teeth, and

his face purple. He could hardly speak with indignation. "Trum!" he shouted. "Did you say
'trum'? You could trum her with the wan hand
behind your back and you lookin' the other way. To
the duvvle with your trum! And they would be sayin'
she wass wet! If Dougie wass here he would tell you.
She would not take in wan cup of watter unless it wass
for synin' oot the dishes. She wass that dry she would
not wet a postage stamp unless we slung it over the
side in a pail. She wass sublime, chust sublime!

"I am telling you there iss not many men following
the sea that could sail the *Fital Spark* the way I could.
There iss not a rock, no, nor a chuckie stone inside the
Cumbrie Heid that I do not have a name for. I would
ken them fine in the dark by the smell, and that iss
not easy, I'm telling you. And I am not wan of your
dry-land sailors. I wass wance at Londonderry with
her. We went at night, and did Dougie no' go away
and forget oil, so that we had no lamps, and chust had
to sail in the dark with our ears wide open. If Dougie
wass here he would tell you. Now and then Dougie
would be striking a match for fear of a collusion."

"Where did he show it?" I asked innocently.
"Forward or aft?"

"Aft," said the mariner suspiciously. "What for
would it be aft? Do you mean to say there could be
a collusion aft? I am telling you she could do her six
knots before she cracked her shaft. It wass in the
bow, of course; Dougie had the matches. She wass
chust sublime. A gold bead oot of my own pocket,
four men and a derrick, and a watter-butt and a pan
loaf in the fo'c'sle. My bonnie wee *Fital Spark*!"

He began to show symptoms of tears, and I hate to

see an ancient mariner's tears, so I hurriedly asked
him how he had lost the command.

" I will tell you that," said he. " It was Dougie's
fault. We had yonder a cargo of coals for Tarbert,
and we got doon the length of Greenock, going fine,
fine. It wass the day after the New Year, and I wass
in fine trum, and Dougie said, ' Wull we stand in here
for orders? ' and so we went into Greenock for some
marmalade, and did we no' stay three days? Dougie
and me wass going about Greenock looking for sign-
boards with Hielan' names on them, and every sign-
board we could see with Campbell, or Macintyre, on
it, or Morrison, Dougie would go in and ask if the
man came from Kilmartin or anyway roond aboot
there, and if the man said no, Dougie would say, ' It's
a great peety, for I have cousins of the same name, but
maybe you'll have time to come oot for a dram? '
Dougie was chust sublime!

" Every day we would be getting sixpenny telegrams
from the man the coals was for at Tarbert, but och!
we did not think he wass in such an aawful hurry, and
then he came himself to Greenock with the *Grenadier*,
and the only wans that wass not in the polis-office
wass myself and the derrick. He bailed the laads out
of the polis-office, and ' Now,' he said, ' you will chust
sail her up as fast as you can, like smert laads, for my
customers iss waiting for their coals, and I will go over
and see my good-sister at Helensburgh, and go back
to Tarbert the day efter to-morrow.' ' Hoo can we be
going and us with no money? ' said Dougie—man, he
wass sublime! So the man gave me a paper pound of
money, and went away to Helensburgh, and Dougie
wass coilin' up a hawser forrit ready to start from the

quay. When he wass away, Dougie said we would maybe chust be as weel to wait another tide, and I said I didna know, but what did he think, and he said, 'Ach, of course!' and we went aal back into Greenock. 'Let me see that pound!' said Dougie, and did I not give it to him? and then he rang the bell of the public-hoose we were in, and asked for four tacks and a wee hammer. When he got the four tacks and the wee hammer he nailed the pound note on the door, and said to the man, 'Chust come in with a dram every time we ring the bell till that's done!' If Dougie wass here he would tell you. Two days efter that the owner of the *Fital Spark* came doon from Gleska and five men with him, and they went away with her to Tarbert."

"And so you lost the old command," I said, preparing to go off. "Well, I hope something will turn up soon."

"There wass some talk aboot a dram," said the mariner. "I thought you said something aboot a dram, but och! there's no occasion!"

A week later, I am glad to say, the Captain and his old crew were reinstated on the *Vital Spark*.

II

THE PRIZE CANARY

"CANARIES!" said Para Handy contemptuously, "I have a canary yonder at home that would give you a sore heid to hear him singing. He's chust sublime. Have I no', Dougie?"

It was the first time the mate had ever heard of the Captain as a bird-fancier, but he was a loyal friend, and at Para Handy's wink he said promptly, "You have that, Peter. Wan of the finest ever stepped. Many a sore heid I had wi't."

"What kind of a canary is it?" asked the Brodick man jealously. "Is it a Norwich?"

Para Handy put up his hand as usual to scratch his ear, and checked the act half-way. "No, nor a Sandwich; it's chust a plain yellow wan," he said coolly. "I'll wudger ye a pound it could sing the best you have blin'. It whustles even-on, night and day, till I have to put it under a bowl o' watter if I'm wantin' my night's sleep."

The competitive passions of the Brodick man were roused. He considered that among his dozen prize canaries he had at least one that could beat anything likely to be in the possession of the Captain of the *Vital Spark*, which was lying at Brodick when this conversation took place. He produced it—an emaciated, sickle-shaped, small-headed, bead-eyed, business-looking bird, which he called the Wee Free. He was prepared to put up the pound for a singing contest anywhere in Arran, date hereafter to be arranged.

"That's all right," said Para Handy, "I'll take you on. We'll be doon this way for a cargo of grevel in a week, and if the money's wi' the man in the shippin'-box at the quay, my canary 'll lift it."

"But what aboot your pound?" asked the Brodick man. "You must wudger a pound too."

"Is that the way o't?" said the Captain. "I wass never up to the gemblin', but I'll risk the pound," and so the contest was arranged.

" But you havena a canary at aal, have you? " said
Dougie, later in the day, as the *Vital Spark* was puffing
on her deliberate way to Glasgow.

" Me? " said Para Handy, " I would as soon think
of keepin' a hoolet. But och, there's plenty in Gleska
if you have the money. From the needle to the anchor.
Forbye, I ken a gentleman that breeds canaries; he's
a riveter, and if I wass gettin' him in good trum he
would maybe give me a lend o' wan. If no', we'll take
a dander up to the Bird Market, and pick up a smert
wan that'll put the hems on Sandy Kerr's Wee Free.
No man wi' any releegion aboot him would caal his
canary a Wee Free."

The Captain and the mate of the *Vital Spark* left
their noble ship at the wharf that evening—it was a
Saturday—and went in quest of the gentleman who
bred canaries. He was discovered in the midst of an
altercation with his wife which involved the total
destruction of all the dishes on the kitchen-dresser,
and, with a shrewdness and consideration that were
never absent in the Captain, he apologised for the
untimely intrusion and prepared to go away. " I see
you're busy," he said, looking in on a floor covered
with the debris of the delf which this ardent lover of
bird life was smashing in order to impress his wife
with the fact that he was really annoyed about something—" I see you're busy. Fine, man, fine! A wife
need never weary in this hoose—it's that cheery.
Dougie and me wass chust wantin' a wee lend of a
canary for a day or two, but och, it doesna matter,
seein' ye're so throng; we'll chust try the shops."

It was indicative of the fine kindly humanity of the
riveter who loved canaries that this one unhesitatingly

stopped his labours, having disposed of the last plate, and said, " I couldna dae't, chaps; I wadna trust a canary oot o' the hoose; there's nae sayin' the ill-usage it micht get. It would break my he'rt to ha'e onything gang wrang wi' ony o' my birds."

" Chust that, Wull, chust that! " said Para Handy agreeably. " Your feelings does you credit. I would be awful vexed if you broke your he'rt; it'll soon be the only hale thing left in the hoose. If I wass you, and had such a spite at the delf, I would use dunny-mite," and Dougie and he departed.

" That's the sort of thing that keeps me from gettin' merrit," the Captain, with a sigh, confided to his mate, when they got down the stair. " Look at the money it costs for dishes every Setturday night."

" Them riveters iss awfu' chaps for sport," said Dougie irrelevantly.

" There's nothing for't now but the Bird Market," said the Captain, leading the way east along Argyle Street. They had no clear idea where that institution was, but at the corner of Jamaica Street consulted several Celtic compatriots, who put them on the right track. Having reached the Bird Market, the Captain explained his wants to a party who had " Guaranteed A1 Songsters " to sell at two shillings. This person was particularly enthusiastic about one bird which in the meantime was as silent as " the harp that once through Tara's halls." He gave them his solemn assurance it was a genuine prize roller canary; that when it started whistling, as it generally did at break-fast time, it sang till the gas was lit, with not even a pause for refreshment. For that reason it was an economical canary to keep; it practically cost nothing for seed for this canary. If it was a songster suitable for use on a ship that was wanted, he went on, with a rapid assumption that his customers were of a maritime profession, this bird was peculiarly adapted for the post. It was a genuine imported bird, and had already made a sea voyage. To sell a bird of such exquisite parts for two shillings was sheer commercial suicide; he admitted it, but he was anxious that it should have a good home.

" I wish I could hear it whustlin'," said the Captain, peering through the spars at the very dejected bird, which was a moulting hen.

" It never sings efter the gas is lighted," said the vendor regretfully, " that's the only thing that's wrang wi't. If that bird wad sing at nicht when the gas was lit, it wad solve the problem o' perpetual motion."

Para Handy, considerably impressed by this high warrandice, bought the canary, which was removed from the cage and placed in a brown paper sugar-bag, ventilated by holes which the bird-seller made in it with the stub of a lead pencil.

" Will you no' need a cage? " asked Dougie.

" Not at aal, not at aal! " the Captain protested; " wance we get him doon to Brodick we'll get plenty o' cages," and away they went with their purchase, Para Handy elate at the imminent prospect of his prize canary winning an easy pound. Dougie carefully carried the bag containing the bird.

Some days after, the *Vital Spark* arrived at Brodick, but the Captain, who had not yet staked his pound with the man in the shipping-box as agreed on, curiously enough showed no disposition to bring off the challenge meeting between the birds. It was by accident he met the Brodick man one day on the quay.

" Talking about birds," said Para Handy, with some diffidence, " Dougie and me had a canary yonder——"

" That's aal off," said the Brodick man hurriedly, getting very red in the face, showing so much embarrassment, indeed, that the Captain of the *Vital Spark* smelt a rat.

" What way off?" he asked. " It sticks in my mind that there wass a kind of a wudger, and that there's a pound note in the shupping-box for the best canary."

" Did you bring your canary? " asked the Brodick man anxiously.

" It's doon there in the vessel singin' like to take the rivets oot o' her," said Para Handy. " It's chust sublime to listen to."

" Weel, the fact iss, I'm not goin' to challenge," said the Brodick man. " I have a wife yonder, and she's sore against bettin' and wudgerin' and gemblin', and she'll no let me take my champion bird Wee Free over the door."

" Chust that! " said Para Handy. " That's a peety. Weel, weel, the pund'll come in handy. I'll chust go away down to the shupping-box and lift it. Seeing I won, I'll stand you a drink."

The Brodick man maintained with warmth that as Para Handy had not yet lodged his stake of a pound the match was off; an excited discussion followed, and the upshot was a compromise. The Brodick man, having failed to produce his bird, was to forfeit ten shillings, and treat the crew of the *Vital Spark*.

They were being treated, and the ten shillings were in Para Handy's possession, when the Brodick sportsman rose to make some disconcerting remark.

" You think you are very smert, Macfarlane," he said, addressing the Captain. " You are thinkin' you did a good stroke to get the ten shullin's, but if you wass smerter it iss not the ten shullin's you would have at aal, but the pound. I had you fine, Macfarlane. My wife never said a word aboot the wudger, but my bird is in the pook, and couldna sing a note this week. That's the way I backed oot."

Para Handy displayed neither resentment nor surprise. He took a deep draught of beer out of a quart pot, and then smiled with mingled tolerance and pity on the Brodick man.

"Ay, ay! " he said, " and you think you have done a smert thing. You have mich caause to be ashamed of yourself. You are nothing better than a common swundler. But och, it doesna matter; the fact iss, oor bird's deid."

" Deid! " cried the Brodick man. " What do you mean by deid? "

" Chust that it's no' livin'," said Para Handy coolly. " Dougie and me bought wan in the Bird Market, and Dougie was carryin' it doon to the vessel in a sugar-poke when he met some fellows he kent in Chamaica Street, and went for a dram, or maybe two. Efter a while he didna mind what he had in the poke, and he put it in his troosers pockets, thinkin' it wass something extra for the Sunday's dinner. When he brought the poor wee bird oot of his pocket in the mornin', it wass chust a' remains."

III

THE MALINGERER

THE crew of the *Vital Spark* were all willing workers, except The Tar, who was usually as tired when he rose in the morning as when he went to bed. He said himself it was his health, and that he had never got his strength right back since he had the whooping-cough twice when he was a boy. The Captain was generally sympathetic, and was inclined to believe The Tar was destined to have a short life unless he got married and had a wife to look after him. "A wife's the very thing for you," he would urge; " it's no' canny, a man as delicate as you to be having nobody to depend on."

" I couldna afford a wife," The Tar always maintained. " They're all too grand for the like of me."

" Och ay! but you might look aboot you and find a wee, no' aawfu' bonny wan," said Para Handy.

" If she was blin', or the like of that, you would have a better chance of gettin' her," chimed in Dougie, who always scoffed at The Tar's periodical illnesses, and cruelly ascribed his lack of energy to sheer laziness.

The unfortunate Tar's weaknesses always seemed to come on him when there was most to do. It generally took the form of sleepiness, so that sometimes when he was supposed to be preparing the dinner he would be found sound asleep on the head of a bucket, with a half-peeled potato in his hand. He once crept out of the fo'c'sle rubbing his eyes after a twelve-hours' sleep, saying, " Tell me this and tell me no more, am I going to my bed or comin' from it? "

But there was something unusual and alarming about

the illness which overtook The Tar on their way up
Loch Fyne to lift a cargo of timber. First he had
shivers all down his back; then he got so stiff that he
could not bend to lift a bucket, but had to kick it
along the deck in front of him, which made Dougie
admiringly say, " Man! you are an aawful handy man
with your feet, Colin "; his appetite, he declared,
totally disappeared immediately after an unusually
hearty breakfast composed of six herrings and two
eggs; and finally he expressed his belief that there was
nothing for it but his bed.

" I'll maybe no trouble you long, boys," he moaned
lugubriously. " My heid's birling roond that fast that
I canna even mind my own name two meenutes."

" You should write it on a wee bit paper," said
Dougie unfeelingly, " and keep it inside your bonnet,
so that you could look it up at any time you were
needin'."

Para Handy had kinder feelings, and told The Tar
to go and lie down for an hour or two and take a wee
drop of something.

" Maybe a drop of brandy would help me," said
The Tar, promptly preparing to avail himself of the
Captain's advice.

" No, not brandy; a drop of good Brutish spurits
will suit you better, Colin," said the Captain, and went
below to dispense the prescription himself.

The gusto with which The Tar swallowed the pre-
scribed dram of British spirits and took a chew of
tobacco after it to enhance the effect, made Para
Handy somewhat suspicious, and he said so to Dougie
when he got on deck, leaving The Tar already in a
gentle slumber.

"The rascal's chust scheming," said Dougie emphatically. "There iss nothing in the world wrong with him but the laziness. If you'll notice, he aalways gets no weel when we're going to lift timber, because it iss harder on him at the winch."

The Captain was indignant, and was for going down there and then with a rope's-end to rouse the patient, but Dougie confided to him a method of punishing the malingerer and at the same time getting some innocent amusement for themselves.

Dinner-time came round. The Tar instinctively wakened and lay wondering what they would take down to him to eat. The *Vital Spark* was puff-puffing her deliberate way up the loch, and there was an unusual stillness on deck. It seemed to The Tar that the Captain and Dougie were moving about on tiptoe and speaking in whispers. The uncomfortable feeling this created in his mind was increased when his two shipmates came down with slippers on instead of their ordinary sea-boots, creeping down the companion with great caution, carrying a bowl of gruel.

"What's that for?" asked The Tar sharply. "Are you going to paste up any bills?"

"Wheest, Colin," said Para Handy, in a sick-room whisper. "You must not excite yourself, but take this gruel. It'll do you no herm. Poor fellow, you're looking aawful bad." They hung over his bunk with an attitude of chastened grief, and Dougie made to help him to the gruel with a spoon as if he were unable to feed himself.

"Have you no beef?" asked The Tar, looking at the gruel with disgust. "I'll need to keep up my strength with something more than gruel."

" You daurna for your life take anything but gruel,"
said the Captain sorrowfully. " It would be the daith
of you at wance to take beef, though there's plenty in
the pot. Chust take this, like a good laad, and don't
speak. My Chove! you are looking far through."

" You're nose is as sherp as a preen," said Dougie
in an awed whisper, and with a piece of engine-room
waste wiped the brow of The Tar, who was beginning
to perspire with alarm.

" I don't think I'm so bad ass aal that," said the
patient. " It wass chust a turn; a day in my bed 'll
put me aal right—or maybe two."

They shook their heads sorrowfully, and the Captain
turned away as if to hide a tear. Dougie blew his nose
with much ostentation and stifled a sob.

" What's the metter wi' you? " asked The Tar, looking at them in amazement and fear.

" Nothing, nothing, Colin," said the Captain.
" Don't say a word. Iss there anything we could get
for you? "

" My heid's bad yet," the patient replied. " Perhaps a drop of spurits——"

" There's no' another drop in the ship," said the
Captain.

The patient moaned. " And I don't suppose there's
any beer either? " he said hopelessly.

He was told there was no beer, and instructed to
cry if he was requiring any one to come to his assistance, after which the two nurses crept quietly on deck
again, leaving him in a very uneasy frame of mind.

They got into the quay late in the afternoon, and the
Captain and mate came down again quietly, with their
caps in their hands, to discover The Tar surreptitiously

smoking in his bunk to dull the pangs of hunger that
now beset him, for they had given him nothing since
the gruel.

"It's not for you, it's not for you at aal, smokin'!"
cried Para Handy in horror, taking the pipe out of his
hand. "With the trouble you have, smoking drives it
in to the hert and kills you at wance."

"What trouble do you think it iss?" asked the
patient seriously.

"Dougie says it's—it's—what did you say it wass,
Dougie?"

"It's convolvulus in the inside," said Dougie
solemnly; "I had two aunties that died of it in their
unfancy."

"I'm going to get up at wance!" said The Tar,
making to rise, but they thrust him back in his blankets,
saying the convolvulus would burst at the first effort of
the kind he made.

He began to weep. "Fancy a trouble like that
coming on me, and me quite young!" he said, pitying
himself seriously. "There wass never wan in oor
femily had it."

"It's sleep brings it on," said Dougie, with the air
of a specialist who would ordinarily charge a fee of ten
guineas—"sleep and sitting doon. There iss nothing
to keep off convolvulus but exercise and rising early
in the morning. Poor fellow! But you'll maybe get
better; when there's hope there's life. The Captain
and me wass wondering if there wass anything we could
buy ashore for you—some grapes, maybe, or a shullin'
bottle of sherry wine."

"Mercy on me! am I ass far through ass that?"
said The Tar.

" Or maybe you would like Macphail, the enchineer, to come doon and read the Scruptures a while to you," said Para Handy.

" Macphail! " cried the poor Tar; " I wudna let a man like that read a song-book to me."

They clapped him affectionately on the shoulders; Dougie made as if to shake his hand, and checked himself; then the Captain and mate went softly on deck again, and the patient was left with his fears. He felt utterly incapable of getting up.

Para Handy and his mate went up the town and had a dram with the local joiner, who was also undertaker. With this functionary in their company they were moving towards the quay when Dougie saw in a grocer's shop-door a pictorial card bearing the well-known monkey portrait advertising a certain soap that won't wash clothes. He went chuckling into the shop, made some small purchase, and came out the possessor of the picture. Half an hour later, when it was dark, and The Tar was lying in an agony of hunger which he took to be the pains of internal convolvulus, Para Handy, Dougie, and the joiner came quietly down to the fo'c'sle, where he lay. They had no lamp, but they struck matches and looked at him in his bunk with countenances full of pity.

"A nose as sherp as a preen," said Dougie; " it must be the galloping kind of convolvulus."

" Here's Macintyre the joiner would like to see you, Colin," said Para Handy, and in the light of a match the patient saw the joiner cast a rapid professional eye over his proportions.

" What's the joiner wantin' here? " said The Tar, with a frightful suspicion.

"Nothing, Colin, nothing—six by two—I wass chust passing—six by two—chust passing, and the Captain asked me in to see you. It's—six by two, six by two—it's no' very healthy weather we're havin'. Chust that!"

The fo'c'sle was in darkness and The Tar felt already as if he was dead and buried. "Am I lookin' very bad?" he ventured to ask Dougie.

"Bad's no' the name for it," said Dougie. "Chust look at yourself in the enchineer's looking-gless." He produced from under his arm the engineer's little mirror, on the face of which he had gummed the portrait of the monkey cut out from the soap advertisement, which fitted neatly into the frame. The Captain struck a match, and in its brief and insufficient light The Tar looked at himself, as he thought, reflected in the glass.

"Man, I'm no' that awful changed either; if I had a shave and my face washed. I don't believe it's convolvulus at aal," said he, quite hopefully, and jumped from his bunk.

For the rest of the week he put in the work of two men.

IV

WEE TEENY

THE last passenger steamer to sail that day from Ardrishaig was a trip from Rothesay. It was Glasgow Fair Saturday, and Ardrishaig Quay was black with people. There was a marvellously stimulating odour of dulse, herring, and shell-fish, for everybody carried away in a handkerchief a few samples of these marine products that are now the only seaside souvenirs not made in Germany. The *Vital Spark*, in ballast, Clydeward bound, lay inside the passenger steamer, ready to start when the latter had got under weigh, and Para Handy and his mate meanwhile sat on the fo'c'sle-head of "the smertest boat in the tred" watching the frantic efforts of lady excursionists to get their husbands on the steamer before it was too late, and the deliberate efforts of the said husbands to slink away up the village again just for one more drink. Wildly the steamer hooted from her siren, fiercely clanged her bell, vociferously the Captain roared upon his bridge, people aboard yelled eagerly to friends ashore to hurry up, and the people ashore as eagerly demanded to know what all the hurry was about, and where the bleezes was Wull. Women loudly defied the purser to let the ship go away without their John, for he had paid his money for his ticket, and though he was only a working man his money was as good as anybody else's; and John, on the quay, with his hat thrust back on his head, his thumbs in the armholes of his waistcoat and a red handkerchief full of dulse at his feet, gave a display of step-dancing that was responsible for a great deal of the congestion of traffic at the shore end of the gangway.

Among the crowd who had got on board was a woman with eleven children. She was standing on the paddle-box counting them to make sure—five attached to the basket that had contained their food for the day, other four clinging to her gown, and one in her arms. " Yin, twa, three, fower, and fower's eight, and twa's ten, and then there's Wee Teeny wi' her faither

B

doon the caibin." She was quite serene. If she could have seen that the father—at that moment in the fore-saloon singing

> " In the guid auld summer time,
> In the guid auld summer time,
> She'll be your tootsy-wootsy
> In the guid auld summer time."

had no Wee Teeny with him, she would have been distracted. As it was, however, the steamer was miles on her way when a frantic woman with ten crying children all in a row behind her, and a husband miraculously sobered, made a vain appeal to the Captain to go back to Ardrishaig for her lost child.

The child was discovered on the quay by the local police ten minutes after the excursion steamer had started, and just when Para Handy was about to cast off the pawls. She was somewhere about three years old, and the only fact that could be extracted from her was that her name was Teeny. There had probably not been a more contented and self-possessed person on Ardrishaig Quay that day: she sucked her thumb with an air of positive relish, smiled on the slightest provocation, and showed the utmost willingness to go anywhere with anybody.

" The poor wee cratur! " said Para Handy sympathetically. " She minds me fearfully of my brother Cherlie's twuns. I wudna wonder but she'a twuns too; that would be the way the mistake would be made in leavin' her; it's such a terrible thing drink. I'm no' goin' to ask you, Dougie, to do anything you wudna like, but what would you be sayin' to us takin' the wean wi' us and puttin' her ashore at Rothesay? Mind you, chust if you like yoursel'."

" It's your own vessel, you're the skipper of her, and I'm sure and I have no objections, at aal at aal," said Dougie quite heartily, and it was speedily arranged with the police that a telegram should be sent to wait the Captain of the excursion steamer at Rothesay, telling him the lost child was following in the steam-lighter *Vital Spark*.

Macphail the engineer, and The Tar, kept the child in amusement with pocket-knives, oil-cans, cotton-waste, and other maritime toys, while the Captain and Dougie went hurriedly up the village for stores for the unexpected passenger.

" You'll not need that mich," was Dougie's opinion; " she'll fall asleep as soon as it's dark, and no' wake till we put her ashore at Rothesay."

" Ah, but you canna be sure o' them at that age," said the Captain. " My brother Cherlie wass merrit on a low-country woman, and the twuns used to sit up at night and greet in the two languages, Gaalic and Gleska, till he had to put plugs in them."

" God bless me! plugs? " said Dougie astonished.

" Ay, chust plugs," said the Captain emphatically. " You'll see them often. They're made of kahouchy, with a bone ring on them for screwing them on and off. It's the only thing for stopping them greetin'."

The adventures of Wee Teeny from this stage may be better told as Para Handy told it to me some time afterwards.

" To let you ken," he said, " I wass feared the wean would sterve. Nothing in the ship but sea biscuits and salt beef. I went into wan shop and got a quart of milk on draught, half a pound of boiled ham the same as they have at funerals, and a tin tinny For a Good

Girl. Dougie wasna slack either; he went into another shop and got thruppence worth of sweeties and a jumpin'-jeck. It wass as nice a thing ass ever you saw to see the wee cratur sittin' on the hatches eatin' away and drinkin' wi' the wan hand, and laughing like anything at the jumpin'-jeck wi' the other. I never saw the ship cheerier; it wass chust sublime. If Dougie wass here himsel' he would tell you. Everything wass going first-rate, and I wass doon below washing my face and puttin' on my other jecket and my watch-chain oot o' respect for the passenger, when Dougie came doon in a hurry wi' a long face on him, and says—

" ' She's wantin' ta-ta.'

" ' Mercy on us, she canna be more ta-ta than she iss unless we throw her over the side,' I says to Dougie. But I went up on dake and told her she would be ta-ta in no time becaase the ship was loggin' six knots and the wind wi' us.

" ' Ta-ta,' says she, tuggin' my whuskers the same as if I wass merrit on her—ah, man! she wass a nice wee thing. And that good-natured! The best I could do wass to make The Tar show her the tattoo marks on his legs, and Dougie play the trump (Jew's harp), and when she wass tired o' that I carried her up and doon the dake singin' 'Auld Lang Syne' till she was doverin' over.

" ' She's goin' to sleep noo,' I says to Dougie, and we put her in my bunk wi' her clothes on. She wanted her clothes off, but I said, ' Och! never mind puttin' them off, Teeny; it's only a habit.' Dougie said, if he minded right, they always put up a kind of prayer at that age. ' Give her a start,' I says to Dougie, and he said the 23rd Psalm in Gaalic, but she didn't understand wan word of it, and went to sleep wi' a poke o' sweeties in her hand.

"We were off Ardlamont, and Macphail wass keepin' the boat bangin' at it to get to Rothesay before the mother went oot of her wuts, when I heard a noise doon below where Teeny wass. I ran doon and found her sittin' up chokin' wi' a sweetie that wass a size too lerge for her. She wass black in the face.

"'Hut her on the back, Peter!' said Dougie.

"'Hut her yoursel'; I wudna hurt her for the world,' I says, and Dougie said he wudna do it either, but he ran up for The Tar, that hasna mich feelin's, and The Tar saved her life. I'm tellin' you it wass a start! We couldna trust her below, herself, efter that, so we took her on dake again. In ten meenutes she fell down among Macphail's engines, and nearly spoiled them. She wasna hurt a bit, but Macphail's feelin's wass, for she wass wantin' the engines to her bed wi' her. She thought they were a kind of a toy. We aye keep that up on him yet.

"'My Chove! this wean's no' canny,' said Dougie, and we took her up on dake again, and put up the sail to get as mich speed oot of the vessel as we could for Rothesay. Dougie played the trump even-on to her, and The Tar walked on his hands till she was sore laughing at him. Efter a bit we took oor eyes off her for maybe two meenutes, and when we turned roond again Teeny wass fallin' doon into the fo'c'sle.

"'This iss the worst cargo ever we had,' I says, takin' her up again no' a bit the worse. 'If we don't watch her like a hawk aal the time she'll do something desperate before we reach Rothesay. She'll jump over the side or crawl doon the funnel, and we'll be black affronted.'

" ' I wudna say but you're right,' said Dougie. We put her sittin' on the hatch wi' the jumpin'-jeck, and the tin tinny For a Good Girl, and my watch and chain, Dougie's trump, the photygraph of The Tar's lass, and Macphail's new carpet sluppers to play wi', and the three of us sat roond her watchin' she didna swallow the watch and chain.

" When I handed her over to her mother and father on Rothesay Quay, I says to them, ' I'm gled I'm no' a mother; I would a hunder times sooner be a sailor.'

" But it's a nice thing a wean, too; for a week efter that we missed her awful," concluded the Captain pensively.

V

THE MATE'S WIFE

THAT the Captain of the *Vital Spark* should so persistently remain a bachelor surprised many people. He was just the sort of man, in many respects, who would fall an easy prey to the first woman on the look-out for a good home. He had rather a gallant way with the sex, generally said " mem " to them all, regardless of class; liked their society when he had his Sunday clothes on, and never contradicted them. If he had pursued any other calling than that of mariner I think he would have been captured long ago; his escape doubtless lay in the fact that sailing about from place to place, only briefly touching at West-

Coast quays, and then being usually grimed with coal-dust, he had never properly roused their interest and natural sporting instincts. They never knew what a grand opportunity they were losing.

" I'm astonished you never got married, Captain," I said to him recently.

" Ach, I couldn't be bothered," he replied, like a man who had given the matter his consideration before now. " I'm that busy wi' the ship I havena time. There's an aawful lot of bother aboot a wife. Forbye, my hert's in the *Fital Spark*—there's no' a smerter boat in the tred. Wait you till I get her pented! "

" But a ship's not a wife, Captain," I protested.

" No," said he, " but it's a responsibulity. You can get a wife any time that'll stick to you the same as if she wass riveted as long's you draw your pay, but it takes a man with aal his senses aboot him to get a ship and keep her. And chust think on the expense! Oh, I'm not sayin', mind you, that I'll not try wan some day, but there's no hurry, no, not a bit."

" But perhaps you'll put it off too long," I said, " and when you're in the humour to have them they won't have you."

He laughed at the very idea.

" Man! " he said, " it's easy seen you have not studied them. I ken them like the Kyles of Bute. The captain of a steamer iss the most popular man in the wide world—popul_er than the munisters themselves, and the munisters iss that popular the weemen put bird-lime in front of the Manses to catch them, the same ass if they were green-linties. It's worse with sea-captains—they're that dashing, and they're not aalways hinging aboot the hoose wi' their sluppers on."

" There's another thing," he added, after a little
pause, " I couldna put up with a woman comin' aboot
the vessel every pay-day. No, no, I'm for none o'
that. Dougie's wife's plenty."

" But surely she does not invade you weekly? " I
said, surprised.

" If the *Fital Spark's* anywhere inside Ardlamont on
a Setturday," said Para Handy, " she's doon wi' the
first steamer from Gleska, and her door-key in her
hand, the same ass if it wass a pistol to put to his heid.
If Dougie was here himsel' he would tell you. She's
a low-country woman, wi' no' a word o' Gaalic, so
that she canna understand Dougie at his best. When
it comes to bein' angry in English, she can easy bate
him. Oh, a cluvver woman: she made Dougie a
Rechabite, and he's aalways wan when he's at home,
and at keepin' him trum and tidy in his clothes she's
chust sublime. But she's no' canny aboot a ship. The
first week efter she merried him we were lyin' at
Innellan, and doon she came on the Setturday wi' her
door-key at full cock. When Dougie saw her comin'
doon the quay he got white, and turned to me, sayin',
' Peter, here's the Mustress; I wish I hadna touched
that dram, she'll can tell it on me, and I'm no' feared
for her, but it would hurt her feelings.'

" ' Man! ' I said, ' you're an aawful tumid man for
a sailor; but haste you doon the fo'c'sle and you'll
get a poke of peppermint sweeties in my other pocket
I had for the church to-morrow. Chust you go like
the duvvle, and I'll keep her in conversation till you
get your breath shifted.'

" Dougie bolted doon below, and wass up in a shot.
' I got the sweeties, Peter,' he said, ' but, oh! she's as

cunning as a jyler, and she'll chalouse something if she smells the peppermints. What would you say to the whole of us takin' wan or two sweeties so that we would be aal the same, and she wouldna suspect me?'
'Very weel,' I said, 'anything to obleege a mate,' and when the good leddy reached the side of the vessel the enchineer and The Tar and me and Dougie wass standin' in a row eating peppermints till you would think it wass the front sate of the Tobermory Free Church.

" ' It's a fine day and an awfu' smell o' losengers,' was the first words she said when she put her two feet on the deck. And she looked very keen at her man.

" ' It is that, mem,' I said. ' It's the cargo.'

" ' What cargo?' said she, looking at Dougie harder than ever. ' I'll cargo him! '

" ' I mean the cargo of the boat, mem,' I said quite smert. ' It's a cheneral cargo, and there's six ton of peppermint sweeties for the Tarbert fishermen.'

" ' What in the wide world dae the Tarbert fishermen dae wi' sae mony sweeties?' said she.

" ' Och, it's chust to keep them from frightening away the herrin' when they're oot at the fishin',' I said. Man! I'm tellin' you I had aal my wuts aboot me that day! It wass lucky for us the hatches wass doon, so that she couldna see the cargo we had in the hold. There wasna wan sweetie in it.

" I couldna but be nice to the woman, for she wasna my wife, so I turned a bucket upside doon and gave her a sate, and let on that Dougie was chust ass mich a man of consequence on the *Fital Spark* as myself. It does not do to let a wife see wi' her own eyes that her man iss under you in your chob, for when she'll get

him at home she'll egg him on to work harder and get
your place, and where are you then, eh! where are
you then, I'm asking? She wass a cluvver woman,
but she had no sense. ' Weel,' said she, ' I don't think
muckle o' yer boat. I thocht it was a great big boat,
wi' a cabin in it. Instead o' that, it's jist a wee coal
yin.'

" Man! do you know that vexed me; I say she
wasna the kind of woman Dougie should have married
at aal, at aal. Dougie's a chentleman like mysel'; he
would never hurt your feelings unless he wass tryin'.

" ' There's nothing wrong with the *Fital Spark*,
mem,' I said to her. ' She's the most namely ship in
the tred; they'll be writing things aboot her in the
papers, and men often come to take photographs of
her.'

" She chust sniffed her nose at that, the way merrit
women have, and said, ' Jist fancy that! '

" ' Yes; chust fancy it! ' I said to her. ' Six knots
in a gale of wind if Macphail the enchineer is in good
trum, and maybe seven if it's Setturday, and him in a
hurry to get home. She has the finest lines of any
steamboat of her size coming oot of Clyde; if her lum
wass pented yellow and she had a bottom strake or
two of green, you would take her for a yat. Perhaps
you would be thinkin' we should have a German band
on board of her, with the heid fuddler goin' aboot
gaitherin' pennies in a shell, and the others keekin'
over the ends of their flutes and cornucopias for fear
he'll pocket some. What? H'm! Chust that! '

" Efter a bit she said she would like to see what sort
of place her man and the rest of us slept in, so there
was nothing for it but to take her doon to the fo'c's'le,

though it wass mich against my will. When she saw
the fo'c'sle she wass nestier than ever. She said,
' Surely this iss not a place for Christian men '; and
I said, ' No, mem, but we're chust sailors.'

" ' There's nae richt furniture in't,' she said.

" ' Not at present, mem,' I said. ' Perhaps you were
expectin' a piano,' but, och! she wass chust wan of
them Gleska women, she didna know life. She went
away up the toon there and then, and came back wi'
a bit of waxcloth, a tin of black soap, a grocer's
calendar, and a wee lookin'-gless, hung her bonnet
and the door-key on a cleat, and started scrubbin' oot
the fo'c'sle. Man, it wass chust peetiful! There wass
a damp smell in the fo'c'sle I could feel for months
efter, and I had a cold in my heid for a fortnight.
When she had the floor of the fo'c'sle scrubbed, she
laid the bit of waxcloth, got two nails from The Tar,
and looked for a place to hang up the calendar and the
wee lookin'-gless, though there wass not mich room for
ornaments of the kind. ' That's a little mair tidy-like,'
she said when she was feenished, and she came up
lookin' for something else to wash. The Tar saw the
danger and went ashore in a hurry.

" ' Are ye merrit? ' she asked me before she left the
vessel wi' Dougie's pay.

" ' No, mem,' I said, ' I'm not merrit yet.'

" ' I could easy see that,' she said, sniffin' her nose
again, the same ass if I wass not a captain at aal, but
chust before the mast. ' I could easy see that. It's
time you were hurryin' up. I ken the very wife wad
suit you; she's a kizzen o' my ain, a weedow wumman
no' a bit the worse o' the wear.'

" ' Chust that! ' said I, ' but I'm engaged.'

" ' Wha to?' she asked quite sherp, no' very sure o' me.

" ' To wan of the Maids of Bute, mem,' I told her, meanin' yon two pented stones you see from the steamer in the Kyles of Bute; and her bein' a Gleska woman, and not traivelled mich, she thocht I wass in earnest.

" ' I don't ken the faimily,' she said, ' but it's my opeenion you wad be better wi' a sensible weedow.'

" ' Not at aal, mem,' I said, ' a sailor couldna have a better wife nor wan of the Maids of Bute; he'll maybe no' get mich tocher with her, but she'll no' come huntin' the quays for him or his wages on the Setturday.' "

VI

PARA HANDY—POACHER

THE *Vital Spark* was lying at Greenock with a cargo of scrap-iron, on the top of which was stowed loosely an extraordinary variety of domestic furniture, from bird cages to cottage pianos. Para Handy had just had the hatches off when I came to the quay-side, and he was contemplating the contents of his hold with no very pleasant aspect.

" Rather a mixed cargo! " I ventured to say.

" Muxed's no' the word for't," he said bitterly. " It puts me in mind of an explosion. It's a flittin' from Dunoon. There would be no flittin's in the *Fital Spark* if she wass my boat. But I'm only the captain, och aye! I'm only the captain, thirty-five shullin's a-week and liberty to put on a pea-jecket. To be puttin' scrap-iron and flittin's in a fine smert boat like this iss carryin' coals aboot in a coach and twice. It would make any man use Abyssinian language."

" Abyssinian language? " I repeated, wondering.

" Chust that, Abyssinian language—swearing, and the like of that, you ken fine, yoursel', withoot me tellin' you. Fancy puttin' a flittin' in the *Fital Spark*! You would think she wass a coal-laary, and her with two new coats of pent out of my own pocket since the New Year."

" Have you been fishing? " I asked, desirous to change the subject, which was, plainly, a sore one with the Captain. And I indicated a small fishing-net which was lying in the bows.

" Chust the least wee bit touch," he said, with a very profound wink. " I have a bit of a net there no' the size of a pocket-naipkin, that I use noo and then at the river-mooths. I chust put it doon—me and Dougie— and whiles a salmon or a sea-troot meets wi' an accident and gets into't. Chust a small bit of a net, no' worth speakin' aboot, no' mich bigger nor a pocket-naipkin. They'll be calling it a splash-net, you ken yoursel' withoot me tellin' you." And he winked knowingly again.

"Ah, Captain! " I said, "that's bad! Poaching with a splash-net! I didn't think you would have done it."

" It's no' me; it's Dougie," he retorted promptly. "A fair duvvle for high jeenks, you canna keep him from it. I told him many a time that it wasna right, becaause we might be found oot and get the jyle for't, but he says they do it on aal the smertest yats. Yes, that iss what he said to me—' They do it on aal the first-cless yats; you'll be bragging the *Fital Spark* iss chust ass good ass any yat, and what for would you grudge a splash-net?' "

" Still it's theft, Captain," I insisted. " And it's very, very bad for the rivers."

" Chust that! " he said complacently. " You'll likely be wan of them fellows that goes to the hotels for the fushing in the rivers. There's more sport aboot a splash-net; if Dougie wass here he would tell you."

" I don't see where the sport comes in," I remarked, and he laughed contemptuously.

" Sport! " he exclaimed. " The best going. There wass wan time yonder we were up Loch Fyne on a Fast Day, and no' a shop open in the place to buy onything for the next mornin's breakfast. Dougie says to me, ' What do you think yoursel' aboot takin' the punt and the small bit of net no' worth mentionin', and going doon to the river mooth when it's dark and seeing if we'll no' get a fush?'

" ' It's a peety to be poaching on the Fast Day,' I said to him.

" ' But it's no' the Fast Day in oor parish,' he said. ' We'll chust give it a trial, and if there's no fush at the start we'll come away back again.' Oh! a consuderate fellow, Dougie; he saw my poseetion at wance, and that I wasna awfu' keen to be fushin' wi' a splash-net on the Fast Day. The end and the short of it wass that when it wass dark we took the net and the punt and rowed doon to the river and began to splash. We had got a fine haul at wance of six great big salmon, and every salmon Dougie would be takin' oot of the net he would be feeling it all over in a droll way, till I said to him, ' What are you feel-feelin' for,

Dougie, the same ass if they had pockets on them? I'm sure they're all right.'

" 'Oh, yes,' he says, ' right enough, but I wass frightened they might be the laird's salmon, and I wass lookin' for the luggage label on them. There's none. It's all right; they're chust wild salmon that nobody planted.'

" Weel, we had got chust ass many salmon ass we had any need for when somebody birled a whustle, and the river watchers put off in a small boat from a point outside of us to catch us. There wass no gettin' oot of the river mooth, so we left the boat and the net and the fush and ran ashore, and by-and-by we got up to the quay and on board the *Fital Spark*, and paaused and consudered things.

" 'They'll ken it's oor boat,' said Dougie, and his clothes wass up to the eyes in salmon scales.

" 'There's no doo't aboot that,' I says. 'If it wassna the Fast Day I wouldna be so vexed; it'll be an awful disgrace to be found oot workin' a splash-net on the Fast Day. And it's a peety aboot the boat, it wass a good boat, I wish we could get her back.'

" 'Ay, it's a peety we lost her,' said Dougie; 'I wonder in the wide world who could have stole her when we were doon the fo'c'sle at oor supper?' Oh, a smert fellow, Dougie! when he said that I saw at wance what he meant.

" 'I'll go up this meenute and report it to the polis office,' I said quite firm, and Dougie said he would go with me too, but that we would need to change oor clothes, for they were covered with fush-scales. We changed oor clothes and went up to the sercheant of polis, and reported that somebody had stolen oor boat.

He wass sittin' readin' his Bible, it bein' the Fast Day, wi' specs on, and he keeked up at us, and said, ' You are very spruce, boys, with your good clothes on at this time of the night.'

" ' We aalways put on oor good clothes on the *Fital Spark* on a Fast Day,' I says to him; ' it's as little as we can do, though we don't belong to the parish.'

" Next day there wass a great commotion in the place aboot some blackguards doon at the river mooth poachin' with a splash-net. The Factor wass busy, and the heid gamekeeper wass busy, and the polis wass busy. We could see them from the dake of the *Fital Spark* goin' aboot buzzin' like bum-bees.

" ' Stop you! ' said Dougie to me aal of a sudden. ' They'll be doon here in a chiffy, and findin' us with them scales on oor clothes—we'll have to put on the Sunday wans again.'

" ' But they'll smell something if they see us in oor Sunday clothes,' I said. ' It's no' the Fast Day the day.'

" ' Maybe no' here,' said Dougie, ' but what's to hinder it bein' the Fast Day in oor own parish? '

" We put on oor Sunday clothes again, and looked the Almanac to see if there wass any word in it of a Fast Day any place that day, but there wass nothing in the Almanac but tides, and the Battle of Waterloo, and the weather for next winter. That's the worst of Almanacs; there's nothing in them you want. We were fair bate for a Fast Day any place, when The Tar came up and asked me if he could get to the funeral of a cousin of his in the place at two o'clock.

" ' A funeral! ' said Dougie. ' The very thing. The Captain and me'll go to the funeral too. That's the way we have on oor Sunday clothes.' Oh, a smert, smert fellow, Dougie!

"We had chust made up oor mind it wass the funeral we were dressed for, and no' a Fast Day any place, when the polisman and the heid gamekeeper came doon very suspeecious, and said they had oor boat. 'And what's more,' said the gamekeeper, 'there's a splash-net and five stone of salmon in it. It hass been used, your boat, for poaching.'

"'Iss that a fact?' I says. 'I hope you'll find the blackguards,' and the gamekeeper gave a grunt, and said somebody would suffer for it, and went away busier than ever. But the polis sercheant stopped behind. 'You're still in your Sunday clothes, boys,' said he; 'what iss the occasion to-day?'

"'We're going to the funeral,' I said.

"'Chust that! I did not know you were untimate with the diseased,' said the sercheant.

"'Neither we were,' I said, 'but we are going oot of respect for Colin.' And we went to the funeral, and nobody suspected nothin', but we never got back the boat, for the gamekeeper wass chust needin' wan for a brother o' his own. Och, ay! there's wonderful sport in a splash-net."

VII

THE SEA COOK

THE TAR's duties included cooking for the ship's company. He was not exactly a chef who would bring credit to a first-class club or restaurant, but for some time after he joined the *Vital Spark* there was no

occasion to complain of him. Quite often he would
wash the breakfast-cups to have them clean for tea
in the evening, and it was only when in a great hurry
he dried plates with the ship's towel. But as time
passed, and he found his shipmates not very particular
about what they ate, he grew a little careless. For
instance, Para Handy was one day very much annoyed
to see The Tar carry forward the potatoes for dinner
in his cap.

"That's a droll way to carry potatoes, Colin," he
said mildly.

"Och! they'll do no herm; it's only an old kep
anyway," said The Tar. "Catch me usin' my other
kep for potatoes!"

"It wass not exactly your kep I wass put aboot for,"
said the Captain. "It wass chust running in my mind
that maybe some sort of a dish would be nater and
genteeler. I'm no' compleenin', mind you, I'm chust
mentioning it."

"Holy smoke!" said The Tar. "You're getting to
be aawful polite wi' your plates for potatoes, and them
no peeled!"

But the want of variety in The Tar's cooking grew
worse and worse each voyage, and finally created a
feeling of great annoyance to the crew. It was always
essence of coffee, and herring—fresh, salt, kippered,
or red—for breakfast, sausages or stewed steak and
potatoes for dinner, and a special treat in the shape of
ham and eggs for Sundays. One unlucky day for the
others of the crew, however, he discovered the con-
venience of tinned corned beef, and would feed them
on that for dinner three or four days a week. Of
course they commented on this prevalence of tinned

food, which the engineer with some humour always called " malleable mule," but The Tar had any number of reasons ready for its presence on the midday board.

" Sorry, boys," he would say affably, " but this is the duvvle of a place; no' a bit of butcher meat to be got in't till Wednesday, when it comes wi' the boat from Gleska." Or " The fire went oot on me, chaps, chust when I wass making a fine thing. Wait you till Setturday, and we'll have something rare! "

"Ay, ay; live, old horse, and you'll get corn," the Captain would say under these circumstances, as he artistically carved the wedge of American meat. " It's a mercy to get anything; back in your plate, Dougie."

It became at last unbearable, and while The Tar was ashore one day in Tarbert, buying bottled coffee and tinned meat in bulk, a conference between the captain, the engineer, and the mate took place.

" I'm no' going to put up wi't any longer," said the engineer emphatically. " It's all very well for them that has no thinking to do wi' their heids to eat tinned mule even on, but an engineer that's thinking aboot his engines all the time, and sweatin' doon in a temperature o' 120, needs to keep his strength up."

" What sort o' heid-work are you talking aboot? " said the Captain. " Iss it readin' your penny novelles? Hoo's Lady Fitzgerald's man gettin' on? " This last allusion was to Macphail's passion for penny fiction, and particularly to a novelette story over which the engineer had once been foolish enough some years before to show great emotion.

" I move," said Dougie, breaking in on what promised to be an unprofitable altercation,—" I move that The Tar be concurred."

" Concurred! " said the engineer, with a contemptuous snort. " I suppose you mean censured? "

" It's the same thing, only spelled different," said the mate.

" What's censured? " asked the Captain.

" It's giving a fellow a duvvle of a clourin'," answered Dougie promptly.

" No, no, I wouldna care to do that to The Tar. Maybe he's doin' the best he can, poor chap. The Tar never saw mich high life before he came on my boat, and we'll have to make an allowance for that."

" Herrin' for breakfast seven days a week! it's a fair scandal," said the engineer. " If you were maister in your own boat, Macfarlane, you would have a very different kind of man makin' your meat for you."

" There's not mich that iss wholesomer than a good herrin'," said Para Handy. " It's a fush that's chust sublime. But I'll not deny it would be good to have a change noo and then, if it wass only a finnen haddie."

" I have a cookery book o' the wife's yonder at home I'll bring wi' me the next time we're in Gleska, and it'll maybe give him a tip or two," said the engineer, and this was, in the meantime, considered the most expedient thing to do.

Next trip, on the way to Brodick on a Saturday with a cargo of bricks, The Tar was delicately approached by the Captain, who had the cookery book in his hand. " That wass a nice tender bit of tinned beef we had the day, Colin," he said graciously. " Capital, aaltogether! I could live myself on tinned beef from wan end of the year to the other, but Dougie and the enchineer there's compleenin' that you're givin' it to them too often. You would think they were lords! But perhaps I shouldna blame them, for the doctor told the enchineer he should take something tasty every day, and Dougie's aye frightened for tinned meat since ever he heard that the enchineer wance killed a man in the Australian bush. What do you say yoursel' to tryin' something fancy in the cookery line?"

"There's some people hard to please," said The Tar; "I'm sure I'm doin' the best I can to satisfy you aal. Look at them red herrin's I made this mornin'!"

"They were chust sublime!" said the Captain, clapping him on the back. "But chust try a change to keep their mooths shut. It'll only need to be for a little, for they'll soon tire o' fancy things. I have a kind of a cookery book here you might get some tips in. It's no' mine, mind you, it's Macphail's."

The Tar took the cookery book and turned over some pages with contemptuous and horny fingers.

"A lot o' nonsense!" he said. "Listen to this: 'Take the remains of any cold chicken, mix with the potatoes, put in a pie-dish, and brown with a salamander.' Where are you to get the cold chucken? and where are you to take it? Fancy callin' it a remains; it would be enough to keep you from eatin' chucken. And what's a salamander? There's no' wan on this vessel, at any rate."

"It's chust another name for cinnamon, but you could leave it oot," said the Captain.

"Holy smoke! listen to this," proceeded The Tar: "'How to make clear stock. Take six or seven pounds of knuckle of beef or veal, half a pound of ham or bacon, a quarter of a pound of butter, two onions, one carrot, one turnip, half a head of salary, and two gallons of water.' You couldna sup that in a week."

"Smaal quantities, smaal quantities, Colin," explained the Captain. " I'm sorry to put you to bother, but there's no other way of pleasin' them other fellows."

" There's no' a thing in this book I would eat except a fowl that's described here," said The Tar, after a further glance through the volume.

" The very thing! " cried the Captain, delighted. " Try a fowl for Sunday," and The Tar said he would do his best.

" I soon showed him who wass skipper on this boat," said the Captain going aft to Dougie and the engineer. " It's to be fowls on Sunday."

There was an old-fashioned cutter yacht at anchor in Brodick Bay with a leg of mutton and two plucked fowls hanging openly under the overhang of her stern, which is sometimes even yet the only pantry a yacht of that type has, though the result is not very decorative.

" Look at that! " said the engineer to The Tar as the *Vital Spark* puffed past the yacht. " There's sensible meat for sailors; no malleable mule. I'll bate you them fellows has a cook wi' aal his wuts aboot him."

" It's aal right, Macphail," said The Tar; "chust you wait till to-morrow and I'll give you fancy cookin'."

And sure enough on Sunday he had two boiled fowls for dinner. It was such an excellent dinner that even the engineer was delighted.

" I'll bate you that you made them hens ready oot o' the wife's cookery book," he said. " There's no' a better cookery book on the South-side of Gleska; the genuine Aunt Kate's. People come far and near

for the lend o' that when they're havin' anything
extra."

"Where did you buy the hens?" inquired the
Captain, nibbling contentedly at the last bone left after
the repast.

"I didna buy them at aal," said The Tar. "I
couldna be expected to buy chuckens on the money
you alloo me. Forbye, it doesna say anything aboot
buying in Macphail's cookery book. It says, 'Take
two chickens and boil slowly.' So I chust had to take
them."

"What do you mean by that?" asked Para Handy,
with great apprehension.

"I chust went oot in a wee boat late last night and
took them from the stern o' yon wee yacht," said The
Tar coolly; and a great silence fell upon the crew of
the *Vital Spark*.

"To-morrow," said the Captain emphatically at last
—" to-morrow you'll have tinned meat; do you know
that, Colin? And you'll never have chucken on the
boat again, not if Macphail was breakin' his he'rt
for it."

VIII

LODGERS ON A HOUSE-BOAT

A MAN and his wife came down Crarae Quay from the
village. The man carried a spotted yellow tin box in
one hand and a bottle of milk in the other. He looked
annoyed at something. His wife had one child in her
arms, and another walked weeping behind her, occasionally stopping the weeping to suck a stalk of The
Original Crarae Rock. There was a chilly air of

separation about the little procession that made it
plain there had been an awful row. At the quay the
Vital Spark lay with her hold half covered by the
hatches, after discharging a cargo. Her gallant commander, with Dougie, stood beside the winch and
watched the family coming down the quay.

" Take my word for it, Dougie," said Para Handy,
" that man's no' in very good trum; you can see by
the way he's banging the box against his legs and
speaking to himsel'. It's no' a hymn he's going over,
I'll bate you. And hersel's no' mich better, or she
wouldna be lettin' the poor fellow carry the box."

The man came forward to the edge of the quay,
looked at the newly painted red funnel of the *Vital
Spark*, and seemed, from his countenance, to have been
seized by some bright idea.

" Hey! you with the skipped kep," he cried down
eagerly to Dougie, " when does this steamer start? "

Para Handy looked at his mate with a pride there
was no concealing. " My Chove! Dougie," he said
in a low tone to him. " My Chove! he thinks we're
opposeetion to the *Lord of the Isles* or the *King Edward*.
I'm aye tellin' you this boat iss built on smert lines;
if you and me had brass buttons we could make money
carryin' passengers."

" Are ye deaf? " cried the man on the quay impatiently, putting down the tin box, and rubbing the
sweat from his brow. " When does this boat start? "

" This iss not a boat that starts at aal," said the
Captain. " It's a—it's a kind of a yat."

" Dalmighty! " exclaimed the man, greatly crestfallen, " that settles it. I thocht we could get back to
Gleska wi' ye. We canna get ludgin's in this place,

and whit the bleezes are we to dae when we canna get ludgin's? "

" That's a peety," said the Captain. " It's no' a very nice thing to happen on a Setturday, and there's no way you can get oot of Crarae till Monday unless you have wan of them motor cars."

" We havena oors wi' us," said the wife, taking up a position beside her husband and the tin box. " I'm vexed the only thing o' the kind I ha'e 's a cuddy, and if it wasna for him we would ha'e stayed at Rothesay, whaur you can aye get ludgin's o' some kind. Do ye no' think ye could gie us twa nicht's ludgin's on your boat? I'm shair there's plenty o' room."

" Bless my sowl, where's the plenty o' room? " asked the Captain. " This boat cairries three men and an enchineer, and we're crooded enough in the fo'c'sle."

" Where's that? " she asked, taking all the negotiations out of the hands of her husband, who sat down on the spotted tin box and began to cut tobacco.

" Yonder it is," said Para Handy, indicating the place with a lazy, inelegant, but eloquent gesture of his leg.

" Weel, there's plenty o' room," persisted the woman,—" ye can surely see for yersel' there's plenty o' room; you and your men could sleep at the—at the—the stroup o' the boat there, and ye could mak' us ony kind o' a shake-down doon the stair there "— and she pointed at the hold.

" My coodness! the stroup o' the boat! " exclaimed Para Handy; " you would think it wass a teapot you were taalkin' aboot. And that's no' a doon-stairs at aal, it's the howld. We're no' in the habit of takin' in ludgers in the coastin' tred; I never had wan in the

Fital Spark in aal my life except the time I cairried Wee Teeny. We havena right accommodation for ludgers; we have no napery, nor enough knives and forks——"

" Onything wad dae for a shove-bye," said the woman. " I'm shair ye wouldna see a dacent man and his wife and twa wee hameless lambs sleepin' in the quarry as lang as ye could gie them a corner to sit doon in on that nice clean boat o' yours."

She was a shrewd woman; her compliment to the *Vital Spark* found the soft side of its captain's nature, and, to the disgust of Macphail the engineer and the annoyance of The Tar—though with the hearty consent of the mate—Jack Flood and his family, with the tin box and the bottle of milk, were ten minutes later installed in the fo'c'sle of the *Vital Spark* as paying guests. The terms arranged were two shillings a night. " You couldna get ludgin's in a good hotel for mich less," said the Captain, and Mrs Flood agreed that that was reasonable.

The crew slept somewhat uncomfortably in the hold, and in the middle watches of the night the Captain wakened at the sound of an infant crying. He sat up, nudged Dougie awake, and moralised.

" Chust listen to that, Dougie," he said, " the wee cratur's greetin' ass naitural ass anything, the same ass if it wass a rale ludgin's or on board wan of them ships that carries passengers to America. It's me that likes to hear it; it's ass homely a thing ass ever happened on this vessel. I wouldna say but maybe it'll be good luck. I'm tellin' you what, Dougie, we'll no' cherge them a d—— ha'penny; what do you think, mate? "

" Whatever you say yoursel'," said Dougie.

The wail of the infant continued; they heard Jack Flood get up at the request of his wife and sing. He sang " Rocked in the Cradle of the Deep "—at least he sang two lines of it over and over again, taking liberties with the air that would have much annoyed the original composer if he could have heard him.

" It's chust sublime! " said Para Handy, stretched on a rolled-up sail. " You're a lucky man, Dougie, that iss mairried and has a hoose of your own. Oor two ludgers iss maybe pretty cross when it comes to the quarrelling, but they have no spite at the weans. You would not think that man Flood had the sense to rise up in the muddle of the night and sing ' Rocked in the Cradle of the Deep ' at his child. It chust shows you us workin'-men have good he'rts."

" Jeck may have a cood enough he'rt," said Dougie, " but, man! he has a poor, poor ear for music! I wish he would stop it and no' be frightenin' the wean. I'm sure it never did him any herm."

By-and-by the crying and the music ceased, and the only sound to be heard was the snore of The Tar and the lapping of the tide against the run of the vessel.

Sunday was calm and bright, but there was no sign of the lodgers coming on deck till late in the forenoon, much to the surprise of the Captain. At last he heard a loud peremptory whistle from the fo'c'sle, and went forward to see what was wanted. Flood threw up four pairs of boots at him. " Gie them a bit polish," he said airily. " Ye needna be awfu' parteecular," he added, " but they're a' glaur, and we like to be dacent on Sunday."

The Captain, in a daze, lifted the boots and told

The Tar to oil them, saying emphatically at the same
time to Dougie, " Efter aal, we'll no' let them off with
the two shillin's. They're too dirty parteecular."

There was another whistle ten minutes later, and
Dougie went to see what was wanted.

" I say, my lad," remarked Mr Flood calmly, " look
slippy with the breakfast; we canna sterve here ony
langer."

"Are you no' comin' up for't? " asked Dougie in
amazement. " It's a fine dry day."

" Dry my auntie! " said Mr Flood. " The wife aye
gets her breakfast in her bed on Sundays whether it's
wet or dry. Ye'll get the kippered herrin' and the loaf
she brung last nicht beside the lum."

The Tar cooked the lodgers' breakfast under pro-
test, saying he was not paid wages for being a saloon
steward, and he passed it down to the fo'c'sle.

" Two shilling's a night! " said the Captain. " If I
had known what it wass to keep ludgers, it wouldna be
two shillin's a night I would be cherging them."

He was even more emphatic on this point when a
third whistle came from the fo'c'sle, and The Tar, on
going to see what was wanted now, was informed by
Mrs Flood that the cooking was not what she was
accustomed to. " I never saw a steamer like this in
my life," she said, " first cless, as ye micht say,
and no' a table to tak' yer meat aff, and only
shelfs to sleep on, and sea-sick nearly the hale nicht
to the bargain! Send us doon a pail o' water to clean
oor faces."

Para Handy could stand no more. He washed himself carefully, put on his Sunday clothes and his watch
chain, which always gave him great confidence and

courage, and went to the fo'c'sle-head. He addressed the lodgers from above.

" Leezy," he said ingratiatingly (for so he had heard Mr Flood designate his wife), " Leezy, you're missing aal the fun doon there; you should come up and see the folk goin' to the church; you never saw such style among the women in aal your days."

" I'll be up in a meenute," she replied quickly; " Jeck, hurry up and hook this."

On the whole, the lodgers and the crew of the *Vital Spark* spent a fairly pleasant Sunday. When the Flood family was not ashore walking in the neighbourhood, it was lying about the deck eating dulse and picking whelks culled from the shore by Jack. The mother kindly supplied the infant with as much dulse and shell-fish as it wanted, and it had for these a most insatiable appetite.

" You shouldna eat any wulks or things of that sort when there's no ' r's ' in the month," Para Handy advised her. " They're no' very wholesome then."

" Fiddlesticks! " said Mrs Flood. " I've ett wulks every Fair since I was a wee lassie, and look at me noo! Besides, there's an ' r ' in Fair, that puts it a' richt."

That night the infant wailed from the moment they went to bed till it was time to rise in the morning; Jack Flood sang " Rocked in the Cradle of the Deep " till he was hoarse, and the crew in the hold got up next morning very sorry for themselves.

" You'll be takin' the early steamer? " said Para Handy at the first opportunity.

" Och! we're gettin' on fine," said Jack cheerfully; " Leezy and me thinks we'll just put in the week wi' ye," and the wife indicated her hearty concurrence.

" You canna stay here," said the Captain firmly.

" Weel, we're no' goin' to leave, onywye," said Mr
Flood, lighting his clay pipe. " We took the ludgin's,
and though they're no' as nice as we would like,
we're wullin' to put up with them, and ye canna put
us oot withoot a week's warnin'."

" My Chove! do you say that? " said Para Handy
in amazement. " You're the first and last ludger I'll
have on this vessel! "

" A week's notice; it's the law o' the land," said the
admirable Mr Flood, " isn't that so, Leezy? "

" Everybody that has sense kens that that's richt,"
said Mrs Flood. And the Flood family retired *en
masse* to the fo'c'sle.

Ten minutes later the *Vital Spark* was getting up
steam, and soon there were signs of her immediate
departure from the quay.

" Whaur are ye gaun? " cried Jack, coming hurriedly
on deck.

" Outward bound," said Para Handy with indifference. " That's a sailor's life for you, here the day and
away yesterday."

" To Gleska? " said Mr Flood hopefully.

" Gleska! " said Para Handy. " We'll no' see it for
ten months; we're bound for the Rio Grande."

" Whaur's that in a' the warld? " asked Mrs Flood,
who had joined her husband on deck.

" Oh! chust in foreign perts," said Para Handy.
" Away past the Bay of Biscay, and the first place on
your left-hand side after you pass New Zealand. It's
where the beasts for the Zoo comes from."

In four minutes the Flood family were off the ship,

and struggling up the quay with the spotted tin trunk, and the *Vital Spark* was starting for Bowling.

" I'm a stupid man," said Para Handy in a few minutes after leaving the quay. " Here we're away and forgot aal aboot the money for the ludgin's."

IX

A LOST MAN

IT was a dirty evening, coming on to dusk, and the *Vital Spark* went walloping drunkenly down Loch Fyne with a cargo of oak bark, badly trimmed. She staggered to every shock of the sea; the waves came combing over her quarter, and Dougie the mate began to wish they had never sailed that day from Kilcatrine. They had struggled round the point of Pennymore, the prospect looking every moment blacker, and he turned a dozen projects over in his mind for inducing Para Handy to anchor somewhere till the morning. At last he remembered Para's partiality for anything in the way of long-shore gaiety, and the lights of the village of Furnace gave him an idea.

"Ach! man, Peter," said he, " did we no' go away and forget this wass the night of the baal at Furnace? What do you say to going in and joining the spree? "

" You're feared, Dougie," said the Captain; " you're scaared to daith for your life, in case you'll have to die and leave your money. You're thinkin' you'll be drooned, and that's the way you want to put her into Furnace. Man! but you're tumid, tumid! Chust

look at me—no' the least put aboot. That's becaause
I'm a Macfarlane, and a Macfarlane never was bate
yet, never in this world! I'm no' goin' to stop the night
for any baal—we must be in Clyde on Friday; besides,
we havena the clothes wi' us for a baal. Forbye, who'll
buy the tickets? Eh? Tell me that! Who'll buy the
tickets?"

"Ach! you don't need tickets for a Furnace baal,"
said Dougie, flicking the spray from his ear, and looking longingly at the village they were nearing. " You
don't need tickets for a Furnace baal as long as you
ken the man at the door and taalk the Gaalic at him.
And your clothes 'll do fine if you oil your boots and
put on a kind of a collar. What's the hurry for Clyde?
It'll no' run dry. In weather like this, too! It's chust
a temptin' of Providence. I had a dream yonder
last night that wasna canny. Chust a temptin' of
Providence."

" I wudna say but it is," agreed the Captain weakly,
putting the vessel a little to starboard; " it's many a
day since I was at a spree in Furnace. Are you sure
the baal's the night? "

" Of course I am," said Dougie emphatically; " it
only started yesterday."

" Weel, if you're that keen on't, we'll maybe be chust
as weel to put her in till the mornin'," said Para Handy,
steering hard for Furnace Bay; and in a little he
knocked down to the engines with the usual, " Stop
her, Macphail, when you're ready."

All the crew of the *Vital Spark* went to the ball, but
they did not dance much, though it was the boast of
Para Handy that he was " a fine strong dancer." The
last to come down to the vessel in the morning when

the ball stopped, because the paraffin-oil was done, was the Captain, walking on his heels, with his pea-jacket tightly buttoned on his chest, and his round, go-ashore pot hat, as he used to say himself, " on three hairs." It was a sign that he felt intensely satisfied with everything.

" I'm feeling chust sublime," he said to Dougie, smacking his lips and thumping himself on the chest as he took his place at the wheel, and the *Vital Spark* resumed her voyage down the loch. " I am chust like the eagle that knew the youth in the Scruptures. It's a fine, fine thing a spree, though I wass not in the trum for dancing. I met sixteen cousins yonder, and them all in the committee. They were the proud men last night to be having a captain for a cousin, and them only quarry-men. It's the educaation, Dougie; educaation gives you the nerve, and if you have the nerve you can go round the world."

" You werena very far roond the world, whatever o't," unkindly interjected the engineer, who stuck up his head at the moment.

The Captain made a push at him angrily with his foot. " Go down, Macphail," he said, " and do not be making a display of your ignorance on this ship. Stop you till I get you at Bowling! Not round the world! Man, I wass twice at Ullapool, and took the *Fital Spark* to Ireland wance, without a light on her. There iss not a port I am not acquent with from the Tail of the Bank to Cairndow, where they keep the two New Years. And Campbeltown, ay, or Barra, or Tobermory. I'm telling you when I am in them places it's Captain Peter Macfarlane iss the mich-respected man. If you were a rale enchineer and not chust a

c

fireman, I would be asking you to my ludgings to let you see the things I brought from my voyages."

The engineer drew in his head and resumed the perusal of a penny novelette.

"He thinks I'm frightened for him," said the Captain, winking darkly to his mate. "It iss because I am too cuvil to him: if he angers me, I'll show him. It is chust spoiling the boat having a man like that in cherge of her enchines, and her such a fine smert boat, with me, and a man like me, in command of her."

"And there's mysel', too, the mate," said Dougie; "I'm no' bad mysel'."

Below Minard rocks the weather grew worse again: the same old seas smashed over the *Vital Spark*. "She's pitching aboot chust like a washin'-boyne," said Dougie apprehensively. "That's the worst of them oak-bark cargoes."

"Like a washin'-boyne!" cried Para Handy indignantly; "she's chust doing sublime. I wass in boats in my time where you would need to be bailing the watter out of your top-boots every here and there. The smertest boat in the tred; stop you till I have a pound of my own, and I will paint her till you'll take her for a yat if it wasna for the lum. You and your washin'-boyne! A washin'-boyne wudna do you any herm, my laad, and that's telling you."

They were passing Lochgair; the steamer *Cygnet* overtook and passed them as if they had been standing, somebody shouting to them from her deck.

Para Handy refrained from looking. It always annoyed him to be passed this way by other craft; and in summer time, when the turbine *King Edward* or the

Lord of the Isles went past him like a streak of lightning, he always retired below to hide his feelings. He did not look at the *Cygnet*. " Ay, ay," he said to Dougie, " if I was telling Mr Macbrayne the umpudence of them fellows, he would put a stop to it in a meenute, but I will not lose them their chobs; poor sowls! maybe they have wifes and femilies. That'll be Chonny Mactavish takin' his fun of me; you would think he wass a wean. Chust like them brats of boys that come to the riverside when we'll be going up the Clyde at Yoker and cry, ' *Columbia*, ahoy! ' at us—the duvvle's own! "

As the *Cygnet* disappeared in the distance, with a figure waving at her stern, a huge sea struck the *Vital Spark* and swept her from stem to stern, almost washing the mate, who was hanging on to a stay, overboard.

" Tar! Tar! " cried the Captain. " Go and get a ha'ad o' that bucket or it'll be over the side."

There was no response. The Tar was not visible, and a wild dread took possession of Para Handy.

" Let us pause and consider," said he to himself; " was The Tar on board when we left Furnace? "

They searched the vessel high and low for the missing member of the crew, who was sometimes given to fall asleep in the fo'c'sle at the time he was most needed. But there was no sign of him. " I ken fine he wass on board when we started," said the Captain, distracted, " for I heard him sputtin'. Look again, Dougie, like a good laad." Dougie looked again, for he, too, was sure The Tar had returned from the ball with him. " I saw him with my own eyes," he said, " two of him, the same as if he was a twins; that iss the curse of drink in a place like Furance." But the

search was in vain, even though the engineer said he
had seen The Tar an hour ago.

" Weel, there's a good man gone! " said Para Handy.
" Och! poor Tar! It was yon last smasher of a sea.
He's over the side. Poor laad! poor laad! Cot bless
me, dyin' without a word of Gaalic in his mooth! It's
a chudgment on us for the way we were carryin' on,
chust a chudgment; not another drop of drink will I
drink, except maybe beer. Or at a New Year time.
I'm blaming you, Dougie, for making us stop at
Furnace for a baal I wudna give a snuff for. You are
chust a disgrace to the vessel, with your smokin' and
your drinkin', and your ignorance. It iss time you
were livin' a better life for the sake of your wife and
femily. If it wass not for you makin' me go into
Furnace last night, The Tar would be to the fore yet,
and I would not need to be sending a telegram to his
folk from Ardrishaig. If I wass not steering the boat,
I would break my he'rt greetin' for the poor laad that
never did anybody any herm. Get oot the flag from
below my bunk, give it a syne in the pail, and put it at
half-mast, and we'll go into Ardrishaig and send a
telegram—it'll be a sixpence. It'll be a telegram with
a sore he'rt, I'll assure you. I do not know what I
will say in it, Dougie. It will not do to break it too
much to them; maybe we will send the two telegrams
—that'll be a shilling. We'll say in the first wan—
' Your son, Colin, left the boat to-day ': and in the
next wan we will say—' He iss not coming back, he iss
drooned.' Och! och! poor Tar, amn't I sorry for
him? I was chust going to put up his wages a shillin'
on Setturday."

The *Vital Spark* went in close to Ardrishaig pier just

as the *Cygnet* was leaving after taking in a cargo of herring-boxes. Para Handy and Dougie went ashore in the punt, the Captain with his hands washed and his watch-chain on as a tribute of respect for the deceased. Before they could send off the telegram it was necessary that they should brace themselves for the melancholy occasion. " No drinking, chust wan gless of beer," said Para Handy, and they entered a discreet contiguous public-house for this purpose.

The Tar himself was standing at the counter having a refreshment, with one eye wrapped up in a handkerchief.

" Dalmighty! " cried the Captain, staggered at the sight, and turning pale. " What are you doing here with your eye in a sling? "

" What's your business? " retorted The Tar coolly. " I'm no' in your employ anyway."

" What way that? " asked Para Handy sharply.

" Did you no' give me this black eye and the sack last night at the baal, and tell me I wass never to set foot on the *Vital Spark* again? It was gey mean o' you to go away withoot lettin' me get my dunnage oot, and that's the way I came here with the *Cygnet* to meet you. Did you no' hear me roarin' on you when we passed? "

" Weel done! weel done! " said Para Handy soothingly, with a wink at his mate. " But ach! I wass only in fun, Colin; it wass a jeenk; it wass chust a baur aalthegither. Come away back to the boat like a smert laad. I have a shilling here I wass going to spend anyway. Colin, what'll you take? We thought you were over the side and drooned, and you are here, quite dry as usual."

X

HURRICANE JACK

I VERY often hear my friend the Captain speak of Hurricane Jack in terms of admiration and devotion, which would suggest that Jack is a sort of demigod. The Captain always refers to Hurricane Jack as the most experienced seaman of modern times, as the most fearless soul that ever wore oilskins, the handsomest man in Britain, so free with his money he would fling it at the birds, so generally accomplished that it would be a treat to be left a month on a desert island alone with him.

" Why is he called Hurricane Jack? " I asked the Captain once.

" What the duvvle else would you caal him? " asked Para Handy. " Nobody ever caals him anything else than Hurricane Jeck."

" Quite so, but why? " I persisted.

Para Handy scratched the back of his neck, made the usual gesture as if he were going to scratch his ear, and then checked himself in the usual way to survey his hand as if it were a beautiful example of Greek sculpture. His hand, I may say, is almost as large as a Belfast ham.

" What way wass he called Hurricane Jeck? " said he. " Well, I'll soon tell you that. He wass not always known by that name; that wass a name he got for the time he stole the sheep."

" Stole the sheep! " I said, a little bewildered, for I

failed to see how an incident of that kind would give
rise to such a name.

" Yes; what you might call stole," said Para Handy
hastily; " but, och! it wass only wan smaal wee sheep
he lifted on a man that never went to the church, and
chust let him take it! Hurricane Jeck would not steal
a fly—no, nor two flies, from a Chrustian; he's the
perfect chentleman in that."

" Tell me all about it," I said.

" I'll soon do that," said he, putting out his hand
to admire it again, and in doing so upsetting his glass.
" Tut, tut! " he said. " Look what I have done—
knocked doon my gless; it wass a good thing there wass
nothing in it.

" Hurricane Jeck," said the Captain, when I had
taken the hint and put something in it, " iss a man that
can sail anything and go anywhere, and aalways be
the perfect chentleman. A millionaire's yat or a
washing-boyne—it's aal the same to Jeck; he would
sail the wan chust as smert as the other, and land on the
quay as spruce ass if he wass newly come from a baal.
Oh, man! the cut of his jeckets! And never anything
else but 'lastic-sided boots, even in the coorsest
weather! If you would see him, you would see a man
that's chust sublime, and that careful about his 'lastic-
sided boots he would never stand at the wheel unless
there wass a bass below his feet. He'll aye be oil-
oiling at his hair, and buying hard hats for going ashore
with: I never saw a man wi' a finer heid for the hat,
and in some of the vessels he wass in he would have
the full of a bunker of hats. Hurricane Jeck wass
brought up in the China clupper tred, only he wassna
called Hurricane Jeck then, for he hadna stole the sheep

till efter that. He wass captain of the *Dora Young*, wan of them cluppers; he's a hand on a gaabert the now, but aalways the perfect chentleman."

" It seems a sad downcome for a man to be a gabbart hand after having commanded a China clipper," I ventured to remark. " What was the reason of his change? "

" Bad luck," said Para Handy. " Chust bad luck. The fellow never got fair-play. He would aye be somewhere takin' a gless of something wi' somebody, for he's a fine big cheery chap. I mind splendid when he wass captain on the clupper, he had a fine hoose of three rooms and a big decanter, wi' hot and cold watter, oot at Pollokshaws. When you went oot to the hoose to see Hurricane Jeck in them days, time slupped bye. But he wassna known as Hurricane Jeck then, for it wass before he stole the sheep."

" You were just going to tell me something about that," I said.

" Jeck iss wan man in a hundred, and ass good ass two if there wass anything in the way of trouble, for, man! he's strong, strong! He has a back on him like a shipping-box, and when he will come down Tarbert quay on a Friday night after a good fishing, and the trawlers are arguing, it's two yerds to the step with him and a bash in the side of his hat for fair defiance. But he never hit a man twice, for he's aye the perfect chentleman iss Hurricane Jeck. Of course, you must understand, he wass not known as Hurricane Jeck till the time I'm going to tell you of, when he stole the sheep.

" I have not trevelled far mysel' yet, except Ullapool and the time I wass at Ireland; but Hurricane Jeck in his time has been at every place on the map, and some that's no'. Chust wan of Brutain's hardy sons—that's what he iss. As weel kent in Calcutta as if he wass in the Coocaddens, and he could taalk a dozen of their foreign kinds of languages if he cared to take the bother. When he would be leaving a port, there wassna a leddy in the place but what would be doon on the quay wi' her Sunday clothes on and a bunch o' floo'ers for his cabin. And when he would be sayin' good-bye to them from the brudge, he would chust take off his hat and give it a shoogle, and put it on again; his manners wass complete. The first thing he would do when he reached any place wass to go ashore and get his boots brushed, and then sing ' Rule Britannia ' roond aboot the docks. It wass a sure way to get freend or foe aboot you, he said, and he wass aye as ready for the wan as for the other. Brutain's hardy son!

" He made the fastest passages in his time that wass ever made in the tea trade, and still and on he would meet you like a common working-man. There wass no pride or nonsense of that sort aboot Hurricane Jeck; but, mind you, though I'm callin' him Hurricane Jeck, he wasna Hurricane Jeck till the time he stole the sheep."

" I don't like to press you, Captain, but I'm anxious to hear about that sheep," I said patiently.

" I'm comin' to't," said Para Handy. " Jeck had the duvvle's own bad luck; he couldna take a gless by-ordinar' but the ship went wrong on him, and he lost wan job efter the other, but he wass never anything else but the perfect chentleman. When he had not a penny in his pocket, he would borrow a shilling from

c 2

you, and buy you a stick pipe for yourself chust for good nature——"

"A stick pipe?" I repeated interrogatively.

"Chust a stick pipe—or a wudden pipe, or whatever you like to call it. He had three medals and a clock that wouldna go for saving life at sea, but that wass before he wass Hurricane Jeck, mind you; for at that time he hadna stole the sheep."

"I'm dying to hear about that sheep," I said.

"I'll soon tell you about the sheep," said Para Handy. "It wass a thing that happened when him and me wass sailing on the *Elizabeth Ann*, a boat that belonged to Girvan, and a smert wan too, if she wass in any kind of trum at aal. We would be going here and there aboot the West Coast with wan thing and another, and not costing the owners mich for coals if coals wass our cargo. It wass wan Sunday we were passing Caticol in Arran, and in a place yonder where there wass not a hoose in sight we saw a herd of sheep eating gress near the shore. As luck would have it, there wass not a bit of butcher-meat on board the *Elizabeth Ann* for the Sunday dinner, and Jeck cocked his eye at the sheep and says to me, ' Yonder's some sheep lost, poor things; what do you say to taking the punt and going ashore to see if there's anybody's address on them? '

" ' Whatever you say yoursel',' I said to Jeck, and we stopped the vessel and went ashore, the two of us, and looked the sheep high and low, but there wass no address on them. ' They're lost, sure enough,' said Jeck, pulling some heather and putting it in his pocket —he wassna Hurricane Jeck then—' they're lost, sure enough, Peter. Here's a nice wee wan nobody would ever miss, that chust the very thing for a coal vessel,' and before you could say ' knife ' he had it killed and carried to the punt. Oh, he iss a smert, smert fellow with his hands; he could do anything.

" We rowed ass caalm ass we could oot to the vessel, and we had chust got the deid sheep on board when we heard a roarin' and whustling.

" ' Taalk about Arran being releegious! " said Jeck. ' Who's that whustling on the Lord's day? '

" The man that wass whustling wass away up on the hill, and we could see him coming running doon the hill the same ass if he would break every leg he had on him.

" ' I'll bate you he'll say it's his sheep,' said Jeck. ' Weel, we'll chust anchor the vessel here till we hear what he hass to say, for if we go away and never mind the cratur he'll find oot somewhere else it's the *Elizabeth Ann*.'

" When the fermer and two shepherds came oot to the *Elizabeth Ann* in a boat, she wass lying at anchor, and we were all on deck, every man wi' a piece o' heather in his jecket.

" ' I saw you stealing my sheep,' said the fermer, coming on deck, furious. ' I'll have every man of you jiled for this.'

" ' Iss the man oot of his wuts? ' said Jeck. ' Drink —chust drink! Nothing else but drink! If you were a sober Christian man, you would be in the church at this 'oor in Arran, and not oot on the hill recovering from last night's carry-on in Loch Ranza, and imagining you are seeing things that's not there at aal, at aal.'

" ' I saw you with my own eyes steal the sheep and

take it on board,' said the fermer, nearly choking with rage.

" ' What you saw was my freend and me gathering a puckle heather for oor jeckets,' said Jeck, ' and if ye don't believe me you can search the ship from stem to stern.'

" ' I'll soon do that,' said the fermer, and him and his shepherds went over every bit of the *Elizabeth Ann*. They never missed a corner you could hide a moose in, but there wass no sheep nor sign of sheep anywhere.

" ' Look at that, Macalpine,' said Jeck. ' I have a good mind to have you up for inflammation of character. But what could you expect from a man that would be whustling on the hill like a peesweep on a Sabbath when he should be in the church. It iss a good thing for you, Macalpine, it iss a Sabbath, and I can keep my temper.'

" ' I could swear I saw you lift the sheep,' said the fermer, quite vexed.

" ' Saw your auntie! Drink; nothing but the cursed drink! " said Jeck, and the fermer and his shepherds went away with their tails behind their legs.

" We lay at anchor till it was getting dark, and then we lifted the anchor and took off the sheep that wass tied to it when we put it oot. ' It's a good thing salt mutton,' said Hurricane Jeck as we sailed away from Caticol, and efter that the name he always got wass Hurricane Jeck."

" But why ' Hurricane Jeck '? " I asked, more bewildered than ever.

" Holy smoke! am I no' tellin' ye? " said Para Handy. " It wass because he stole the sheep."

But I don't understand it yet.

XI

PARA HANDY'S APPRENTICE

THE owner of the *Vital Spark* one day sent for her
Captain, who oiled his hair, washed himself with hot
water and a scrubbing-brush, got The Tar to put three
coats of blacking on his boots, attired himself in his
good clothes, and went up to the office in a state of
some anxiety. " It's either a rise in pay," he said to
himself, " or he's heard aboot the night we had in
Campbeltown. That's the worst of high jeenks;
they're aye stottin' back and hittin' you on the nose;
if it's no' a sore heid, you've lost a pound-note, and
if it's nothing you lost, it's somebody clypin' on you."
But when he got to the office and was shown into the
owner's room, he was agreeably enough surprised to
find that though there was at first no talk about a rise
of pay, there was, on the other hand, no complaint.

" What I wanted to see you about, Peter," said the
owner, " is my oldest boy Alick. He's tired of school
and wants to go to sea."

" Does he, does he? Poor fellow! " said Para
Handy. " Och, he's but young yet, he'll maybe get
better. Hoo's the mustress keepin'? "

" She's very well, thank you, Peter," said the owner.
" But I'm anxious about that boy of mine. I feel sure
that he'll run away some day on a ship; he's just the
very sort to do it and I want you to help me. I'm going
to send him one trip with you, and I want you to see
that he's put off the notion of being a sailor—you
understand? I don't care what you do to him so long

as you don't break a leg on him, or let him fall over the side. Give him it stiff."

" Chust that! " said the Captain. " Iss he a boy that reads novelles? "

" Fair daft for them! " said the owner. " That's the cause of the whole thing."

" Then I think I can cure him in wan trip, and it'll no' hurt him either."

" I'll send him down to the *Vital Spark* on Wednesday, just before you start," said the owner. "And, by the way, if you manage to sicken him of the idea, I wouldn't say but there might be a small increase in your wages."

" Och, there's no occasion for that," said Para Handy.

On the Wednesday a boy about twelve years of age, with an Eton suit and a Saturday-to-Monday hand-bag, came down to the wharf in a cab alone, opened the door of the cab hurriedly, and almost fell into the arms of Para Handy, who was on shore to meet him.

"Are you the apprentice for the *Fital Spark*? " asked the Captain affably. " Your name'll be Alick? "

" Yes," said the boy. "Are you the Captain? "

" That's me," said the Captain. " Gie me a haad o' your portmanta," and taking it out of Alick's hand, he led the way to the side of the wharf, where the *Vital Spark* was lying, with a cargo of coals that left her very little free-board, and all her crew on deck awaiting developments. " I'm sorry," he said, " we havena any gangway, but I'll hand you doon to Dougie, and you'll be aal right if your gallowses 'll no' give way."

" What! is THAT the boat I'm to go on? " cried the boy, astounded.

" Yes," said the Captain, with a little natural irritation. "And what's wrong with her? The smertest boat in the tred. Stop you till you see her goin' roond Ardlamont! "

" But she's only a coal boat; she's very wee," said Alick. " I never thought my father would apprentice me on a boat like that."

" But it's aye a beginnin'," explained the Captain, with remarkable patience. " You must aye start sailorin' some way, and there's many a man on the brudge of Atlantic liners the day that began on boats no bigger than the *Fital Spark*. If you don't believe me, Dougie 'll tell you himsel'. Here, Dougie, catch a haad o' oor new apprentice, and watch you don't dirty his clean collar wi' your hands." So saying, he slung Alick down to the mate, and ten minutes later the *Vital Spark*, with her new apprentice on board, was coughing her asthmatic way down the river outward bound for Tarbert. The boy watched the receding wharf with mixed feelings.

" What do you say to something to eat? " asked the Captain, as soon as his command was under way. " I'll tell The Tar to boil you an egg, and you'll have a cup of tea. You're a fine high-spurited boy, and a growin' boy needs aal the meat he can get. Watch that rope; see and no' dirty your collar; it would never do to see an apprentice wi' a dirty collar."

Alick took the tea and the boiled egg, and thought regretfully that life at sea, so far, was proving very different from what he had expected.

" Where are we bound for? " he asked.

"Oh! a good long trup," said the Captain. "As far as Tarbert and back again. You'll be an A.B. by the time you come back."

"And will I get wearing brass buttons?" inquired Alick.

"Brass buttons!" exclaimed Para Handy. "Man, they're oot o' date at sea aalthegither; it's nothing but hooks and eyes, and far less trouble to keep them clean."

"Can I start learning to climb the mast now?" asked Alick, who was naturally impatient to acquire the elements of his new profession.

"Climb the mast!" cried Para Handy, horrified. "There wass never an apprentice did that on my vessel, and never will; it would dirty aal your hands! I see a shoo'er o' rain comin'; there's nothing worse for the young sailor than gettin' damp; away doon below like a good boy, and rest you, and I'll give you a roar when the rain's past."

Alick went below bewildered. In all the books he had read there had been nothing to prepare him for such coddling on a first trip to sea; so far, there was less romance about the business than he could have found at home in Athole Gardens. It rained all afternoon, and he was not permitted on deck; jelly "pieces" were sent down to him at intervals. The Tar was continually boiling him eggs; he vaguely felt some dreadful indignity in eating them, but his appetite compelled him, and the climax of the most hum-drum day he had ever spent came at night when the Captain insisted on his taking gruel to keep off the cold, and on his fastening his stocking round his neck.

Alick was wakened next morning by The Tar standing at the side of his bunk with tea on a tray.

"Apprentices aye get their breakfast in their bed," said The Tar, who had been carefully coached by the Captain what he was to do. " Sit up and take this, and then have a nice sleep to yoursel', for it's like to be rainin' aal day, and you canna get on deck."

" Surely I can't melt," said the boy, exasperated. " I'll not learn much seamanship lying here."

" You would maybe get your daith o' cold," said The Tar, " and a nice-like job we would have nursin' you." He turned to go on deck when an idea that Para Handy had not given him came into his head, and with great solemnity he said to the boy, " Perhaps you would like to see a newspaper; we could put ashore and buy wan for you to keep you from wearyin'."

" I wouldn't object to ' Comic Cuts,' " said Alick, finding the whole illusion of life on the deep slipping from him.

But " Comic Cuts " did not come down. Instead, there came the Captain with a frightful and familiar thing—the strapful of school-books to escape from which Alick had first proposed a sailor's life. Para Handy had sent to Athole Gardens for them the previous day.

" Shipmate ahoy! " he cried, cheerily stumping down to the fo'c'sle. " You'll be frightened you left your books behind, but I sent The Tar for them, and here they are," and, unbuckling the strap, he poured the unwelcome volumes on the apprentice's lap.

" Who ever heard of an apprentice sailor taking his school-books to sea with him? " said Alick, greatly disgusted.

" Who ever heard o' anything else? " retorted the

Captain. "Do you think a sailor doesna need any educaation? Every apprentice has to keep going at his Latin and Greek, and Bills of Parcels, and the height of Ben Nevis, and Grammar, and aal the rest of it. That's what they call navigation, and if you havena the navigation, where are you? Chust that, where are you?"

"Do you meant to tell me that when you were an apprentice you learned Latin and Greek, and all the rest of that rot?" asked Alick, amazed.

"Of course I did," said the Captain unblushingly. "Every day till my heid wass sore!"

"Nature Knowledge, too?" asked Alick.

"Nature Knowledge!" cried Para Handy. "At Nature Knowledge I wass chust sublime! I could do it with my eyes shut. Chust you take your books, Alick, like a sailor, and wire into your navigation, and it'll be the brudge for you aal the sooner."

There were several days of this unromantic life for the boy, who had confidently expected to find the career of a sea apprentice something very different. He had to wash and dress himself every morning as scrupulously as ever he did at home for Kelvinside Academy; Para Handy said that was a thing that was always expected from apprentices, and he even went further and sent Alick back to the water-bucket on the ground that his neck and ears required a little more attention. A certain number of hours each day, at least, were ostensibly devoted to the study of " Navigation," which, the boy was disgusted to find, was only another name for the lessons he had had at the Academy. He was not allowed on deck when it was wet without an umbrella, which the Captain had unearthed from somewhere; it was in vain he rebelled against breakfast in bed, gruel, and jelly " pieces."

" If this is being a sailor, I would sooner be in a Sunday School," said Alick finally.

" Och! you're doin' splendid," said Para Handy. "A fine high-spurited laad! We'll make a sailor of you by the time we're back at Bowling if you keep your health. It's pretty cold the night; away doon to your bunk like a smert laad, and The Tar'll take doon a hot-watter bottle for your feet in a meenute or two."

When the *Vital Spark* got back to the Clyde, she was not three minutes at the wharf when her apprentice deserted her.

Para Handy went up to the owner's office in the afternoon with the boy's school-books and the Saturday-to-Monday bag.

" I don't know how you managed it," said Alick's father, quite pleased; " but he's back yonder this morning saying a sailor's life's a fraud, and that he wouldn't be a sailor for any money. And by the fatness of him, I should say you fed him pretty well."

" Chust that! " said Para Handy. " The Tar would be aye boilin' an egg for him noo and then. Advice to a boy iss not much use; the only thing for it iss kindness, chust kindness. If I wass wantin' to keep that boy at the sailin', I would have taken the rope's-end to him, and he would be a sailor chust to spite me. There wass some taalk aboot a small rise in the pay, but och——"

" That's all right, Peter; I've told the cashier," said the owner, and the Captain of the *Vital Spark* went down the stair beaming.

XII

QUEER CARGOES

" THE worst cargo ever I sailed wi'," said Macphail
the engineer, " was a wheen o' thae Mahommedan
pilgrims: it wasna Eau de Colong they had on their
hankies."

" Mahommedans! " said Para Handy, with his
usual suspicions of the engineer's foreign experience—
" Mahommedans! Where were they bound for?
Was't Kirkintilloch? "

" Kirkintilloch's no' in Mahommeda," said Macphail
nastily. " I'm talkin' aboot rale sailin', no' wyding in
dubs, the way some folk does a' their days."

" Chust that! chust that! " retorted the Captain,
sniffing. " I thought it wass maybe on the Port-
Dundas Canal ye had them."

" There was ten or eleeven o' them died every
nicht," proceeded Macphail, contemptuous of these
interruptions. " We just gied them the heave over the
side, and then full speed aheid to make up for the
seven meenutes."

" Like enough you would ripe their pockets first,"
chimed in Dougie. " The worst cargo ever I sailed
with wass leemonade bottles; you could hear them
clinking aal night, and not wan drop of stumulents on
board! It wass duvilish vexing."

" The worst cargo ever I set eyes on," ventured The
Tar timidly, in presence of these hardened mariners,
" wass sawdust for stuffing dolls."

" Sawdust would suit you fine, Colin," said the

Captain. " I'll warrant you got plenty of sleep that trup.

" You're there and you're taalking about cargoes," proceeded Para Handy, " but there's not wan of you had the experience I had, and that wass with a cargo of shows for Tarbert Fair. They were to go with a luggage-steamer, but the luggage-steamer met with a kind of an accident, and wass late of getting to the Broomielaw: she twisted wan of her port-holes or something like that, and we got the chob. It's me that wassna wantin' it, for it wass no credit to a smert boat like the *Fital Spark*, but you ken yoursel' what owners iss; they would carry coal tar made up in delf crates if they get the freight for it."

" I wouldna say but what you're right," remarked Dougie agreeably.

"A stevedore would go wrong in the mind if he saw the hold of the vessel efter them showmen got their stuff on board. You would think it wass a pawn-shop struck wi' a sheet o' lightning. There wass every-thing ever you saw at a show except the coconuts and the comic polisman. We started at three o'clock in the mornin', and a lot of the show people made a bargain to come wi' us to look efter their stuff. There wass the Fattest Woman in the World, No-Boned Billy or the Boy Serpent, the Mesmerising Man, another man very namely among the Crowned Heads for walkin' on stilts, and the heid man o' the shows, a chap they called Mr Archer. At the last meenute they put on a wee piebald pony that could pick oot any card you asked from a pack. If you don't believe me, Macphail, there's Dougie; you can ask him yoursel'."

" You're quite right, Peter," said Dougie emphati-

cally. " I'll never forget it. What are you goin' to tell
them aboot the Fair? " he added suspiciously.

" It's a terrible life them show folk has! " resumed
the Captain, without heeding the question. " Only
English people would put up with it; poor craturs, I
wass sorry for them! Fancy them goin' aboot from
place to place aal the year roond, wi' no homes! I
would a hundred times sooner be a sailor the way I
am. But they were nice enough to us, and we got on
fine, and before you could say ' knife ' Dougie wass
flirtin' wi' the Fattest Woman in the World."

" Don't believe him, boys," said the mate, greatly
embarrassed. " I never even kent her Chrustian
name."

" When we got the shows discherged at Tarbert,
Mr Archer came and presented us aal with a free pass
for everything except the stilts. ' You'll no' need to
put on your dress clothes,' says he. He wass a cheery
wee chap, though he wass chust an Englishman.
Dougie and me went ashore and had a royal night of
it. I don't know if ever you wass at a Tarbert Fair,
Macphail—you were aye that busy learnin' the names
of the foreign places you say you traivelled to, that
you wouldn't have the time; but I'll warrant you it's
worth while seein'. There's things to be seen there
you couldna see the like of in London. Dougie made
for the tent of the mesmeriser and the Fattest Woman
in the World whenever we got there: he thought she
would maybe be dancin' or something of that sort,
but aal she did was to sit on a chair and look fat.
There wass a crood roond her nippin' her to make sure
she wasna padded, and when we got in she cried,
' Here's my intended man, Mr Dugald; stand aside

and let him to the front to see his bonny wee rosebud. Dugald, darling, you see I'm true to you and wearin' your ring yet,' and she showed the crood a brass ring you could tie boats to."

" She wass a caaution! " said Dougie. " But what's the use of rakin' up them old stories? "

" Then we went to the place where No-Boned Billy or the Boy Serpent wass tying himself in knots and jumpin' through girrs. It was truly sublime! It bates me to know hoo they do it, but I suppose it's chust educaation."

" It's nothing else," said the mate. " Educaation'll do anything for you if you take it when you're young, and have the money as weel."

" Every noo and then we would be takin' a gless of yon red lemonade they sell at aal the Fairs, till Dougie got dizzy and had to go to a public-house for beer."

" Don't say a word aboot yon," interrupted the mate anxiously.

" It's aal right, Dougie, we're among oorsel's. Weel, as I wass sayin', when he got the beer, Dougie, right or wrong, wass for goin' to see the fortune-teller. She wass an Italian-lookin' body that did the spaein', and for a sixpence she gave Dougie the finest fortune ever you heard of. He wass to be left a lot of money when he wass fifty-two, and mairry the dochter of a landed chentleman. But he wass to watch a man wi' curly hair that would cross his path, and he wass to mind and never go a voyage abroad in the month o' September. Dougie came out of the Italian spaewife's in fine trum wi' himsel', and nothing would do him but another vusit to the Fattest Woman in the World."

" Noo, chust you be canny what you're at next! "

again broke in the mate. " You said you would never tell anybody."

" Who's tellin' anybody? " asked Para Handy impatiently. " I'm only mentionin' it to Macphail and Colin here. The mesmeriser wass readin' bumps when we got into the tent, and Dougie wass that full o' the fine fortune the Italian promised him that he must be up to have his bumps read. The mesmeriser felt aal the bumps on Dougie's heid, no' forgettin' the wan he got on the old New Year at Cairndow, and he said it wass wan of the sublimest heids he ever passed under his hands. ' You are a sailor,' he said to Dougie, ' but accordin' to your bumps you should have been a munister. You had a fine, fine heid for waggin'. There's great strength of will behind the ears, and the back of the foreheid's packed wi' animosity.'

" When the readin' of the bumps wass done, and Dougie wass nearly greetin' because his mother didna send him to the College in time, the mesmeriser said he would put him in a trance, and then he would see fine fun."

" Stop it, Peter," protested the mate. " If you tell them, I'll never speak to you again."

Para Handy paid no attention, but went on with his narrative. " He got Dougie to stare him in the eye the time he wass working his hands like anything, and Dougie was in a trance in five meenutes. Then the man made him think he wass a railway train, and Dougie went on his hands and knees up and doon the pletform whustlin' for tunnels. Efter that he made him think he wass a singer—and a plank of wud— and a soger—and a hen. I wass black affronted to see the mate of the *Fital Spark* a hen. But the best of the baur was when he took the Fattest Woman in the World up on the pletform and mairried her to Dougie in front of the whole of Tarbert."

" You gave me your word you would never mention it," interrupted the mate, perspiring with annoyance.

" Then the mesmeriser made Dougie promise he would come back at twelve o'clock the next day and take his new wife on the honeymoon. When Dougie wass wakened oot of the trance, he didn't mind ony-thing aboot it."

" Neither I did," said the mate.

" Next day, at ten meenutes to twelve, when we were makin' ready to start for the Clyde, my mate here took a kind of a tirrivee, and wass for the shows again. I saw the dregs of the mesmerisin' wass on the poor laad, so I took him and gave him a gill of whisky with sulphur in it, and whipped him on board the boat and off to the Clyde before the trance came on at its worst. It never came back."

" Iss that true? " asked The Tar.

" If Dougie wass here—— Of course it iss true," said the Captain.

"All I can mind aboot it is the whisky and sulphur," said Dougie. " That's true enough."

XIII

IN SEARCH OF A WIFE

THE TAR had only got his first week's wages after they were raised a shilling, when the sense of boundless wealth took possession of him, and went to his head like glory. He wondered how on earth he could spend a pound a week. Nineteen shillings were only some loose coins in your pocket, that always fell through as if they were red-hot: a pound-note was different, the pleasure of not changing it till maybe to-morrow was like a wage in itself. He kept the pound-note untouched for three days, and then dreamed one night that he lost it through a hole in his pocket. There were really holes in his pockets, a fact that had never troubled him before; so the idea of getting a wife to mend them flashed on him. He was alarmed at the notion at first —it was so much out of his daily routine of getting up and putting on the fire, and cooking for the crew, and working the winch, and eating and sleeping—so he put it out of his head; but it always came back when he thought of the responsibility of a pound a week, so at last he went up to Para Handy and said to him sheepishly, " I wass thinking to mysel' yonder that maybe it wouldna be a bad plan for me to be takin' a kind of a wife."

" Capital! First-rate! Good for you, Colin! " said the Captain. "A wife's chust the very thing you're needing. Your guernsays iss no credit to the *Fital Spark*—indeed they'll be giving the boat a bad name; and I aalways like to see everything in nice trum aboot her. I would maybe try wan mysel', but I'm that busy on the boat with wan thing and another, me being Captain of her, I havena mich time for keeping a hoose. But och! there's no hurry for me; I am chust nine and two-twenties of years old, no' countin' the year I wass workin' in the sawmull. What wass the gyurl you were thinkin' on? "

" Och, I didna get that length," said The Tar, getting very red in the face at having the business rushed like that.

"Weel, you would need to look slippy," said Para Handy. "There's fellows on shore with white collars on aal the time going aboot picking up the smert wans."

"I wass chust thinkin' maybe you would hear of somebody aboot Loch Fyne that would be suitable: you ken the place better nor me."

"I ken every bit of it," said Para Handy, throwing out his chest. "I wass born aal along this loch-side, and brocht up wi' an auntie. What kind of a wan would you be wantin'?"

"Och, I would chust leave that to yoursel'," said The Tar. "Maybe if she had a puckle money it wouldna be any herm."

"Money!" cried the Captain. "You canna be expectin' money wi' the first. But we'll consuder, Colin. We'll paause and consuder."

Two days later the *Vital Spark* was going up to Inveraray for a cargo of timber, Para Handy steering, and singing softly to himself—

> "As I gaed up yon Hieland hill,
>   I met a bonny lassie;
>   She looked at me and I at her,
>   And oh, but she was saucy.
>   With my rolling eye,
>   Fal tee diddle dye,
>   Rolling eye dum derry,
>   With my rolling eye."

The Tar stood by him peeling potatoes, and the charming domestic sentiment of the song could not fail to suggest the subject of his recent thoughts. "Did you have time to consuder yon?" he asked the Captain, looking up at him with comical coyness.

"Am I no' consudering it as hard as I'm able?" said Para Handy. "Chust you swept aal them peelin's over the side and no' be spoiling the boat, my good laad."

"I wass mindin', mysel', of a femily of gyurls called Macphail up in Easdale, or maybe it wass Luing," said The Tar.

"Macphails!" cried Para Handy. "I never hear the name of Macphail but I need to scratch mysel'. I wouldna alloo any man on the *Fital Spark* to mairry a Macphail, even if she wass the Prunce of Wales. Look at that man of oors that caals himsel' an enchineer; he's a Macphail, that's the way he canna help it."

"Och, I wass chust in fun," The Tar hastened to say soothingly. "I don't think I would care for any of them Macphail gyurls whatever. Maybe you'll mind of something suitable before long."

Para Handy slapped himself on the knee. "My Chove!" said he, "I have the very article that would fit you."

"What's—what's her name?" asked The Tar alarmed at the way destiny seemed to be rushing him into matrimony.

"Man, I don't know," said the Captain, "but she's the laandry-maid up here in the Shurriff's—chust a regular beauty. I'll take you up and show her you to-morrow."

"Will we no' be awfu' busy to-morrow?" said The Tar hastily. "Maybe it would be better to wait till we come back again. There's no' an awfu' hurry."

"No hurry!" cried the Captain. "It's the poor heid for business you have, Colin; a gyurl the same as

I'm thinkin' on for you will be snapped up whenever she gets her Mertinmas wages."

" I'm afraid she'll be too cluver for me, her being a laandry-maid," said The Tar. " They're aawfu' high-steppers, laandry-maids, and aawfu' stiff."

" That's wi' working among starch," explained Para Handy. " It'll aal come oot in the washin'. Not another word, Colin; leave it to me. And maybe Dougie, och ay, Dougie and me'll see you right."

So keenly did the Captain and Dougie enter into the matrimonial projects of The Tar that they did not even wait till the morrow, but set out to interview the young lady that evening. " I'll no' put on my pea-jecket or my watch-chain in case she might take a fancy to my-sel'," the Captain said to his mate. "A man in a good poseetion like me canna be too caautious." The Tar, at the critical moment, showed the utmost reluctance to join the expedition. He hummed and hawed, pro-tested he " didna like," and would prefer that they settled the business without him; but this was not according to Para Handy's ideas of business, and ultimately the three set out together with an arrange-ment that The Tar was to wait out in the Sheriff's garden while his ambassadors laid his suit in a pre-liminary form before a lady he had never set eyes on and who had never seen him.

There was a shower of rain, and the Captain and his mate had scarcely been ushered into the kitchen on a plea of " important business " by the Captain, than The Tar took shelter in a large wooden larder at the back of the house.

Para Handy and Dougie took a seat in the kitchen

at the invitation of its single occupant, a stout cook with a humorous eye.

"It was the laandry-maid we were wantin' to see, mem," said the Captain, ducking his head forward several times and grinning widely to inspire confidence and create a genial atmosphere without any loss of time. "We were chust passing the door, and we thought we would give her a roar in the by-going."

"You mean Kate?" asked the cook.

"Ay! chust that, chust that—Kate," said the Captain, beaming warmly till his whiskers curled. "Hoo's the Shurriff keeping himsel'?" he added as an afterthought. "Iss he in good trum them days?" And he winked expansively at the cook.

"Kate's not in," said the domestic. "She'll be back in a while if you wait."

The Captain's face fell for a moment. "Och perhaps you'll do fine yoursel'," said he cordially, at last. "We have a fellow yonder on my boat that's come into some money, and what iss he determined on but to get mairried? He's aawfu' backward, for he never saw much Life except the Tarbert Fair, and he asked us to come up here and put in a word for him."

"Is that the way you do your courtin' on the coal-gabbarts?" said the cook, greatly amused.

"Coal-gaabert!" cried Para Handy, indignant. "There iss no coal-gaabert in the business; I am the Captain of the *Fital Spark*, the smertest steamboat in the coastin' tred——"

"And I'm no' slack mysel'; I'm the mate," said Dougie, wishing he had brought his trump.

"He must be a soft creature not to speak for himself," said the cook.

" Never mind that," said the Captain; " are you game to take him? "

The cook laughed. " What about yoursel'? " she asked chaffingly, and the Captain blenched.

" Me! " he cried. " I peety the wumman that would mairry me. If I wass not here, Dougie would tell you —would you no', Dougie?—I'm a fair duvvle for high jeenks. Forbye, I'm sometimes frightened for my health."

"And what is he like, this awfu' blate chap?" asked the cook.

"As smert a laad as ever stepped," protested Para Handy. " Us sailors iss sometimes pretty wild; it's wi' followin' the sea and fightin' hurricanes, here the day and away yesterday; but Colin iss ass dacent a laad ass ever came oot of Knapdale if he wass chust letting himself go. Dougie himsel' will tell you."

" There's nothing wrong wi' the fellow," said Dougie. "A fine riser in the mornin'."

"And for cookin', there's no' his equal," added the Captain.

" It seems to me it's my mistress you should have asked for," said the cook; " she's advertising for a scullery-maid." But this sarcasm passed over the heads of the eager ambassadors.

" Stop you! " said the Captain, " and I'll take him in himsel'; he's oot in the garden waiting on us." And he and the mate went outside.

" Colin! " cried Para Handy, " come away and be engaged, like a smert laad." But there was no answer, and it was after considerable searching they discovered the ardent suitor sound asleep in the larder.

" It's no' the laandry-maid; but it's a far bigger

wan," explained the Captain. " She's chust sublime. Aal you have to do now is to come in and taalk nice to her."

The Tar protested he couldn't talk to her unless he had some conversation lozenges. Besides, it was the laundry-maid he had arranged for, not the cook.

" She'll do fine for a start; a fine gyurl," the Captain assured him, and with some difficulty they induced The Tar to go with them to the back-door, only to find it emphatically shut in their faces.

" Let us paause and consuder, what day iss this? " asked the Captain, when the emphasis of the rebuff had got time to sink into his understanding.

" Friday," said Dougie.

" Tuts! wass I not sure of it? It's no' a lucky day for this kind of business. Never mind, Colin, we'll come to-morrow when the laandry-maid's in, and you'll bring a poke of conversation lozenges. You mustna be so stupid, man; you were awfu' tumid!"

" I wasna a bit tumid, but I wasna in trum," said The Tar, who was walking down to the quay with a curious and unusual straddle.

"And what for would you not come at wance when I cried you in? " asked the Captain.

" Because," said The Tar pathetically, " I had a kind of an accident yonder in the larder: I sat doon on a basket of country eggs."

XIV

PARA HANDY'S PIPER

IF you haven't been at your favourite coast resort except at the time of summer holidays, you don't know much about it. At other seasons of the year it looks different, smells different, and sounds different—that is, when there's any sound at all in it. In those dozing, dreamy days before you come down with your yellow tin trunk or your kit-bag, there's only one sound in the morning in the coast resort — the sizzling of frying herring. If it is an extra lively day, you may also hear the baker's van-driver telling a dead secret to the deaf bellman at the other end of the village, and the cry of sea-gulls. Peace broods on that place then like a benediction, and (by the odour) some one is having a sheep's head singed at the smithy.

I was standing one day on Brodick quay with Para Handy when the place looked so vacant, and was so quiet we unconsciously talked in whispers for fear of wakening somebody. The *Vital Spark* shared the peace of that benign hour: she nodded idly at the quay, her engineer half asleep with a penny novelette in his hands; The Tar, sound asleep and snoring, unashamed, with his back against the winch; Dougie, the mate, smoking in silent solemnity, and occasionally scratching his nose, otherwise you would have taken him for an ingenious automatic smoking-machine, set agoing by putting a penny in the slot. If anybody had dropped a postage-stamp in Brodick that day, it would have sounded like a dynamite explosion. It was the breakfast hour.

Suddenly a thing happened that seemed to rend the very heavens: it was the unexpected outburst of a tinker piper, who came into sight round the corner of a house, with his instrument in the preliminary stages of the attack.

D

" My Chove! " said Para Handy, " isn't that fine?
Splendid aalthegither! "

" What's your favourite instrument? " I asked.

" When Dougie's in trum it's the trump," said he
in a low voice, lest the mate (who was certainly very
vain of his skill on the trump—that is to say, the Jew's
harp) should hear him; " but, man! for gaiety, the
pipes. They're truly sublime! A trump's fine for small
occasions, but for style you need the pipes. And good
pipers iss difficult nooadays to get; there's not many
in it. You'll maybe can get a kind of a plain piper
going aboot the streets of Gleska noo and then, but
they're like the herrin', and the turnips, and rhubarb,
and things like that—you don't get them fresh in
Gleska; if you want them at their best, you have to
go up to the right Hielands and pull them off the tree.
You ken what I mean yoursel'."

And the Captain of the *Vital Spark* widely opened
his mouth and inhaled the sound of the bagpipe with
an air of great refreshment.

" That's ' The Barren Rocks of Aden ' he iss on
now," he informed me by and by. " I can tell by the
sound of it. Oh, music! music! it's me that's fond
of it. It makes me feel that droll I could bound over
the mountains, if you understand. Do you know that
I wance had a piper of my own? "

" A piper of your own! "

" Ay, chust that, a piper of my own, the same ass
if I wass the Marquis of Bute. You'll be thinkin' I
couldna afford it," Para Handy went on, smiling slyly,
" but a Macfarlane never wass bate. Aal the fine
gentry hass their piper that plays to them in the
mornin' to put them up, and goes playin' roond the

table at dinner-time when there's any English vusitors there, and let them chust take it! It serves them right; they should stay in their own country. My piper wass a Macdonald."

" You mean one of the tinker pipers? " I said mischievously, for I knew a tribe of tinker pipers of that name.

Para Handy was a little annoyed. " Well," he said, " I wouldna deny but he wass a kind of a tinker, but he wass in the Militia when he wass workin', and looked quite smert when he wass sober."

" How long did you keep the piper? " I asked, really curious about this unexpected incident in the Captain's career.

" Nearly a whole day," he answered. " Whiles I kept him and whiles he wass going ashore for a dram.

" To let you understand, it wass the time of the fine fushin's in Loch Fyne, and I had a cousin yonder that wass gettin' mairried at Kilfinan. The weddin' wass to be on a Friday, and I wass passin' up the loch with a cargo of salt, when my cousin hailed me from the shore, and came oot in a small boat to speak to me.

" ' Peter,' he said to me, quite bashful, ' they're sayin' I'm goin' to get mairried on Friday, and I'm lookin' for you to be at the thing.'

" ' You can depend on me bein' there, Dougald,' I assured him. ' It would be a poor thing if the Macfarlanes would not stick by wan another at a time of trial.'

" ' Chust that! ' said my cousin; ' there's to be sixteen hens on the table and plenty of refreshment. What's botherin' me iss that there's not a piper in Kilfinan. I wass thinkin' that maybe between this and

Friday you would meet wan on your trevels, and take him back with you on your shup.'

" ' Mercy on us! You would think it wass a parrot from foreign perts I wass to get for you,' I said. ' But I'll do my best,' and off we went. I watched the hill-sides aal the way up the loch to see if I could see a piper; but it wass the time of the year when there's lots of work at the hay, and the pipers wass keepin' oot of sight, till I came to Cairndow. Dougie and me wass ashore at Cairndow in the mornin', when we saw this Macdonald I'm telling you aboot standin' in front of the Inns with pipes under his oxter. He wass not playin' them at the time. I said to him, ' There's a weddin' yonder at Kilfinan to-morrow, that they're wantin' a piper for. What would you take to come away doon on my vessel and play for them? '

" ' Ten shillin's and my drink,' he said, as quick as anything.

" ' Say five and it's a bargain,' I said; and he engaged himself on the spot. He wass a great big fellow with a tartan trooser and a cocketty bonnet, and oh, my goodness! but his hair wass rud! I couldna but offer him a dram before we left Cairndow, for we were startin' there and then, but he wouldna set foot in the Inns, and we went on board the *Fital Spark* withoot anything at all, and started doon the loch. I thought it wass a droll kind of a piper I had that would lose a chance.

" When we would be a mile or two on the passage, I said to him, ' Macdonald, tune up your pipes and give us the Macfarlanes' Merch.'

" He said he didna know the Macfarlanes had a Merch, but would do the best he could by the ear, and he began to screw the bits of his pipes together. It took him aboot an hour, and by that time we were off Strachur.

" ' Stop you the boat,' he said, ' I'll need to get ashore a meenute to get something to soften the bag of this pipes; it's ass hard ass a bit of stick.'

" ' You can get oil from the enchineer,' I said to him.

" ' Oil! ' said he; ' do you think it's a clock I'm mendin'? No, no; there's nothing will put a pipe bag in trum but some treacle poured in by the stock.'

" Well, we went ashore and up to the Inns, and he asked if they could give him treacle for his bagpipes. They said they had none. ' Weel,' said he, ' next to that the best thing for it iss whusky—give me a gill of the best, and the Captain here will pay for it; I'm his piper.' He got the gill, and what did he do but pour a small sensation of it into the inside of his pipes and drink the rest? ' It comes to the same thing in the long-run,' said he, and we got aboard again, and away we started.

" ' There's another tune I am very fond of,' I said to him, watchin' him workin' away puttin' his drones in order. ' It's " The 93rd's Farewell to Gibraltar." '

" ' I ken it fine,' he said, ' but I don't ken the tune. Stop you, and I'll give you a trate if I could get this cursed pipe in order. What aboot the dinner? '

" The dinner wass nearly ready, so he put the pipes past till he wass done eatin', and then he had a smoke, and by the time that wass done we were off Lochgair. ' That puts me in mind,' said he; ' I wonder if I could get a chanter reed from Maclachlan the innkeeper? He plays the pipes himself. The chanter reed I have iss bad, and I would like to do the best I could at your cousin's weddin'.'

" We stopped, and Dougie went ashore in the smaal boat with him, and when they came back in half-an-hour the piper said it wass a peety, but the innkeeper wasna a piper efter aal, and didna have a reed, but maybe we would get wan in Ardrishaig.

" ' We're no' goin' to Ardrishaig, we're goin' to Kilfinan,' I told him, and he said he couldna help it, but we must make for Ardrishaig, right or wrong, for he couldna play the pipes right withoot a new reed. ' When you hear me playing,' he said, ' you will be glad you took the trouble. There iss not my equal in the three parishes,' and, man, but his hair wass rud, rud!

" We wouldna be half-an-oor oot from Lochgair when he asked if the tea would soon be ready. He wass that busy puttin' his pipes in order, he said, he was quite fatigued. Pipers iss like canaries, you have to keep them going weel with meat and drink if you want music from them. We gave him his tea, and by the time it wass finished we were off Ardrishaig, and he made me put her in there to see if he could get a reed for his chanter. Him and Dougie went ashore in the smaal boat. Dougie came back in an oor wi' his hair awfu' tousy and nobody wi' him.

" ' Where's my piper? ' I said to him.

" ' Man, it's terrible! ' said Dougie; ' the man's no a piper at aal, and he's away on the road to Kilmertin. When he wass standin' at Cairndow Inns yonder, he was chust holdin' the pipes for a man that wass inside for his mornin', and you and me 'll maybe get into trouble for helpin' him to steal a pair o' pipes.'

" That wass the time I kept a piper of my own," said Para Handy, in conclusion. "And Dougie had to play the trump to the dancin' at my cousin's weddin'."

XV

THE SAILORS AND THE SALE

PARA HANDY'S great delight was to attend farm sales. "A sale's a sublime thing," he said, " for if you don't like a thing you don't need to buy it. It's at the sales a good many of the other vessels in the tred get their sailors." This passion for sales was so strong in him that if there was one anywhere within twelve miles of any port the *Vital Spark* was lying at, he would lose a tide or risk demurrage rather than miss it. By working most part of a night he got a cargo of coals discharged at Lochgoilhead one day in time to permit of his attending a displenishing sale ten miles away. He and the mate, Dougie, started in a brake that was conveying people to the sale; they were scarcely half-way there when the Captain sniffed.

" Hold on a meenute and listen, Dougie," said he. " Do you no' smell anything? "

Dougie sniffed too, and his face was lit up by a beautiful smile as of one who recognises a friend. " It's not lemon kali at any rate," he said knowingly, and chuckled in his beard.

" Boys! " said the Captain, turning round to address the other passengers in the brake, who were mainly cattle dealers and farmers—" Boys! this iss going to be a majestic sale; we're five miles from the place and I can smell the whisky already."

At that moment the driver of the brake bent to look under his seat, and looked up again with great vexation written on his countenance. " Isn't it not chust duvvelish? " he said. " Have I not gone away and put my left foot through a bottle of good spurits I wass bringing up wi' me in case anybody would take ill through the night."

" Through the night! " exclaimed one of the farmers, who was plainly not long at the business. " What night are you taalking aboot? "

" This night," replied the driver promptly.

" But surely we'll be back at Lochgoilhead before night? " said the farmer, and all the others in the coach looked at him with mingled pity and surprise.

" It's a ferm sale we're going to, and not a rent collection," said the driver. "And there's thirty-six gallons of ale ordered for it, no' to speak of refreshments. If we're home in time for breakfast from this sale it's me that'll be the bonny surprised man, I'm telling you."

At these farm sales old custom demands that food and drink should be supplied " ad lib." by the outgoing tenant. It costs money, but it is a courtesy that pays in the long-run, for if the bidding hangs fire a brisk circulation of the refreshments stimulates competition among the buyers, and adds twenty per cent to the price of stots. It would be an injustice to Para Handy and Dougie to say they attended sales from any consideration of this sort; they went because of the high jeenks. At the close of the day sometimes they found that they had purchased a variety of things not likely to be of much use on board a steam-lighter, as on the occasion when Dougie bought the rotary churn.

" Keep away from the hoosehold furniture aaltogither! " said the Captain, this day. " We have too mich money in oor pockets between us, and it'll be safer no' to be in sight of the unctioneer till the beasts iss on, for we'll no' be tempted to buy beasts."

" I would buy an elephant for the fun of the thing, let alone a coo or two," said Dougie.

" That's put me in mind," said the Captain, " there's a cousin of my own yonder in Kilfinan wantin' a milk coo for the last twelvemonth; if I saw a bargain maybe I would take it. But we'll do nothing rash, Dougie, nothing rash; maybe we're chust sailors, but we're no' daft aalthegither."

By this time they were standing on the outside of a crowd of prospective purchasers interested in a collection of farm utensils and household sundries, the disposal of which preceded the rouping of the beasts. The forenoon was chilly; the chill appeared to affect the mood of the crowd, who looked coldly on the chain harrows, turnip-cutters, and other articles offered to them at prices which the auctioneer said it broke his heart to mention, and it was to instil a little warmth into the proceedings that a handy man with red whiskers went round with refreshments on a tray.

" Streetch your hand and take a gless," he said to the Captain. " It'll do you no herm."

" Man, I'm not mich caring for it," drawled the Captain. " I had wan yesterday. What do you think, Dougie? Would it do any herm chust to take wan gless to show we're freendly to the sale of impliments and things? "

" Whatever you say yoursel'," replied Dougie diffi-

D 2

dently, but at the same time grasping the glass nearest him with no uncertain hand.

" Weel, here's good prices! " said the Captain, fixing to another glass, and after that the sun seemed to come out with a genial glow.

The lamentable fact must be recorded that before the beasts came up to the hammer the mate of the *Vital Spark* had become possessor of a pair of curling-stones—one of them badly chipped—a Dutch hoe, and a baking-board.

" What in the world are you going to do with that trash? " asked the Captain, returning from a visit to the outhouse where the ale was, to find his mate with the purchases at his feet.

" Och! it's aal right," said Dougie, cocking his eye at him. " I wassna giving a docken for the things mysel', but I saw the unctioneer aye look-looking at me, and I didna like no' to take nothing. It's chust, as you might say, for the good of the hoose. Stop you and you'll see some fun."

" But it's a rideeculous thing buying curling-stones at this time of the year, and you no' a curler. What? "

Dougie scratched his neck and looked at his purchases. " They didn't cost mich," he said; " and they're aye handy to have aboot you."

When the cattle came under the hammer it was discovered that prices were going to be very low. All the likely buyers seemed to be concentrated round the beer-barrel in the barn, with the result that stots, queys, cows, and calves were going at prices that brought the tears to the auctioneer's eyes. He hung so long on the sale of one particular cow for which he could only squeeze out offers up to five pounds that Para Handy took pity on him, and could not resist giving a nod that put ten shillings on to its price and secured the animal.

" Name, please? " said the auctioneer, cheering up wonderfully.

" Captain Macfarlane," said Para Handy, and, very much distressed at his own impetuosity, took his mate aside. " There you are, I bought your coo for you," he said to Dougie.

" For me! " exclaimed his mate. " What in the world would I be doing with a coo? "

" You said yoursel' you would take a coo or two for the fun o' the thing," said Para Handy.

" When I'm buying coos I'm buying them by my own word o' mooth; you can chust keep it for your cousin in Kilfinan. If I wass buyin' a coo it wouldna be wan you could hang your hat on in fifty places No, no, Peter, I'm Hielan', but I'm no' so Hielan' ass aal that."

" My goodness! " said Para Handy, " this iss the scrape! I will have to be taking her to Lochgoilhead, and hoisting her on the vessel, and milking her, and keeping her goodness knows what time till I'll have a cargo the length of Kilfinan. Forbye, my cousin and me's no' speakin' since Whitsunday last."

" Go up to the unctioneer and tell him you didna buy it at aal, that you were only noddin' because you had a tight collar," suggested the mate, and the Captain acted on the suggestion; but the auctioneer was not to be taken in by any such story, and Para Handy and his mate were accordingly seen on the road to Lochgoil late that night with a cow, the possession of which took all the pleasure out of their day's outing. Dougie's curling-stones, hoe, and baking-board were to follow in a cart.

It was a long time after this before the *Vital Spark* had any occasion to go to Lochgoilhead. Macphail the engineer had only to mention the name of the place and allude casually to the price of beef or winter feeding, and the Captain would show the most extraordinary ill-temper. The fact was he had left his purchase at a farmer's at Lochgoil to keep for him till called for, and he never liked to think upon the day of reckoning. But the *Vital Spark* had to go to Lochgoilhead sooner or later, and the first time she did so the Captain went somewhat mournfully up to the farm where his cow was being kept for him.

" It's a fine day; hoo's the mustress? " he said to the farmer, who showed some irritation at never having heard from the owner of the cow for months.

" Fine, but what aboot your coo, Peter? "

" My Chove! iss she living yet? " said the Captain. " I'll be due you a penny or two."

" Five pounds, to be exact; and it'll be five pounds ten at the end of next month."

" Chust the money I paid for her," said Para Handy. " Chust you keep her for me till the end of next month, and then pay yoursel' with her when my account iss up to the five pound ten," a bargain which was agreed on; and so ended Para Handy's most expensive high jeenk.

XVI

A NIGHT ALARM

THE wheel of the *Vital Spark* was so close to the engines that the Captain could have given his orders in a whisper, but he was so proud of the boat that he liked to sail her with all the honours, so he always used the knocker. He would catch the brass knob and give one, two, or three knocks as the circumstances demanded, and then put his mouth to the speaking-tube and cry coaxingly down to the engineer, " Stop her, Dan, when you're ready." That would be when she was a few lengths off the quay. Dan, the engineer, never let on he heard the bell; he was very fond of reading penny novelettes, and it was only when he was spoken to soothingly down the tube that he would put aside ' Lady Winifred's Legacy,' give a sigh, and stop his engine. Then he would stand upright—which brought his head over the level of the deck, and beside the Captain's top-boots—wiping his brow with a piece of waste the way real engineers do on the steamers that go to America. His great aim in taking a quay was to suggest to anybody hanging about it that it was frightfully hot in the engine-room—just like the Red Sea—while the fact was that most of the time there was a draught in the engine-room of the *Vital Spark* that would keep a cold store going without ice.

When he stuck up his head he always said to the Captain, " You're aye wantin' something or other; fancy goin' awa' and spoilin' me in the middle o' a fine baur."

" I'm sorry, Dan," Para Handy would say to him in an agony of remorse, for he was afraid of the engineer because that functionary had once been on a ship that made a voyage to Australia, and used to say he had killed a man in the Bush. When he was not sober it was two men, and he would weep. " I'm sorry, Dan, but I did not know you would be busy." Then he would knock formally to reverse the engine, and cry down the tube, " Back her, Dan, when you're ready; there's no hurry," though the engineer was, as I have said, so close that he could have put his hand on his head.

Dan drew in his head, did a bit of juggling with the machinery, and resumed his novelette at the place where Lady Winifred lost her jewels at the ball. There was something breezy in the way he pulled in his head and moved in the engine-room that disturbed the Captain. " Dan's no' in good trum the day," he would say, in a hoarse whisper to the mate Dougie under these circumstances. " You daurna say wan word to him but he flies in a tiravee."

" It's them cursed novelles," was always Dougie's explanation; " they would put any man wrong in the heid, let alone an enchineer. If it wass me wass skipper of this boat, I wadna be so soft with him, I'll assure you."

" Ach, you couldna be hard on the chap and him a Macphail," said the Captain. " There wass never any holdin' o' them in. He's an aawful fellow for high jeenks; he killed a man in the Bush."

One afternoon the *Vital Spark* came into Tarbert with a cargo of coals that could not be discharged till the morning, for Sandy Sinclair's horse and cart were engaged at a country funeral. The Captain hinted at repainting a strake or two of the vessel, but his crew said they couldn't be bothered, forbye Dougie had three shillings; so they washed their faces after tea and went up the town. Peace brooded on the *Vital Spark*, though by some overlook Macphail had left her with almost a full head of steam. Sergeant Macleod, of the constabulary, came down when she lay deserted. " By Cheorge! " said he to himself, " them fellows iss coing to get into trouble this night, I'm tellin' you," for he knew the *Vital Spark* of old. He drew his tippit more firmly about him, breathed hard, and went up the town to survey the front of all the public-houses. Peace brooded on the *Vital Spark* —a benign and beautiful calm.

It was ten o'clock at night when her crew returned. They came down the quay in a condition which the most rigid moralist could only have described as jovial, and went to their bunks in the fo'c'sle. A drizzling rain was falling. That day the Captain had mounted a new cord on the steam whistle, so that he could blow it by a jerk from his position at the wheel. It was drawn back taut, and the free end of it was fastened to a stanchion. As the night passed and the rain continued falling, the cord contracted till at last it acted on the whistle, which opened with a loud and croupy hoot that rang through the harbour and over the town. Otherwise peace still brooded on the *Vital Spark*. It took fifteen minutes to waken the Captain, and he started up in wild alarm. His crew were snoring in the light of a small globe lamp, and the engineer had a ' Family Herald Supplement ' on his chest.

" That's either some duvvlement of somebody's or

a warnin'," said Para Handy, half irritated, half in superstitious alarm. " Dougie, are you sleepin'? "

" What would I be here for if I wass not sleepin'? " said Dougie.

" Go up like a smert laad and see who's meddlin' my whustle."

" I canna," said Dougie; " I havena but the wan o' my boots on. Send up The Tar." The Tar was so plainly asleep from his snoring that it seemed no use to tackle him. The Captain looked at him. " Man! " he said, " he hass a nose that minds me o' a winter day, it's so short and dirty. He would be no use any way. It's the enchineer's chob, but I daurna waken him, he's such a man for high jeenks." And still the whistle waked the echoes of Tarbert.

" If I wass skipper of this boat I would show him," said Dougie, turning in his bunk, but showing no sign of any willingness to turn out. " Give him a roar, Peter, or throw the heel of yon pan loaf at him."

" I would do it in a meenute if he wasna a Macphail," said the Captain, distracted. " He wance killed a man in the Bush. But he's the enchineer; the whustle's in his depairtment. Maybe if I spoke nice to him he would see aboot it. Dan! " he cried softly across the fo'c'sle to the man with the ' Family Herald Supplement ' on his chest—" Dan, show a leg, like a good laad, and go up and stop that cursed whustle."

"Are you speakin' to me? " said the engineer, who was awake all the time.

" I was chust makin' a remark," explained the Captain hurriedly. " It's not of any great importance, but there's a whustle there, and it's wakin' the whole toon of Tarbert. If you werena awfu' throng sleepin', you might take a bit turn on dake and see what is't. Chust when you're ready, Dan, chust when you're ready."

Dan ostentatiously turned on his side and loudly went to sleep again. And the whistle roared louder than ever.

The Captain began to lose his temper. " Stop you till I get back to Bowling," he said, " and I'll give every man of you the whole jeeng-bang, and get rale men for the *Fital Spark*. Not a wan of you iss worth a spittle in the hour of dancher and trial. Look at Macphail there tryin' to snore like an enchineer with a certeeficate, and him only a fireman! I am not a bit frightened for him; I do not believe he ever killed a man in the Bush at aal—he hass not the game for it; I'll bate you he never wass near Australia—and what wass his mother but wan of the Macleans of Kenmore? Chust that; wan of the Macleans of Kenmore! Him and his pride! If I had my Sunday clothes on I would give him my opeenion. And there you are, Dougie! I thocht you were a man and not a mice. You are lying there in your ignorance, and never wass the length of Ullapool. Look at me—on the vessels three over twenty years, and twice wrecked in the North at places that's not on the maps."

The two worthies thus addressed paid no attention and snored with suspicious steadiness, and the Captain turned his attention to The Tar.

" Colin! " he said more quietly, " show a leg, like a cluvver fellow, and go up and put on the fire for the breakfast." But The Tar made no response, and in the depth of the fo'c'sle Para Handy's angry voice rose up again, as he got out of his bunk and prepared to pull on some clothes and go up on deck himself.

" Tar by by-name and Tar by nature! " said he. " You will stick to your bed that hard they could not take you off without half-a-pound of saalt butter. My goodness! have I not a bonny crew? You are chust a wheen of crofters. When the owners of vessels wass wantin' men like you, they go to the Kilmichael cattle-market and drag you down with a rope to the seaside. You will not do the wan word I tell you. I'll wudger I'll not hammer down to you again, Dan, or use the speakin'-tube, the same ass if you were a rale enchineer; I'll chust touch you with the toe of my boot when I want you to back her, mind that! There iss not a finer nor a faster vessel than the *Fital Spark* in the tred; she iss chust sublime, and you go and make a fool of her with your drinking and your laziness and your ignorance."

He got up on deck in a passion, to find a great many Tarbert people running down the quay to see what was wrong, and Sergeant Macleod at the head of them.

" Come! come ! Peter, what iss this whustlin' for on a wet night like this at two o'clock in the mornin'? " asked the sergeant, with a foot on the bulwark. " What are you blow-blow-blowin' at your whustle like that for? "

" Chust for fun," said the Captain. " I'm a terrible fellow for high jeenks. I have three fine stots from the Kilmichael market down below here, and they canna sleep unless they hear a whustle."

" The man's in the horrors! " said the sergeant in a whisper to some townsmen beside him on the quay. " I must take him to the lock-up and make a case of him, and it's no' a very nice chob, for he's ass strong ass a horse. Wass I not sure there would be trouble when I saw the *Fital Spark* the day? It must be the lock-up for him, and maybe Lochgilphead, but it iss a case for deleeberation and caaution—great caaution.

" Captain Macfarlane," he said in a bland voice to the Captain, who stood defiant on the deck, making no attempt to stop the whistling. " Mr Campbell the banker wass wantin' to see you for a meenute up the toon. Chust a meenute! He asked me to come doon and tell you."

" What will the banker be wantin' wi' me? " said the Captain, cooling down and suspecting nothing. " It's a droll time o' night to be sendin' for onybody."

" So it is, Captain Macfarlane," admitted the constable mildly. " I do not know exactly what he wants, but it iss in a great hurry. He said he would not keep you wan meenute. I think it will be to taalk about your cousin Cherlie's money."

" I'll go wi' you whenever I get on my bonnet," said the Captain, preparing to go below.

" Never mind your bonnet; it iss chust a step or two, and you'll be back in five meenutes," said the sergeant; and, thus cajoled, the Captain of the *Vital Spark*, having cut the cord and stopped the whistle, went lamb-like to the police office.

Peace fell again upon the *Vital Spark*.

XVII

A DESPERATE CHARACTER

THOUGH Para Handy went, like a lamb, with Sergeant Macleod, he had not to suffer the ignominy of the police office, for the sergeant found out on the way that the Captain belonged to the Wee Free, and that made a great deal of difference. Instead of putting the mariner into a cell, he took him into his own house, made a summary investigation into the cause of the whistling of the *Vital Spark*, found the whole thing was an accident, dismissed the accused without a stain on his character, gave him a dram, and promised to take him down a pair of white hares for a present before the vessel left Tarbert.

" I am glad to see you belong to the right Church, Peter," he said. " Did I not think you were chust wan of them unfuduls that carries the rud-edged hime-books and sits at the prayer, and here you are chust a dacent Christian like mysel'. My goodness! It shows you a man cannot be too caautious. Last year there wass but a small remnant of us Christians to the fore here—myself and Macdougall the merchant, and myself and the Campbells up in Clonary Farm, and myself and the steamboat aagent, and myself and my cousins at Dunmore; but it'll be changed days when we get a ha'ad o' the church. They'll be sayin' there's no hell; we'll show them, I'll assure you! We are few, but firm—firm; there's no bowin' of the knee with us, and many a pair of white hares I'll be gettin' from the Campbells up in Clonary. I have chust got to say the word that wan of the rale old Frees iss in a vessel at the quay, and there will be a pair of white hares doon for you to-morrow."

" I'm a staunch Free," said Para Handy, upsetting his glass, which by this time had hardly a drop left in it. " Tut! tut! " he exclaimed apologetically, " it's a

good thing I never broke the gless. Stop! stop! stop
in a meenute; I'm sure I'm no needin' any more. But
it's a cold wet nicht, whatever. I'm a staunch Free.
I never had a hime-book on board my boat; if Dougie
wass here he would tell you."

" You'll no' get very often to the church, wi' you
goin' about from place to place followin' the sea? "
said the sergeant.

" That's the worst of it," said Para Handy, heaving
a tremendous sigh. " There's no mich fun on a coal
vessel; if it wasna the *Fital Spark* wass the smertest
in the tred, and me the skipper of her, I would mairry
a fine strong wife and start a business. There wass
wan time yonder, when I wass younger, I wass very
keen to be a polisman."

" The last chob! " cried the sergeant. " The very
last chob on earth! You would be better to be trap-
ping rabbits. It iss not an occupation for any man
that has a kind he'rt, and I have a he'rt mysel' that's
no slack in that direction, I'm tellin' you. Many a
time I'll have to take a poor laad in and cherge him,
and he'll be fined, and it's mysel' that's the first to get
the money for his fine."

" Do you tell me you pay the fine oot of your own
pocket? " asked Para Handy, astonished.

" Not a bit of it; I have aal my faculties about me.
I go roond and raise a subscruption," explained the
sergeant. " I chust go roond and say the poor laad
didna mean any herm, and his mother wass a weedow,
and it iss aal right, och aye! it iss aal right at wance
wi' the folk in Tarbert. Kind, kind he'rts in Tarbert
—if there's any fushing. But the polis iss no chob for

a man like me. Still and on it's a good pay, and the uniform, and a fine pair of boots, and an honour, so I'm no' complaining. Not a bit! "

Para Handy put up his hand with his customary gesture to scratch his ear, but as usual thought better of it, and sheered off. " Do you ken oor Dougie? " he asked.

" Iss it your mate? " replied the constable. " They're telling me aboot him, but I never had him in my hands."

" It's easy seen you're no' long in Tarbert," said the Captain. " He wass wan time namely here for makin' trouble; but that wass before he wass a kind of a Rechabite. Did you hear aboot him up in Castlebay in Barra? "

" No," said the sergeant.

" Dougie will be aye bouncin' he wass wan time on the yats, and wearing a red night-kep aal the time, and whitening on his boots, the same ass if he wass a door-step, but, man! he's tumid, tumid! If there's a touch of a gale he starts at his prayers, and says he'll throw his trump over the side. He can play the trump sub-lime—reels and things you never heard the like of; and if he wass here, and him in trum, it's himself would show you. But when the weather's scoury, and the *Fital Spark* not at the quay, he'll make up his mind to live a better life, and the first thing that he's going to stop 's the trump. ' Hold you on, Dougie,' I'll be sayin' to him; ' don't do anything desperate till we see if the weather 'll no lift on the other side of Minard.' It's a long way from Oban out to Barra; many a man that hass gold braid on his kep in the Clyde never went so far, but it's nothing at aal to the *Fital Spark*. But

Dougie does not like that trup at aal, at aal. Give him Bowling to Blairmore in the month of Aagust, and there's no' a finer sailor ever put on oilskins."

" Och, the poor fellow! " said the sergeant, with true sympathy.

" Stop you! " proceeded Para Handy. " When we would be crossing the Munch, Dougie would be going to sacrifice his trump, and start releegion every noo and then; but when we had the vessel tied to the quay at Castlebay, the merchants had to shut their shops and make a holiday."

" My Chove! do you tell me? " cried the sergeant.

" If Dougie was here himsel' he would tell you," said the Captain. " It needed but the wan or two drams, and Dougie would start walkin' on his heels to put an end to Castlebay. There iss not many shops in the place aaltogither, and the shopkeepers are aal MacNeils, and cousins to wan another; so when Dougie was waalkin' on his heels and in trum for high jeenks, they had a taalk together, and agreed it would be better chust to put on the shutters."

" Isn't he the desperate character! " said the constable. " Could they no' have got the polis? "

" There's no a polisman in the island of Barra," said Para Handy. " If there wass any need for polismen they would have to send to Lochmaddy, and it would be two or three days before they could put Dougie on his trial. Forbye, they kent Dougie fine; they hadna any ill-wull to the laad, and maybe it wass a time there wasna very mich business doin' anyway. When Dougie would find the shops shut he would be as vexed as anything, and make for the school. He would go into the school and give the children a lecture

on music and the curse of drink, with illustrations on
the trump. At last they used to shut the school, too,
and give the weans a holiday, whenever the *Fital Spark*
was seen off Castle Kismul. He wass awfu' popular,
Dougie, wi' the weans in Castlebay."

"A man like that should not be at lerge," said the
constable emphatically.

"Och! he wass only in fun; there wass no more
herm in Dougie than a fly. Chust fond of high jeenks
and recreation; many a place in the Highlands would
be gled to get the lend of him to keep them cheery in
the winter-time. There's no herm in Dougie, not at
aal, chust a love of sport and recreation. If he wass
here himsel' he would tell you."

"It iss a good thing for him he does not come to
Tarbert for his recreation," said the constable sternly;
"we're no' so Hielan' in Tarbert ass to shut the shops
when a man iss makin' himsel' a nuisance. By
Cheorge! if he starts any of his high jeenks in Tarbert
he'll suffer the Laaw."

"There iss no fear of Tarbert nowadays," said the
Captain, "for Dougie iss a changed man. He mairried
a kind of a wife yonder at Greenock, and she made
him a Good Templar, or a Rechabite, or something of
the sort where you get ten shillin's a week if your leg's
broken fallin' doon the stair, and nobody saw you.
Dougie's noo a staunch teetotaller except aboot the
time of the old New Year, or when he'll maybe be
takin' a dram for medicine. It iss a good thing for his
wife, but it leaves an awfu' want in Barra and them
other places where they kent him in his best trum."

XVIII

THE TAR'S WEDDING

It was months after The Tar's consultation with Para Handy about a wife: The Tar seemed to have given up the idea of indulgence in any such extravagance, and Para Handy had ceased to recommend various " smert, muddle-aged ones wi' a puckle money " to the consideration of the young man, when the latter one day sheepishly approached him, spat awkwardly through the clefts of his teeth at a patch in the funnel of the *Vital Spark*, and remarked, " I wass thinkin' to mysel' yonder, Captain, that if there wass nothing parteecular doing next Setturday, I would maybe get mairried."

" Holy smoke! " said the Captain; " you canna expect me to get a wife suitable for you in that time. It's no reasonable. Man, you're gettin' droll—chust droll! "

" Och, I needn't be puttin' you to any trouble," said The Tar, rubbing the back of his neck with a hand as rough as a rasp. " I wass lookin' aboot mysel', and there's wan yonder in Campbeltown 'll have me. In fact, it's settled. I thocht that when we were in Campbeltown next Setturday, we could do the chob and be dune wi't. We were roared last Sunday——"

" Roared! " said the Captain. " Iss it cried, you mean? "

" Yes, chust cried," said The Tar, " but the gyurl's kind of dull in the hearing, and it would likely need to be a roar. You'll maybe ken her—she's wan of the MacCallums."

"A fine gyurl," said the Captain, who had not the
faintest idea of her identity, and had never set eyes on
her, but could always be depended on for politeness.
"A fine gyurl! Truly sublime! I'm not askin' if
there's any money; eh?—not a word! It's none of
my business, but, tuts! what's the money anyway,
when there's love?"

"Shut up aboot that!" said the scandalised Tar,
getting very red. "If you're goin' to speak aboot love,
be dacent and speak aboot it in the Gaalic. But we're
no' taalkin' aboot love; we're taalkin' aboot my merrage. Is it aal right for Setturday?"

"You're a cunning man to keep it dark till this,"
said the Captain, "but I'll put nothing in the way,
seein' it's your first caper of the kind. We'll have high
jeenks at Campbeltown."

The marriage took place in the bride's mother's
house, up a stair that was greatly impeded by festoons
of fishing-nets, old oars, and net-bows on the walls,
and the presence of six stalwart Tarbert trawlers,
cousins of The Tar's, who were asked to the wedding,
but were so large and had so many guernseys on, they
would of themselves have filled the room in which the
ceremony took place; so they had agreed, while the
minister was there at all events, to take turn about of
going in to countenance the proceedings. What space
there was within was monopolised by the relatives of
the bride, by Para Handy and Dougie, The Tar in a
new slop-shop serge suit, apparently cut out by means
of a hatchet, the bride—a good deal prettier than a
Goth like The Tar deserved—and the minister. The
wedding-supper was laid out in a neighbour's house
on the same stair-landing.

A solemn hush marked the early part of the proceedings, married only by the sound of something frying in the other house and the shouts of children crying for bowl-money in the street. The minister was a teetotaller, an unfortunate circumstance which the Captain had discovered very early, and he was very pleased with the decorum of the company. The MacCallums were not church-goers in any satisfactory sense, but they and their company seemed to understand what was due to a Saturday night marriage and the presence of " the cloth." The clergyman had hardly finished the ceremony when the Captain began manœuvring for his removal. He had possessed himself of a bottle of ginger cordial and a plate of cake.

" You must drink the young couple's health, Mr Grant," he said. " We ken it's you that's the busy man on the Setturday night, and indeed it's a night for the whole of us goin' home early. I have a ship yonder, the *Fital Spark*, that I left in cherge of an enchineer by the name of Macphail, no' to be trusted with such a responsibulity."

The minister drank the cheerful potion, nibbled the corner of a piece of cake, and squeezed his way downstairs between the Tarbert trawlers.

" We're chust goin' away oorsel's in ten meenutes," said the Captain after him.

" Noo that's aal right," said Para Handy, who in virtue of his office had constituted himself master of ceremonies. " He's a nice man, Mr Grant, but he's not strong, and it would be a peety to be keeping him late out of his bed on a Setturday night. I like, mysel', yon old-fashioned munisters that had nothing wrong wi' them, and took a Chrustian dram. Pass oot that bottle of chinger cordial to the laads from Tarbert and you'll see fine fun."

He was the life and soul of the evening after that. It was he who pulled the corks, who cut the cold ham, who kissed the bride first, who sang the first song, and danced with the new mother-in-law. " You're an aawful man, Captain Macfarlane," she said in fits of laughter at his fun.

" Not me!" said he, lumberingly dragging her round in a polka to the strains of Dougie's trump. " I'm a quate fellow, but when I'm in trum I like a high jeenk noo and then. Excuse my feet. It's no' every day we're merryin' The Tar. A fine, smert, handy fellow, Mrs MacCallum; you didn't make a bad bargain of it with your son-in-law. Excuse my feet. A sailor every inch of him, once you get him wakened. A pound a-week of wages an' no incumbrance. My feet again, excuse them!"

" It's little enough for two," said Mrs MacCallum; " but a man's aye a man," and she looked the Captain in the eye with disconcerting admiration.

" My Chove! she's a weedow wuman," thought the Captain; " I'll have to ca' canny, or I'll be in for an engagement."

" I aye liked sailors," said Mrs MacCallum; " John —that's the depairted, I'm his relic—was wan."

" A poor life, though," said the Captain, " especially on the steamers, like us. But your man, maybe, was sailin' foreign, an' made money? It's always a consuderation for a weedow."

" Not a penny," said the indiscreet Mrs MacCallum, as Para Handy wheeled her into a chair.

At eleven o'clock The Tar was missing. He had last been seen pulling off his new boots, which were too small for him, on the stair-head; and it was only after considerable searching the Captain and one of the Tarbert cousins found him sound asleep on the top of a chest in the neighbour's house.

" Colin," said the Captain, shaking him awake, " sit up and try and take something. See at the rest of us, as jovial as anything, and no' a man hit yet. Sit up and be smert for the credit of the *Fital Spark*."

"Are you angry wi' me, Captain?" asked The Tar.

" Not a bit of it, Colin! But you have the corkscrew in your pocket. I'm no' caring myself, but the Tarbert gentlemen will take it amiss. Forbye, there's your wife; you'll maybe have mind of her—wan Lucy MacCallum? She's in yonder, fine and cheery, wi' two of your Tarbert cousins holding her hand."

" Stop you! I'll hand them! " cried the exasperated bridegroom, and bounded into the presence of the marriage-party in the house opposite, with a demonstration that finally led to the breaking-up of the party.

Next day took place The Tar's curious kirking. The MacCallums, as has been said, were not very regular churchgoers; in fact, they had overlooked the ordinances since the departed John died, and forgot that the church bell rang for the Sabbath-school an hour before it rang for the ordinary forenoon service.

Campbeltown itself witnessed the bewildering spectacle of The Tar and his bride, followed by the mother and Para Handy, marching deliberately up the street and into the church among the children. Five minutes later they emerged, looking very red and ashamed of themselves.

" If I knew there wass so mich bother to mind things, I would never have got merried at all," said the bridegroom.

XIX

A STROKE OF LUCK

It was a night of harmony on the good ship *Vital Spark*. She was fast in the mud at Colintraive quay, and, in the den of her, Para Handy was giving his song, " The Dancing Master "—

" Set to Jeanie Mertin, tee-teedalum, tee-tadulam,
Up the back and doon the muddle, tee-tadulam, tee-tadulam.
Ye're wrong, Jeck, I'm certain; tee-tadulam, tee-tadulam,"

while the mate played an accompaniment on the trump —that is to say, the Jew's harp, a favourite instrument on steam-lighters where the melodeon has not intruded. The Captain knew only two verses, but he sang them over several times. " You're getting better and better at it every time," The Tar assured him, for The Tar had got the promise of a rise that day of a shilling a week on his pay. " If I had chust on my other boots," said the Captain, delighted at this appreciation. " This ones iss too light for singin' with——" and he stamped harder than ever as he went on with the song, for it was his idea that the singing of a song was a very ineffective and uninteresting performance unless you beat time with your foot on the floor.

The reason for the harmony on the vessel was that Dougie the mate had had a stroke of luck that evening. He had picked up at the quay-side a large and very coarse fish called a stenlock, or coal-fish, and had succeeded, by sheer effrontery, in passing it off as a cod worth two shillings on a guileless Glasgow woman who had come for the week to one of the Colintraive cottages.

" I'm only vexed I didna say it wass a salmon," said Dougie, when he came back to the vessel with his ill-got florin. " I could have got twice ass much for't."

" She would ken fine it wasna a salmon when it wasna in a tin," said the Captain.

" There's many a salmon that iss not in a canister," said the mate.

" Och ay, but she's from Gleska; they're awfu' Hielan' in Gleska aboot fush and things like that," said the Captain. " But it's maybe a peety you didn't say it wass a salmon, for two shullin's iss not mich among four of us."

"Among four of us!" repeated Dougie emphatically. " It's little enough among wan, let alone four; I'm going to keep her to mysel'."

" If that iss your opeenion, Dougie, you are maakin' a great mistake, and it'll maybe be better for you to shift your mind," the Captain said meaningly. " It iss the jyle you could be getting for swundling a poor cratur from Gleska that thinks a stenlock iss a cod. Forbye, it iss a tremendous risk, for you might be found oot, and it would be a disgrace to the *Fital Spark*."

Dougie was impressed by the possibility of trouble with the law as a result of his fish transaction, which, to do him justice, he had gone about more as a practical joke than anything else. " I'm vexed I did it, Peter," he said, turning the two shillings over in his hand. " I have a good mind to go up and tell the woman it wass chust a baur."

" Not at aal! not at aal! " cried Para Handy. " It

wass a fine cod right enough; we'll chust send The Tar
up to the Inns with the two shullin's and the jar, and
we'll drink the Gleska woman's health that does not
ken wan fish from another. It will be a lesson to her
to be careful; chust that, to be careful."

So The Tar had gone to the Inn for the ale, and thus
it was that harmony prevailed in the fo'c'sle of the
Vital Spark.

" Iss that a song of your own doing? " asked Dougie,
when the Captain was done.

" No," said Para Handy, " it iss a low-country song
I heard wance in the Broomielaw. Yon iss the place
for seeing life. I'm telling you it iss Gleska for gaiety
if you have the money. There iss more life in wan day
in the Broomielaw of Gleska than there iss in a fortnight on Loch Fyne."

" I daarsay there iss," said Dougie; " no' coontin'
the herring."

" Och! life, life! " said the Captain, with a pensive
air of ancient memory; " Gleska's the place for it.
And the fellows iss there that iss not frightened, I'm
telling you."

" I learned my tred there," mentioned the engineer,
who had no accomplishments, and had not contributed
anything to the evening's entertainment, and felt that
it was time he was shining somehow.

" Iss that a fact, Macphail? I thocht it wass in a
coal-ree in the country," said Para Handy. " I wass
chust sayin', when Macphail put in his oar, that yon's
the place for life. If I had my way of it, the *Fital
Spark* would be going up every day to the Chamaica
Brudge the same as the *Columba*, and I would be step-
ping ashore quite spruce with my Sunday clothes on,

and no' lying here in a place like Colintraive, where there's no' even a polisman, with people that swundle a Gleska woman oot of only two shullin's. It wass not hardly worth your while, Dougie." The ale was now finished.

The mate contributed a reel and strathspey on the trump to the evening's programme, during which The Tar fell fast asleep, from which he wakened to suggest that he should give them a guess.

" Weel done, Colin! " said the Captain, who had never before seen such enterprise on the part of The Tar. " Tell us the guess if you can mind it."

" It begins something like this," said The Tar nervously: " ' Whether would you raither——' That's the start of it."

" Fine, Colin, fine! " said the Captain encouragingly. " Take your breath and start again."

" ' Whether would you raither,' " proceeded The Tar—" ' whether would you raither or walk there? ' "

" Say 't again, slow," said Dougie, and The Tar repeated his extraordinary conundrum.

" If I had a piece of keelivine (lead pencil) and a lump of paper I could soon answer that guess," said the engineer, and the Captain laughed.

" Man Colin," he said, " you're missing half of the guess oot. There's no sense at aal in ' Whether would you raither or walk there? ' "

" That's the way I heard it, anyway," said The Tar, sorry he had volunteered. " ' Whether would you raither or walk there? ' I mind fine it wass that."

" Weel, we give it up anyway; what's the answer? " said the Captain.

" Man, I don't mind whether there wass an answer

E

or no'," confessed The Tar, scratching his head; and
the Captain irritably hit him with a cap on the ear,
after which the entertainment terminated, and the crew
of the *Vital Spark* went to bed.

Next forenoon a very irate-looking Glasgow woman
was to be observed coming down the quay, and Dougie
promptly retired into the hold of the *Vital Spark*,
leaving the lady's reception to the Captain.

" Where's that man away to? " she asked Para
Handy. " I want to speak to him."

" He's engaged, mem," said the Captain.

" I don't care if he's merried," said the Glasgow
woman; " I'm no' wantin' him. I jist wanted to say
yon was a bonny-like cod he sell't me yesterday. I
biled it three oors this mornin', and it was like leather
when a' was done."

" That's droll," said the Captain. " It wass a fine
fush, I'll assure you; if Dougie was here himsel' he
would tell you. Maybe you didna boil it right. Cods
iss curious that way. What did you use? "

" Watter! " snapped the Glasgow woman; " did
you think I would use sand? "

" Chust that! chust that! Watter? Weel, you
couldna use anything better for boilin' with than chust
watter. What kind of coals did you use? "

" Jist plain black yins," said the woman. " I bocht
them frae Cameron along the road there," referring
to a coal agent who was a trade rival to the local
charterer of the *Vital Spark*.

" Cameron! " cried Para Handy. " Wass I not sure
there wass something or other wrong? Cameron's
coals wouldna boil a wulk, let alone a fine cod. If
Dougie wass here he would tell you that himsel'."

XX

DOUGIE'S FAMILY

THE size of Dougie the mate's family might be considered a matter which was of importance to himself alone, but it was astonishing how much interest his shipmates took in it. When there was nothing else funny to talk about on the *Vital Spark*, they would turn their attention to the father of ten, and cunningly extract information from him about the frightful cost of boys' boots and the small measure of milk to be got for sixpence at Dwight's dairy in Plantation.

They would listen sympathetically, and later on roast him unmercifully with comments upon the domestic facts he had innocently revealed to them.

It might happen that the vessel would be lying at a West Highland quay, and the Captain sitting on deck reading a week-old newspaper, when he would wink at Macphail and The Tar, and say, " Cot bless me! boys, here's the price of boots goin' up; peety the poor faithers of big femilies." Or, " I see there's to be a new school started in Partick, Dougie; did you flit again? "

" You think you're smert, Peter," the mate would retort lugubriously. " Fun's fun, but I'll no' stand fun aboot my femily."

" Och! no offence, Dougald, no offence," Para Handy would say soothingly. " Hoo's the mustress keepin'? " and then ask a fill of tobacco to show his feelings were quite friendly.

In an ill-advised moment the parental pride and joy of the mate brought on board one day a cabinet photograph of himself and his wife and the ten children.

"What do you think of that?" he said to Para Handy, who took the extreme tip of one corner of the card between the finger and thumb of a hand black with coal-grime, glanced at the group, and said—

"Whatna Sunday School trup's this?"

"It's no' a trup at aal," said Dougie with annoyance.

"Beg pardon, beg pardon," said the Captain, "I see noo I wass wrong; it's Quarrier's Homes. Who's the chap wi' the whuskers in the muddle, that's greetin'?"

"Where's your eyes?" said Dougie. "It's no' a Homes at aal; that's me, and I'm no' greetin'. What would I greet for?"

"Faith, I believe you're right," said the Captain. "It's yoursel' plain enough, when I shut wan eye to look at it; but the collar and a clean face make a terrible dufference. Well, well, allooin' that it's you, and you're no greetin', it's rideeculous for you to be goin' to a dancin'-school."

"It's no' a dancin'-school, it's the femily," said the mate, losing his temper. "Fun's fun, but if you think I'll stand——"

"Keep caalm, keep caalm!" interrupted the Captain hurriedly, realising that he had carried the joke far enough. "I might have kent fine it wass the femily; they're aal ass like you both ass anything, and that'll be Susan the eldest."

"That!" said Dougie, quite mollified—"that's the mustress hersel'."

"Well, I'm jeegered," said the Captain, with well-acted amazement. "She's younger-looking than ever; that's a woman that's chust sublime."

The mate was so pleased he made him a present of the photograph.

But it always had been, and always would be, a distressing task to Dougie to have to intimate to the crew (as he had to do once a year) that there was a new addition to the family, for it was on these occasions that the chaff of his shipmates was most ingenious and galling. Only once, by a trick, had he got the better of them and evaded his annual roastings. On that occasion he came to the *Vital Spark* with a black muffler on, and a sad countenance.

" I've lost my best freend," said he, rubbing his eyes to make them red.

" Holy smoke! " said Para Handy, " is Macmillan the pawnbroker deid? "

" It's no' him," said Dougie, manfully restraining a sob, and he went on to tell them that it was his favourite uncle, Jamie. He put so much pathos into his description of Uncle Jamie's last hours, that when he wound up by mentioning, in an off-hand way, that his worries were complicated by the arrival of another daughter that morning, the crew had, naturally, not the heart to say anything about it.

Some weeks afterwards they discovered by accident that he never had an Uncle Jamie.

" Man! he's cunning! " said Para Handy, when this black evidence of Dougie's astuteness came out. " Stop you till the next time, and we'll make him pay for it."

The suitable occasion for making the mate smart doubly for his deceit came in due course. Macphail the engineer lived in the next tenement to Dougie's family in Plantation, and he came down to the quay one morning before the mate, with the important intelligence for the Captain that the portrait group was now incomplete.

" Poor Dugald! " said the Captain sympathetically. " Iss it a child or a lassie? "

" I don't ken," said the engineer. " I just got a rumour frae the night polisman, and he said the wife was fine."

" Stop you and you'll see some fun with Dougie," said the Captain. " I'm mich mistaken if he'll swundle us this twict."

Para Handy had gone ashore for something, and was back before his mate appeared on board the *Vital Spark*, which was just starting for Campbeltown with a cargo of bricks. The mate took the wheel, smoked ceaselessly at a short cutty pipe, and said nothing; and nobody said anything to him.

" He's plannin' some other way oot of the scrape," whispered the Captain once to the engineer; " but he'll not get off so easy this time. Hold you on! "

It was dinner-time, and the captain, mate, and engineer were round the pot on deck aft, with The Tar at the wheel, within comfortable hearing distance, when Para Handy slyly broached the topic.

" Man, Dougie," he said, " what wass I doin' yonder last night but dreamin' in the Gaalic aboot you? I wass dreamin' you took a charter of the *Fital Spark* doon to Ardkinglas with a picnic, and there wass not a park in the place would hold the company."

Dougie simply grunted.

" It wass a droll dream," continued the Captain, diving for another potato. " I wass chust wonderin' hoo you found them aal at home. Hoo's the mustress keepin'? "

The mate got very red. " I wass chust goin' to tell you aboot her," he said with considerable embarrassment.

" A curious dream it wass," said Para Handy, postponing his pleasure, like the shrewd man he is, that he might enjoy it all the more when it came. " I saw you ass plain ass anything, and the *Fital Spark* crooded high and low with the picnic, and you in the muddle playing your trump. The mustress wass there, too, quite spruce, and— But you were goin' to say something aboot the mustress, Dougie. I hope she's in her usual? "

" That's chust it," said Dougie, more and more embarrassed as he saw his news had to be given now, if ever. " You would be thinkin' to yourself I wass late this mornin', but the fact iss we were in an aawful habble in oor hoose——"

" Bless me! I hope the lum didn't take fire nor nothing like that? " said Para Handy anxiously; and The Tar, at the wheel behind, was almost in a fit with suppressed laughter.

" Not at aal! worse nor that! " said Dougie in melancholy tones. " There's—there's—dash it! there's more boots than ever needed yonder! "

" Man, you're gettin' quite droll," said Para Handy. " Do you no' mind you told me aboot that wan chust three or four months ago? "

" You're a liar! " said Dougie, exasperated; " it's a twelvemonth since I told you aboot the last."

" Not at aal! not at aal! your mind's failin'," protested the Captain. " Five months ago at the most; you told me aboot it at the time. Surely there's some mistake? "

" No mistake at aal aboot it," said the mate, shaking his head so sadly that the Captain's heart was melted.

" Never mind, Dougald," he said, taking a little parcel out of his pocket. " I'm only in fun. I heard aboot it this mornin' from Macphail, and here's a wee bit peeny and a pair o' sluppers that I bought for't."

" To the muschief! It's no' an ' it,' " said Dougie; " it's—it's—it's a twuns! "

" Holy smoke! " exclaimed Para Handy. " Iss that no chust desperate? " And the mate was so much moved that he left half his dinner and went forward towards the bow.

Para Handy went forward to him in a little and said, " Cheer up, Dougie; hoo wass I to ken it wass a twuns? If I had kent, it wouldna be the wan peeny and the wan sluppers; but I have two or three shillin's here, and I'll buy something else in Campbeltown."

" I can only—I can only say thankye the noo, Peter; it wass very good of you," said the mate, deeply touched, and attempting to shake the Captain's hand.

"Away! away! " said Para Handy, getting very red himself; " none of your chat! I'll buy peenies and sluppers if I like."

XXI

THE BAKER'S LITTLE WIDOW

ON the night after New Year's Day the Captain did a high-spirited thing he had done on the corresponding day for the previous six years; he had his hair cut and his beard trimmed by Dougie the mate, made a specially careful toilet—taking all the tar out of his hands by copious applications of salt butter—wound up his watch (which was never honoured in this way more than once or twice a twelvemonth), and went up the quay to propose to Mrs Crawford. It was one of the rare occasions upon which he wore a topcoat, and envied Macphail his Cairngorm scarfpin. There was little otherwise to suggest the ardent wooer, for ardent wooers do not look as solemn as Para Handy looked. The truth, is, he was becoming afraid that his persistency might wear down a heart of granite, and that this time the lady might accept him.

The crew of the *Vital Spark*, whom he thought quite ignorant of his tender passion for the baker's widow, took a secret but intense interest in this annual enterprise. He was supposed to be going to take tea with a cousin (as if captains took the tar off their hands to visit their own cousins!), and in order to make the deception more complete and allay any suspicions on the part, especially, of Macphail, who, as a great student of penny novelettes, was up to all the intrigues of love, the Captain casually mentioned that if it wasn't that it would vex his cousin he would sooner stay on the vessel and play Catch the Ten with them.

" I hate them tea-pairties," he said; " chust a way of wasting the New Year. But stay you here, boys, and I'll come back ass soon ass ever I can."

" Bring back some buns, or cookies, or buscuits wi' you," cried Dougie, as the Captain stepped on to the quay.

" What do you mean? " said Para Handy sharply, afraid he was discovered.

" Nothing, Peter, nothing at aal," the mate assured

E 2

him, nudging The Tar in the dark. " Only it's likely
you'll have more of them that you can eat at your
cousin's tea-pairty."

Reassured thus that his secret was still safe, Para
Handy went slowly up the quay. As he went he
stopped a moment to exchange a genial word with
everybody he met, as if time was of no importance,
and he was only ashore for a daunder. This was
because, dressed as he was, if he walked quickly and
was not particularly civil to everybody, the whole of
Campbeltown (which is a very observant place) would
suspect he was up to something and watch him.

The widow's shop was at a conveniently quiet corner.
He tacked back and forward off it in the darkness
several times till a customer, who was being served, as
he could see through the glass door, had come out,
and a number of boys playing at " guesses " at the
window had passed on, and then he cleared his throat,
unbuttoned his topcoat and jacket to show his watch-
chain, and slid as gently as he could in at the glass
door.

" Dear me, fancy seeing you, Captain Macfarlane! "
said the widow Crawford, coming from the room at
the back of the shop. " Is it really yourself? "

"A good New Year to you," said the Captain,
hurried and confused. " I wass chust goin' up the
toon, and I thought I would give you a roar in the
by-going. Are you keeping tip-top, Mery? "

His heart beat wildly; he looked at her sideways
with a timid eye, for, hang it! she was more irresistible
than ever. She was little, plump, smiling, rosy-cheeked,
neat in dress, and just the exact age to make the Captain
think he was young again.

" Will you not come ben and warm yourself? It's a nasty, damp night," said Mrs Crawford, pushing the back door, so that he got the most tempting vision of an interior with firelight dancing in it, a genial lamp, and a tea-table set.

" I'll chust sit doon and draw my breath for a meenute or two. You'll be busy? " said the Captain, rolling into the back room with an elephantine attempt (which she skilfully evaded) at playfully putting his arm round the widow's waist as he did so.

" You're as daft as ever, I see, Captain," said the lady. " I was just making myself a cup of tea; will you take one? "

" Och, it's puttin' you to bother," said the Captain.

" Not a bit of it," said the widow, and she whipped out a cup, which was suspiciously handy in a cupboard, and told the Captain to take off his coat and he would get the good of it when he went out.

People talk about young girls as entrancing. To men of experience like the Captain girls are insipid. The prime of life in the other sex is something under fifty; and the widow, briskly making tea, smiling on him, shaking her head at him, pushing him on the shoulder when he was impudent, chaffing him, surrounding him with an intoxicating atmosphere of homeliness, comfort, and cuddleability, seemed to Para Handy there and then the most angelic creature on earth. The rain could be heard falling heavily outside, no customers were coming in, and the back room of the baker's shop was, under the circumstances, as fine an earthly makeshift for Paradise as man could ask for.

Para Handy dived his hand into his coat pocket.

" That minds me," said he; " I have a kind of a bottle of scent here a friend o' mine, by the name of Hurricane Jeck, took home for me from America last week. It's the rale Florida Water; no' the like o't to be got here, and if you put the least sensation on your hanky you'll feel the smell of it a mile away. It's chust sublime."

" Oh! it's so kind of you! " said the widow, beaming on him with the merriest, brownest, deepest, meltingest of eyes, and letting her plump little fingers linger a moment on his as she took the perfume bottle. The Captain felt as if golden harps were singing in the air, and fairies were tickling him down the back with pea-cocks' feathers.

" Mery," he said in a little, " this iss splendid tea. Capital, aalthegither! "

" Tuts! Captain," said she, " is it only my tea you come to pay compliments to once a year? Good tea's common enough if you're willing to pay for it. What do you think of myself? "

The Captain neatly edged his chair round the corner of the table to get it close beside hers, and she just as neatly edged her chair round the other corner, leaving their relative positions exactly as they had been.

" No, no, Captain," said she, twinkling; " hands off the widow. I'm a done old woman, and it's very good of you to come and have tea with me; but I always thought sailors, with a sweetheart, as they say, in every port, could say nice things to cheer up a lonely female heart. What we women need, Captain—the real necessity of our lives—is some one to love us. Even if he's at the other end of the world, and unlikely ever to be any nearer, it makes the work of the day cheery. But what am I haverin' about? " she added,

with a delicious, cosy, melting, musical sigh that
bewitchingly heaved her blouse. " Nobody cares for
me, I'm too old."

" Too old! " exclaimed the Captain, amused at the
very idea. " You're not a day over fifty. You're
chust sublime."

" Forty-nine past, to be particular," said the widow,
" and feel like twenty. Oh! Captain, Captain! you
men! "

" Mery," entreated Para Handy, putting his head to
one side, " caal me Peter, and gie me a haad o' your
hand." This time he edged his chair round quicker
than she did hers, and captured her fingers. Now
that he had them he didn't know very well what to do
with them, but he decided after a little that a cute
thing to do was to pull them one by one and try to
make them crack. He did so, and got slapped on the
ear for his pains.

" What do you mean by that? " said she.

" Och, it was chust a baur, Mery," said Para Handy.
" Man, you're strong, strong! You would make a
sublime wife for any sober, decent, good-looking,
capable man. You would make a fine wife for a
sailor, and I'm naming no names, mind ye; but "—
here he winked in a manner that seemed to obliterate
one complete side of his face—" they caal him Peter.
Eh? What? "

" Nobody would have me," said the widow, quite
cheerfully, enjoying herself immensely. " I'm old—
well, kind of old, and plain, and I have no money."

" Money! " said Para Handy contemptuously; " the
man I'm thinking of does not give wan docken for
money. And you're no more old than I am mysel',

and as for bein' plain, chust look at the lovely polka
you have on and the rudness of your face. If Dougie
was here he would tell—no, no, don't mention a cheep
to Dougie—not a cheep; he would maybe jalouse
something."

" This is the sixth time of asking, Captain," said
the widow. " You must have your mind dreadful
firm made up. But it's only at the New Year I see
you; I'm afraid you're like all sailors—when you're
away you forget all about me. Stretch your hand and
have another London bun."

" London buns iss no cure for my case," said the
Captain, taking one, however. " I hope you'll say yes
this time."

" I'll—I'll think about it," said the widow, still
smiling; " and if you're passing this way next New
Year and call in, I'll let you know."

The crew of the *Vital Spark* waited on deck for the
return of the skipper. Long before he came in sight
they heard him clamping down the quay singing cheerfully to himself—

> " Rolling home to bonnie Scotland,
>   Rolling home, dear land, to thee ;
> Rolling home to bonnie Scotland,
>   Rolling home across the sea."

" Iss your cousin's tea-pairty over already? " said
Dougie innocently. " Wass there many at it? "

" Seven or eight," said Para Handy promptly. " I
chust came away. And I'm feeling chust sublime.
Wan of Brutain's hardy sons."

He went down below, and hung up his topcoat and
his watch and took off his collar, which uncomfortably
rasped his neck. " Mery's the right sort," said he to

himself; " she's no' going ram-stam into the business.
She's caautious like mysel'. Maybe next New Year
she'll make her mind up."

And the widow, putting up her shutters that night,
hummed cheerfully to herself, and looked quite happy.
" I wish I HAD called him Peter," she thought; " next
year I'll not be so blate."

XXII

THREE DRY DAYS

ON the first day of February the Captain of the *Vital
Spark* made an amazing resolution. Life in the leisure
hours of himself and his crew had been rather strenuous
during the whole of January, for Dougie had broken
the Rechabites. When Dougie was not a Rechabite,
he always carried about with him an infectious atmosphere of gaiety and a half-crown, and the whole ship's
company took its tone from him. This is a great moral
lesson. It shows how powerful for good or evil is the
influence and example of One Strong Man. If Dougie
had been more at home that month, instead of trading
up the West Coast, his wife would have easily dispelled
his spirit of gaiety by making him nurse the twins, and
she would have taken him herself to be reinstalled in
the Rechabites, for she was " a fine, smert, managin'
woman," as he admitted himself; but when sailors are
so often and so far away from the benign influences of
home, with nobody to search their pockets, it is little
wonder they should sometimes be foolish.

So the Captain rose on the first day of the month

with a frightful headache, and emphatically refused to adopt the customary method of curing it. " No," he said to his astonished mates, " I'm no' goin' up to the Ferry Hoose nor anywhere else; I'm teetotal."

" Teetotal! " exclaimed Dougie, much shocked. " You shouldna make a joke aboot things like that, and you no' feelin' very weel; come on up and take your mornin'."

" Not a drop! " said Para Handy firmly.

" Tut, tut, Peter; chust wan beer," persisted the mate patiently.

" Not even if it wass jampaigne," said the Captain, drying his head, which he had been treating to a cold douche. " My mind's made up. Drink's a curse, and I'm done wi't, for I canna stand it."

" There's nobody askin' you to stand it," explained the mate. " I have a half-croon o' my own here."

" It's no odds," said the Captain. " I'm on the teetotal tack. Not another drop will I taste——"

" Stop, stop! " interrupted Dougie, more shocked than ever. " Don't do anything rash. You might be struck doon deid, and then you would be sorry for what you said. Do you mean to tell us that you're goin' to be teetotal aalthegether? "

" No," said the Captain, " I'm no' that desperate. I wouldna care chust to go aal that length, but I'm goin' to be teetotal for the month o' February."

" Man, I think you're daft, Peter," said the mate. " February, of aal months! In February the New Year's no' right bye, and the Gleska Fair's chust comin' on; could you no' put it off for a more sensible time? "

" No," said the Captain firmly, " February's the

month for me; there's two or three days less in't than any other month in the year."

So the crew filed ashore almost speechless with astonishment—annoyed and depressed to some extent by this inflexible virtue on the part of Para Handy.

" He's gettin' quite droll in his old age," was Dougie's explanation.

" Fancy him goin' away and spoilin' the fun like that! " said The Tar incredulously.

" I aye said he hadna the game in him," was the comment of Macphail the engineer.

Para Handy watched them going up to the Ferry House, and wished it was the month of March.

The first day of his abstinence would have passed without much more inclination on his part to repent his new resolution were it not for the fact that half a score of circumstances conspired to make it a day of unusual trial. He met friends that day he had not met for months, all with plenty of time on their hands; Hurricane Jack, the irresistible, came alongside in another vessel, and was immediately for celebrating this coincidence by having half a day off, a proposal the Captain evaded for a while only by pretending to be seriously ill and under medical treatment; the coal merchant, whose cargo they had just discharged, presented the crew with a bottle of whisky; there was a ball at the George Hotel; there was a travelling piper on the streets, with most inspiring melodies; the headache was away by noon—only a giant will-power could resist so many circumstances conducive to gaiety. But Para Handy never swerved in his resolution. He compromised with the friends who had plenty of time and the inclination for merriment by taking fills of tobacco from them; confiscated the bottle of whisky as Captain, and locked it past with the assurance to his crew that it would be very much the more matured if kept till March; and the second time Hurricane Jack came along the quay to see if the Captain of the *Vital Spark* was not better yet, he accompanied him to the Ferry House, and startled him by saying he would have " Wan small half of lime-juice on draught."

" What's that, Peter? " said Hurricane Jack. " Did I hear you say something aboot lime-juice, or does my ears deceive me? "

" It's chust for a bate, Jeck—no offence," explained the Captain hurriedly. " I have a bate on wi' a chap that I'll no' drink anything stronger this month; but och! next month, if we're spared, wait you and you'll see some fine fun."

Hurricane Jack looked at him with great disapproval. " Macfarlane," he said solemnly, " you're goin' far, far wrong, and mind you I'm watchin' you. A gembler iss an abomination, and gemblin' at the expense of your inside iss worse than gemblin' on horses. Us workin' men have nothing but oor strength to go on, and if we do not keep up oor strength noo and then, where are we? You will chust have a smaal gill, and the man that made the bate wi' you 'll never be any the wiser."

" No, Jeck, thank you aal the same," said the Captain, " but I'll chust take the lime-juice. Where'll you be on the first o' Merch? "

Hurricane Jack grudgingly ordered the lime-juice, and asked the landlady to give the Captain a sweetie with it to put away the taste, then looked on with an aspect of mingled incredulity and disgust as Para

Handy hurriedly gulped the unaccustomed beverage and chased it down with a drink of water.

" It's a fine thing a drap watter," said Para Handy, gasping.

" No' a worse thing you could drink," said Hurricane Jack. " It rots your boots; what'll it no' do on your inside? Watter's fine for sailin' on—there's nothing better—but it's no' drink for sailors."

On the second day of the great reform Para Handy spent his leisure hours fishing for saithe from the side of the vessel, and was, to all appearance, firmer than ever. He was threatened for a while by a good deal of interference from his crew, who resented the confiscation of the presentation bottle, but he turned the tables on them by coming out in the *rôle* of temperance lecturer. When they approached him, he sniffed suspiciously, and stared at their faces in a way that was simply galling—to Dougie particularly, who was naturally of a rubicund countenance. Then he sighed deeply, shook his head solemnly, and put on a fresh bait.

" Are you no' better yet? " Dougie asked. " You're looking ass dull ass if the shup wass tied up to a heid-stone in the Necropolis o' Gleska. None o' your didoes, Peter; give us oot the spurits we got the present o'. It's Candlemas."

Para Handy stared at his fishing-line, and said gently, as if he were speaking to himself, " Poor sowls! poor sowls! Nothing in their heids but drink. It wass a happy day for me the day I gave it up, or I might be like the rest o' them. There's poor Dougald lettin' it get a terrible grup o' him; and The Tar chust driftin', driftin' to the poor's-hoose, and Macphail iss sure to be in the horrors before Setturday, for he hasna the heid for drink, him no' bein' right Hielan'."

"Don't be rash; don't do anything you would be vexed for, but come on away up the toon and have a pant," said Dougie coaxingly. "Man, you have only to make up your mind and shake it off, and you'll be ass cheery ass ever you were."

"He's chust takin' a rise oot o' us; are you no', Captain?" said The Tar, anxious to leave his commander an honourable way of retreat from his preposterous position.

Para Handy went on fishing as if they were not present.

"Married men, too, with wifes and femilies," he said musingly. "If they chust knew what it wass, like me, to be risin' in the mornin' wi' a clear heid, and a good conscience, they would never touch it again. I never knew what happiness wass till I joined the teetotal, and it'll be money in my pocket forbye."

"You'll go on, and you'll go on with them expuriments too far till you'll be a vegetarian next," said Dougie, turning away. "Chust a vegetarian, tryin' to live on turnips and gress, the same ass a coo. If I was a Macfarlane I wouldna care to be a coo."

Then they left him with an aspect more of sorrow than of anger, and he went on fishing.

The third day of the month was Saturday; there was nothing to do on the *Vital Spark*, which was waiting on a cargo of timber, so all the crew except the Captain spent the time ashore. Him they left severely alone, and the joys of fishing saithe and reading a week-old newspaper palled.

" The worst of bein' good iss that it leaves you duvelish lonely," said the Captain to himself.

An hour later, he discovered that he had a touch of toothache, and, strongly inclined for a temporary suspension of the new rules for February, he went to the locker for the presentation bottle.

It was gone!

XXIII

THE VALENTINE THAT MISSED FIRE

A FORTNIGHT of strict teetotalism on the part of the Captain was too much of a joke for his crew. " It's just bounce," said the mate; " he's showin' off. I'm a Rechabite for six years, every time I'm in Gleska; but I never let it put between me and a gless of good Brutish spurits wi' a shipmate in any port, Loch Fyne or foreign."

" It's most annoyin'," said The Tar. " He asked me yesterday if my health wassna breakin' doon wi' drink, the same ass it would break doon wi' aal I take."

" Chust what I told you; nothing but bounce! " said Dougie gloomily. " Stop you! Next time he's in trum, I'll no' be so handy at pullin' corks for him. If I wass losin' my temper wi' him, I would give him a bit o' my mind."

The engineer, wiping his brow with a wad of oily waste, put down the penny novelette he was reading and gave a contemptuous snort. " I wonder to hear the two o' ye talkin'," said he. " Ye're baith feared for him. I could soon fix him."

" Could you, Macphail? " said Dougie. " You're aawful game: what would you do? "

" I would send him a valentine that would vex him," replied the engineer promptly; " a fizzer o' a valentine that would mak' his hair curl for him."

The mate impulsively smacked his thigh. " My Chove! Macphail," said he, " it's the very ticket! What do you say to a valentine for the Captain, Colin? "

" Whatever you think yersel'," said The Tar.

That night Dougie and The Tar went ashore at Tarbert for a valentine. There was one shop-window up the town with a gorgeous display of penny " mocks," designed and composed to give the recipient in every instance a dull, sickening thud on the bump of his self-esteem. The two mariners saw no valentine, however, that quite met the Captain's case.

" There'll be plenty o' other wans inside on the coonter," said Dougie diplomatically. " Away you in, Colin, and pick wan suitable, and I'll stand here and watch."

" Watch what? " inquired The Tar suspiciously. " It would be more like the thing if you went in and bought it yoursel'; I'll maybe no' get wan that'll please you."

"Aal you need to ask for iss a mock valentine, lerge size, and pretty broad, for a skipper wi' big feet. I would go in mysel' in a meenute if it wassna that—if it wassna that it would look droll, and me a muddle-aged man wi' whuskers."

The Tar went into the shop reluctantly, and was horrified to find a rather pretty girl behind the counter. He couldn't for his life suggest mock valentines to her, and he could not with decency back out without explanation.

" Have you any—have you any nice unvelopes? " he inquired bashfully, as she stood waiting his order.

" What size? " she asked.

" Lerge size, and pretty broad, for a skipper wi' big feet," said The Tar in his confusion. Then he corrected himself, adding, "Any size, muss, suitable for holdin' letters."

" There's a great run on that kind of envelope this winter," the lady remarked, being a humorist. " How many? "

"A ha'pennyworth," said The Tar. " I'll chust take them wi' me."

When The Tar came out of the shop the mate was invisible, and it was only after some search he found him in a neighbouring public-house.

" I chust came in here to put by the time," said Dougie; " but seein' you're here, what am I for? "

The Tar, realising that there must be an unpleasant revelation immediately, produced the essential threepence and paid for beer.

" I hope you got yon? " said the mate anxiously.

"Ass sure ass daith, Dougie, I didna like to ask for it," explained the young man pathetically. " There's a gasalier and two paraffin lamps bleezin' in the shop, and it would gie me a rud face to ask for a mock valentine in such an illumination. Iss there no other wee dark shop in the toon we could get what we want in? "

The mate surveyed him with a disgusted countenance. " Man, you're a coward, Colin," he said. " The best in the land goes in and buys mock valentines, and it's

no disgrace to nobody so long ass he has the money
in his hand. If I had another gless o' beer I would go
in mysel'."

" You'll get that! " said The Tar gladly, and produced another threepence, after which they returned
to the shop-window, where Dougie's courage apparently failed him, in spite of the extra glass of beer.
" It's no' that I give a docken for anybody," he
explained, " but you see I'm that weel kent in Tarbert.
What sort o' body keeps the shop? "

" Och, it's chust an old done man wi' a sore hand and
wan eye no' neebours," replied The Tar strategically.
" Ye needna be frightened for him; he'll no' say a
cheep. To bleezes wi' him! "

Dougie was greatly relieved at this intelligence.
" Toots! " he said. " Iss that aal? Watch me! " and
he went banging in at the door in three strides.

The lady of the shop was in a room behind. To call
her attention Dougie cried, " Shop! " and kicked the
front of the counter, with his eyes already on a pile of
valentines ready for a rush of business in that elegant
form of billet-doux. When the pretty girl came skipping out of the back room, he was even more astounded
and alarmed than The Tar had been.

" A fine night," he remarked affably: " iss your
faither at the back? "

" I think you must have made a mistake in the shop,"
said the lady. " Who do you want? "

" Him with the sore hand and the wan eye no' right
neebours," said the mate, not for a moment suspecting
that The Tar had misled him. " It's parteecular
business; I'll no' keep him wan meenute."

" There's nobody here but myself," the girl informed

him, and then he saw he had been deceived by his shipmate.

" Stop you till I get that Tar! " he exclaimed with natural exasperation, and was on the point of leaving when the pile of valentines met his eye again, and he decided to brazen it out.

" Maybe you'll do yoursel'," said he, with an insinuating leer at the shopkeeper. " There iss a shipmate o' mine standin' oot there took a kind o' notion o' a mock valentine and doesna like to ask for't. He wass in a meenute or two ago—you would know him by the warts on his hand—but he hadna the nerve to ask for it."

" There you are, all kinds," said the lady, indicating the pile on the counter, with a smile of comprehension. "A penny each."

Dougie wet his thumb and clumsily turned over the valentines, seeking for one appropriate to a sea captain silly enough to be teetotal. " It's chust for a baur, mind you," he explained to the lady. " No herm at aal, at aal; chust a bit of a high jeenk. Forbye, it's no' for me: it's for the other fellow, and his name's Colin Turner, but he's blate, blate." He raised his voice so that The Tar, standing outside the window, could hear him quite plainly; with the result that The Tar was so ashamed, he pulled down his cap on his face and hurriedly walked off to the quay.

" There's an awful lot o' them valentines for governesses and tylers and polismen," said Dougie; " the merchant service doesna get mich of a chance. Have you nothing smert and nippy that'll fit a sea captain, and him teetotal? "

The shopkeeper hurriedly went over her stock, and

discovered that teetotalism was the one eccentricity valentines never dealt with; on the contrary, they were all for people with red noses and bibulous propensities.

"There's none for teetotal captains," said she; "but here's one for a captain that's not teetotal," and she shoved a valentine with a most unpleasant-looking seaman, in a state of intoxication, walking arm-in-arm with a respectable-looking young woman.

"Man, that's the very tup!" said Dougie, delighted. "It's ass clever a thing ass ever I seen. I wonder the way they can put them valentines thegather. Read what it says below, I havena my specs."

The shopkeeper read the verse on the valentine:

> "The girl that would marry a man like you
> Would have all the rest of her life to rue;
> A sailor soaked in salt water and rum
> Could never provide a happy home."

"Capital!" exclaimed the mate, highly delighted. "Ass smert ass anything in the works of Burns. That wan'll do splendid."

"I thought it was for a teetotal captain you wanted one," said the lady, as she folded up the valentine.

"He's only teetotal to spite us," said Dougie. "And that valentine fits him fine, for he's coortin' a baker's weedow, and he thinks we don't know. Mind you, it's no' me that's goin' to send the valentine, it's Colin Turner; but there's no herm, chust a bit of a baur. You ken yoursel'."

Then an embarrassing idea occurred to him—Who was to address the envelope?

"Do you keep mournin' unvelopes?" he asked.

"Black-edged envelopes—yes," said the shopkeeper.

"Wan," said Dougie; and when he got it he put the valentine inside and ventured to propose to the lady that, seeing she had pen and ink handy, she might address the envelope for him, otherwise the recipient would recognise Colin Turner's hand-of-write.

The lady obliged, and addressed the document to

CAPTAIN PETER MACFARLANE,
SS. VITAL SPARK,
TARBERT.

Dougie thanked her effusively on behalf of The Tar, paid for his purchases and a penny stamp, and went out. As he found his shipmate gone, he sealed the envelope and posted it.

When the letter-carrier came down Tarbert quay next morning, all the crew of the *Vital Spark* were on deck—the Captain in blissful unconsciousness of what was in store for him, the others anxious not to lose the expression of his countenance when he should open his valentine.

It was a busy day on the *Vital Spark*; all hands had to help to get in a cargo of wood.

"A mournin' letter for you, Captain," said the letter-carrier, handing down the missive.

Para Handy looked startled, and walked aft to open it. He took one short but sufficient glimpse at the valentine, with a suspicious glance at the crew, who were apparently engrossed in admiration of the scenery round Tarbert. Then he went down the fo'c'sle, to come up a quarter of an hour later with his good clothes on, his hat, and a black tie.

"What the duvvle game iss he up to noo?" said Dougie, greatly astonished.

" I hope it didna turn his brain," said The Tar. "A fright sometimes does it. Wass it a very wild valentine, Dougie? "

Para Handy moved aft with a sad, resigned aspect, the mourning envelope in his hand. " I'm sorry I'll have to go away till the efternoon, boys," he said softly. " See and get in that wud nice and smert before I come back."

" What's wrong? " asked Dougie, mystified.

The Captain ostentatiously blew his nose, and explained that they might have noticed he had just got a mourning letter.

" Was't a mournin' wan? I never noticed," said Dougie.

" Neither did I," added The Tar hurriedly.

" Yes," said the Captain sadly, showing them the envelope; " my poor cousin Cherlie over in Dunmore iss no more; he just slipped away yesterday, and I'm goin' to take the day off and make arrangements."

" Well, I'm jiggered! " exclaimed Dougie, as they watched Para Handy walking off on what they realised was to be a nice holiday at their expense, for they would now have his share of the day's work to do as well as their own.

" Did ye ever see such a nate liar? " said The Tar, lost in admiration at the cunning of the Captain.

And then they fell upon the engineer, and abused him for suggesting the valentine.

XXIV

THE DISAPPOINTMENT OF ERCHIE'S NIECE

PARA HANDY never had been at a Glasgow ball till he went to the Knapdale Natives', and he went there simply to please Hurricane Jack. That gallant and dashing mariner came to him one day at Bowling, treated him to three substantial refreshments in an incredibly short space of time, and then delivered a brilliant lecture on the duty of being patriotic to one's native place, " backing up the boys," and buying a ticket for the assembly in question.

" But I'm not a native of Knapdale," said the Captain. " Forbye, I'm kind of oot o' the dancin'; except La Va and Petronella I don't mind wan step."

" That's aal right, Peter," said Hurricane Jack encouragingly; " there's nobody 'll make you dance at a Knapdale ball if you're no' in trum for dancin'. I can get you on the committee, and aal you'll have to do will be to stand at the door of the committee room and keep the crood back from the beer-bottles. I'm no' there mysel' for amusement: do you ken Jean Mactaggart? "

" Not me," said Para Handy. " What Mactaggarts iss she off, Jeck? "

" Carradale," said Hurricane Jack modestly. " A perfect beauty! We're engaged."

The Captain shook hands mournfully with his friend and cheerlessly congratulated him. " It's a responsibulity, Jeck," he said, " there's no doot it's a responsibulity, but you ken yoursel' best."

" She's a nice enough gyurl so far ass I know," said Hurricane Jack. " Her brother's in the Western Ocean tred. What I'm wantin' you on the committee for iss to keep me back from the committee room, so that I'll not take a drop too much and affront the lassie. If you see me desperate keen on takin' more than would be dacent, take a dozen strong smert fellows in wi' you at my expense and barricade the door. I'll maybe taalk aboot tearin' the hoose doon, but och, that'll only be my nonsense."

The Captain accepted the office, not without reluctance, and went to the ball, but Hurricane Jack failed to put in any appearance all night, and Para Handy considered himself the victim of a very stupid practical joke on the part of his friend.

Early next forenoon Hurricane Jack presented himself on board the *Vital Spark* and made an explanation. " I'm black affronted, Peter," he said, " but I couldna help it. I had a bit of an accident. You see it wass this way, Peter. Miss Mactaggart wass comin' special up from Carradale and stayin' with her uncle, old Macpherson. She wass to put her clothes on there, and I wass to caal for her in wan of them cabs at seven o'clock. I wass ready at five, all spruce from clew to earing, and my heid wass that sore wi' wearin' a hat for baals that I got hold of a couple of men I knew in the China tred and went for chust wan small wee gless. What happened efter that for an oor or two's a mystery, but I think I wass drugged. When I got my senses I wass in a cab, and the driver roarin' doon the hatch to me askin' the address.

" ' What street iss it you're for? " said he.

" ' What streets have you? ' I asked.

" 'Aal you told me wass Macfarlane's shup,' he said; ' do you think we're anyway near it? '

" When he said that I put my heid oot by the gless and took an observation.

" ' Iss this Carrick Street or Monday mornin'? ' says I to him, and then he put me oot of his cab. The poor sowl had no fear in him; he must have been Irish. It wass not much of a cab; here's the door handles, a piece of the wud, and the man's brass number; I chust took them with me for identification, and went home to my bed. When I wakened this mornin' and thought of Jean sittin' up aal night waitin' on me, I wass clean demented."

" It's a kind of a peety, too, the way it happened," said Para Handy sympathetically. " It would put herself a bit aboot sittin' aal night wi' her sluppers on."

"And a full set o' new sails," said Hurricane Jack pathetically. " She was sparin' no expense. This'll be a lesson to me. It'll do me good; I wish it hadna happened. What I called for wass to see if you'll be kind enough, seein' you were on the committee, to go up to 191 Barr Street, where she's stayin' wi' Macpherson, and put the thing ass nicely for me ass you can."

Para Handy was naturally shy of the proposal. " I never saw the lassie," said he. " Would it no' look droll for me to go instead of yoursel' ? "

" It would look droll if you didna," said Hurricane Jack emphatically. " What are you on the committee for, and in cherge of aal the beer, unless you're to explain things? I'll show you the close, and you'll go up and ask for two meenutes' private conversation with Miss Mactaggart, and you'll tell her that I'm far

from weel. Say I wass on my way up last night in fine
time and the cab collided with a tramway car. Break
it nice, and no' frighten the poor gyurl oot of her
senses. Say I was oot of my conscience for seven
'oors, but that I'm gettin' the turn, and I'm no' a bit
disfigured."

Para Handy was still irresolute. " She'll maybe
want to nurse you, the way they do in Macphail's
novelles," said he, " and what'll I tell her then? "

This was a staggerer for Hurricane Jack. He recognised the danger of arousing the womanly sympathies
of Miss Mactaggart. But he was equal to all difficulties
of this kind. " Tell her," said he, " there's nobody to
get speakin' to me for forty-eight 'oors, but that I'll
likely be oot on Monday."

The Captain agreed to undertake this delicate
mission, but only on condition that Dougie the mate
should accompany him to back him up in case his own
resourcefulness as a liar should fail him at the critical
moment.

" Very well," said Hurricane Jack, " take Dougie
wi' you, but watch her uncle; I'm told he's cunning,
cunning, though I never met him—a man Macpherson,
by the name of Erchie. Whatever you tell her, if he's
there at the time, tell it to her in the Gaalic."

Para Handy and his mate that evening left Hurricane Jack at a discreet public bar called the " Hot
Blast," and went up to the house of Erchie Macpherson. It was himself who came to answer their
knock at his door, for he was alone in the house.

" We're no' for ony strings o' onions, or parrots,
or onything o' that sort," he said, keeping one foot
against the door and peering at them in the dim light

of the rat-tail burner on the stair-landing. "And if it's the stair windows ye want to clean, they were done yesterday."

"You should buy specs," said the Captain promptly —"they're no' that dear. Iss Miss Mactaggart in?"

Erchie opened the door widely, and gave his visitors admission to the kitchen.

"She's no' in the noo," said he. "Which o' ye happens to be the sailor chap that was to tak' her to the ball last nicht?"

"It wasna any o' us," said Para Handy. "It wass another gentleman aalthegither."

"I micht hae kent that," said Erchie. "Whit lock-up is he in? If it's his bail ye're here for, ye needna bother. I aye tell't my guid-sister's dochter she wasna ill to please when she took up wi' a sailor. I had a son that was yince a sailor himself, but thank the Lord he's better, and he's in the Corporation noo. Were ye wantin' to see Jean?"

"Chust for a meenute," said Para Handy, quietly taking a seat on the jawbox. "Will she be long?"

"Five feet three," said Erchie, "and broad in pro-portion. She hasna come doon sae much as ye wad think at her disappointment."

"That's nice," said Para Handy. "A thing o' the kind would tell terribly on some weemen. You're no' in the shuppin' tred yoursel', I suppose? I ken a lot o' Macphersons in the coast line. But I'm no' askin', mind ye; it's chust for conversation. There wass a femily of Macphersons came from the same place ass mysel' on Lochfyne-side; fine smert fellows they were, but I daresay no relation. Most respectable. Perhaps you ken the Gaalic?"

F

" Not me! " said Erchie frankly—" jist plain Gleska. If I'm Hielan' I canna help it; my faither took the boat to the Broomielaw as soon as he got his senses."

The conversation would have languished here if Dougie had not come to the rescue. " What's your tred? " he asked bluntly.

" Whiles I beadle and whiles I wait," replied Erchie, who was not the man to be ashamed of his calling. "At ither times I jist mind my ain affairs; ye should gie 't a trial—it'll no hurt ye."

The seamen laughed at this sally: it was always a virtue of both of them that they could appreciate a joke at their own expense.

" No offence, no offence, Mr Macpherson," said Para Handy. " I wish your niece would look slippy. You'll be sorry to hear aboot what happened to poor Jeck."

Erchie turned quite serious. " What's the maitter wi' him? " he said.

" The cab broke doon last night," said the Captain solemnly, " and he got a duvvle of a smash."

" Puir sowl! " said Erchie, honestly distressed. " This'll be a sair blow for Jeanie."

" He lost his conscience for 'oors, but there's no disfeegurement, and he'll be speechless till Monday mornin'. It's a great peety. Such a splendid voice ass he had, too; it wass truly sublime. He's lyin' yonder wi' his heid in a sling and not wan word in him. He tell't me I was to say to——"

Here Dougie, seeing an inconsistency in the report, slyly nudged his captain, who stopped short and made a very good effort at a sigh of deep regret.

" I thocht ye said he couldna speak," said Erchie suspiciously.

" My mistake, my mistake," said the Captain. " What I meant wass that he could only speak in the Gaalic; the man's fair off his usual. Dougie 'll tell you himsel'."

Dougie shook his head lugubriously. "Ay," said he, " he's yonder wi' fifteen doctors roond him waitin' for the turn."

" What time did it happen? " inquired Erchie. " Was it efter he was here? "

" He wass on his way here," said Para Handy. " It was exactly half-past seven, for his watch stopped in the smash."

At this Erchie sat back in his chair and gave a disconcerting laugh. " Man," he said, " ye're no' bad at a baur, but ye've baith put yer feet in't this time. Will ye tak' a refreshment? There's a drop speerits in the hoose and a bottle or two o' porter."

" I'm teetotal mysel' at present," said Para Handy, " but I have a nesty cold. I'll chust take the spurits while you're pullin' the porter. We'll drink a quick recovery to Jeck."

" Wi' a' my he'rt," said Erchie agreeably. " I hope he'll be oot again afore Monday. Do ye no' ken he came here last nicht wi' the cab a' richt, but was that dazed Jeanie wadna gang wi' him. But she got to the ball a' the same, for she went wi' Mackay the polisman."

" My Chove! " said the Captain, quite dumbfoundered. " He doesna mind, himsel', a thing aboot it."

" I daresay no'," said Erchie, " that's the warst o' trevellin' in cabs; he should hae come in a motor-caur."

When the Captain and Dougie came down Macpherson's stair, they considered the situation in the
close.

" I think mysel'," said the Captain, " it wouldna be
salubrious for neither o' the two of us to go to the
' Hot Blast ' and break the news to Jeck the night."

" Whatever ye think yoursel'," said Dougie, and
they headed straight for home.

XXV

PARA HANDY'S WEDDING

IT is possible that Para Handy might still have been a
bachelor if Calum Cameron had not been jilted.
Three days before Calum was to have been married,
the girl exercised a girl's privilege and changed her
mind. She explained her sad inconstancy by saying
she had never cared for him, and only said " yes " to
get him off her face. It was an awkward business,
because it left the baker's widow, Mrs Crawford, with
a large bride's-cake on her hands. It is true the bride's-
cake had been paid for, but in the painful circumstances
neither of the parties to the broken contract would have
anything to do with it, and it continued to lie in the
baker's window, a pathetic evidence of woman's per-
fidy. All Campbeltown talked about it; people came
five and six miles in from the country to look at it.
When they saw what a handsome example of the con-
fectioner's art it was, they shook their heads and said
the lassie could have no heart, let alone good taste.

Mrs Crawford, being a smart business woman, put a bill in the window with the legend—

EXCELLENT BRIDE'S-CAKE

SECOND-HAND

17/6

But there were no offers, and she was on the point of disposing of it on the Art Union principle, when, by one of those providential accidents that are very hard on the sufferer but lead by a myriad consequent circumstances to the most beneficent ends, a man in Carrick Street, Glasgow, broke his leg. The man never heard of Para Handy in all his life, nor of the *Vital Spark*; he had never been in Campbeltown, and if he had not kept a pet tortoise he would never have figured in this book, and Para Handy might not have been married, even though Calum Cameron's girl had been a jilt.

The Carrick Street man's tortoise had wandered out into the close in the evening; the owner, rushing out hurriedly at three minutes to ten to do some shopping, tripped over it, and was not prevented by the agony of his injured limb from seizing the offending animal and throwing it into the street, where it fell at the feet of Para Handy, who was passing at the time.

"A tortoise!" said the Captain, picking it up. "The first time ever I kent they flew. I'll take it to Macphail —he's keen on birds anyway," and down he took it to the engineer of the *Vital Spark*.

But Macphail refused to interest himself in a pet which commended itself neither by beauty of plumage nor sweetness of song, and for several days the unhappy tortoise took a deck passage on the *Vital Spark*, its

constitution apparently little impaired by the fact that
at times The Tar used it as a coal-hammer.

" I'll no' see the poor tortoise abused this way,"
said Para Handy, when they got to Campbeltown one
day; " I'll take it up and give it to a friend o' mine,"
and, putting it into his pocket in the evening, he went
up to the baker's shop.

The widow was at the moment fixing a card on the
bride's-cake intimating that tickets for the raffle of it
would cost sixpence each, and that the drawing would
take place on the following Saturday. Her plump
form was revealed in the small shop-window; the
flush of exertion charmingly irradiated her countenance
as she bent among her penny buns and bottles of fancy
biscuits; Para Handy, gazing at her from the outside,
thought he had never seen her look more attractive.
She blushed more deeply when she saw him looking
in at her, and retired from the window with some
embarrassment as he entered the shop.

" Fine night, Mery," said the Captain. " You're
pushin' business desperate, surely, when you're raffling
bride's-cakes."

" Will you not buy a ticket? " said the lady, smiling.
" You might be the lucky man to get the prize."

"And what in the world would I do wi' a bride's-
cake? " asked the Captain, his manly sailor's heart in
a gentle palpitation. " Where would I get a bride to
—to—to fit it? "

" I'm sure and I don't know," said the widow hurriedly, and she went on to explain the circumstances
that had left it on her hands. The Captain listened
attentively, eyed the elegant proportions of the cake
in the window, and was seized by a desperate resolve.

" I never saw a finer bride's-cake," he said; " it's chust sublime! Do you think it would keep till the Gleska Fair? "

" It would keep a year for that part o't," said the widow. " What are you askin' that for? "

" If it'll keep to the Fair, and the Fair suits yoursel'," said Para Handy boldly, " we'll have it between us. What do you say to that, Mery? " and he leaned amorously over the counter.

" Mercy on me! this is no' the New Year time," exclaimed the widow; " I thought you never had any mind of me except at the New Year. Is this a proposal, Captain? "

" Don't caal me, Captain, caal me Peter, and gie me a haad o' your hand," entreated Para Handy languishingly.

" Well, then—Peter," murmured the widow, and the Captain went back to the *Vital Spark* that night an engaged man: the bride's-cake was withdrawn from the window, and the tortoise took up its quarters in the back shop.

. . . .

Of all the ordeals Para Handy had to pass through before his marriage, there was none that troubled him more than his introduction to her relatives, and the worst of them was Uncle Alick, who was very old, very deaf, and very averse to his niece marrying again. The Captain and his " fiancée " visited him as in duty bound, and found him in a decidedly unfavourable temper.

" This is Peter," said the widow by way of introduction; and the Captain stood awkwardly by her side, with his pea-jacket tightly buttoned to give him an appearance of slim, sprightly, and dashing youth-fulness.

" What Peter? " asked the uncle, not taking his pipe out of his mouth, and looking with a cold, indifferent eye upon his prospective relative.

" You know fine," said the lady, flushing. " It's my lad."

" What did you say? " inquired Uncle Alick, with a hand behind his ear.

" My lad," she cried. " Peter Macfarlane—him that's Captain on the *Vital Spark*."

" Catched him in a park," said Uncle Alick. " I'll wudger you didna need to run fast to catch him. Whatna park was it? "

" The *Fital Spark*," roared the Captain, coming to Mary's assistance. " I'm captain on her."

"Are you, are you? " said Uncle Alick querulously. " Weel, you needna roar at me like that; I'm no' that deaf. You'll be wan o' the Macfarlanes from Ach-natra; they were aal kind of droll in the mind, but hermless."

The Captain explained that he was a member of a different family altogether, but Uncle Alick displayed no interest in the explanation. " It's none of my business," said he.

" Mery thinks it is," rejoined the Captain. " That's the reason we're here."

" Beer! " said Uncle Alick. " No, no, I have no beer for you. I never keep drink of any sort in the hoose."

" I never said beer," exclaimed Para Handy.

" I'll be telling a lie then," said Uncle Alick. " The

same ass if I didn't hear you with my own ears. You'll be the man that Mery's goin' to merry. I canna understand her; I'm sure she had plenty of trouble wi' Donald Crawford before he went and died on her. But it's none o' my business: I'm only an old done man, no' long for this world, and I'm not goin' to interfere wi' her if she wass to merry a bleck. She never consulted me, though I'm the only uncle she has. You shouldna put yoursel's to bother tellin' me anything aboot it; I'm sure I would have heard aboot it from some o' the neebours. The neebours iss very good to me. They're sayin' it's a droll-like thing Mery merryin' again, and her wi' a nice wee shop o' her own. What I says to them iss, ' It's her own business: perhaps she sees something takin' in the man that nobody else does. Maybe,' I says to them, ' he'll give up his vessel and help her in the shop.' "

" Och, you're chust an old haiver! " remarked the Captain *sotto voce*, and of course the deaf man heard him.

"A haiver! " said he. "A nice-like thing to say aboot the only uncle Mery has, and him over eighty-six. But you're no' young yoursel'. Maybe it wass time for you to be givin' up the boats."

" I'm no' thinkin' o' givin' them up, Uncle," said Para Handy cheerfully. " The *Vital Spark*'s the smertest boat in the tred. A bonny-like hand I would be in a shop. No, no, herself here — Mery, can keep the shop or leave it, chust ass it pleases hersel', it's aal wan to me; I'm quite joco. I hope you'll turn up at the weddin' on the fufteenth, for aal langsyne."

" What's your wull? " inquired Uncle Alick.

F 2

" I hope you'll turn up at the weddin' and give us support," bellowed the Captain.

" Give you sport," said the old man indignantly. " You'll surely get plenty of sport withoot takin' it off a poor old man like me."

" Och! to the muschief! " exclaimed the Captain somewhat impatiently. " Here's a half pound o' tobacco me and Mery brought you, and surely that'll put you in better trum."

" What wey did you no' say that at first? " said Uncle Alick. " Hoo wass I to know you werena wantin' the lend o' money for the weddin'? Stop you and I'll see if there's any spurits handy."

. . . . .

I was not at the wedding, but the Captain told me all about it some days afterwards. " It would be worth a bit in the papers," he said with considerable elation. " I'll wudger there wasna another weddin' like it in Kintyre for chenerations. The herrin' trawlers iss not back at their work yet, and herrin's up ten shullin's a box in Gleska. Dougie and The Tar and their wifes wass there, quite nate and tidy, and every noo and then Macphail would be comin' doon to the boat and blowin' her whustle. Och, he's not a bad chap Macphail, either, but chust stupid with readin' them novelles.

" I never saw Mery lookin' more majestic; she wass chust sublime! Some of them said I wassna lookin' slack mysel', and I daarsay no', for I wass in splendid trum. When the knot was tied, and we sat doon to a bite, I found it wass a different bride's-cake aal-thegither from the wan that julted Cameron.

" ' What's the meanin' of that? ' I whuspered to the mustress. ' That's no' the bride's-cake you had in the window.'

" ' No,' says she, ' but it's a far better one, isn't it? '

" ' It's a better-lookin' wan,' I says, ' but the other wan might have done the business.'

" ' Maybe it would,' she said, ' but I have all my wuts aboot me, and I wasna goin' to have the neighbours say that both the bride and bride's-cake were second-hand.' Oh! I'm tellin' you she's a smert wan the mustress! "

" Well, I wish you and your good lady long life and happiness, Captain," I said.

" Thanky, thanky," said he. " I'll tell the mustress. Could you no put a bit in the papers sayin', ' The rale and only belle o' Captain Macfarlane's weddin' wass the young lady first in the grand merch, dressed in broon silk.' "

" Who was the young lady dressed in brown? " I asked.

" What need you ask for? " he replied. " Who would it be but the mustress? "

IN HIGHLAND
HARBOURS WITH
PARA HANDY
S.S. *VITAL SPARK*

IN HIGHLAND
HARBOURS WITH
PARA HANDY

A NEW COOK

THE s.s. *Texa* made a triumphal entry to the
harbour by steaming in between two square-
rigged schooners, the *Volant* and *Jehu*, of Wick, and
slid silently, with the exactitude of long experience,
against the piles of Rothesay quay, where Para Handy
sat on a log of wood. The throb of her engine, the
wash of her propeller, gave place to the strains of a
melodeon, which was playing " Stop yer ticklin,
Jock," and Para Handy felt some sense of gaiety
suffuse him, but business was business, and it was
only for a moment he permitted himself to be carried
away on the divine wings of music.

" Have you anything for me, M‘Kay? " he hailed
the *Texa's* clerk.

The purser cast a rapid glance over the deck,
encumbered with planks, crates, casks of paraffin oil,
and herring-boxes, and seeing nothing there that
looked like a consignment for the questioner, leaned
across the rail, and made a rapid survey of the open
hold. It held nothing maritime—only hay-bales,
flour-bags, soap-boxes, shrouded mutton carcases,

rolls of plumbers' lead, two head-stones for Ardrishaig, and the dismantled slates, cushions, and legs
of a billiard-table for Strachur.

" Naething the day for you, Peter," said the clerk;
" unless it's yin o' the heid-stanes," and he ran his eye
down the manifest which he held in his hand.

" Ye're aawful smert, M'Kay," said Para Handy.
"If ye wass a rale purser wi' brass buttons and a yellow-
and-black strippit tie on your neck, there would be no
haadin' ye in! It's no' luggage I'm lookin' for; it's
a kind o' a man I'm expectin'. Maybe he's no' in
your depairtment; he'll be traivellin' saloon. Look
behind wan o' them herring-boxes, Lachie, and see if
ye canna see a sailor."

His intuition was right; the *Texa's* only passenger
that afternoon was discovered sitting behind the
herring-boxes playing a melodeon, and smiling beatifi-
cally to himself, with blissful unconsciousness that he
had arrived at his destination. He came to himself
with a start when the purser asked him if he was going
off here; terminated the melody of his instrument in
a melancholy squawk, picked up a carelessly tied
canvas bag that lay at his feet, and hurried over the
plank to the quay, shedding from the bag as he went
a trail of socks, shoes, collars, penny ballads, and seamen's biscuits, whose exposure in this awkward fashion
seemed to cause him no distress of mind, for he only
laughed when Para Handy called them to his attention,
and left to one of the *Texa's* hands the trouble of col-
lecting them, though he obligingly held the mouth of
the sack open himself while the other restored the
dunnage. He was a round, short, red-faced, clean-
shaven fellow of five-and-twenty, with a thin serge

suit, well polished at all the bulgy parts, and a laugh that sprang from a merry heart.

"Are you The Tar's kizzen? Are you Davie Green?" asked Para Handy.

"Right-oh! The very chap," said the stranger. "And you'll be Peter? Haud my melodeon, will ye, till I draw my breath. Right-oh!"

"Are ye sure there's no mistake?" asked Para Handy as they moved along to the other end of the quay where the *Vital Spark* was lying. "You're the new hand I wass expectin', and you name's Davie?"

"My name's Davie, richt enough," said the stranger, "but I seldom got it; when I was on the Cluthas they always ca'd me Sunny Jim."

"Sunny Jum!" said the Captain. "Man! I've often heard aboot ye; you were namely for chumpin' fences?"

"Not me!" said Davie. "Catch me jumpin' ony-thing if there was a hole to get through. Is that your vessel? She's a tipper! You and me'll get on A1. Wait you till ye see the fun I'll gie ye! That was the worst o' the Cluthas—awfu' short trips, and every noo and then a quay; ye hadn't a meenute to yerself for a baur at all. Whit sort o' chaps hae ye for a crew?"

"The very pick!" said Para Handy, as they came alongside the *Vital Spark*, whose crew, as a matter of fact, were all on deck to see the new hand. "That's Macphail, the chief enchineer, wan of Brutain's hardy sons, wi' the wan gallows; and the other chap's Dougie, the first mate, a Cowal laad; you'll see him plainer efter his face iss washed for the tea. Then there's me, mysel', the Captain. Laads, this iss Colin's kizzen, Sunny Jum."

Sunny Jim stood on the edge of the quay, and smiled like a sunset on his future shipmates. " Hoo are yez, chaps? " he cried genially, waving his hand.

" We canna compleen," said Dougie solemnly. "Are ye in good trum yersel'? See's a grup o' your hold-aal, and excuse the gangway."

Sunny Jim jumped on board, throwing his dunnage-bag before him, and his feet had no sooner touched the deck than he indulged in a step or two of the sailor's hornpipe with that proficiency which only years of practice in a close-mouth in Crown Street, S.S., could confer. The Captain looked a little embarrassed; such conduct was hardly business-like, but it was a relief to find that The Tar's nominee and successor was a cheery chap at any rate. Dougie looked on with no disapproval, but Macphail grunted and turned his gaze to sea, disgusted at such free-and-easy informality.

" I hope ye can cook as weel's ye can dance," he remarked coldly.

Sunny Jim stopped immediately. " Am I supposed to cook? " he asked, concealing his surprise as he best could.

" Ye are that! " said Macphail. " Did ye think ye were to be the German band on board, and go roon' liftin' pennies? Cookin's the main thing wi' the second mate o' the *Vital Spark*, and I can tell ye we're gey particular; are we no', Dougie? "

"Aawful!" said Dougie sadly. "Macphail here hass been cookin' since The Tar left; he'll gie ye his receipt for haddies made wi' enchine-oil."

The *Vital Spark* cast off from Rothesay quay on her way for Bowling, and Sunny Jim was introduced to several pounds of sausages to be fried for dinner, a bag of potatoes, and a jar of salt, with which he was left to juggle as he could, while the others, with expectant appetites, performed their respective duties. Life on the open sea, he found, was likely to be as humdrum as it used to be on the Cluthas, and he determined to initiate a little harmless gaiety. With some difficulty he extracted all the meat from the uncooked sausages, and substituted salt. Then he put them on the frying-pan. They had no sooner heated than they began to dance in the pan with curious little crackling explosions. He started playing his melodeon, and cried on the crew, who hurried to see this unusual phenomenon.

" Well, I'm jeegered," said the Captain; " what in aal the world iss the matter wi' them? "

" It's a waarnin'," said Dougie lugubriously, with wide-staring eyes.

" Warnin', my auntie! " said Sunny Jim, playing a jig-tune. " They started jumpin' like that whenever I begood to play my bonnie wee melodeon."

" I daarsay that," said Para Handy; " for you're a fine, fine player, Jum, but—but it wassna any invitation to a baal I gave them when I paid for them in Ro'sa'."

" I aye said sausages werena meat for sailors," remarked the engineer, with bitterness, for he was very hungry. " Ye'll notice it's an Irish jig they're dancin' to," he added with dark significance.

" I don't see mysel'," said the Captain, " that it maitters whether it iss an Irish jeeg or the Gourock Waltz and Circassian Circle."

" Does it no'? " retorted Macphail. " I suppose ye'll never hae heard o' Irish terrier dugs? I've ett my last sausage onywye! Sling us ower that pan-loaf," and seizing the bread for himself he proceeded to make a spartan meal.

Sunny Jim laughed till the tears ran down his jovial countenance. " Chaps," he exclaimed, with firm conviction, " this is the cheeriest ship ever I was on; I'm awful gled I brung my music."

Dougie took a fork and gingerly investigated. "As hard ass whun-stanes! " he proclaimed; " they'll no' be ready by the time we're at the Tail o' the Bank. Did you ever in your mortal life see the like of it? " and he jabbed ferociously with the fork at the bewitched sausages.

" That's richt! " said Macphail. " Put them oot o' pain."

" Stop you! " said Para Handy. " Let us pause and consuder. It iss the first time ever I saw sassages with such a desperate fine ear for music. If they'll no' fry, they'll maybe boil. Put them in a pot, Jum."

" Right-oh! " said Sunny Jim, delighted at the prospect of a second scene to his farce, and the terpsichorean sausages were consigned to the pot of water which had boiled the potatoes. The crew sat round, staving off the acuter pangs of hunger with potatoes and bread.

" You never told us what for they called you Sunny Jum, Davie," remarked the Captain. " Do you think it would be for your complexion? "

" I couldna say," replied the new hand, " but I think mysel' it was because I was aye such a cheery wee chap. The favourite Clutha on the Clyde, when the Cluthas was rinnin', was the yin I was on; hunners o' trips used to come wi' her on the Setturdays on the aff-chance that I wad maybe gie them a baur. Mony a pant we had! I could hae got a job at the Finnieston Ferry richt enough, chaps, but they wouldna alloo the melodeon, and I wad sooner want my wages."

" A fine, fine unstrument!" said Para Handy agreeably. " Wi' it and Dougie's trump we'll no' be slack in passin' the time."

" Be happy!—that's my motto," said Sunny Jim, beaming upon his auditors like one who brings a new and glorious evangel. " Whatever happens, be happy, and then ye can defy onything. It's a' in the wye ye look at things. See?"

" That's what I aalways say mysel' to the wife," said Dougie in heart-broken tones, and his eye on the pot, which was beginning to boil briskly.

"As shair as daith, chaps, I canna stand the Jock o' Hazeldean kind o' thing at a'—folk gaun aboot lettin' the tear doon-fa a' the time. Gie me a hearty laugh and it's right-oh! BE HAPPY!—that's the Golden Text for the day, as we used to say in the Sunday School."

" I could be happy easy enough if it wassna that I wass so desperate hungry," said Dougie in melancholy accents, lifting the lid to look into the pot. He could see no sign of sausages, and with new forebodings he began to feel for them with a stick. They had disappeared! " I said from the very first it wass a waarnin'!" he exclaimed, resigning the stick to the incredulous engineer.

" This boat's haunted," said Macphail, who also failed to find anything in the pot. " I saw ye puttin' them in wi' my ain eyes, and noo they're no' there."

Para Handy grabbed the spirtle, and feverishly

explored on his own account, with the same extraordinary results.

" My Chove! " he exclaimed, " did you ever see the
like of that, and I havena tasted wan drop of stimulants
since last Monday. Laads! I don't know what you
think aboot it, but it's the church twice for me
to-morrow! "

.   .   .   .   .

Sunny Jim quite justified his nickname by giving a
pleasant surprise to his shipmates in the shape of a
meat-tea later in the afternoon.

PENSION FARMS

THE *Vital Spark* was making for Lochgoilhead, Dougie
at the wheel, and the Captain straddled on a water-
breaker, humming Gaelic songs, because he felt magnificent after his weekly shave. The chug-chug-chug
of the engines was the only other sound that broke
the silence of the afternoon, and Sunny Jim deplored
the fact that in the hurry of embarking early in the
morning he had quite forgotten his melodeon—those
peaceful days at sea hung heavy on his urban spirit.

" That's Ardgoil," remarked Macphail, pointing
with the stroup of an oil-can at the Glasgow promon-
tory, and Para Handy gazed at the land with affected
interest.

" So it iss, Macphail," he said ironically. " That
wass it the last time we were here, and the time before,
and the time before that again. You would think it
would be shifted. It's wan of them guides for towerists

you should be, Macphail, you're such a splendid hand
for information. What way do you spell it?"

"Oh, shut up!" said the engineer with petulance;
"ye think ye're awfu' clever. I mind when that wee
hoose at the p'int was a hen farm, and there's no' a
road to't. Ye could only get near the place wi' a
boat."

"If that wass the way of it," said Dougie, "ducks
would suit them better; they could swim. It's a fine
thing a duck."

"But a goose is more extraordinar'," said Macphail
with meaning. "Anyway it was hens, and mony a
time I wished I had a ferm for hens."

"You're better where you are," said the Captain,
"oilin' engines like a chentleman. A hen ferm iss an
aawful speculation, and you need your wuts aboot you
if you start wan. All your relations expect their eggs
for nothing, and the very time o' the year when eggs
iss dearest, hens takes a tirrievee and stop the layin'.
Am I no' tellin' the truth, Dougie?"

"You are that!" said the mate agreeably; "I have
noticed it mysel'."

"If ye didna get eggs ye could live aff the chickens,"
suggested Sunny Jim. "I think a hen ferm would be
top, richt enough!"

"It's not the kind o' ferm I would have mysel'
whatever o't," said Para Handy; "there's far more
chance o' a dacent livin' oot o' rearin' pensioners."

"Rearin' pensioners?" remarked Macphail; "ye
would lie oot o' your money a lang while rearin'
pensioners; ye micht as weel start growin' trees."

"Not at aal! not at aal!" said Para Handy;
"there's quick returns in pensioners if you put your

mind to the thing and use a little caation. Up in the
Islands, now, the folks iss givin' up their crofts and
makin' a kind o' ferm o' their aged relations. I have a
cousin yonder oot in Gigha wi' a stock o' five fine
healthy uncles—no' a man o' them under seventy.
There's another frien' o' my own in Mull wi' thirteen
heid o' chenuine old Macleans. He gaithered them
aboot the islands wi' a boat whenever the rumours o'
the pensions started. Their frien's had no idea what
he wanted wi' them, and were glad to get them off
their hands. ' It's chust a notion that I took,' he said,
' for company; they're great amusement on a winter
night,' and he got his pick o' the best o' them. It
wassna every wan he would take; they must be aal
Macleans, for the Mull Macleans never die till they're
centurions, and he wouldna take a man that wass over
five and seventy. They're yonder, noo, in Loch
Scridain, kept like fightin' cocks; he puts them oot on
the hill each day for exercise, and if wan o' them takes
a cough they dry his clothes and give him something
from a bottle."

" Holy smoke! " said Dougie; " where's the profits
comin' from? "

" From the Government," said Para Handy. " Nothing simpler! He gets five shillings a heid in the week
for them, and that's £169 in the year for the whole
thirteen—enough to feed a regiment! Wan pensioner
maybe wadna pay you, but if you have a herd like my
frien' in Mull, there's money in it. He buys their meal
in bulk from Oban, and they'll grow their own
potatoes; the only thing he's vexed for iss that they
havena wool, and he canna clip them. If he keeps his
health himsel', and doesna lose his heid for a year or

twa, he'll have the lergest pension ferm in Scotland, and be able to keep a gig. I'm no' a bit feared for Donald, though; he's a man o' business chust ass good ass you'll get on the streets o' Gleska."

"Thirteen auld chaps like that aboot a hoose wad be an awfu' handful," suggested Sunny Jim.

"Not if it's at Loch Scridain," answered Para Handy; "half the time they're on the gress, and there's any amount o' fanks. They're quite delighted swappin' baurs wi' wan another aboot the way they could throw the hammer fifty years ago, and they feel they're more important noo than ever they were in a' their lives afore. When my frien' collected them, they hadna what you would caal an object for to live for except it wass their own funerals; noo they're daft for almanacs, and makin' plans for living to a hundred, when the fermer tells them that he'll gie them each a medal and a uniform. Oh! a smert, smert laad, Donal'. Wan o' Brutain's hardy sons! Nobody could be kinder!"

"It's a fine way o' makin' a livin'," said Macphail. "I hope they'll no' go wrang wi' him."

"Fine enough," said Para Handy, "but the chob iss not withoot responsibilities. Yonder's my cousin in Gigha wi' his stock o' five, and a nice bit ground for them, and you wouldna believe what it needs in management. He got two of them pretty cheap in Salen, wan o' them over ninety, and the other eighty-six; you wouldna believe it, but they're worse to manage than the other three that's ten years younger. The wan over ninety's very cocky of his age, and thinks the other wans iss chust a lot o' boys. He says it's a scandal givin' them a pension; pensions should be kept for men that's up in years, and then it should be something sensible—something like a pound. The wan that iss eighty-six iss desperate dour, and if my cousin doesna please him, stays in his bed and says he'll die for spite."

" That's gey mean, richt enough! " said Sunny Jim; " efter your kizzen takin' a' that trouble! "

" But the worst o' the lot's an uncle that he got in Eigg; he's seventy-six, and talkin' aboot a wife! "

" Holy smoke! " said Dougie; " isn't that chust desperate! "

"Ay; he hass a terrible conceity notion o' his five shillin's a-week; you would think he wass a million-aire. ' I could keep a wife on it if she wass young and strong,' he tells my cousin, and it takes my cousin and the mustress aal their time to keep him oot o' the way o' likely girls. They don't ken the day they'll lose him."

" Could they no' put a brand on him? " asked Dougie.

" Ye daurna brand them," said the Captain, " nor keel them either. The law 'll not allo' it. So you see yersel's there's aye a risk, and it needs a little capital. My cousin had a bit of a shop, and he gave it up to start the pension ferm; he'll be sayin' sometimes it wass a happier man he wass when he wass a merchant, but he's awfu' prood that noo he hass a chob, as you might say, wi' the Brutish Government."

PARA HANDY'S PUP

ONE night when the *Vital Spark* lay at Port Ellen quay, and all the crew were up the village at a shinty concert, some one got on board the vessel and stole her best chronometer. It was the property of Macphail, had cost exactly 1s. 11½d., and kept approximate time for hours on end if laid upon its side. Macphail at frequent intervals repaired it with pieces of lemonade wire, the selvedges of postage stamps, and a tube of seccotine.

" Holy smoke! " said the Captain, when the loss was discovered; " we'll be sleepin' in in the efternoons as sure as anything. Isn't this the depredation! "

" The champion wee nock! " said Macphail, on the verge of tears. " Set it to the time fornenst yon nock o' Singerses at Kilbowie, and it would tick as nate as onything to the Cloch."

" Right enough! " said Sunny Jim impressively; " I've biled eggs wi't. There's the very nail it hung on! "

" It's the first time I ever knew that nock to go without Macphail doin' something to it wi' the stroup o' an oil-can," said Dougie.

It was decided that no more risks of quay-head burglary were to be run, and that when evening entertainments called the rest of the crew ashore, the charge of the ship should depend on Sunny Jim.

" I couldna tak' it in haund, chaps! " he protested feelingly. " Ye've nae idea hoo silly I am at nicht when I'm my lane; I cod mysel' I'm seein' ghosts till every hair on my heid's on end."

" I'm like that mysel'! " confessed Para Handy. " I can gie mysel' a duvvle o' a fright, but it's only nonsense, chust fair nonsense! there's no' a ghost this side o' the Sound o' Sleat; nothing but imagination."

" Ye shouldna be tumid! " counselled Dougie, who never could stay in the fo'c'sle alone at night himself for fear of spirits.

" Ye'll can play your melodeon," said Macphail; " if there's onything to scare the life oot o' ghosts it's that."

But Sunny Jim was not to be induced to run the risk, and the Captain wasn't the sort of man to compel a body to do a thing he didn't like to do, against his will. Evening entertainments at the ports of call were on the point of being regretfully foresworn, when Sunny Jim proposed the purchase of a watch-dog. "A watch-dug's the very ticket," he exclaimed. " It's an awfu' cheery thing on a boat. We can gie't the rin o' the deck when we're ashore at nicht, and naebody 'll come near't. I ken the very dug—it belangs to a chap in Fairfield, a rale Pompanion, and he ca's it Biler. It has a pedigree and a brass-mounted collar, and a' its P's and Q's."

" Faith! there's worse things than a good dog; there's some o' them chust sublime! " said Para Handy, quite enamoured of the notion. " Iss it well trained, your frien's Pompanion? "

" Top! " Sunny Jim assured him. " If ye jist seen it! It would face a regiment o' sodgers, and has a bark ye could hear from here to Campbeltown. It's no awfu' fancy-lookin', mind; it's no' the kind ye'll see the women carryin' doon Buchanan Street in their oxters; but if ye want sagaciosity——! " and Sunny

Jim held up his hands in speechless admiration of the animal's intelligence. " It belangs to a riveter ca'd Willie Stevenson, and it's jist a pup. There's only the wan fau't wi't, or Willie could live aff the prizes it wad lift at shows—it's deaf."

" That's the very sort o' dug we wad need for a boat like this," said Macphail, with his usual cynicism. " Could ye no' get yin that was blin' too? " But nobody paid any attention to him; there were moments when silent contempt was the obvious attitude to the engineer.

" The worst about a fine, fine dog like that," said Para Handy reflectively, " iss that it would cost a lot o' money, and aal we want iss a dog to watch the boat and bark daily or hourly ass required."

" Cost! " retorted Sunny Jim; " it wad cost nae-thing! I wad ask Willie Stevenson for the len' o't, and then say we lost it ower the side. It has far mair sense than Willie himsel'. It goes aboot Govan wi' him on pay Setturdays, and sleeps between his feet when he's sittin' in the public-hooses backin' up the Celts. Sometimes Willie forget's it's wi' him, and gangs awa' without waukenin' 't, but when Biler waukens up and sees its maister's no there, it stands on its hind legs and looks at the gless that Willie was drinkin' frae. If there's ony drink left in't it kens he'll be back, and it waits for him."

" Capital! " said Para Handy. " There's dogs like that. It's born in them. It's chust a gift! "

The dog Biler was duly borrowed by Sunny Jim on the next run to Glasgow, and formally installed as watch of the *Vital Spark*. It was distinctly not the sort of dog to make a lady's pet; its lines were generously large, but crude and erratic; its coat was hopelessly unkempt and ragged, its head incredibly massive, and its face undeniably villainous. Even Sunny Jim was apologetic when he produced it on a chain. " Mind, I never said he was onything awfu' fancy," he pleaded. " But he's a dug that grows on ye."

" He's no' like what I thocht he would be like at aal, at aal," admitted the Captain, somewhat disappointed. " Iss he a rale Pompanion? "

" Pure bred! " said Sunny Jim; " never lets go the grip. Examine his jaw."

" Look you at his jaw, Dougie, and see if he's the rale Pompanion," said the Captain; but Dougie declined. " I'll wait till we're better acquent," he said. " Man! doesn't he look desperate dour? "

" Oor new nock's a' richt wi' a dug like that to watch it," said Macphail; " he's as guid as a guardship."

Biler surveyed them curiously, not very favourably impressed, and deaf, of course, to all blandishments. For a day or two the slightest hasty movement on the part of any of his new companions made him growl ferociously and display an appalling arsenal of teeth. As a watch-dog he was perfect; nobody dared come down a quay within a hundred yards of the *Vital Spark* without his loud, alarming bay. Biler spoiled the quay-head angling all along Loch Fyne.

In a week or two Para Handy got to love him, and bragged incessantly of his remarkable intelligence. " Chust a pup! " he would say, " but as long in the heid as a weedow woman. If he had aal his faculties he would not be canny, and indeed he doesna seem to want his hearin' much; he's ass sharp in the eye ass

a polisman. A dog like that should have a Board of
Tred certuficate."

Dougie, however, was always dubious of the pet.
" Take my word, Peter," he would say solemnly,
" there's muschief in him; he's no a dog you can take
to your he'rt at aal, at aal, and he barks himsel' black
in the face wi' animosity at Macphail."

" Didn't I tell you? " would the Captain cry,
exultant. "Ass deaf ass a door, and still he can take
the measure o' Macphail! I hope, Jum, your frien' in
Fairfield's no' in a hurry to get him back."

" Not him," said Sunny Jim. " He's no expectin'
him back at a'. I tell't him Biler was drooned at Colintraive, and a' he said was ' ye micht hae tried to save
his collar.' "

And Dougie's doubts were fully justified in course
of time. The *Vital Spark* was up with coals at Skipness, at a pier a mile away from the village, and Para
Handy had an invitation to a party. He dressed himself in his Sunday clothes, and, redolent of scented
soap, was confessed the lion of the evening, though
Biler unaccountably refused to accompany him. At
midnight he came back along the shore, to the ship,
walking airily on his heels, with his hat at a dashing
angle. The crew of the *Vital Spark* were all asleep,
but the faithful Biler held the deck, and the Captain
heard his bark.

" Pure Pompanion bred! " he said to himself. "As
wise as a weedow woman! For the rale sagacity give
me a dog! "

He made to step from the quay to the vessel's gunnel,
but a rush and a growl from the dog restrained him;
Biler's celebrated grip was almost on his leg.

" Tuts, man," said the Captain, " I'm sure you can see it's me; it's Peter. Good old Biler; stop you and I'll give you a buscuit! "

He ventured a foot on the gunnel again, and this time Biler sampled the tweed of his trousers. Nothing else was stirring in the *Vital Spark*. The Captain hailed his shipmates for assistance; if they heard, they never heeded, and the situation was sufficiently unpleasant to annoy a man of better temper even than Para Handy. No matter how he tried to get on board, the trusty watch-dog kept him back. In one attempt his hat fell off, and Biler tore it into the most impressive fragments.

" My Cot," said the Captain, " issn't this the happy evenin'? Stop you till I'll be pickin' a dog again, and it'll be wan wi' aal his faculties."

He had to walk back to the village and take shelter ashore for the night; in the morning Biler received him with the friendliest overtures, and was apparently astonished at the way they were received.

" Jum," said the Captain firmly, " you'll take back that dog to your frien' in Fairfield, and tell him there's no' a bit o' the rale Pompanion in him. He's chust a common Gleska dog, and he doesna know a skipper when he sees him, if he's in his Sunday clothes."

TREASURE TROVE

SUNNY JIM proved a most valuable acquisition to the *Vital Spark*. He was a person of humour and resource, and though they were sometimes the victims of his practical jokes, the others of the crew forgave him readily because of the fun he made. It is true that

when they were getting the greatest entertainment
from him they were, without thinking it, generally
doing his work for him—for indeed he was no sailor,
only a Clutha mariner—but at least he was better value
for his wages than The Tar, who could neither take
his fair share of the work nor tell a baur. Sunny Jim's
finest gift was imagination; the most wonderful things
in the world had happened to him when he was on the
Cluthas—all intensely interesting, if incredible: and
Para Handy, looking at him with admiration and even
envy, after a narrative more extraordinary than usual,
would remark, " Man! it's a peety listenin' to such
d——d lies iss a sin, for there iss no doobt it iss a most
pleeasant amuusement! "

Macphail the engineer, the misanthrope, could not
stand the new hand. " He's no' a sailor at a'! " he
protested; " he's a clown; I've see'd better men
jumpin' through girrs at a penny show."

" Weel, he's maybe no' aawful steady at the wheel,
but he hass a kyind, kyind he'rt! " Dougie said.

" He's chust sublime! " said Para Handy. " If he
wass managed right there would be money in him! "

Para Handy's conviction that there was money to
be made out of Sunny Jim was confirmed by an episode
at Tobermory, of which the memory will be redolent
in Mull for years to come.

The *Vital Spark*, having discharged a cargo of coal
at Oban, went up the Sound to load with timber, and
on Calve Island, which forms a natural breakwater for
Tobermory harbour, Dougie spied a stranded whale.
He was not very much of a whale as whales go in
Greenland, being merely a tiny fellow of about five-
and-twenty tons, but as dead whales here are as rarely

G

to be seen as dead donkeys, the *Vital Spark* was steered close in to afford a better view, and even stopped for a while that Para Handy and his mate might land with the punt on the islet and examine the unfortunate cetacean.

" My Chove! he's a whupper!" was Dougie's comment, as he reached up and clapped the huge mountain of sea-flesh on its ponderous side. " It wass right enough, I can see, Peter, aboot yon fellow Jonah; chust look at the accommodation! "

" Chust waste, pure waste," said the skipper; " you can make a meal off a herrin', but whales iss only lumber, goin' aboot ass big as a land o' hooses, blowin' aal the time, and puttin' the fear o' daith on aal the other fushes. I never had mich respect for them."

" If they had a whale like that aground on Clyde," said Dougie, as they returned to the vessel, " they would stick bills on't; it's chust thrown away on the Tobermory folk."

Sunny Jim was enchanted when he heard the whale's dimensions. " Chaps," he said with enthusiasm, " there's a fortune in't; right-oh! I've see'd them chargin' tuppence to get into a tent at Vinegar Hill, whaur they had naethin' fancier nor a sea-lion or a seal."

" But they wouldna be deid," said Para Handy; " and there's no' mich fun aboot a whale's remains. Even if there was, we couldna tow him up to Gleska, and if we could, he wouldna keep."

" Jim'll be goin' to embalm him, rig up a mast on him, and sail him up the river; are ye no', Jim?" said Macphail with irony.

" I've a faur better idea than that," said Sunny Jim.

" Whit's to hinder us clappin' them tarpaulins roon'
the whale whaur it's lyin', and showin' 't at a sixpence
a heid to the Tobermory folk? Man! ye'll see them
rowin' across in hunners, for I'll bate ye there's no
much fun in Tobermory in the summer time unless it's
a Band o' Hope soiree. Give it a fancy name—the
' Tobermory Treasure '; send the bellman roond the
toon, sayin' it's on view to-morrow from ten till five,
and then goin' on to Oban; Dougie 'll lift the money,
and the skipper and me'll tell the audience a' aboot
the customs o' the whale when he's in life. Macphail
can stand by the ship at Tobermory quay."

" Jist what I said a' alang," remarked Macphail
darkly. " Jumpin' through girrs! Ye'll need a big
drum and a naphtha lamp."

" Let us first paause and consider," remarked Para
Handy, with his usual caution; " iss the whale oors? "

" Wha's else wad it be? " retorted Sunny Jim. " It
was us that fun' it, and naebody seen it afore us, for
it's no' mony oors ashore."

" Everything cast up on the shore belangs to the
Crown; it's the King's whale," said Macphail.

" Weel, let him come for 't," said Sunny Jim; " by
the time he's here we'll be done wi 't."

The presumption that Tobermory could be interested in a dead whale proved quite right; it was the
Glasgow Fair week, and the local boat-hirers did good
business taking parties over to the island where an
improvised enclosure of oars, spars, and tarpaulin and
dry sails concealed the " Tobermory Treasure " from
all but those who were prepared to pay for admission.
Para Handy, with his hands in his pockets and a studied
air of indifference, as if the enterprise was none of his,

chimed in at intervals with facts in the natural history
of the whale, which Sunny Jim might overlook in the
course of his introductory lecture.

" The biggest whale by three feet that's ever been
seen in Scotland," Sunny Jim announced. " Lots o'
folk thinks a whale's a fish, but it's naething o' the
kind; it's a hot-blooded mammoth, and couldna live
in the watter mair nor a wee while at a time withoot
comin' up to draw its breath. This is no' yin of thae
common whales that chases herrin', and goes pechin'
up and doon Kilbrannan Sound; it's the kind that's
catched wi' the harpoons and lives on naething but
roary borealises and icebergs."

" They used to make umbrella-rubs wi' this parteecular kind," chimed in the skipper diffidently;
" forbye, they're full o' blubber. It's an aawful useful
thing a whale, chentlemen." He had apparently
changed his mind about the animal, for which the
previous day he had said he had no respect.

" Be shair and tell a' your friends when ye get ashore
that it's maybe gaun on to Oban to-morrow," requested
Sunny Jim. " We'll hae it up on the Esplanade there
and chairge a shillin' a heid; if we get it the length o'
Gleska, the price 'll be up to hauf-a-croon."

" Is it a ' right ' whale? " asked one of the audience
in the interests of exact science.

" Right enough, as shair's onything; isn't it, Captain? " said Sunny Jim.

" What else would it be? " said Para Handy indignantly. " Does the chentleman think there iss onything
wrong with it? Perhaps he would like to take a look
through it; eh, Jum? Or maybe he would want a
doctor's certeeficate that it's no a dromedary."

The exhibition of the "Tobermory Treasure"
proved so popular that its discoverers determined to
run their entertainment for about a week. On the
third day passengers coming into Tobermory with the
steamer *Claymore* sniffed with appreciation, and talked
about the beneficial influence of ozone; the English
tourists debated whether it was due to peat or heather.
In the afternoon several yachts in the bay hurriedly
got up their anchors and went up Loch Sunart, where
the air seemed fresher. On the fourth day the residents
of Tobermory overwhelmed the local chemist with
demands for camphor, carbolic powder, permanganate
of potash, and other deodorants and disinfectants;
and several plumbers were telegraphed for to Oban.
The public patronage of the exhibition on Calve
Island fell off.

"If there's ony mair o' them wantin' to see this
whale," said Sunny Jim, "they'll hae to look slippy."

"It's no' that bad to windward," said Para Handy.
"What would you say to coverin' it up wi' more
tarpaulins?"

"You might as weel cover't up wi' crape or muslin,"
was Dougie's verdict. "What you would need iss
armour-plate, the same ass they have roond the
cannons in the man-o'-wars. If this wind doesn't
change to the west, half the folk in Tobermory 'll be
goin' to live in the cellar o' the Mishnish Hotel."

Suspicion fell on the "Tobermory Treasure" on
the following day, and an influential deputation waited
on the police sergeant, while the crew of the *Vital
Spark*, with much discretion, abandoned their whale,
and kept to their vessel's fo'c'sle. The sergeant
informed the deputation that he had a valuable clue

to the source of these extraordinary odours, but that unfortunately he could take no steps without a warrant from the Sheriff, and the Sheriff was in Oban. The deputation pointed out that the circumstances were too serious to permit of any protracted legal forms and ceremonies; the whale must be removed from Calve Island by its owners immediately, otherwise there would be a plague. With regret the police sergeant repeated that he could do nothing without authority, but he added casually that if the deputation visited the owners of the whale and scared the life out of them, he would be the last man to interfere.

"Hullo, chaps! pull the hatch efter yez, and keep oot the cold air!" said Sunny Jim, as the spokesman of the deputation came seeking for the crew in the fo'c'sle. "Ye'd be the better o' some odecolong on your hankies."

"We thought you were going to remove your whale to Oban before this," said the deputation sadly.

"I'm afraid," said Para Handy, "that whale hass seen its best days, and wouldna be at aal popular in Oban."

"Well, you'll have to take it out of here immediately anyway," said the deputation. "It appears to be your property."

"Not at aal, not at aal!" Para Handy assured him; "it belongs by right to His Majesty, and we were chust takin' care of it for him till he would turn up, chairgin' a trifle for the use o' the tarpaulins and the management. It iss too great a responsibility now, and we've given up the job; aren't we, Jum?"

"Right-oh!" said Sunny Jim, reaching for his melodeon; "and it's time you Tobermory folk were shiftin' that whale."

"It's impossible," said the deputation, "a carcase weighing nearly thirty tons—and in such a condition!"

"Indeed it is pretty bad," said Para Handy; "perhaps it would be easier to shift the toon o' Tobermory."

But that was, luckily, not necessary, as a high tide restored the "Tobermory Treasure" to its natural element that very afternoon.

LUCK

PARA HANDY, gossiping with his crew, and speaking generally of "luck" and the rewards of industry and intelligence, always counted luck the strongest agent in the destiny of man. "Since ever I wass a skipper," he said, "I had nobody in my crew that was not lucky; I would sooner have lucky chaps on board wi' me than tip-top sailors that had a great experience o' wrecks. If the *Fital Spark* hass the reputation o' bein' the smertest vessel in the coastin' tred, it's no' aalthegither wi' navigation; it's chust because I had luck mysel', and aalways had a lot o' lucky laads aboot me. Dougie himsel' 'll tell you that."

"We have plenty o' luck," admitted Dougie, nursing a wounded head he had got that day by carelessly using it as a fender to keep the side of the ship from the piles of Tarbert quay. "We have plenty of luck, but there must be a lot o' cluver people never mindin' mich aboot their luck, and gettin' aal the money."

"Money!" said the Captain with contempt; "there's other things to think aboot than money. If I had as mich money ass I needed, I wouldna ask for a penny more. There's nothing bates contentment and a

pleesant way o' speakin' to the owners. You needna
empty aal the jar o' jam, Macphail; give him a rap on
the knuckles, Jum, and tak' it from him."

Macphail relinquished the jam-jar readily, because
he had finished all that was in it. " If ye had mair luck
and less jaw aboot it," said he snappishly, " ye wadna
hae to wait so lang on the money ye're expectin' frae
your cousin Cherlie in Dunmore. Is he no deid yet?"

" No," said Para Handy dolefully; " he's still
hangin' on; I never heard o' a man o' ninety-three so
desperate deleeberate aboot dyin', and it the winter-
time. Last Friday week wass the fifth time they sent
to Tarbert for the munister, and he wasna needed."

" That was your cousin Cherlie's luck," said the
engineer, who was not without logic.

" I don't caal that luck at aal," retorted Para
Handy; " I call it just manœuvrin'. Forbye, it wasna
very lucky for the munister."

Cousin Cherlie's deliberation terminated a week
later, when the *Vital Spark* was in Loch Fyne, and the
Captain borrowed a hat and went to the funeral.
" My own roond hat iss a good enough hat and quite
respectable," he said, " but someway it doesna fit for
funerals since I canna wear it on my heid except it's
cocked a little to the side. You see, I have been at so
many Tarbert Fairs with it, and high jeenks chenerally."

The crew helped to make his toilet. Macphail, with
a piece of oily engine-room waste, imparted a resplen-
dent polish to the borrowed hat, which belonged to a
Tarbert citizen, and had lost a good deal of its original
lustre. Dougie contributed a waistcoat, and Sunny
Jim cheerfully sacrificed his thumb-nails in fastening
the essential, but unaccustomed, collar on his Captain's

neck. "There ye are, skipper," he said; "ye look A1 if ye only had a clean hanky."

"I'm no feelin' in very good trum, though," said the Captain, who seemed to be almost throttled by the collar; "there's no' mich fun for us sailor chaps in bein' chentlemen. But of course it's no' every day we're buryin' Cherlie, and I'm his only cousin, no' coontin' them MacNeills."

"Hoo much did ye say he had?" asked Macphail. "Was it a hunder pounds and a free hoose? or a hunder free hooses and a pound?"

"Do you know, laads," said the Captain, "his money wasna in my mind!"

"That's wi' the ticht collar," said the engineer unfeelingly; "lowse yer collar and mak' up yer mind whit yer gaun to dae wi' the hunder pounds. That's to say, if the MacNeills don't get it."

The Captain's heart, at the very thought of such disaster, came to his throat, and burst the fastenings of his collar, which had to be rigged up anew by Sunny Jim.

"The MacNeills," he said, "'ll no' touch a penny. Cherlie couldna stand them, and I wass aye his favourite, me bein' a captain. Money would be wasted on the MacNeills; they wouldna know what to do wi't."

"I ken whit I wad dae wi' a hunder pound if I had it," said Macphail emphatically.

"You would likely gie up the sea and retire to the free hoose wi' a ton or two o' your penny novelles," suggested the Captain.

"I wad trevel," said the engineer, heedless of the unpleasant innuendo. "There's naething like trevel

G 2

for widenin' the mind. When I was sailin' foreign I
saw a lot o' life, but I didna see near sae much as I
wad hae seen if I had the money."

" Fancy a sailor traivellin'! " remarked Sunny Jim.
" There's no much fun in that."

" I don't mean traivellin' in boats," explained
Macphail. " Ye never see onything trevellin' in boats;
I mean trains. The only places abroad worth seein'
's no' to be seen at the heid o' a quay; ye must tak' a
train to them. Rome, and Paris, and the Eyetalian
Lakes—that sort o' thing. Ye live in hotels and any
amount o' men's ready to carry yer bag. Wi' a hunder
pound a man could trevel the world."

" Never heed him, Peter," said Dougie; " trevellin's
an anxious business; you're aye losin' your tickets,
and the tips you have to give folk 's a fair ruination.
If I had a hunder pound and a free hoose, I would let
the hoose and tak' a ferm."

"A ferm's no' bad," admitted Para Handy, " but
there's a desperate lot o' work aboot a ferm."

" There's a desperate lot o' work aboot anything
ye can put your hand to, except enchineerin'," said
Dougie sadly, " but you can do wonders if you have a
good horse and a fine strong wife. You wouldna need
to be a rale fermer, but chust wan o' them chentleman
fermers that wears knickerbockers and yellow leggin's."

" There's a good dale in what you say, Dougie,
admitted the Captain, who saw a pleasing vision of
himself in yellow leggings. " It's no' a bad tred,
chentleman fermin'."

" Tred! " said Dougie; " it's no a tred—it's a
recreation, like sailin' a yat. Plooin'-matches and 'ool-
markets every other day; your own eggs and all the

mutton and milk you need for nothing. Buy you a ferm, Peter, I'm tellin' you!"

" Chust that!" said the Captain cunningly. "And then maybe you would be skipper of the *Fital Spark*, Dougie."

" I wasna thinkin' aboot that at aal!" protested the mate.

" I wasna sayin' you were," said the Captain, " but the mustress would give you the notion."

" If I was you I wad tak' a shop in Gleska," said Sunny Jim. " No' an awfu' big shop, but a handy wee wan ye could shut when there was any sport on withoot mony people noticin'."

Para Handy buttoned his coat, and prepared to set out for the funeral. " Whether it wass trevellin', or a ferm, or a shop, I would get on sublime, for I'm a lucky, lucky man, laads; but I'm no lettin' my mind dwell on Cherlie's money, oot o' respect for my relative. I'll see you aal when I come back, and maybe it might be an Occasion."

Dougie cried after him when he was a little up the quay, " Captain, your hat's chust a little to the side."

Para Handy was back from the funeral much sooner than was expected, his collar in his pocket, and the borrowed hat in his hand. He went below to resume his ordinary habiliments without a word to the crew, who concluded that he was discreetly concealing the legacy. When he came up, they asked no questions, from a sense of proper decorum, but the Captain seemed surcharged with great emotion.

" Dougie," he said to the mate, " what would be the cost o' a pair o' yellow leggin's?"

"Aboot a pound," said the mate, with some exultation. " Have you made up your mind for fermin'? "

" No," said the Captain bitterly; " but I might afford the leggin's off my cousin Cherlie's legacy, but it wouldna go the length o' knickerbockers."

SALVAGE FOR THE *VITAL SPARK*

THE vessel was rounding Ardlamont in a sou'-wester that set her all awash like an empty herring-box. Over her snub nose combed appalling sprays; green seas swept her fore and aft; she was glucking with internal waters, and her squat red funnel whooped dolorously with wind. " Holy smoke! " gasped Para Handy, " isn't this the hammerin'! "

"A sailor's life!" said Dougie bitterly, drawing a soaking sleeve across his nose; " I would sooner be a linen-draper."

In flaws of the wind they could hear Macphail break coals in the engine-room, and the wheezy tones of Sunny Jim's melodeon as he lay on his bunk in the fo'c'sle quelling his apprehensions to the air of " The Good Old Summer-Time." Together at the wheel the Captain and his mate were dismal objects, drenched to the hide, even below their oil-skins, which gave them the glistening look of walruses or seals. They had rigged a piece of jib up for a dodger; it poorly served its purpose, and seemed as inefficient as a handkerchief as they raised their blinking eyes above it and longingly looked for the sheltering arms of the Kyles.

" I wish to the Lord it wass Bowlin' quay and me sound sleepin'," said the mate. " Yonder's the mustress in Plantation snug and cosy on't, and I'll wager she's no' a bit put aboot for her man on the heavin' bullow. It makes me quite angry to think of it. Eggs for her tea and all her orders, and me with not a bite since breakfast-time but biscuits."

" Holy smoke! you surely wouldna like her to be wi' you here," said Para Handy, shocked.

" No," said Dougie, " but I wish she could see me noo, and I wish I could get her and her high tea at the fireside oot on' my heid; it's bad enough to be standing here like a flag-pole thinkin' every meenute 'll be my next."

" Toot! man, Dougie, you're tumid, tumid," said the Captain. " Draw your braith as deep's you can, throw oot your chest, and be a hero. Look at me! my name's Macfarlane and I'm wan of Brutain's hardy sons! "

The *Vital Spark* got round the Point, and met a wave that smashed across her counter and struck full in the face the mariners at the wheel. Dougie, with his mouth inelegantly open, swallowed a pint or two, and spluttered. Para Handy shook the water from his beard like a spaniel, and looking more anxiously than before through smarting eyes, saw a gabbart labouring awkwardly close on the shore of Ettrick Bay.

" Dougie," said he, " stop giggling a bit, and throw your eye to starboard—is yon no' the *Katherine-Anne*? "

" It wassna giggling I wass," said Dougie irritably, coughing brine, " but I nearly spoiled the Kyles o'

Bute. It's the *Katherine-Anne* right enough, and they've lost command o' her; stop you a meenute and you'll hear an awfu' dunt."

" She'll be ashore in a juffy," said the Captain tragically. " Man! iss it no' chust desperate! I'm no' makin' a proposeetion, mind, but what would you say to givin' a slant across and throwin' a bit o' a rope to her? "

Dougie looked wistfully at Tighnabruaich ahead of them, and now to be reached in comfort, and another at the welter of waves between them and the struggling gabbart. " Whatever you say yoursel', Peter," he replied, and for twenty minutes more they risked disaster. At one wild moment Para Handy made his way to the fo'c'sle hatch and bellowed down to Sunny Jim, " You there wi' your melodeon—it would fit you better if you tried to mind your Psalms."

When they reached the *Katherine-Anne*, and found she had been abandoned, Para Handy cursed at first his own soft heart that had been moved to the distress of a crew who were comfortably on their way to Rothesay. He was for leaving the gabbart to her fate, but Macphail, the engineer, and Sunny Jim remarked that a quite good gabbart lacking any obvious owners wasn't to be picked up every day. If they towed her up to Tighnabruaich they would have a very pretty claim for salvage.

" Fifty pounds at least for ship and cargo," said Macphail; " my share 'll pay for my flittin' at the term, jist nate."

" Fifty pounds! " said Para Handy. " It's a tidy sum, and there might be more than fifty in't when it came to the bit, for fifty pounds iss not an aawful lot when the owner gets his wheck of it. What do you think yoursel', Dougie? "

" I wass chust thinkin'," said Dougie, " that fifty pounds would be a terrible lot for poor MacCallum, him that owns the *Katherine-Anne*; he hasna been very lucky wi' her."

" If we're no' gaun to get the fifty pound then, we can just tow her up to Tighnabruaich for a baur," said Sunny Jim. " It doesna dae to be stickin'. If there's naething else in't, we'll get a' oor names in the papers for a darin' deed at sea. Come on, chaps, be game! "

" I wish to peace the *Katherine-Anne* belonged to any other man than John MacCallum," said the skipper. " You're an aawful cluver laad, Macphail; what iss the law aboot salvage? "

" Under the Merchant Shippin' Act," said Macphail glibly, " ye're bound to get your salvage; if ye divna claim't, it goes to the King the same as whales or onything that's cast up by the sea."

"Ach! it disna maitter a docken aboot the salvage," said Sunny Jim. " Look at the fun we'll hae comin' into Tighnabruaich wi' a boat we fun' the same as it was a kitlin. See's a rope, and I'll go on board and mak' her fast."

When they had towed the *Katherine-Anne* to Tighna-bruaich, Dougie was sent ashore with a telegram for the owner of the *Vital Spark*, suggesting his immediate appearance on the scene. Later in the afternoon the crew of the *Katherine-Anne* came by steamer to Tighnabruaich, to which port she and they belonged, and the captain and owner ruefully surveyed the vessel he had abandoned, now lying safe and sound at his

native quay. He sat on a barrel of paraffin-oil and
looked at Para Handy in possession.

" Where did you pick her up? " said MacCallum
sadly.

" Oh, chust doon the road a bit," said Para Handy.
" It's clearin' up a nice day."

" It's a terrible business this," said MacCallum,
nervously wiping his forehead with his handkerchief.

" Bless me! what is't? " exclaimed Para Handy.
" I havena seen the paper this week yet."

" I mean about havin' to leave the *Katie-Anne*
almost at our own door, and you finding her."

" Chust that; it wass Providence," remarked Para
Handy piously, " chust Providence."

" I'll hae to gie you something for your bother,"
said MacCallum.

" I wouldna say but you would," replied the skipper.
" It's a mercy your lifes wass saved. Hoo are they
keepin', aal, in Ro'sa'? "

" Are ye no' comin' ashore for a dram? " remarked
MacCallum, and Para cocked at him a cunning eye.

" No, John," he said; " I'm no' carin' mich aboot
a dram the day; I had wan yesterday."

But he succumbed to the genial impulse an hour
later, and leaving his mate in possession of the
Katherine-Anne, went up the village with the owner of
that unhappy craft. MacCallum took him to his
home, where Para Handy found himself in the uncomfortable presence of a wife and three daughters dress-
making. The four women sewed so assiduously, and
were so moist about the eyes with weeping, that he
was sorry he came.

" This is the gentleman that found the *Katie-Anne*,"

remarked MacCallum by way of introduction, and the eldest daughter sobbed.

" Ye're aal busy!" said Para Handy, with a desperate air of cheerfulness.

" Indeed, aye! we're busy enough," said the mother bitterly. " We're workin' oor fingers to the bane, but we're no' makin' much o't; it's come wi' the wind and gang wi' the water," and the second daughter sobbed in unison with her sister as they furiously plied their needles.

" By Chove! " thought Para Handy, " a man would need to have the he'rt o' a hoose-factor on a chob like this; it puts me aal oot o' trum," and he drank his glass uncomfortably.

" I think ye mentioned aboot fifty pounds?" said MacCallum mournfully, and at these words all the four women laid their sewing on their knees and wept without restraint. " Fi-fi-fifty p-p-pounds! " exclaimed the mother, " where in the wide world is John MacCallum to get fifty pounds? "

Para Handy came hurriedly down the quay and called Dougie ashore from the *Katherine-Anne*.

" Somebody must stay on board of her, or we'll have trouble wi' the salvage," said the mate.

" Come ashore this meenute," commanded the Captain, " for I'm needin' some refreshment. There's four women yonder greetin' their eyes oot at the loss o' fifty pounds."

" Chust that! " said Dougie sympathetically. " Poor things! "

" I would see the salvage to the duvvle," said the Captain warmly, " if we hadna sent that telegram to oor owner. Four o' them sew-sew-sewing yonder.

and dreepin', like the fountain oot in Kelvingrove! "

"Man, it wass lucky, too, aboot the telegram," said Dougie, "for I didna like to send it and it's no' away."

Para Handy slapped him on the shoulder. "Man!" he said, "that's capital! To the muschief with their fifty pounds! Believe you me, I'm feelin' quite sublime!"

PARA HANDY HAS AN EYE TO BUSINESS

IT was a lovely day, and the *Vital Spark*, without a cargo, lay at the pier of Ormidale, her newly painted under-strakes reflected in a loch like a mirror, making a crimson blotch in a scene that was otherwise winter-brown. For a day and a half more there was nothing to be done. "It's the life of a Perfect Chentleman," said Dougie. The engineer, with a novelette he had bought in Glasgow, was lost in the love affairs of a girl called Gladys, who was excessively poor, but looked, at Chapter Five, like marrying a Colonel of Hussars who seemed to have no suspicion of the fate in store for him; and Sunny Jim, with the back of his head showing at the fo'c'sle scuttle, was making with his melodeon what sounded like a dastardly attack on "The Merry Widow."

"I wass thinkin', seein' we're here and nothing else doin', we might be givin' her the least wee bit touch o' the tar-brush," remarked Para Handy, who never cared to lose a chance of beautifying his vessel.

"There it is again!" exclaimed Macphail, laying down his novelette in exasperation. "A chap canna

get sittin' doon five meenutes in this boat for a read
to himsel' withoot somebody breakin' their legs to
find him a job. Ye micht as weel be in a man-o'-war."
Even Dougie looked reproachfully at the Captain; he
had just been about to pull his cap down over his eyes
and have a little sleep before his tea.

" It wass only a proposeetion," said the Captain
soothingly. " No offence! Maybe it'll do fine when
we get to Tarbert. It's an awfu' peety they're no'
buildin' boats o' this size wi' a kind of a study in them
for the use o' the enchineers," and he turned for
sympathy to the mate, who was usually in the mood to
rag Macphail. But this time Dougie was on Macphail's
side.

" There's some o' your jokes like the Carradale
funerals—there's no' much fun in them," he remarked.
" Ye think it's great sport to be tar-tar-tarring away
at the ship; ye never consult either oor healths or oor
inclinations. Am I right, Macphail? "

" Slave-drivin'! that's whit I ca't," said Macphail
emphatically. " If Lloyd George kent aboot it, he
would bring it before the Board o' Tred."

The Captain withdrew, moodily, from his crew, and
ostentatiously scraped old varnish off the mast. This
business engaged him only for a little; the weather
was so plainly made for idleness that he speedily put
the scraper aside and entered into discourse with Sunny
Jim.

" Whatever you do, don't you be a Captain, Jum,"
he advised him.

" I wisht I got the chance! " said Sunny Jim.

" There's nothing in't but the honour o' the thing,
and a shilling or two extra; no' enough to pay the

drinks to keep up the poseetion. Here am I, and I'm
anxious to be frien'ly wi' the chaps, trate them the
same's I wass their equal, and aalways ready to come-
and-go a bit, and they go and give me the name o' a
slave-driver! Iss it no' chust desperate?"

"If I was a Captain," said Sunny Jim philo-
sophically, "I wad dae the comin' and mak' the ither
chaps dae the goin', and d——d smert aboot it."

"That's aal right for a Gleska man, but it's no' the
way we're brocht up on Loch Long; us Arrochar folk,
when we're Captains, believe in a bit o' compromise
wi' the crews. If they don't do a thing when we ask
them cuvilly, we do't oorsel's, and that's the way to
vex them."

"Did ye never think ye wad like to change your
job and try something ashore?" asked Sunny Jim.

"Many a time!" confessed the Captain. "There's
yonder jobs that would suit me fine. I wass nearly,
once, an innkeeper. It wass at a place called Cladich;
the man came into a puckle money wi' his wife, and
advertised the goodwull at a great reduction. I left
the boat for a day and walked across to see him. He
wass a man they caalled MacDiarmid, and he wass
yonder wi' his sleeves up puttin' corks in bottles wi' a
wonderful machine. Did you ever see them corkin'
bottles, Jum?"

"I never noticed if I did," said Sunny Jim; "but
I've seen them takin' them oot."

"Chust that! This innkeeper wass corkin' away
like hey-my-nanny.

"'You're sellin' the business?' says I.

"'I am,' says he; and him throng corkin' away at
the bottles.

" ' What's your price? ' says I.

" ' A hundred and fifty pounds for the goodwull and the stock the way it stands,' says he.

" ' What aboot the fixtures? ' then says I.

" ' Oh, they're aal right! " said the innkeeper, cork-cork-corkin' away at the bottles; ' the fixtures goes along with the goodwull.'

" ' What fixtures iss there? ' says I.

" ' There's three sheep fermers, the shoemaker doon the road, and Macintyre the mail-driver, and that's no' coontin' a lot o' my Sunday customers,' said the innkeeper."

" You didna tak' the business, then? " said Sunny Jim.

" Not me! " said Para Handy. " To be corkin' away at bottles aal my lone yonder would put me crazy. Forbye, I hadna the half o' the hunder-and-fifty. There wass another time I went kind o' into a business buyin' eggs——"

" Eggs! " exclaimed Sunny Jim with some astonishment—" whit kin' o' eggs? "

" Och! chust egg eggs," said the Captain. " It wass a man in Arran said there wass a heap o' money in them if you had the talent and a wee bit powney to go roond the countryside. To let you ken: it wass before the *Fital Spark* changed owners; the chentleman that had her then wass a wee bit foolish; nothing at aal against his moral and releegious reputaation, mind, but apt to go over the score with it, and forget whereaboots the vessel would be lying. This time we were for a week or more doin' nothin' in Loch Ranza, and waitin' for his orders. He couldna mind for the life o' him where he sent us, and wass telegraphin' aal

the harbour-masters aboot the coast to see if they kent
the whereaboots o' the *Fital Spark*, but it never came
into his heid that we might be near Loch Ranza, and
there we were wi' the best o' times doin' nothing."

" Could ye no' hae sent him a telegraph tellin' him
where ye wiz? " asked Sunny Jim.

" That's what he said himsel', but we're no' that
daft, us folk from Arrochar; I can tell you we have
aal oor faculties. Dougie did better than that; he
put a bit o' paper in a bottle efter writin' on't a message
from the sea—' s.s. *Fital Spark* stranded for a fortnight
in a fit o' absent-mind; aal hands quite joco, but the
owner lost.'

" We might have been lyin' in Loch Ranza yet if it
wassna that I tried Peter Carmichael's business.
' When you're doin' nothing better here,' he said to
me, ' you micht be makin' your fortune buyin' and
sellin' eggs, for Arran's fair hotchin' wi' them.'

" ' What way do you do it? ' says I.

" ' You need a wee cairt and a powney,' said Peter
Carmichael, ' and I've the very cairt and powney that
would suit you. You go roond the island gatherin'
eggs from aal the hooses, and pay them sixpence a
dozen—champion eggs ass fresh ass the mornin'
breeze. Then you pack them in boxes and send them
to Gleska and sell them at a profit.'

" ' What profit do you chenerally allow yoursel'? '
I asked Peter.

" ' Oh! chust nate wan per cent,' said Peter; ' you
chairge a shillin' in Gleska for the eggs; rale Arran
eggs, no' foreign rubbadge. Folk 'll tell you to put
your money in stone and lime; believe me, nothing
bates the Arran egg for quick returns. If the people

in Gleska have a guarantee that any parteecular egg
wass made in Arran, they'll pay any money for it; it's
ass good ass a day at the coast for them, poor craturs!'

" Seein' there wass no prospeck o' the owner findin'
where we were unless he sent a bloodhound oot to
look for us, I asked Carmichael hoo long it would take
to learn the business, and he said I could pick it up in
a week. I agreed to buy the cairt and powney and the
goodwull o' the business if the chob at the end o' the
week wass like to bring in a pleasin' wage, and Dougie
himsel' looked efter the shup. You never went roond
the country buyin' eggs? It's a chob you need a lot
o' skill for. Yonder wass Peter Carmichael and me
goin' roond by Pirnmill, Machrie, and Blackwaterfoot,
Sliddery, and Shiskine——"

"Ach! ye're coddin'!" exclaimed Sunny Jim;
" there's no such places."

" It's easy seen you were a' your days on the Clutha
steamers," said the Captain patiently; " I'll assure
you that there's Slidderys and Shiskines oot in Arran.
Full o' eggs! The hens oot yonder's no' puttin' bye
their time!

" Three days runnin' Peter and me and the powney
scoured the country and gaithered so many eggs that
I begun to get rud in the face whenever I passed the
least wee hen. We couldna get boxes enough to hold
them in Loch Ranza, so we got some bales o' hay and
packed them in the hold of the *Fital Spark*, and then
consudered. ' There's nothing to do noo but to take
them to the Broomielaw and sell them quick at a
shillin',' said Carmichael. ' The great thing iss to keep
them on the move, and off your hands before they
change their minds and start for to be chuckens. Up

steam, smert, and off wi' ye! And here's the cairt and powney—fifteen pounds.'

" ' Not at aal, Carmichael! ' I said to him; ' I'll wait till I'll see if you wass right aboot the wan per cent of profits. Stop you here till I'll come back.'

" I telegraphed that day to the owner o' the vessel, sayin' I was comin' into the Clyde wi' a cargo, and when we got to Gleska he wass standin' on the quay, and not in the best o' trum.

" ' Where in a' the world were you? ' says he; ' and me lookin' high and low for you! What's your cargo? '

" ' Eggs from Arran, Mr Smuth,' says I, ' and a bonny job I had gettin' them at sixpence the dozen.'

" ' Who are they from? ' he asked, glowerin' under the hatches.

" ' Chust the cheneral population, Mr Smuth,' says I.

" ' Who are they consigned to? ' he asked then— and man he wassna in trum at aal, at aal!

" ' Anybody that'll buy them, sir," said I; ' it's a bit of a speculation.'

" He scratched his heid and looked at me. ' I mind o' orderin' eggs,' says he, ' but I never dreamt I wass daft enough to send for a boat-load o' them. But noo they're here I suppose we'll have to make the best o' them.' So he sold the eggs, and kept the wan per cent for freight and responsibeelity, and I made nothin' off it except that I shifted my mind aboot takin' a chob ashore, and didn't buy Carmichael's cairt and powney."

A VEGETARIAN EXPERIMENT

THE *Vital Spark* had been lying for some time in the Clyde getting in a new boiler, and her crew, who had been dispersed about the city in their respective homes, returned to the wharf on a Monday morning to make ready for a trip to Tobermory.

" She's a better boat than ever she was," said Macphail with satisfaction, having made a casual survey. " Built like a lever watch! We'll can get the speed oot o' her noo. There's boats gaun up and doon the river wi' red funnels, saloon caibins, and German bands in them, that havena finer engines. When I get that crank and crossheid tightened, thae glands packed and nuts slacked, she'll be the gem o' the sea."

" She's chust sublime! " said Para Handy, patting the tarred old hull as if he were caressing a kitten; " it's no' coals and timber she should be carryin' at aal, but towrist passengers. Man! if we chust had the accommodation! "

" Ye should hae seen the engines we had on the Cluthas! " remarked Sunny Jim, who had no illusions about the *Vital Spark* in that respect. " They were that shiney I could see my face in them."

" Could ye, 'faith? " said Macphail; " a sicht like that must have put ye aff yer work. We're no' that fond o' polish in the coastin' tred that we mak' oor engines shine like an Eyetalian ice-cream shop; it's only vanity. Wi' us it's speed——"

" Eight knots," murmured Sunny Jim, who was in

a nasty Monday-morning humour. " Eight knots, and the chance o' nine wi' wind and tide."

" You're a liar! " said the Captain irritably, " and that's my advice to you. Ten knots many a time between the Cloch and the Holy Isle," and an argument ensued which it took Dougie all his tact to put an end to short of bloodshed.

" It's me that's gled to be back on board of her anyway," remarked Para Handy later; " I suppose you'll soon be gettin' the dinner ready, Jum? See and have something nice, for I'm tired o' sago puddin'."

" Capital stuff for pastin' up bills," said Dougie; " I've seen it often in the cookin'-depots. Wass the wife plyin' ye wi' sago? "

" Sago, and apples, potatoes, cabbage, cheese, and a new kind o' patent coffee that agrees wi' the indigestion; I havena put my two eyes on a bit of Christian beef since I went ashore; the wife's in wan of her tirravees, and she's turned to be a vegetarian."

" My Chove! " said Dougie incredulously; " are you sure, Peter? "

" Sure enough! I told her this mornin' when I left I would bring her home a bale of hay from Mull, and it would keep her goin' for a month or two. Women's a curious article! "

" You should get the munister to speak to her," said Dougie sympathetically. " When a wife goes wrong like that, there's nothing bates the munister. She'll no' be goin' to the church; it's aalways the way wi' them fancy new releegions. Put you her at wance in the hands o' a dacent munister."

" I canna be harsh wi' her, or she'll greet," said Para Handy sadly.

" It's no harshness that's wanted," counselled the mate, speaking from years of personal experience; " what you need iss to be firm. What way did this calamity come on her? Don't be standin' there, Jum, like a soda-water bottle, but hurry and make a bit of steak for the Captain; man! I noticed you werena in trum whenever I saw you come on board. I saw at wance you hadn't the agility. What way did the trouble come on her? "

" She took it off a neighbour woman," explained the Captain. " She wass aal right on the Sunday, and on the Monday mornin' she couldna bear to look at ham and eggs. It might happen to anybody. The thing was at its heid when I got home, and the only thing on the table wass a plate of maccaroni."

" Eyetalian! " chimed in the engineer. " I've seen them makin' it in Genoa and hingin' it up to bleach on the washin'-greens. It's no' meat for men; it's only for passin' the time o' organ-grinders and ship-riggers."

" ' Mery,' I said to her, ' I never saw nicer decorations, but hurry up like a darlin' wi' the meat.' ' There'll be no more meat in this hoose, Peter,' she said, aal trumblin'; ' if you saw them busy in a slaughter-hoose you wadna eat a chop. Forbye, there's uric acid in butcher meat, and there's more nourishment in half a pound o' beans than there iss in half a bullock.' ' That's three beans for a sailor's dinner; it's no' for nourishment a man eats always; half the time it's only for amusement, Mery,' said I to her, but it wass not the time for argyment. ' You'll be a better man in every way if you're a vegetarian,' she said to me. ' If it iss a better man you are wantin',' I says to her,

wonderful caalm in my temper, ' you are on the right
tack, sure enough; you have only to go on with them
expuriments wi' my meat and you'll soon be a weedow
woman.'

" But she wouldna listen to reason, Mery, and for a
fortnight back I have been feedin' like the Scribes and
Sadducees in the Scruptures."

" Man! iss it no chust desperate? " said Dougie
compassionately, and he admiringly watched his Captain a little later make the first hearty meal for a fortnight. " You're lookin' a dufferent man already," he
told him; " what's for the tea, Jum? "

" I kent a vegetarian yince," said Sunny Jim, " and
he lived maist o' the time on chuckie soup."

" Chucken soup? " repeated Dougie interrogatively.

" No; chuckie soup. There was nae meat o' ony
kind in't. A' ye needed was some vegetables, a pot
o' hot water, and a parteecular kind o' chuckie-stane.
It was fine and strengthenin'."

" You would need good teeth for't, I'm thinkin',"
remarked the Captain dubiously.

" Of course ye didna eat the chuckie-stane," Sunny
Jim explained; " it made the stock; it was instead o'
a bane, and it did ower and ower again."

" It would be a great savin'," said Dougie, fascinated
with the idea. " Where do you get them parteecular
kinds of chuckies? "

" Onywhere under high water," replied Sunny Jim,
who saw prospects of a little innocent entertainment.

" We'll get them the first time we're ashore, then,"
said the mate, " and if they're ass good ass what you
say, the Captain could take home a lot of them for his
vegetarian mustress."

At the first opportunity, when he got ashore, Sunny Jim perambulated the beach and selected a couple of substantial pieces of quartz, and elsewhere bought a pound of margarine which he put in his pocket. " Here yez are, chaps—the very chuckie! I'll soon show ye soup," he said, coming aboard with the stones, in which the crew showed no little interest. " A' ye have to do is to scrub them weel, and put them in wi' the vegetables when the pot's boilin'."

They watched his culinary preparations closely. He prepared the water and vegetables, cleaned the stones, and solemnly popped them in the pot when the water boiled. At a moment when their eyes were off him he dexterously added the unsuspected pound of margarine. By and by the soup was ready, and when dished, had all the aspect of the ordinary article. Sunny Jim himself was the first to taste it *pour encourager les autres.*

" Fair champion! " he exclaimed.

The engineer could not be prevailed to try the soup on any consideration, but the Captain and the mate had a plate apiece, and voted it extraordinary.

" It's a genius you are, Jum! " said the delighted Captain; " if the folk in Gleska knew that soup like this was to be made from chuckie-stanes they wouldna waste their time at the Fair wi' gaitherin' cockles."

And the next time Para Handy reached the Clyde he had on board in all good faith a basket-load of stones culled from the beach at Tobermory for his vegetarian mistress.

THE COMPLETE GENTLEMAN

" THE finest chentleman I ever knew was Hurricane Jeck," said Para Handy. " His manners wass complete. Dougie himsel' will tell you."

" A nice laad," said the mate agreeably; " he had a great, great faculty."

" Whaur did he mak' his money? " asked Sunny Jim, and they looked at him with compassion.

" There iss men that iss chentlemen, and there iss men that hass a puckle money," said the Captain impressively; " Hurricane Jeck wass seldom very rife with money, but he came from Kinlochaline, and that iss ass good ass a Board of Tred certuficate. Stop you till you're long enough on the *Fital Spark*, and you'll get your educaation. Hurricane Jeck was a chentleman. What money he had he would spend like the wave of the sea."

" It didna maitter wha's money it was, either," chimed in Macphail unsympathetically. " I kent him! Fine! "

" Like the wave of the sea," repeated the Captain, meeting the engineer's qualification with the silence of contempt. " Men like Jeck should never be oot of money, they distribute it with such a taste."

" I've seen chaps like that," remarked Sunny Jim, who was sympathetic to that kind of character. " When I was on the Cluthas——"

" When you was on the Cluthas, Jum, you were handlin' nothing but ha'pennies; Hurricane Jeck was a chentleman in pound notes, and that's the dufference."

" My Jove! " said Sunny Jim, " he must hae been weel aff! "

" There wass wan time yonder," proceeded the Captain, " when Jeck came into a lot o' money from a relative that died—fifty pounds if it wass a penny, and he spent it in a manner that was chust sublime. The very day he got it, he came down to the *Fital Spark* at Bowlin' for a consultation. ' You'll no' guess what's the trouble, Peter,' said he; ' I'm a chentleman of fortune,' and he spread the fifty notes fornent him, with a bit of stone on each of them to keep them doon, the same as it wass a bleachin'- green. ' Fifty pounds and a fortnight to spend it in, before we sail for China. Put bye your boat, put on your Sunday clothes, and you and me'll have a little recreaation.'

" ' I canna, Jeck,' says I—and Dougie himsel' 'll tell you—' I canna, Jeck; the cargo's in, and we're sailin' in the mornin'.'

" ' That's the worst o' money," said Hurricane Jeck; ' there's never enough o't. If Uncle Willy had left me plenty I would buy your boat and no' let a cargo o' coals interfere wi' oor diversion.'

" ' Put it in the bank,' I said to him.

" ' I'm no' that daft,' he said. ' There's no' a worst place in the world for money than the banks; you never get the good o't."

" ' Oh, there's plenty of other ways of gettin' rid of it,' I told him.

" ' Not of fifty pounds,' said Jeck. ' It's easy spendin' a pound or two, but you canna get rid o' a legacy withoot assistance.' Wassn't that the very words of him, Dougie? "

" Chust his own words! " said the mate; " your memory iss capital."

" ' There's a lot o' fun I used to think I would indulge in if I had the money,' said Hurricane Jeck, ' and now I have the opportunity if I only had a friend like yoursel' to see me doin' it. I'm goin' to spend it aal in trevellin'.' "

" And him a sailor! " commented the astonished Sunny Jim.

" He wass meanin' trevellin' on shore," said Para Handy. " Trains, and tramway cars, and things like that, and he had a brulliant notion. It wass aye a grief to Jeck that there wass so many things ashore you darena do withoot a prosecution. ' The land o' the Free! ' he would say, ' and ye canna take a tack on a train the length o' Paisley withoot a bit of a paste-board ticket! ' He put in the rest of that day that I speak of trevellin' the Underground till he wass dizzy, and every other hour he had an altercaation wi' the railway folk aboot his ticket. ' Take it oot o' that,' he would tell them, handin' them a pound or two, and he quite upset the traffic. On the next day he got a Gladstone bag, filled it with empty bottles, and took the train to Greenock. ' Don't throw bottles oot at the windows,' it says in the railway cairrages; Jeck opened the windows and slipped oot a bottle or two at every quarter mile, till the Caledonian system looked like the mornin' efter a Good Templars' trip. They catched him doin' it at Pollokshields.

" ' What's the damage? ' he asked them, hangin' his arm on the inside strap o' a first-cless cairrage and smokin' a fine cigar. You never saw a fellow that could be more genteel.

" ' It might be a pound a bottle,' said the railway people; ' we have the law for it.'

" 'Any reduction on takin' a quantity?' said Jeck; ' I'm havin' the time o' my life; it's most refreshin'.'

" That day he took the train to Edinburgh—didn't he, Dougie? "

" He did that! " said Dougie. " You have the story exactly."

" He took the train to Edinburgh. It was an express, and every noo and then he would pull the chain communication wi' the guard. The train would stop, and the guard would come and talk with Jeck. The first time he came along Jeck shook him by the hand, and said he only wanted to congratulate him.

" ' What aboot? ' said the guard, no' lookin' very well pleased.

" ' On your cheneral agility,' said Hurricane Jeck. ' Your cairrages iss first-rate; your speed iss astonishin' quick; your telegraph communication iss workin' A1; and you stopped her in two lengths. I thocht I would chust like you to take my compliments to the owners.'

" ' It's five pounds o' a fine for pullin' the cord,' said the guard.

" ' That's only for the wan cord; I pulled the two o' them,' said Jeck, quite nice to him; ' first the port and then the starboard. You canna be too parteecular. There's the money and a shillin' extra for a dram.'

" The guard refused the money, and said he would see aboot it at Edinburgh, and the train went on. Jeck pulled the cords till he had them all in the cairrage wi' him, but the train never stopped till it came to

H

Edinburgh, and then a score o' the offeecials came to
the cairrage.

"'What are you doin' with them cords?' they asked
him.

"'Here they are, all coiled up and flemished-down,'
said Jeck, lightin' another cigar. 'When does this
train go back?' and he hands them over a bunch o'
notes, and told them never to mind the change."

"Man! he was the comic!" exclaimed Sunny Jim.
"Fair champion!"

"In Edinburgh," proceeded Pary Handy, "he
waalked aboot till he came on a fire alarm where it
said it would cost a heavy fine to work it unless there
wass a fire. Jeck rung the bell, and waited whustlin'
till the Fire Brigade came clatterin' up the street.

"'Two meenutes and fifty seconds,' he says to them,
holdin' his watch; 'they couldna do better in Gleska.
I like your helmets. Noo that we're aal here, what iss
it goin' to be, boys?'

"'Are you drunk, or daft?' said the Captain o' the
Fire Brigade, grippin' him by the collar.

"'Not a drop since yesterday!' said Jeck. 'And
I'm no' daft, but chust an honest Brutish sailor,
puttin' bye the time and spreadin' aboot my money.
There's me and there's Mr Carnegie. His hobby is
libraries; on the other hand I'm for Liberty. The Land
of the Free and the Brave; it says on the fire alarm
that I mustna break it, and I proved I could. Take
your money oot o' that,'—and he hands the Captain
the bundle of notes. 'If there iss any change left when
you pay yoursel's for your bother, send home the
enchines and we'll aal adjourn to a place.'"

"Capital!" exclaimed Dougie.

" It took three days for Jeck to get rid of his fortune in cheneral amusement of that kind, and then he came to see me before he joined his shup for China.

" ' I had a fine time, Peter,' he said; ' couldna have better. You would wonder the way the week slipped by. But it's the Land of the Free, right enough; there's no' half enough o' laws a chentleman can break for his diversion; I hadna very mich of a selection.' "

AN OCEAN TRAGEDY

IT was a lovely afternoon at the end of May, and the *Vital Spark* was puffing down Kilbrannan Sound with a farmer's flitting. Macphail, the engineer, sat " with his feet among the enchines and his heid in the clouds," as Dougie put it—in other words, on the ladder of his engine-room, with his perspiring brow catching the cool breeze made by the vessel's progress, and his emotions rioting through the adventures of a governess in the ' Family Herald Supplement.' Peace breathed like an exhalation from the starboard hills; the sea was like a mirror, broken only by the wheel of a stray porpoise, and Sunny Jim indulged the Captain and the mate with a medley on his melodeon.

" You're a capital player, Jum," said the Captain in a pause of the entertainment. " Oh, yes, there's no doot you are cluver on it; it's a gift, but you havena the selection; no, you havena the selection, and if you havena the selection where are you? "

" He's doin' his best," said Dougie sympathetically, and then, in one of those flashes of philosophy that

come to the most thoughtless of us at times—"A man
can do no more."

" Whit selections was ye wantin'? " asked the
musician, with a little irritation; " if it's Gaelic sangs
ye're meanin' I wad need a drum and the nicht aff."

" No, I wassna thinkin' aboot Gaalic sangs,"
explained Para Handy; " when we're consuderin'
them we're consuderin' music; I wass taalkin' of the
bits of things you put on the melodeon; did you ever
hear ' Napoleon '? " and clearing his throat he
warbled—

" Wa-a-an night sad and dree-ary
    Ass I lay on my bed,
And my head scarce reclined on the pillow;
A vision surprisin' came into my head,
And I dreamt I wass crossin' the billow.
And ass my proud vessel she dashed o'er the deep——"

" It wasna the *Vital Spark*, onywye," remarked
Macphail cynically; " afore I got her biler sorted she
couldna dash doon a waterfall——"

" I beheld a rude rock, it was craggy and steep,"

(proceeded the vocalist, paying no attention),

" 'Twas the rock where the willow iss now seen to weep,
    O'er the grave of the once-famed Napo-o-o-ole-on! "

" I never heard better, Peter," said the mate approv-
ingly. " Take your breath and give us another touch
of it. There's nothing bates the old songs."

" Let me see, noo, what wass the second verse? "
asked the Captain, with his vanity as an artist fully
roused; " it was something like this—

"And ass my proud vessel she near-ed the land,
    I beheld clad in green, his bold figure;
The trumpet of fame clasped firm in his hand,
On his brow there wass valour and vigour."

"Balloons! balloons!" cried Macphail, imitating some Glasgow street barrow-vendor. "Fine balloons for rags and banes."

"Fair do! gie the Captain a chance," expostulated Sunny Jim. "Ye're daein' fine, Captain; Macphail's jist chawed because he canna get readin'."

"'Oh, stranger,' he cried, 'dost thou come unto me,
From the land of thy fathers who boast they are free;
Then, if so, a true story I'll tell unto thee
Concerning myself—I'm Napo-o-o-ole-on,'"

proceeded the Captain, no way discouraged, and he had no sooner concluded the final doleful note than a raucous voice from the uncovered hold cried "Co-co-coals!"

Even Dougie sniggered; Macphail fell into convulsions of laughter, and Sunny Jim showed symptoms of choking.

"I can stand Macphail's umpudence, but I'll no' stand that nonsense from a hoolit on my own shup," exclaimed the outraged vocalist, and, stretching over the coamings, he grabbed from the top of a chest of drawers in the hold a cage with a cockatoo. "Come oot like a man," said he, "and say't again."

"Toots! Peter, it's only a stupid animal; I wouldna put myself a bit aboot," remarked Dougie soothingly. "It's weel enough known them cockatoos have no ear for music. Forbye, he wassna meanin' anything when he cried 'Coals!' he was chust in fun."

"Fun or no," said Macphail, "a bird wi' sense like that's no' canny. Try him wi' another verse, Captain, and see if he cries on the polis."

"If he says another word I'll throw him over the side," said Para Handy. "It's nothing else but mutiny," and with a wary eye on the unsuspecting cockatoo he sang another verse—

> " ' You remember that year so immortal,' he cried,
>   ' When I crossed the rude Alps famed in story,
>   With the legions of France, for her sons were my pride,
>   And I led them to honour and glory——' "

" Oh, crickey! Chase me, girls! " exclaimed the cockatoo, and the next moment was swinging over the side of the *Vital Spark* to a watery grave.

The fury of the outraged Captain lasted but a moment; he had the vessel stopped and the punt out instantly for a rescue; but the unhappy bird was irrecoverably gone, and the tea-hour on the *Vital Spark* that afternoon was very melancholy. Macphail, particularly, was inexpressibly galling in the way he over and over again brought up the painful topic.

" I canna get it oot o' my heid," he said; " the look it gied when ye were gaun to swing it roon' your heid and gie't the heave! I'll cairry that cockatoo's last look to my grave."

" Whit kin' o' look was it? " asked Sunny Jim, eager for details; " I missed it."

" It was a look that showed ye the puir bird kent his last oor was come," explained the engineer. " It wasna anger, and it wasna exactly fricht; it was— man! I canna picture it to ye, but efter this ye needna tell me beasts have nae sowls; it's a' my aunty. Yon bird——"

" I wish I hadna put a finger on him," said the Captain, sore stricken with remorse. " Change the subject."

" The puir bird didna mean ony hairm," remarked Sunny Jim, winking at the engineer. " ' Coals! ' or

' Chase me, girls! ' is jist a thing onybody would say
if they heard a chap singin' a sang like yon; it's oot
o' date. Fair do! ye shouldna hae murdered the beast;
the man it belangs to 'll no' be awfu' weel pleased."

" Murdered the beast! " repeated the conscience-
stricken Captain; " it's no' a human body you're
talkin' aboot," and the engineer snorted his amazement.

"Michty! Captain, is that a' ye ken?" he exclaimed.
" If it's no' murder, it's manslaughter; monkeys,
cockatoos, and parrots a' come under the Act o'
Parliament. A cockatoo's no' like a canary; it's able
to speak the language and give an opeenion, and the
man that wad kill a cockatoo wad kill a wean."

" That's right enough, Peter," said Dougie pathetically; " everybody kens it's manslaughter. I never
saw a nicer cockatoo either; no' a better behaved
bird; it's an awful peety. Perhaps the polis at Carradale will let the affair blow bye."

" I wassna meanin' to herm the bird," pleaded Para
Handy. " It aggravated me. Here wass I standin'
here singin' ' Napoleon,' and the cockatoo wass
yonder, and he hurt my feelin's twice; you would be
angry yoursel' if it wass you. My nerves got the
better o' me."

" If the polis cross-examine me," said the engineer
emphatically, " I'll conceal naething. I'll no' turn
King's evidence or onything like that, mind, but if
I'm asked I'll tell the truth, for I don't want to
be mixed up wi' a case o' manslaughter and risk my
neck."

Thus were the feelings of the penitent Para Handy
lacerated afresh every hour of the day, till he would
have given everything he possessed in the world to

restore the cockatoo to life. The owner's anger at the destruction of his bird was a trifle to be anticipated calmly; the thought that made Para Handy's heart like lead was that cockatoos DID speak, that this one even seemed to have the gift of irony, and that he had drowned a fellow-being; it was, in fact, he admitted to himself, a kind of manslaughter. His shipmates found a hundred ways of presenting his terrible deed to him in fresh aspects.

" Cockatoos iss mentioned in the Scruptures," said Dougie; " I don't exactly mind the place, but I've seen it."

" They live mair nor a hundred years if they're weel trated," was Sunny Jim's contribution to the natural history of the bird.

" Naebody ever saw a deid cockatoo," added the engineer.

" I wish you would talk aboot something else," said the Captain piteously; " I'm troubled enough in mind withoot you bringin' that accursed bird up over and over again," and they apologised, but always came back to the topic again.

" I wid plead guilty and throw mysel' on the mercy o' the coort," was Macphail's suggestion. "At the maist it'll no' be mair nor a sentence for life."

" Ye could say ye did it in self-defence," recommended Sunny Jim. " Thae cockatoos bites like onything."

"A great calamity! " moaned Dougie, shaking his head.

When the cargo of furniture was discharged and delivered, the farmer discovered the absence of his cockatoo, and came down to make inquiries.

" He fell over the side," was the Captain's explanation. " We had his cage hanging on the shrouds, and a gale struck us and blew it off. His last words wass, ' There's nobody to blame but mysel'.' "

" There was no gale aboot here," said the farmer, suspecting nothing. " I'm gey sorry to lose that cage. It was a kind o' a pity, too, the cockatoo bein' drooned."

" Say nothing aboot that," pleaded the Captain. " I have been mournin' about that cockatoo all week; you wouldna believe the worry it haas been for me, and when all iss said and done I consider the cockatoo had the best of it."

THE RETURN OF THE TAR

A YACHTSMAN with " R.Y.S. Dolphin " blazoned on his guernsey came down Campbeltown quay and sentimentally regarded the *Vital Spark*, which had just completed the discharge of a cargo of coals under circumstances pleasing to her crew, since there had been a scarcity of carts, two days of idleness, and two days' demurrage. Para Handy saw him looking— " The smertest shup in the tred," he remarked to Sunny Jim; " you see the way she catches their eye! It's her lines, and cheneral appearance; stop you till I give her a touch of paint next month! "

" He'll ken us again when he sees us," said Sunny Jim, unpleasantly conscious of his own grimy aspect, due to eight hours of coal dust. " Hey, you wi' the sign-board, is't a job you're wantin'? " he cried to the

H 2

yachtsman; and started to souse himself in a bucket of water.

The stranger pensively gazed at the Captain, and said, " Does your eyes deceive me or am I no' Colin? "

" Beg pardon! " replied the Captain cautiously.

" Colin," repeated the stranger. " Surely you must mind The Tar? "

" Holy smoke! " exclaimed Para Handy, " you're no' my old shupmate, surely; if you are, there's a desperate change on you. Pass me up my spy-gless, Dougie."

The yachtsman jumped on board, and barely escaped crashing into the tea-dishes with which Sunny Jim proposed to deal when his toilet was completed. "And there's Dougie himsel'," he genially remarked; "——and Macphail, too; it's chust like comin' home. Are ye aal in good condeetion? "

" We canna complain," said Dougie, shaking the proffered hand with some dubiety. " If you were The Tar we used to have you wouldna miss them plates so handy wi' your feet." They stood around and eyed him shrewdly; he certainly looked a little like The Tar if The Tar could be imagined wideawake, trim, clean-shaven, and devoid of diffidence. The engineer, with a fancy nourished on twenty years' study of novelettes, where fraudulent claimants to fortunes and estates were continually turning up, concluded at once that this was really not The Tar at all, but a clever impersonator, and wondered what the game was. The Captain took up a position more non-committal; he believed he could easily test the bona-fides of the stranger.

"And how's your brother Charles? " he inquired innocently.

" Cherles," said the yachtsman, puzzled. " I never had a brother Cherles."

" Neither you had, when I mind, now; my mistake! " said the Captain; " I wass thinkin' on another hand we used to have that joined the yats. Wass I not at your mairrage over in Colintraive? "

" I wasna mairried in Colintraive at all! " exclaimed the puzzled visitor. " Man, Captain! but your memory's failin'."

" Neither you were," agreed the Captain, thinking for a moment. " It wass such a cheery weddin', I forgot."

" If you're the oreeginal Tar," broke in the engineer, " you'll maybe gie me back my knife: ye mind I gied ye a len' o't the day ye left, and I didna get it back frae ye," but this was an accusation the visitor emphatically denied.

" You'll maybe no' hae an anchor tattooed aboot you anywhere? " asked the mate. " It runs in my mind there wass an anchor."

" Two of them," said the visitor, promptly baring an arm, and revealing these interesting decorations.

" That's anchors right enough," said the Captain, closely examining them, and almost convinced. " I canna say mysel' I mind o' them, but there they are, Dougie."

" It's easy tattooin' anchors," said the engineer; " whaur's your strawberry mark? "

" What's a strawberry mark? " asked the baffled stranger.

" There! " exclaimed Macphail triumphantly. " Everybody kens ye need to hae a strawberry mark. Hoo are we to ken ye're the man ye say ye are if ye

canna produce a strawberry mark?" And again the
confidence of the Captain was obviously shaken.

"Pass me along that pail," said the mate suddenly
to the stranger, who, with his hands in his pockets,
slid the pail along the deck to the petitioner with a
lazy thrust of his foot that was unmistakably familiar.

The Captain slapped him on the shoulder. "It's
you yoursel', Colin!" he exclaimed. "There wass
never another man at sea had the same agility wi' his
feet; it's me that's gled to see you. Many a day we
missed you. It's chust them fancy togs that makes
the difference. That and your hair cut, and your face
washed so parteecular."

"A chentleman's life," said The Tar, later, sitting
on a hatch with his bona-fides now established to the
satisfaction of all but the engineer, who couldn't so
readily forget the teachings of romance. "A chentleman's life. That's oor yat oot there; she comes from
Cowes, and I'm doin' fine on her. I knew the tarry
old hooker here ass soon ass I saw her at the quay."

"You're maybe doin' fine on the yats," said the
Captain coldly, "but it doesna improve the mainners.
She wassna a tarry old hooker when you were earnin'
your pound a-week on her."

"No offence!" said The Tar remorsefully. "I wass
only in fun. I've seen a wheen o' vessels since I left
her, but none that had her style nor nicer shupmates."

"That's the truth!" agreed the Captain, mollified
immediately. "Come doon and I'll show you the
same old bunk you did a lot o' sleepin' in," and The
Tar agreeably followed him with this sentimental purpose. They were below ten minutes, during which time
the engineer summed up the whole evidence for and

against the identity of the claimant, and proclaimed his belief to Dougie that the visitor had come to the *Vital Spark* after no good. He was so righteously indignant at what he considered a deception that he even refused to join the party when it adjourned into the town to celebrate the occasion fittingly at the Captain's invitation.

The Tar retired to his yacht in due course; Para Handy, Dougie, and Sunny Jim returned, on their part, to the *Vital Spark*, exhilarated to the value of half-a-crown handsomely disbursed by the Captain, who had never before been seen with a shilling of his own so far on in the week. They were met on board by Macphail in a singularly sarcastic frame of mind, mingled with a certain degree of restrained indignation.

" I hope your frien' trated ye well," he said.

" Fine! " said the Captain. " Colin was aye the chentleman. He's doin' capital on the yats."

" He'll be daein' time oot o' the yats afore he's done," said the engineer. " I kent he was efter nae guid comin' here, and when ye had him doon below showin' him whaur The Tar bunked, he picked my Sunday pocket o' hauf-a-croon. The man's a fraud, ye're blin' no' to see't; he hadna even a strawberry mark."

" Whatever you say yoursel'," replied the Captain, with an expansive wink at the mate and Sunny Jim. " If he's not The Tar, and took your money, it wass lucky you saw through him."

THE FORTUNE-TELLER

TARBERT FAIR was in full swing; the crew of the
Vital Spark had exhausted the delirious delights of
the hobby-horses, the shooting-gallery, Aunt Sally,
Archer's Lilliputian Circus, and the booth where, after
ten, they got pink fizzing drinks that had "a fine,
fine appearance, but not mich fun in them," as Para
Handy put it, and Dougie stumbled upon a gipsy's
cart on the outskirts of the Fair, where a woman was
telling fortunes. Looking around to assure himself
that he was unobserved by the others, he went behind
the cart tilt and consulted the oracle, a proceeding
which took ten minutes, at the end of which time he
rejoined the Captain, betraying a curious mood of
alternate elation and depression.

" Them high-art fizzy drinks iss not agreeing with
you, Dougie," said the Captain sympathetically;
" you're losing all your joviality, and it not near the
mornin'. Could you not get your eye on Macphail?
I'll wudger he'll have something sensible in a bottle! "

" Macphail! " exclaimed the mate emphatically;
" I wouldna go for a drink to him if I wass dyin'; I
wouldna be in his reverence."

" Holy smoke! but you're gettin' desperate independent," said the Captain; " you had more than wan
refreshment with him the day already," and the mate,
admitting it remorsefully, relapsed into gloomy silence
as they loitered about the Fair-ground.

" Peter," he said in a little, " did you ever try your
fortune? "

" I never tried anything else," said the Captain; " but it's like the herrin' in Loch Fyne the noo—it's no' in't."

" That's no' what I mean," said Dougie; " there's a cluver woman roond in a cairt yonder, workin' wi' cairds and tea-leaves and studyin' the palm o' the hand, and she'll tell you everything that happened past and future. I gave her a caal mysel' the noo, and she told me things that wass most astonishin'."

" What did it cost you? " asked Para Handy, with his interest immediately aroused.

" Ninepence."

" Holy smoke! she would need to be most extra-ordinar' astonishin' for ninepence; look at the chap in Archer's circus tying himself in knots for front sates threepence! Forbye, I don't believe in them spae-wifes; half the time they're only tellin' lies."

" This wan's right enough, I'll warrant you," said the mate; " she told me at once I wass a sailor and came through a lot of trouble."

" What did she predict?—that's the point, Dougie; they're no' mich use unless they can predict; I could tell myself by the look o' you that you had a lot o' trouble, the thing's quite common."

" No, no," said the mate cautiously; " pay nine-pence for yoursel' if you want her to predict. She told me some eye-openers."

The Captain, with a passion for eye-openers, demanded to be led to the fortune-teller, and submitted himself to ninepence worth of divination, while Dougie waited outside on him. He, too, came forth, half elated, half depressed.

" What did she say to you? " asked the mate.

" She said I wass a sailor and seen a lot o' trouble," replied the Captain.

" Yes, but what did she predict? "

" Whatever it wass it cost me ninepence," said the Captain, " and I'm no' givin' away any birthday presents any more than yoursel'; it's time we were back noo on the vessel."

Getting on board the *Vital Spark* at the quay they found that Para Handy's guess at the engineer's possession of something sensible in a bottle was correct. He hospitably passed it round, and was astonished to find the Captain and mate, for the first time in his experience, refuse a drink. They not only refused but were nasty about it.

" A' richt," he said; " there'll be a' the mair in the morn for me an' Jim. I daursay ye ken best yersel's when ye've gane ower faur wi't. I aye believe, mysel', in moderation."

The manner of Para Handy and his mate for a week after this was so peculiar as to be the subject of unending speculation on the part of the engineer and Sunny Jim. The most obvious feature of it was that they both regarded the engineer with suspicion and animosity.

" I'm shair I never did them ony hairm," he protested to Sunny Jim, almost in tears; " I never get a ceevil word frae either o' them. Dougie's that doon on me, he wad raither gang withoot a smoke than ask a match aff me."

" It's cruel, that's whit it is! " said Sunny Jim, who had a feeling heart; " but they're aff the dot ever since the nicht we were at Tarbert. Neither o' them'll eat fish, nor gang ashore efter it's dark. They baith took

to their beds on Monday and wouldna steer oot o'
their bunks a' day, pretendin' to be ill, but wonderfu'
sherp in the appetite."

" I'll give them wan chance, and if they refuse it
I'll wash my hands o' them," said Macphail decisively,
and that evening after tea he produced a half-crown
and extended a general invitation to the nearest
tavern.

" Much obleeged, but I'm not in the need of anything," said the Captain. " Maybe Dougie——"

" No thanky," said the mate with equal emphasis;
" I had a dram this week already "—a remark so
ridiculous that it left the engineer speechless. He
tapped his head significantly with a look at Sunny
Jim, and the two of them went ashore to dispose of
the half-crown without the desired assistance.

Next day there was an auction sale in the village,
and Para Handy and his mate, without consulting
each other, found themselves among the bidders.

" Were you fancyin' anything parteecular? " asked
the Captain, who plainly had an interest in a battered
old eight-day clock.

" No, nothing to mention," said the mate, with an
eye likewise on the clock. " There's capital bargains
here, I see, in crockery."

But the Captain seemed to have no need for crockery;
he hung about an hour or two till the clock was put
to the hammer, and offered fifteen shillings, thus completely discouraging a few of the natives who had concealed the hands and weights of the clock, and hoped
to secure the article at the reasonable figure of about
a crown. To the Captain's surprise and annoyance,
he found his mate his only competitor, and between

them they raised the price to thirty shillings, at which figure it was knocked down to the Captain, who had it promptly placed on a barrow and wheeled down to the quay.

" Were you desperate needin' a nock? " asked the mate, coming after him.

" I wass on the look-out for a nock like that for years," said the Captain, apparently charmed with his possession.

" I'll give you five-and-thirty shillings for't," said the mate, but Para Handy wasn't selling. He had the clock on board, and spent at least an hour investigating its interior, with results that from his aspect seemed thoroughly disappointing. He approached Dougie and informed him that he had changed his mind, and was willing to hand over the clock for five-and-thirty shillings. The bargain was eagerly seized by Dougie, who paid the money and submitted his purchase to an examination even more exhaustive than the Captain.

Half an hour later the engineer and Sunny Jim had to separate the Captain and the mate, who were at each other's throats, the latter frantically demanding back his money or a share of whatever the former had found inside the clock.

" The man's daft," protested Para Handy; " the only thing that was in the nock wass the works and an empty bottle."

" The Tarbert spae-wife said I would find a fortune in a nock like that," spluttered Dougie.

" Holy smoke! She said the same to me," confessed the Captain. "And did she say that eatin' fish wass dangerous? "

" She did that," said the mate. " Did she tell you

to keep your bed on the first o' the month in case o' accidents? "

" Her very words! " said the Captain. " Did she tell you to beware o' a man wi' black whiskers that came from Australia? " and he looked at the engineer.

" She told me he was my bitterest enemy," said the mate.

"And that's the way ye had the pick at me! " exclaimed the engineer. " Ye're a couple o' Hielan' cuddies; man, I never wass nearer Australia than the River Plate."

On the following day a clock went cheap at the head of the quay for fifteen shillings, and the loss was amicably shared by Para Handy and his mate, but any allusion to Tarbert Fair and fortune-telling has ever since been bitterly resented by them both.

THE HAIR LOTION

DOUGIE, the mate, had so long referred to his family album as a proof of the real existence of old friends regarding whom he had marvellous stories to tell, that the crew finally demanded its production. He protested that it would be difficult to get it out of the house, as his wife had it fair in the middle of the parlour table, on top of the Family Bible.

" Ye can ask her for the len' o't, surely," said the Captain. " There's nobody goin' to pawn it on her. Tell her it's to show your shupmates what a tipper she wass hersel' when she wass in her prime."

" She's in her prime yet," said the mate, with some annoyance.

" Chust that! ' said Para Handy. "A handsome gyurl, I'm sure of it; but every woman thinks she wass at her best before her husband mairried her. Let you on that you were bouncin' aboot her beauty, and tell her the enchineer wass dubious——"

" Don't drag me into 't," said the engineer. " You micht hae married Lily Langtry for a' I care; put the blame on the Captain; he's what they ca' a connysure among the girls," a statement on which the Captain darkly brooded for several days after.

The mate ultimately rose to the occasion, and taking advantage of a visit by his wife to her good-sister, came on board one day with the album wrapped in his oil-skin trousers. It created the greatest interest on the *Vital Spark*, and an admiration only marred by the discovery that the owner was attempting to pass off a lithograph portrait of the late John Bright as that of his Uncle Sandy.

" My mistake! " he said politely, when the engineer corrected him; " I thocht it wass Uncle Sandy by the whuskers; when I look again I see he hasna the breadth across the shouthers."

" Wha's this chap like a body-snatcher? " asked the engineer, turning over another page of the album. " If I had a face like that I wad try and no' keep mind o't."

" You're a body-snatcher yoursel'," said the mate warmly, " and that's my advice to you. Buy specs, Macphail; you're spoilin' your eyes wi' readin' them novelles."

" Holy smoke! " cried the Captain; " it's a picture o' yoursel', Dougie. Man! what a heid o' hair! "

" I had a fair quantity," said the mate, passing his

hand sadly over a skull which was now as bare as a bollard. " I'm sure I don't ken what way I lost it."

" Short bunks for sleepin' in," suggested the Captain kindly; " that's the worst o' bein' a sailor."

" I tried everything, from paraffin oil to pumice-stone, but nothing did a bit of good; it came oot in handfuls."

" I wad hae left her," said the engineer. " When a wife tak's her hands to ye the law says ye can leave her and tak' the weans wi' ye."

" I see ye hae been consultin' the lawyers," retorted the mate readily; " what way's your ear keepin' efter your last argument wi' the flet-iron? " and Macphail retired in dudgeon to his engines.

Sunny Jim regarded Dougie's portrait thoughtfully. " Man! " he said, " if the Petroloid Lotion had been invented in them days ye could hae had your hair yet. That's the stuff! Fair champion! Rub it on the door-step and ye didna need to keep a bass. The hair mak's a difference, richt enough; your face is jist the same's it used to be, but the hair in the photo mak's ye twenty years younger. It's as nice a photo as ever I seed; there's money in 't."

" None o' your dydoes noo! " said the mate, remembering how Sunny Jim had found money in the exploitation of the Tobermory whale. " If you think I would make an exhibeetion o' my photygraph——"

" Exhibeetion my aunty! " exclaimed Sunny Jim. " Ye're no' an Edna May. But I'll tell ye whit we could dae. Thae Petroloid Lotion folks is keen on testimonials. A' ye hae to dae is to get Macphail to write a line for ye saying ye lost yer hair in a biler explosion, and tried Petroloid, and it brocht it back in a couple o' weeks. Get a photograph o' yersel' the way ye are the noo and send it, and this yin wi' the testimonial, lettin' on the new yin's the way ye looked immediately efter the explosion, and this yin's the way ye look since ye took to usin' the lotion."

" Capital! " cried the Captain, slapping his knees. " For ingenuity you're chust sublime, Jum."

" Sublime enough," said Dougie cautiously, " but I thocht you said there wass money in it."

" So there is," said Sunny Jim. " The Petroloid Lotion folk'll gie ye a pound or twa for the testimonial; I kent a chap that made his livin' oot o' curin' himsel' o' diseases he never had, wi' pills he never saw except in pictures. He was a fair don at describin' a buzzin' in the ear, a dizzy heid, or a pain alang the spine o' his back, and was dragged back frae the brink o' the grave a thoosand times, by his way o't, under a different name every time. Macphail couldna touch him at a testimonial for anything internal, but there's naething to hinder Macphail puttin' a bit thegither aboot the loss and restoration o' Dougie's hair. Are ye game, Dougie? "

The mate consented dubiously, and the engineer was called upon to indite the requisite document, which took him a couple of evenings, on one of which the mate was taken ashore at Rothesay and photographed in the Captain's best blue pilot pea-jacket. The portraits and the testimonial were duly sent to the address which was found in the advertisement of Petroloid's Lotion for the Hair, a gentle hint being included that some " recognition " would be looked for, the phrase being Sunny Jim's. Then the crew of the *Vital Spark* resigned themselves to a patient wait of several days for an acknowledgment.

Three weeks passed, and Sunny Jim's scheme was sadly confessed a failure, for nothing happened, and the cost of the Rothesay photograph, which had been jointly borne by the crew on the understanding that they were to share alike in the products of it, was a subject of frequent and unfeeling remarks from the engineer, who suggested that the mate had got a remittance and said nothing about it. But one afternoon the Captain picked up a newspaper, and turning, as was his wont, to the pictorial part of it, gave an exclamation on beholding the two portraits of his mate side by side in the midst of a Petroloid advertisement.

" Holy smoke! Dougie," he cried, " here you are ass large ass life like a futbaal player or a man on his trial for manslaughter."

" Michty! iss that me? " said the mate incredulously. " I had no notion they would put me in the papers. If I kent that I would never have gone in for the ploy."

" Ye look guilty," said the engineer, scrutinising the blurred lineaments of his shipmate in the newspaper. " Which is the explosion yin? The testimonial's a' richt onyway; it's fine," and he read his own composition with complete approval—

I unfortunately lost all my hair in a boiler explosion, and tried all the doctors, but none of them could bring it back. Then I heard of your wonderful Petroloid Lotion, and got a small bottle, which I rubbed in night and morning as described. In a week there was a distinct improvement. In a fortnight I had to have my head shorn twice, and now it is as thick as ever it was. I will recommend your Lotion to all my friends, and you are at liberty to make any use of this you like.—(Signed) Dougald Campbell, Captain, *Vital Spark.*

"What's that?" cried Para Handy, jumping up. "Captain! who said he was captain?"

"The advertisement," said the engineer guiltily. "I never wrote 'captain'; they've gone and shifted a lot o' things I wrote, and spiled the grammar and spellin'. Fancy the way they spell distinck!"

. . . . . .

A few days later a box was delivered on the *Vital Spark* which at first was fondly supposed to be a case of whisky lost by somebody's mistake, but was found on examination to be directed to the mate. It was opened eagerly, and revealed a couple of dozen of the Petroloid specific, with a letter containing the grateful acknowledgments of the manufacturers, and expressing a generous hope that as the lotion had done so much to restore their correspondent's hair, he would distribute the accompanying consignments among all his bald-headed friends.

"Jum," said the Captain sadly, "when you're in the trum for makin' money efter this, I'll advise you to tak' the thing in hand yoursel' and leave us oot of it."

PARA HANDY AND THE NAVY

MACPHAIL the engineer sat on an upturned bucket reading the weekly paper, and full of patriotic alarm at the state of the British Navy.

" What are you groanin' and sniffin' at? " asked the Captain querulously. " I should think mysel' that by this time you would be tired o' Mrs Atherton. Whatna prank iss she up to this time? "

" It's no' Mrs Atherton," said the reader; " it's something mair important; it's the Germans."

" Holy smoke! " said Para Handy, " are they findin' them oot, noo? Wass I not convinced there wass something far, far wrong wi' them? Break the full parteeculars to me chently, Mac, and you, Jim, go and get the dinner ready; you're far too young to hear the truth aboot the Chermans. Which o' the Chermans iss it, Mac? Some wan in a good poseetion, I'll be bound! It's a mercy that we're sailors; you'll no' find mich aboot the wickedness o' sailors in the papers."

" The British Navy's a' to bleezes! " said Macphail emphatically. " Here's Germany buildin' Dreadnought men-o'-war as hard's she can, and us palaverin' awa' oor time."

Para Handy looked a little disappointed. " It's politics you're on," said he; " and I wass thinkin' it wass maybe another aawful scandal in Society. That's the worst o' the newspapers—you never know where you are wi' them; a week ago it wass nothing but the high jeenks of the beauteous Mrs Atherton. Do you tell me the Brutish Navy's railly done? "

" Complete! " said the engineer.

" Weel, that's a peety! " said Para Handy sympathetically; " it'll put a lot o' smert young fellows oot o' jobs; I know a Tarbert man called Colin Kerr that had a good poseetion on the *Formidable*. I'm aawful sorry aboot Colin."

The engineer resumed his paper, and the *Vital Spark* chug-chugged her sluggish way between the Gantocks and the Cloch, with Dougie at the wheel, his nether garments hung precariously on the half of a pair of braces. " There's nothing but dull tred everywhere," said he. " They're stoppin' a lot o' the railway steamers, too."

" The state o' the British Navy's mair important than the stoppage o' a wheen passenger steamers," explained the engineer. " If you chaps read the papers ye would see this country's in a bad poseetion. We used to rule the sea——"

" We did that! " said the Captain heartily; " I've seen us doin' it! Brutain's hardy sons! "

"And noo the Germans is gettin' the upper hand o' us; they'll soon hae faur mair Dreadnoughts than we hae. We're only buildin' four. Fancy that! Four Dreadnoughts at a time like this, wi' nae work on the Clyde, and us wi' that few Territorials we hae to go to the fitba' matches and haul them oot to jine by the hair o' the heid. We've lost the two-Power standard."

" Man, it's chust desperate! " said the Captain. " We'll likely advertise for 't. What's the—what's the specialty aboot the Dreadnoughts? "

" It's the only cless o' man-o'-war that's coonted noo," said the engineer; " a tip-top battle-winner.

If ye havena Dreadnoughts ye micht as weel hae dredgers."

" Holy smoke! what a lot o' lumber aal the other men-o'-war must be! " remarked the Captain. " That'll be the way they're givin' them up and payin' off the hands."

" Wha said they were givin' them up? " asked the engineer snappishly.

" Beg pardon! beg pardon ! I thocht I heard you mention it yon time I remarked on Colin Kerr. I thocht that maybe aal the other boats wass absolute, and we would see them next week lyin' in the Kyles o' Bute wi' washin's hung oot on them."

" There's gaun to be nae obsolete boats in the British Navy efter this," said the engineer; " we're needin' every man-o'-war that'll haud thegither. The Germans has their eye on us."

" Dougie," said the Captain firmly, with a glance at the deshabille of his mate, " go doon this instant and put on your jecket! The way you are, you're not a credit to the boat."

A terrific bang broke upon the silence of the Firth; the crew of the *Vital Spark* turned their gaze with one accord towards the neighbourhood of Kilcreggan, whence the report seemed to have proceeded, and were frightfully alarmed a second or two afterwards when a shell burst on the surface of the sea a few hundred yards or so from them, throwing an enormous column of water into the air.

" What did I tell ye! " cried Macphail, as he dived below to his engine-room.

" Holy smoke! " exclaimed Para Handy; " did ye notice anything, Dougie? "

" I think I did! " said the mate, considerably perturbed; " there must be some wan blastin'."

" Yon wassna a blast," said the Captain; " they're firin' cannons at us from Portkill."

" There's a pant for ye! " exclaimed Sunny Jim, dodging behind the funnel.

" What for would they be firin' cannons at us? " asked the mate, with a ludicrous feeling that even the jacket advised a minute or two ago by the Captain would now be a most desirable protection.

Another explosion from the fort at Portkill postponed the Captain's answer, and this time the bursting shell seemed a little closer.

" Jim," said the mate appealingly, " would ye mind takin' haud o' this wheel till I go down below and get my jacket? If I'm to be shot, I'll be shot like a Hielan' chentleman and no' in my shirt-sleeves."

" You'll stay where you are! " exclaimed the Captain, greatly excited; " you'll stay where you are, and die at your post like a Brutish sailor. This iss WAR. Port her heid in for Macinroy's Point, Dougald, and you, Macphail, put on to her every pound of steam she'll cairry. I wish to Providence I had chust the wan wee Union Jeck."

" Whit would ye dae wi' a Union Jeck? " asked the engineer, putting up his head and ducking nervously as another shot boomed over the Firth.

" I would nail it to the mast! " said Para Handy, buttoning his coat. " It would show them Cherman chentlemen we're the reg'lar he'rts of oak."

" Ye don't think it's Germans that's firin', dae ye? " asked the engineer, cautiously putting out his head again. " It's the Garrison Arteelery that's firin' frae Portkill."

" Whit are the silly duvvles firin' at us for, then? "
asked Para Handy; " I'm sure we never did them any
herm."

" I ken whit for they're firin'," said the engineer
maliciously; " they're takin' the *Vital Spark* for yin
o' them German Dreadnoughts. Ye have nae idea o'
the fear o' daith that's on the country since it lost the
two-Power standard."

This notion greatly charmed the Captain, being distinctly complimentary to his vessel; but his vanity was
soon dispelled, for Sunny Jim pointed out that the last
shot had fallen far behind them, in proximity to a
floating target now for the first time seen. " They're
jist at big-gun practice," he remarked with some relief,
" and we're oot o' the line o' fire."

" Of course we are! " said Para Handy. " I kent
that aal along. Man, Macphail, but you were tumid,
tumid! You're losin' aal your nerve wi' readin' aboot
the Chermans."

PIRACY IN THE KYLES

" I'M goin' doon below to put on my sluppers," said
the Captain, as the vessel puffed her leisured way
round Buttock Point; " keep your eye on the *Collingwood*, an' no' run into her; it would terribly vex the
Admiralty."

The mate, with a spoke of the wheel in the small of
his back, and his hands in his trousers pockets, looked
along the Kyles towards Colintraive, and remarked
that he wasn't altogether blind.

" I didna say you were," said the Captain; " I wass
chust advisin' caaution. You canna be too caautious,

and if anything would happen it's mysel' would be the man responsible. Keep her heid a point away, an' no' be fallin' asleep till I get my sluppers on; you'll mind you were up last night pretty late in Tarbert."

Macphail, the engineer, projected a perspiring head from his engine-room, and wiped his brow with a wad of oily waste. " Whit's the argyment?" he asked. " Is this a coal-boat or a Convention o' Royal Burghs? I'm in the middle o' a fine story in the ' People's Frien',' and I canna hear mysel' readin' for you chaps barkin' at each other. I wish ye would talk wee."

Para Handy looked at him with a contemptuous eye, turned his back on him, and confined his address to Dougie. " I'll never feel safe in the Kyles of Bute," he said, " till them men-o'-war iss oot o' here. I'm feared for a collusion."

" There's no' much chance of a collusion wi' a boat like that," said the mate, with a glance at the great sheer hulk of the discarded man-o'-war.

" You would wonder! " said Para Handy. " I haf seen a smert enough sailor before now come into a collusion wi' the whole o' Cowal. And he wassna tryin 't either! Keep her off yet, Dougald."

With his slippers substituted for his sea-boots, the Captain returned on deck, when the *Collingwood* was safely left astern; and, looking back, watched a couple of fishermen culling mussels off the lower plates of the obsolete ship of war. " They're a different cless of men aboot the Kyles from what there used to be," said he, " or it wouldn't be only bait they would be liftin' off a boat like that. If she wass there when Hurricane Jeck wass in his prime, he would have the very cannons off her, sellin' them for junk in Greenock.

There's no' that hardy Brutish spirit in the boys that wass in't when Hurricane Jeck and me wass on the *Aggie*."

" Tell us the baur," pleaded Sunny Jim, seated on an upturned bucket, peeling the day's potatoes.

" It's not the only baur I could tell you about the same chentleman," said the Captain, " but it's wan that shows you his remarkable agility. Gie me a haud o' that wheel, Dougie; I may ass well be restin' my back ass you, and me the skipper. To let you ken, Jum, Hurricane Jeck wass a perfect chentleman, six feet two, ass broad in the back ass a shippin'-box, and the very duvvle for contrivance. He wass a man that wass namely in the clipper tred to China, and the Board o' Tred had never a hand on him; his navigation wass complete. You know that, Dougie, don't you? "

" Whatever you say yoursel'," replied the mate agreeably, cutting himself a generous plug of navy-blue tobacco. " I have nothing to say against the chap —except that he came from Campbeltown."

" He sailed wi' me for three or four years on the *Aggie*," said the Captain, " and a nicer man on a boat you wouldna meet, if you didna contradict him. There wass nothing at aal against his moral character, except that he always shaved himsel' on Sunday, whether he wass needin' it or no'. And a duvvle for recreation! Six feet three, if he wass an inch, and a back like a shippin'-box! "

" Where does the British spirit come in? " inquired the engineer, who was forced to relinquish his story and join his mates.

" Hold you on, and I'll tell you that," said Para

Handy. " We were lyin' wan winter night at Tighnabruaich wi' a cargo o' stones for a place they call Glen
Caladh, that wass buildin' at the time, and we wanted
a bit o' rope for something in parteecular—I think it
wass a bit of a net. There wass lyin' at Tighnabruaich
at the time a nice wee steamer yat belonging to a
chentleman in Gleska that was busy at his business,
and nobody wass near her. ' We'll borrow a rope for
the night from that nice wee yat,' said Hurricane Jeck,
as smert as anything, and when it wass dark he took
the punt and went off and came back wi' a rope that
did the business. ' They havena much sense o' ropes
that moored that boat in the Kyles,' said he; ' they
had it flemished down and nate for liftin'. They must
be naval architects.' The very next night did Jeck no'
take the punt again and go oot to the wee steam-yat,
and come back wi' a couple o' india-rubber basses and
a weather-gless? "

" Holy smoke! " said Dougie. " Wasn't that chust
desperate? "

" We were back at Tighnabruaich a week efter that,"
continued Para Handy, "and Jeck made some inquiries.
Nobody had been near the wee steam-yat, though the
name o' her in the Gaalic was the *Eagle*, and Jeck
made oot it wass a special dispensation. ' The man
that owned her must be deid,' said he, ' or he hasna
his wuts aboot him; I'll take a turn aboard the night
wi' a screw-driver, and see that all's in order.' He
came back that night wi' a bag o' cleats, a binnacle,
half a dozen handy blocks, two dozen o' empty bottles,
and a quite good water-breaker.

" ' They may call her the *Eagle* if they like,' says he,
' but I call her the *Silver Mine*. I wish they would put

lights on her; I nearly broke my neck on the cabin
stairs.'

" ' Mind you, Jeck,' I says to him, ' I don't ken anything aboot it. If you're no' comin' by aal them things
honest, it'll give the *Aggie* a bad name.'

" ' It's aal right, Peter,' says he, quite kind. ' Flot-
sam and jetsam; if you left them there, you don't ken
who might lift them! ' Oh, a smert, smert sailor,
Jeck! Six feet four in his stockin's soles, and a back
like a couple o' shippin'-boxes."

" He's gettin' on! " remarked the engineer sarcastically. " I'm gled I wasna his tailor."

" The Glen Caladh job kept us comin' and goin' aal
winter," pursued the Captain, paying no attention.
" Next week we were back again, and Jeck had a talk
with the polisman at Tighnabruaich aboot the lower
clesses. Jeck said the lower clesses up in Gleska were
the worst you ever saw; they would rob the wheels
off a railway train. The polisman said he could weel
believe it, judgin' from the papers, but, thank the
Lord! there wass only honest folk in the Kyles of
Bute. ' It's aal right yet,' said Jeck to me that night;
' the man that owns the *Silver Mine* 's in the Necropolis, and never said a word aboot the wee yat in his
will.' In the mornin' I saw a clock, a couple o' North
Sea charts, a trysail, a galley-stove, two kettles, and a
nice decanter lyin' in the hold.

" ' Jeck,' I says, ' is this a flittin'? '

" ' I'll not deceive you, Peter,' he says, quite honest,
' it's a gift '; and he sold the lot on Setturday in
Greenock."

" A man like that deserves the jyle," said the engineer
indignantly.

I

" I wouldna caal it aalthegither fair horny," admitted
the Captain, " parteecularly as the rest of us never got
more than a schooner o' beer or the like o't oot of it;
but, man! you must admit the chap's agility! He
cairried the business oot single-handed, and there wass
few wass better able; he wass six feet six, and had a
back on him like a Broomielaw shed. The next time
we were in the Kyles, and he went off wi' the punt at
night, he came back from the *Silver Mine* wi' her
bowsprit, twenty faddom o' chain, two doors, and half
a dozen port-holes."

" Oh, to bleezes! " exclaimed Sunny Jim incredulously, " noo you're coddin'! What wye could he steal
her port-holes? "

" Quite easy! " said Para Handy. " I didna say he
took the holes themsel's, but he twisted off the windows
and the brass aboot them. You must mind the chap's
agility! And that wassna the end of it, for next time
the *Aggie* left the Kyles she had on board a beautiful
vernished dinghy, a couple o' masts, no' bad, and a
fine brass steam-yat funnel."

" Holy smoke! " said Dougie; " it's a wonder he
didna strip the lead off her."

" He had it in his mind," exclaimed the Captain;
" but, mind, he never consulted me aboot anything,
and I only kent, as you might say, by accident, when
he would be standin' me another schooner. It wass
aalways a grief to Jeck that he didna take the boat the
way she wass, and sail her where she would be properly
appreciated. ' My mistake, chaps! ' he would say;
' I might have kent they would miss the masts and
funnel! ' "

AMONG THE YACHTS

MACPHAIL was stoking carefully and often, like a mother feeding her first baby; keeping his steam at the highest pressure short of blowing off the safety valve, on which he had tied a pig-iron bar; and driving the *Vital Spark* for all she was worth past Cowal. The lighter's bluff bows were high out of water, for she was empty, and she left a wake astern of her like a liner.

" She hass a capital turn of speed when you put her to it," said the Captain, quite delighted; " it's easy seen it's Setturday, and you're in a hurry to be home, Macphail. You're passin' roond that oil-can there the same ass if it wass a tea-pairty you were at, and nobody there but women. It's easy seen it wass a cargo of coals we had the last trip, and there's more in your bunkers than the owner paid for. But it's none o' my business; please yoursel'! "

" We'll easy be at Bowlin' before ten," said Dougie, consulting his watch. " You needna be so desperate anxious."

The engineer mopped himself fretfully with a fistful of oily waste and shrugged his shoulders. " If you chaps like to palaver awa' your time," said he, " it's all the same to me, but I was wantin' to see the end o' the racin'."

" Whatna racin'? " asked the Captain.

" Yat-racin'," said the engineer, with irony. " Ye'll maybe hae heard o't. If ye havena, ye should read the papers. There's a club they ca' the Royal Clyde at Hunter's Quay, and a couple o' boats they ca' the *Shamrock* and the *White Heather* are sailin' among a

wheen o' ithers for a cup. I wouldna care if I saw the
feenish; you chaps needna bother; just pull doon the
skips o' your keps on your e'en when ye pass them,
and ye'll no' see onything."

" I don't see much in aal their yat-racin'," said Para
Handy.

" If I was you, then, I would try the Eye Infirmary,"
retorted the engineer, " or wan o' them double-breisted
spy-glesses. Yonder the boats; we're in lots o'
time——" and he dived again among his engines, and
they heard the hurried clatter of his shovel.

"Anything wi' Macphail for sport! " remarked the
Captain sadly. " You would think at his time o' life,
and the morn Sunday, that his meditaations would be
different. . . . Give her a point to starboard, Dougie,
and we'll see them better. Yonder's the *Ma'oona*; if
the duvvle wass wise he would put aboot at wance or
he'll hit that patch o' calm."

" There's an aawful money in them yats! " said the
mate, who was at the wheel.

" I never could see the sense o't," remarked the
Captain. . . . " There's the *Hera* tacking; man, she's
smert! smert! Wan o' them Coats's boats; I wish she
would win; I ken a chap that plays the pipes on her."

Dougie steered as close as he could on the racing
cutters with a sportsman's scrupulous regard for wind
and water. " What wan's that? " he asked, as they
passed a thirty-rater which had struck the calm.

" That's the *Pallas*," said the Captain, who had a
curiously copious knowledge of the craft he couldn't
see the sense of. "Another wan o' the Coats's; every
other wan you see belongs to Paisley. They buy them
by the gross, the same ass they were pirns, and dis-

tribute them every noo and then among the faimely.
If you're a Coats you lose a lot o' time makin' up your
mind what boat you'll sail to-morrow; the whole o'
the Clyde below the Tail o' the Bank is chock-a-block
wi' steamboat-yats and cutters the Coats's canna hail
a boat ashore from to get a sail, for they canna mind
their names. Still-and-on, there's nothing wrong wi'
them—tip-top sportin' chentlemen! "

" I sometimes wish, mysel', I had taken to the yats,"
said Dougie; " it's a suit or two o' clothes in the year,
and a pleasant occupaation. Most o' the time in
canvas sluppers."

" You're better the way you are," said Para Handy;
" there's nothing bates the mercantile marine for
makin' sailors. Brutain's hardy sons! We could do
withoot yats, but where would we be withoot oor coal-
boats? Look at them chaps sprauchlin' on the deck;
if they saw themsel's they would see they want another
fut on that main-sheet. I wass a season or two in the
yats mysel'—the good old *Marjory*. No' a bad job at
aal, but aawful hurried. Holy smoke! the way they
kept you jumpin' here and there the time she would
be racin'! I would chust as soon be in a lawyer's
office. If you stopped to draw your breath a minute
you got yon across the ear from a swingin' boom.
It's a special breed o' sailor-men you need for racin'-
yats, and the worst you'll get iss off the Islands."

" It's a cleaner job at any rate than carryin' coals,"
remarked the mate, with an envious eye on the spotless
decks of a heeling twenty-tonner.

" Clean enough, I'll alloo, and that's the worst of
it," said Para Handy. " You might ass weel be a
chamber-maid—up in the mornin' scourin' brass and

scrubbin' floors, and goin' ashore wi' a fancy can for sixpenceworth o' milk and a dozen o' syphon soda. Not much navigation there, my lad! . . . If I wass that fellow I would gybe her there and set my spinnaker to starboard; what do you think yoursel', Macphail? "

" I thocht you werena interested," said the engineer, who had now reduced his speed.

" I'm not much interested, but I'm duvellish keen," said Para Handy. " Keep her goin' chust like that, Macphail; we'll soon be up wi' the *Shamrock* and the *Heather*; they're yonder off Loch Long."

A motor-boat regatta was going on at Dunoon; the *Vital Spark* seemed hardly to be moving as some of the competitors flashed past her, breathing petrol fumes.

" You canna do anything like that," said Dougie to the engineer, who snorted.

" No," said Macphail contemptuously, " I'm an engineer; I never was much o' a hand at the sewin'-machine. I couldna lower mysel' to handle engines ye could put in your waistcoat pocket."

" Whether you could or no'," said Para Handy, " the times iss changin', and the motor-launch iss coming for to stop."

" That's whit she's aye daein'," retorted the engineer; " stoppin's her strong p'int; gie me a good substantial compound engine; nane o' your hurdy-gurdies! I wish the wind would fresh a bit, for there's the *Shamrock*, and her mainsail shakin'." He dived below, and the *Vital Spark* in a little had her speed reduced to a crawl that kept her just abreast of the drifting racers.

" Paddy's hurricane—up and doon the mast," said Dougie in a tone of disappointment. " I would like, mysel', to see Sir Thomas Lipton winnin', for it's there I get my tea."

Para Handy extracted a gully-knife from the depths of his trousers pockets, opened it, spat on the blade for luck, and, walking forward, stuck it in the mast, where he left it. " That's the way to get wind," said he; " many a time I tried it, and it never fails. Stop you, and you'll see a breeze immediately. Them English skippers, Sycamore and Bevis, havena the heid to think o't."

" Whit's the use o' hangin' on here? " said the engineer, with a wink at Dougie; " it's time we were up the river; I'll better get her under weigh again."

The Captain turned on him with a flashing eye. " You'll do nothing o' the kind, Macphail," said he; " we'll stand by here and watch the feenish, if it's any time before the Gleska Fair."

Shamrock, having split tacks off Kilcreggan, laid away to the west, while *White Heather* stood in for the Holy Loch, seeking the evening breeze that is apt to blow from the setting sun. It was the crisis of the day, and the crew of the *Vital Spark* watched speechlessly for a while the yachts manœuvring. For an hour the cutter drifted on this starboard leg, and Sunny Jim, for reasons of his own, postponed the tea.

" It wants more knifes," said Para Handy; " have you wan, Dougie? " but Dougie had lost his pocket-knife a week ago, and the engineer had none either.

" If stickin' knifes in the mast would raise the wind," said Sunny Jim, " there would be gales by this time, for I stuck the tea-knife in an oor ago."

" Never kent it to fail afore! " said Para Handy. . . . " By George! it's comin'. Yonder's Bevis staying! "

White Heather, catching the wind, reached for the closing lap of the race with a bone in her mouth, and Para Handy watched her, fascinated, twisting the buttons off his waistcoat in his intense excitement. With a turn or two of the wheel the mate put the *Vital Spark* about and headed for the mark; Macphail deserted his engine and ran forward to the bow.

" The *Heather* hass it, Dougald," said the Captain thankfully; " I'm vexed for you, considerin' the place you get your tea."

" Hold you on, Peter," said the mate; " there's the *Shamrock* fetchin'; a race is no' done till it's feenished." His hopes were justified. *Shamrock,* only a few lengths behind, got the same light puff of wind in her sails, and rattled home a winner by half a minute.

" Macphail! " bawled the Captain, " I'll be much obleeged if you take your place again at your bits of engines, and get under weigh; it's any excuse wi' you for a diversion, and it's time we werena here."

FOG

In a silver-grey fog that was not unpleasant, the *Vital Spark* lay at Tarbert quay, and Dougie read a belated evening paper.

" Desperate fog on the Clyde! " he said to his shipmates; " we're the lucky chaps that's here and oot o't! It hasna lifted in Gleska for two days, and there's any amount o' boats amissin' between the Broomielaw and Bowlin'."

" Tck! tck! issn't that deplorable? " said the Captain. " Efter you wi' the paper, Dougald. It must be full o' accidents."

" The Campbeltown boat iss lost since Setturday, and they're lookin' for her wi' lanterns up and doon the river. I hope she hassna many passengers; the poor sowls 'll be stervin'."

" Duvvle the fear! " said Para Handy; " not on the Campbeltown boat ass long ass she has her usual cargo. I would sooner be lost wi' a cargo o' Campbeltown for a week than spend a month in wan o' them hydropathics."

" Two sailors went ashore at Bowlin' from the *Benmore*, and they havena been heard of since," proceeded the mate; " they couldna find their way back to the ship."

"And what happened then? " asked Para Handy.

" Nothing," replied the mate. " That's all; they couldna find their way back."

" Holy smoke! " reflected Para Handy, with genuine surprise; " they're surely ill off for news in the papers nooadays; or they must have a poor opeenion o' sailor-men. They'll be thinkin' they should aalways be teetotalers."

The Captain got the paper to read for himself a little later, and discovered that the missing *Benmore* men had not lost themselves in the orthodox sailor way, but were really victims of the fog, and his heart went out to them. " I've seen the same thing happen to mysel'," he remarked. " It wass the time that Hurricane Jeck and me wass on the *Julia*. There wass a fog come on us wan time there so thick you could almost cut it up and sell it for briquettes."

" Help! " exclaimed Macphail.

1 2

"Away, you, Macphail, and study your novelles; what way's Lady Fitzgerald gettin' on in the chapter you're at the noo? It's a wonder to me you're no' greetin'," retorted the Captain; and this allusion to the sentimental tears of the engineer sent him down, annoyed, among his engines.

" It wass a fog that lasted near a week, and we got into it on a Monday mornin' chust below the Cloch. We were makin' home for Gleska. We fastened up to the quay at Gourock, waitin' for a change, and the thing that vexed us most wass that Hurricane Jeck and me wass both invited for that very night to a smaal tea-party oot in Kelvinside."

" It's yoursel' wass stylish! " said the mate. " It must have been before you lost your money in the City Bank."

" It wassna style at aal, but a Cowal gyurl we knew that wass cook to a chentleman in Kelvinside, and him away on business in Liverpool," explained the Captain. "Hurricane Jeck wass in love wi' the gyurl at the time, and her name wass Bella. ' This fog 'll last for a day or two,' said Jeck in the efternoon; ' it's a peety to lose the ploy at Bella's party.'

" ' What would you propose, yoursel'? ' I asked him, though I wass the skipper. I had aye a great opeenion o' Hurricane Jeck's agility.

" ' What's to hinder us takin' the train to Gleska, and leavin' the *Julia* here? ' said Jeck, ass smert ass anything. ' There's nobody goin' to run away wi' her.'

" Jeck and me took the train for Gleska, and left the enchineer—a chap Macnair—in full command o' the vessel. I never could trust a man o' the name o' Macnair from that day on.

" It wass a splendid perty, and Jeck wass chust sublime. I never partook in a finer perty—two or three hens, a pie the size o' a binnacle, and wine!—the wine was chust miraculous. Bella kept it comin' in in quantities. The coalman wass there, and the letter-carrier, and the man that came for the grocer's orders, and there wassna a gas in the hoose that wassna bleezin'. You could see that Hurricane Jeck had his he'rt on makin' everybody happy. It wass him that danced the hornpipe on the table, and mostly him that carried the piano doon the stair to the dinin'-room. He fastened a clothes-line aft on the legs o' her, laid doon a couple o' planks, and slided her. ' Tail on to the rope, my laads! ' says he, ' and I'll go in front and steady her.' But the clothes-rope broke, and the piano landed on his back. He never had the least suspeecion, but cairried her doon the rest o' the stair himsel', and put her in poseetion. And efter a' oor bother there wass nobody could play. ' That's the worst o' them fore-and-aft pianos! ' said Jeck, ass vexed ass any-thing; ' they're that much complicated! '

" We were chust in the middle o' the second supper, and Bella wass bringin' in cigars, when her maister opened the door wi' his chubb, and dandered in! There wassna a train for Liverpool on account o' the fog!

" ' What's this? ' says he, and Bella nearly fainted.

" ' It's Miss Maclachlan's birthday '—meanin' Bella—answered Jeck, ass nice ass possible. ' You're chust in the nick o' time,' and he wass goin' to introduce the chentleman, for Jeck wass a man that never forgot his mainners.

" ' What's that piano doin' there? ' the chentleman asked, quite furious.

" ' You may weel ask that,' said Jeck, ' for aal the use it iss, we would be better wi' a concertina,' and Bella had to laugh.

" ' I've a good mind to send for the polis,' said her maister.

" ' You needna bother,' said Bella; ' he's comin' anyway, ass soon ass he's off his bate and shifted oot o' his uniform,' and that wass the only intimation and invitation Hurricane Jeck ever got that Bella wass goin' to mairry Macrae the polisman.

" We spent three days in the fog in Gleska, and aal oor money," proceeded Para Handy, " and then, ' It's time we were back on the hooker,' said Hurricane Jeck; ' I can mind her name; it's the *Julia*.'

" ' It's no' so much her name that bothers me,' says I; ' it's her latitude and longitude; where in aal the world did we leave her? '

" ' Them pink wines! ' said Jeck. ' That's the rock we split on, Peter! The fog would never have lasted aal this time if we had taken Brutish spirits.'

" It wass chust luck we found the half o' a railway ticket in Jeck's pocket, and it put us in mind that we left the boat at Gourock. We took the last train doon, and landed there wi' the fog ass bad ass ever; ay, worse! it wass that thick noo, it wassna briquettes you would make wi't, but marble nocks and mantel-pieces.

" ' We left the *Julia* chust fornenst this shippin'-box,' said Jeck, on Gourock quay, and, sure enough, there wass the boat below, and a handy ladder. Him and me went doon the ladder to the deck, and whustled on Macnair. He never paid the least attention.

" ' He'll be in his bed,' said Jeck; ' gie me a ha'ad o' a bit o' marlin'.'

" We went doon below and found him sleepin' in the dark; Jeck took a bit' o' the marlin', and tied him hands and feet, and the two o' us went to bed, ass tired ass anything, wi' oor boots on. You never, never, never saw such fog!

" Jeck wass the first to waken in the mornin', and he struck a match.

" ' Peter,' said he, quite solemn, when it went oot, ' have we a stove wi' the name Eureka printed on the door? '

" ' No, nor Myreeka,' says I; ' there's no' a door at aal on oor stove, and fine ye ken it! '

" He lay a while in the dark, sayin' nothing, and then he struck another match. ' Is Macnair red-heided, do you mind? ' says he when the match went oot.

" ' Ass black ass the ace o' spades! ' says I.

" ' That wass what wass runnin' in my own mind,' said Jeck; ' but I thocht I maybe wass mistaken. WE'RE IN OOR BED IN THE WRONG BOAT! '

" And we were! We lowsed the chap and told him right enough it wass oor mistake, and gave him two or three o' Bella's best cigars, and then we went ashore to look for the *Julia*. You never saw such fog! And it wass Friday mornin'.

" ' Where's the *Julia*? ' we asked the harbour-maister. ' Her! ' says he; ' the enchineer got tired waitin' on ye, and got a couple o' quayheid chaps and went crawlin' up the river wi' the tide on We'nesday! '

" So Hurricane Jeck and me lost more than oorsel's in the fog; we lost oor jobs," concluded Para Handy. " Never put your trust in a man Macnair? "

CHRISTMAS ON THE *VITAL SPARK*

THERE was something, plainly, weighing on Dougie's mind; he let his tea get cold, and merely toyed with his kippered herring; at intervals he sighed—an unsailor-like proceeding which considerably annoyed the engineer, Macphail.

" Whit's the maitter wi' ye? " he querulously inquired. " Ye would think it was the Fast, to hear ye. Are ye ruein' your misspent life? "

" Never you mind Macphail," advised the Captain; " a chentleman should aalways hev respect for another chentleman in tribulation. What way's the mustress, Dougald? " He held a large tablespoonful of marmalade suspended in his hand, while he put the question with genuine solicitude; Dougie's wife was the very woman, he knew, to have something or other seriously wrong with her just when other folk were getting into a nice and jovial spirit for New Year.

" Oh, she's fine, thanky, Peter," said the mate; " there's nothing spashial wrong wi' her except, noo and then, the rheumatism."

" She should aalways keep a raw potato in her pocket," said Para Handy; " it's the only cure."

" She micht as weel keep a nutmeg-grater in her coal-bunker," remarked the engineer. " Whit wye can a raw potato cure the rheumatism? "

" It's the—it's the influence," explained Para Handy vaguely. " Look at them Vibrators! But you'll believe in nothing, Macphail, unless you read aboot it in wan o' them novelles; you're chust an unfidel! "

Dougie sighed again, and the engineer, protesting

that his meal had been spoiled for him by his ship-mate's melancholy, hurriedly finished his fifth cup of tea and went on deck. There were no indications that it was Christmas Eve; two men standing on the quay were strictly sober. Crarae is still a place where they thoroughly celebrate the Old New Year after a first rehearsal with the statutory one.

" If you're not feelin' very brusk you should go to your bed, Dougie," remarked the Captain sympatheti-cally. " The time to stop trouble iss before it starts."

" There's nothing wrong wi' me," the mate assured him sadly; " we're weel off, livin' on the fat o' the land, and some folk stervin'."

" We are that! " agreed Para Handy, helping him-self to Dougie's second kipper. " Were you thinkin' of any wan parteecular? "

" Did you know a quarryman here by the name o' Col Maclachlan? " asked the mate, and Para Handy, having carefully reflected, confessed he didn't.

" Neither did I," said Dougie; " but he died a year ago and left a weedow yonder, and the only thing that's for her iss the poorshouse at Lochgilpheid."

" Holy smoke! " exclaimed the Captain; " isn't that chust desperate! If it wass a cargo of coals we had this trip, we might be givin' her a pickle, but she couldna make mich wi' a bag o' whinstones."

" They tell me she's goin' to start and walk to-morrow mornin' to Lochgilpheid, and she's an old done woman. She says she would be affronted for to go in the *Cygnet* or the *Minard*, for every one on board would ken she was goin' to the poorshouse."

" Oh, to the muschief! " said Para Handy; " Mac-phail wass right—a body might ass weel be at a funeral

ass in your company, and it comin' on to the New
Year!" He fled on deck from this doleful atmosphere
in the fo'c'sle, but came down again in a minute or two.

"I wass thinkin' to mysel'," he remarked with diffidence to the mate, "that if the poor old body would
come wi' us, we could give her a lift to Ardrishaig;
what do you say?"

"Whatever you say yoursel'," said the mate; "but
we would need to be aawfu' careful o' her feelin's, and
she wouldna like to come doon the quay unless it wass
in the dark."

"We'll start at six o'clock, then," said the Captain,
"if you'll go ashore the now and make arrangements,
and you needna bother aboot her feelin's; we'll handle
them like gless."

As an alternative to walking to the poorhouse, the
sail to Lochgilphead by the *Vital Spark* was quite
agreeable to the widow, who turned up at the quay
in the morning quite alone, too proud even to take
her neighbours into her confidence. Para Handy
helped her on board and made her comfortable.

"You're goin' to get a splendid day!" he assured
her cheerfully. "Dougie, iss it nearly time for oor
cup o' tea?"

"It'll be ready in a meenute," said Dougie, with
delightful promptness, and went down to rouse Sunny
Jim.

"We aalways have a cup o' tea at six o'clock on the
Fital Spark," the Captain informed the widow, with
a fluency that astonished even the engineer. "And an
egg; sometimes two. Jum 'll boil you an egg."

"I'm sure I'm an aawful bother to you!" protested
the poor old widow feebly.

" Bother! " said Para Handy; " not the slightest! The tea's there anyway. And the eggs. Efter that we'll have oor breakfast."

" I'll be a terrible expense to you," said the unhappy widow; and Para Handy chuckled jovially.

" Expense! Nonsense, Mrs Maclachlan! Everything's paid for here by the owners; we're allooed more tea and eggs and things than we can eat. I'll be thinkin' mysel' it's a sin the way we hev to throw them sometimes over the side "—at which astounding effort of the imagination Macphail retired among his engines and relieved his feelings by a noisy application of the coaling shovel.

" I have the money for my ticket," said the widow, fumbling nervously for her purse.

" Ticket! " said Para Handy, with magnificent alarm. " If the Board o' Tred heard o' us chergin' money for a passage in the *Fital Spark*, we would never hear the end o't; it would cost us oor certuficate."

The widow enjoyed her tea immensely, and Para Handy talked incessantly about everything and every place but Lochgilphead, while the *Vital Spark* chug-chugged on her fateful way down Loch Fyne to the poorhouse.

" Did you know my man? " the woman suddenly asked, in an interval which even Para Handy's wonderful eloquence couldn't fill up.

" Iss it Col Maclachlan? " he exclaimed. " Fine! me'm; fine! Col and me wass weel acquent; it wass that that made me take the liberty to ask you. There wass never a finer man in Argyllshire than poor Col —a regular chentleman! I mind o' him in the—in the quarry. So do you, Dougie, didn't you? "

" I mind o' him caapital! " said Dougie, without a moment's hesitation. " The last time I saw him he lent me half-a-croon, and I never had the chance to pay him't back."

" I think mysel', if I mind right, it wass five shullin's," suggested Para Handy, putting his hand in his trousers pocket, with a wink to his mate, and Dougie quickly corrected himself; it WAS five shillings, now that he thought of it. But having gone aside for a little and consulted the engineer and Sunny Jim, he came back and said it was really eight-and-sixpence.

" There wass other three-and-six I got the lend o' from him another time," he said; " I could show you the very place it happened, and I wass nearly forgettin' aal aboot it."

" My! ye're an awfu' leear!" said the engineer in a whisper as they stood aside.

" Maybe I am," agreed the mate; " but did you ever, ever, ever hear such a caapital one ass the Captain? "

Sunny Jim had no sooner got the dishes cleaned from this informal meal than Para Handy went to him and commanded a speedy preparation of the breakfast.

" Right-oh! " said Sunny Jim; " I'll be able to tak' a job as a chef in yin o' thae Cunarders efter this. But I've naething else than tea and eggs."

" Weel, boil them! " said the Captain. " Keep on boilin' them! Things never look so black to a woman when she can get a cup o' tea, and an egg or two 'll no' go wrong wi' her. Efter that you'll maybe give us a tune on your melodeon—something nice and cheery, mind; none o' your laments; they're no' the thing at aal for a weedow woman goin' to the poorshouse."

It was a charming day; the sea was calm; the extraordinary high spirits of the crew of the *Vital Spark*
appeared to be contagious, and the widow confessed
she had never enjoyed a sail so much since the year
she had gone with Col on a trip to Rothesay.

" It's five-and-thirty years ago, and I never wass
there again," she added, just a little sadly.

" Faith, you should come wi' us to Ro'say," said
the Captain genially, and then regretted it.

" I canna," said the poor old body; " I'll never see
Ro'say again, for I'm goin' to Lochgilphead."

"And you couldna be goin' to a nicer place! "
declared Para Handy. " Lochgilpheid's chust sublime!
Dougie himsel' 'll tell you! "

" Salubrious! " said the mate. "And forbye, it's
that healthy! "

" There wass nothing wrong wi' Crarae," said the
widow pathetically, and Sunny Jim came to the rescue
with another pot of tea.

" Many a time I'll be thinking to mysel' yonder that
if I had a little money bye me, I would spend the rest
o' my days in Lochgilpheid," said Para Handy. " You
never saw a cheerier place——"

" Crarae wass very cheery, too—in the summer time
—when Col wass livin'," said the widow.

" Oh, but there's an aawful lot to see aboot Lochgilpheid; that's the place for Life! " said Para Handy.
"And such nice walks; there's—there's the road to
Kilmartin, and Argyll Street, full o' splendid shops;
and the steamers comin' to Ardrishaig, and every night
the mail goes bye to Crarae and Inveraray "—here his
knowledge of Lochgilphead's charms began to fail him.

" I didna think it would be so nice ass that," said

the widow, less dispiritedly. " I forgot aboot the mail; I'll aye be seein' it passin' to Crarae."

" Of course you will! " said Para Handy gaily; " that's a thing I wouldna miss, mysel'. And any time you take the notion, you'll can take a drive in the mail to Crarae if the weather's suitable."

" I would like it fine! " said the widow; " but—but maybe they'll no' let me. You would hear—you would hear where I wass goin' in Lochgilpheid? "

" I never heard a word! " protested Para Handy. " That minds me—will you have another egg? Jum, boil another egg for Mrs Maclachlan! "

" You hev been very kind," said the widow gratefully, as the *Vital Spark* came into Ardrishaig pier; " you couldna hev been kinder."

" I'm sorry you have to waalk to Lochgilpheid," said the Captain.

" Oh, I'm no' that old but I can manage the waalk," she answered; " I'm only seventy."

" Seventy! " said Para Handy, with genuine surprise; " I didna think you would be anything like seventy."

" I'll be seventy next Thursday," said the widow, and Para Handy whistled.

"And what in the world are you goin' to Lochgilpheid for?—the last place on God's earth, next to London. Efter Thursday next you'll can get your five shillin's a week in Crarae."

" Five shillin's a week in Crarae! " said the widow mournfully; " I hope I'll be ass weel off ass that when I get to heaven! "

" Then never mind aboot heaven the noo," said Para Handy, clapping her on the back; " go back to

Crarae wi' the *Minard*, and you'll get your pension regular every week—five shillin's."

" My pension! " said the widow, with surprise. " Fancy me wi' a pension; I never wass in the Airmy."

" Did nobody ever tell you that you wass entitled to a pension when they knew you were needin't? " asked the Captain, and the widow bridled.

" Nobody knew that I wass needin' anything," she exclaimed; " I took good care o' that."

.   .   .   .

Late that evening Mrs Maclachlan arrived at Crarae in the *Minard Castle* with a full knowledge for the first time of her glorious rights as an aged British citizen, and the balance of 8s. 6d. forced upon her by the mate, who had so opportunely remembered that he was due that sum to the lamented Col.

THE MAIDS OF BUTE

EVEN the captain of a steam lighter may feel the cheerful, exhilarating influence of spring, and Para Handy, sitting on an upturned pail, with his feet on a coil of rope, beiked himself in the sun and sang like a lintie—a rather croupy lintie. The song he sang was:

> " Blow ye winds aye-oh!
>   For it's roving I will go,
> I'll stay no more on England's shore,
> So let the music play.
> I'm off by the morning train,
> Across the raging main,
> I have booked a trup wi' a Government shup,
> Ten thousand miles away."

" Who's that greetin'? " asked the engineer maliciously, sticking his head out of the engine-room.

The Captain looked at him with contempt. " Nobody's greetin'," he said. " It's a thing you don't know anything at aal about; it's music. Away and read your novelles. What way's Lady Fitzgerald gettin' on wi' her new man? "

The engineer hastily withdrew.

" That's the way to settle him," said the Captain to Dougie and Sunny Jim. " Short and sweet! I could sing him blin'. Do ye know the way it iss that steamboat enchineers is aalways doon in the mooth like that? It's the want o' nature. They never let themselves go. Poor duvvles, workin' away among their bits o' enchines, they never get the wind and the sun aboot them right the same ass us seamen. If I wass always doon in a hole like that place o' Macphail's dabbin' my face wi' an oily rag aal day, I would maybe be ass ugly ass himsel'. Man, I'm feelin' fine! There's nothing like the spring o' the year, when you can get it like this. It's chust sublime! I'm feelin' ass strong ass a lion. I could pull the mast oot o' the boat and bate Brussels carpets wi' it."

" We'll pay for this yet," said Sunny Jim. " Ye'll see it'll rain or snow before night. What do ye say, Dougie? "

" Whatever ye think yoursel'," said Dougie.

"At this time o' the year," said the Captain, " I wish I wass back in MacBrayne's boats. The *Fital Spark* iss a splendid shup, the best in the tred, but there's no diversion. I wass the first man that ever pented the Maids o' Bute."

" Ye don't tell me! " exclaimed Dougie incredulously.

" I wass that," said Para Handy, as modestly as possible. " I'm not sayin' it for a bounce; the job might have come anybody's way, but I wass the man that got it. I wass a hand on the *Inveraray Castle* at the time. The Captain says to me wan day we were passin' the Maids—only they werena the Maids then; they hadna their clothes on—' Peter, what do you think o' them two stones on the hull-side? '

" ' They'll be there a long while before they're small enough to pap at birds wi',' says I.

" ' But do they no' put ye desperate in mind o' a couple o' weemen? ' said he.

" ' Not them! ' say I. ' I have been passin' here for fifteen years, and I never heard them taalkin' yet. If they were like weemen what would they be sittin' waitin' there for so long, and no' a man on the whole o' this side o' Bute? '

" ' Ay, but it's the look o' them,' said the Captain. ' If ye stand here and shut wan eye, they'll put ye aawfu' in mind o' the two MacFadyen gyurls up in Pennymore. I think we'll chust christen them the Maids o' Bute.'

" Well, we aalways caaled them the Maids o' Bute efter that, and pointed them oot to aal the passengers on the steamers. Some o' them said they were desperate like weemen, and others said they were chust like two big stones. The Captain o' the *Inveraray Castle* got quite wild at some passengers that said they werena a bit like weemen. ' That's the worst o' them English towerists,' he would say. ' They have no imachination. I could make myself believe them two stones wass a regiment o' sodgers if I put my mind to't. I'm sure the towerists might streetch a point the same ass other folk, and keep up the amusement.'

" Wan day the skipper came to me and says, 'Are ye on for a nice holiday, Peter?' It wass chust this time o' the year and weather like this, and I wass feelin' fine.

" ' No objections,' says I.

" ' Well,' he says, ' I wish you would go off at Tighnabruaich and take some pent wi' ye in a small boat over to the Maids, and give them a touch o' rud and white that'll make them more like weemen than ever.'

" ' I don't like,' said I.

" ' What way do ye no' like?' said the skipper. ' It's no' even what you would caal work; it's chust amusement! '

" ' But will it no' look droll for a sailor to be pentin' clothes on a couple o' stones, aal his lone by himsel' in the north end o' Bute, and no' a sowl to see him? Chust give it a think yersel', skipper; would it no' look awfu' daft? '

" ' I don't care if it looks daft enough for the Loch-gilphead Asylum, ye'll have to do it,' said the skipper. ' I'll put ye off at Tighnabruaich this efternoon; ye can go over and do the chob, and take a night's ludgin's in the toon, and we'll pick you up to-morrow when we're comin' doon. See you and make the Maids as smert as ye can, and, by Chove, they'll give the towerists a start! '

" Weel, I wass put off at Tighnabruaich, and the rud and white pent wi' me. I got ludgin's, took my tea and a herrin' to't, and rowed mysel' over in a boat to Bute. Some of the boys aboot the quay wass askin' what I wass efter, but it wassna likely I would tell them I wass goin' to pent clothes on the Maids o'

Bute; they would be sure to caal me the manta-maker efter it. So I chust said I wass going over to mark oot the place for a new quay MacBrayne wass buildin'. There's nothing like discretioncy.

"It wass a day that wass chust sublime! The watter wass that calm you could see your face in it, the birds were singing like hey-my-nanny, and the Kyles wass lovely. Two meenutes efter I started pentin' the Maids I wass singin' to mysel' like anything. Now I must let you ken I never had no education at drawin', and it's wonderful how fine I pented them. When you got close to them they were no more like rale maids than I am; ye wouldna take them for maids even in the dark, but before I wass done with them, ye would ask them up to dance. The only thing that vexed me wass that I had only the rud and white; if I had magenta and blue and yellow, and the like o' that, I could have made them far more stylish. I gave them white faces and rud frocks and bonnets, and man, man, it wass a splendid day!

"I took the notion in my heid that maybe the skipper o' the *Inveraray* wass right, and that they were maids at wan time, that looked back the same as Lot's wife in the Scruptures and got turned into stone. When I wassna singin', I would be speakin' away to them, and I'll assure ye it wass the first time maids never gave me any back chat. Wan o' them I called Mery efter— efter a gyurl I knew, and the other I called 'Lizabeth, for she chust looked like it. And it wass a majestic day. 'There ye are, gyurls,' I says to them, 'and you never had clothes that fitted better. Stop you, and if I'm spared till next year, you'll have the magenta too.' The north end o' Bute iss a bleak, wild, lonely place, but when I wass done pentin' the Maids it looked like a lerge population. They looked that nate and cheery among the heather! Mery had a waist ye could get your arm roond, but 'Lizabeth wass a broad, broad gyurl. And I wassna a bad-lookin' chap mysel'."

Here Para Handy stopped and sighed.

" Go on wi' your baur," said Dougie.

" Old times! old times! " said the Captain. " By Chove! I wass in trum that day! I never saw finer weather, nor nicer gyurls. Och! but it wass chust imachination; when we pass the Maids o' Bute now, I know they're only stones, with rud and white pent on them. They're good enough for towerists."

HERRING—A GOSSIP

" OF aal the fish there iss in the sea," said Para Handy, " nothing bates the herrin'; it's a providence they're plentiful and them so cheap! "

" They're no' in Loch Fyne, wherever they are," said Dougie sadly; " the only herrin' that they're gettin' there iss rud ones comin' up in barrels wi' the *Cygnet* or the *Minard Castle*. For five years back the trade wass desperate."

" I wouldna say but you're right," agreeably remarked the Captain. " The herrin' iss a great, great mystery. The more you will be catchin' of them the more there iss; and when they're no' in't at aal they're no' there "—a great philosophic truth which the crew smoked over in silence for a few minutes.

" When I wass a hand on the gabberts," continued the Captain, " the herrin' fishin' of Loch Fyne wass in its prime. You ken yoursel' what I mean; if you don't believe me, Jum, there's Dougie himsel' 'll tell you. Fortunes! chust simply fortunes! You couldna show your face in Tarbert then but a lot of the laads would gaither round at wance and make a jovial day of it. Wi' a barrel of nets in a skiff and a handy wife at the guttin', a man of the least agility could make enough in a month to build a land o' hooses, and the rale Loch Fyne was terrible namely over aal the world."

" I mind o't mysel'," said Sunny Jim; " they never sold onything else but the rale Loch Fyne in Gleska."

" They did that whether or no'," explained Para Handy, " for it wass the herrin's of Loch Fyne that had the reputation."

" I've seen the Rooshians eatin' them raw in the Baltic," said Macphail, the engineer, and Dougie shuddered. " Eating them raw! " said he; " the dirty duvvles! "

" The herrin' wass that thick in Loch Fyne in them days," recalled the Captain, " that you sometimes couldna get your anchor to the ground, and the quality was chust sublime. It wassna a tred at aal so much as an amusement; you went oot at night when the weans wass in their beds, and you had a couple o' cran on the road to Clyde in time for Gleska's breakfast. The quays wass covered wi' John O'Brian's boxes, and man alive! but the wine and spirit tred wass busy. Loch Fyne wass the place for Life in them days—high jeenks and big hauls; you werena very smert if you werena into both o' them. If you don't believe me, Dougie himsel' 'll tell you."

" You have it exact, Peter," guaranteed the mate, who was thus appealed to; " I wass there mysel'."

" Of course I have it exact," said Para Handy; " I'll
assure you it's no' a thing I read in the papers. To-day
there's no a herrin' in Loch Fyne or I'm mistaken."

" If there's wan he'll be kind o' lonely," said the
mate. " I wonder what in the muschief's wrong wi'
them? "

" You might shot miles o' nets for a month and
there's no' a herrin' will come near them."

" Man! aren't they the tumid, frightened idiots! "
said Dougie, with disgust.

" If ye ask me, I think whit spoiled the herrin' fishing
in Loch Fyne was the way they gaed on writin' aboot
it in the papers," said Macphail. " It was enough to
scunner ony self-respectin' fish. Wan day a chap
would write that it was the trawlers that were daein'
a' the damage; next day anither chap would say he
was a liar, and that trawlin' was a thing the herrin'
thrived on. Then a chap would write that there
should be a close time so as to gie the herrin' time to
draw their breaths for anither breenge into the nets;
and anither chap would write from Campbeltoon and
say a close time would be takin' the bread oot o' the
mooths o' his wife and weans. A scientific man said
herrin' came on cycles——"

" He's a liar, anyway," said the Captain, with conviction. " They were in Loch Fyne afore the cycle
was invented. Are you sure, Macphail, it's no' the
cod he means? "

" He said the herrin' fishin' aye missed some years
noo and then in a' the herrin' places in Europe as
weel's in Loch Fyne, and the Gulf Stream had something to dae wi't."

" That's the worst o' science," said the Captain

piously; " it takes aal the credit away from the
Creator. Don't you pay attention to an unfidel like
that; when the herrin' wass in Loch Fyne they stayed
there aal the time, and only maybe took a daunder oot
noo and then the length o' Ballantrae."

" If it's no' the Gulf Stream, then ye'll maybe tell
us whit it is? " said the engineer, with some annoyance.

" I'll soon do that," said Para Handy; " if you
want to ken, it's what I said—the herrin' iss a mystery,
chust a mystery! "

" I'm awfu' gled ye told me," said the engineer
ironically. " I aye wondered. Whit's the parteecular
mysteriousness aboot it? "

" It's a silly fish," replied the Captain; " it's fine
for eatin', but it hasna the sagacity. If it had the
sagacity it wouldna come lower than Otter Ferry, nor
be gallivantin' roond the Kyles o' Bute in daylight.
It's them innovations that's the death o' herrin'. If
the herrin' stayed in Loch Fyne attendin' to its business
and givin' the drift-net crews encouragement, it would
have a happier life and die respected.

" Whenever the herrin' of Loch Fyne puts his nose
below Kilfinan, his character is gone. First the Tarbert
trawlers take him oot to company and turn his heid;
then there iss nothing for it for him but flying trips to
the Kyles o' Bute, the Tail o' the Bank, and Gareloch.
In Loch Fyne we never would touch the herrin' in the
daytime, nor in winter; they need a rest, forbye we're
none the worse o' one oorsel's; but the folk below
Kilfinan have no regard for Chrustian principles, and
they no sooner see an eye o' fish than they're roond
aboot it with trawls, even if it's the middle o' the day
or New-Year's mornin'. They never give the fish a

chance; they keep it on the run till its fins get hot.
If it ventures ass far ass the Tail o' the Bank, it gets
that dizzy wi' the sight o' the shippin' traffic that it
loses the way and never comes back to Loch Fyne
again. A silly fish! If it only had sagacity! Amn't
I right, Dougie? "

" Whatever you say yoursel', Captain; there's wan
thing sure, the herrin's scarce."

" The long and the short of it iss that they're a
mystery," concluded Para Handy.

TO CAMPBELTOWN BY SEA

" MAN, it's hot; most desperate hot! " said Para
Handy, using his hand like a squeegee to remove the
perspiration from his brow. " Life in weather like
thiss iss a burden; a body might ass weel be burnin'
lime or at the bakin'. I wish I wass a fush."

The *Vital Spark* was lying at Skipness, the tar boiling
between her seams in unusually ardent weather, and
Macphail on deck, with a horror of his own engine-
room.

" Bein' a fush wouldna be bad," said Dougie, " if
it wass not for the constant watter. The only thing
you can say for watter iss that it's wet and fine for
sailin' boats on. If you were a fush, Captain, you
would die of thirst."

> " Watter, watter everywhere,
>   And not a single drop of drink,"

quoted the engineer, who was literary.

The Captain looked at him with some annoyance.
" It's bad enough, Macphail," said he, " withoot you

harpin', harpin' on the thing. You have no consuderation! I never mentioned drink. I wass thinkin'
of us plowterin' doon in weather like this to Campbeltown, and wishin' I could swim."

" Can you no' swim? " asked Sunny Jim with some
surprise.

" I daresay I could, but I never tried," said Para
Handy. " I had never the time, havin' aye to attend
to my business."

" Swimmin's aal the rage chust now," remarked
Dougie, who occasionally read a newspaper. " Look
at the Thames in London—there's men and women
swimmin' it in droves; they'll do six or seven miles
before their breakfast. And the Straits o' Dover's
busy wi' splendid swimmers makin' their way to
France."

" What are they wantin' to France for? " asked Para
Handy. " Did they do anything? "

" I wouldna say," replied the mate; " it's like
enough the polis iss efter them, but the story they have
themsel's iss that they're swimmin' for a wudger. The
best this season iss a Gleska man caaled Wolffe; he
swam that close to France the other day he could hear
the natives taalkin'."

" What for did he no' land? " asked Sunny Jim.

" I canna tell," said Dougie, " but it's likely it would
be wan o' the places where they charge a penny at the
quay. Him bein' a Gleska man, he would see them
d——d first, so he chust came back to Dover."

" I don't see the fun of it, mysel'," said Para Handy
reflectively. " But of course, if it's a wudger——"

" That's what I'm throng tellin' you," said the mate.
" It looks a terrible task, but it's simple enough for

any man with the agility. First you put off your clo'es
and leave them in the shippin'-box at Dover if you
have the confidence. Then you oil yoursel' wi' oil,
put on a pair o' goggles, and get your photygraph.
When the crood's big enough you kiss the wife good-bye
and start swimmin' like anything."

" Whit wife? " asked the engineer, whose profound
knowledge of life as depicted in penny novelettes had
rendered him dubious of all adventures designed to
end in France.

" Your own wife, of course," said Para Handy
impatiently. " What other wife would a chap want to
leave and go to France for? Go on wi' your story,
Dougie."

" Three steamers loaded wi' beef-tea, champagne,
chocolate, and pipers follows you aal the way——"

" Beef-tea and chocolate! " exclaimed the Captain,
with astonishment. " What's the sense o' that? Are
you sure it's beef-tea, Dougie? "

" I read it mysel' in the papers," the mate assured
him. " You strike out aalways wi' a firm, powerful,
over-hand stroke, and whenever you're past the heid
o' Dover quay you turn on your back, take your
luncheon oot of a bottle, and tell the folk on the
steamers that you're feelin' fine."

" You might well be feelin' fine, wi' a luncheon oot
o' a bottle," said Para Handy. " It's the beef-tea that
bothers me."

"Aal the time the pipers iss standin' on the paiddle-
boxes o' the steamers playin' ' Hielan' Laddie ' and
' The Campbells iss Comin'.' "

"Aal the time! " repeated Para Handy. " I don't
believe wan word of it! Not aboot pipers; take my

word for it, Dougie, they'll be doon below noo and then; there's nothing in this world thirstier than music."

" Do they no' get ony prizes for soomin' a' that distance? " asked Sunny Jim.

" I'll warrant you there must be money in it some way," said the engineer. " Whatever side they land on, they'll put roond the hat. There's naething the public 'll pay you quicker or better for, than for daein' wi' your legs what an engine 'll dae faur better."

" I could soom ony o' them blin'! " said Sunny Jim. " I was the natest wee soomer ever Geordie Geddes dragged by the hair o' the heid frae the Clyde at Jenny's Burn. Fair champion! Could we no' get up a soom frae here to Campbeltown the morn, and mak' a trifle at the start and feenish? "

" Man! you couldna swim aal that distance," said the Captain. " It would take you a week and a tug to tow you."

" I'm no' daft," explained Sunny Jim; " the hale thing's in the startin', for seemin'ly naebody ever feenishes soomin' ower to France. A' I hae to dae is to ile mysel' and dive, and the *Vital Spark* can keep me company into Kilbrannan Sound."

" There's the photygraphs, and the beef-tea, and the pipers," said the engineer; " unless ye hae them ye micht as well jist walk to Campbeltown."

" Dougie can play his trump, and that'll dae instead o' the pipers," said Sunny Jim. " It's a' in the start. See? I'll jump in at the quay, and you'll collect the money from the Skipness folk, and pick me up whenever they're oot o' sicht. I'll dae the dive again afore we come into Campbeltown, and Dougie 'll haud the watch and gie a guarantee I swam the hale length o'

K

Kintyre in four oors and five-and-twenty minutes. Then—bizz!—bang!—roon' the folk in Campbeltown wi' the bonny wee hat again! See? "

" Man! your cluverness is chust sublime! " said Para Handy; " we'll have the demonstration in the mornin'."

The intelligence that the cook of the *Vital Spark* was to swim to Campbeltown found Skipness curiously indifferent. " If he had been swimming FROM Campbeltown it might be different," said the natives; so the attempts to collect a subscription in recognition of the gallant feat were poorly recognised and Sunny Jim, disgusted, quitted the water, and resumed his clothes on the deck of the vessel less than a hundred yards from the shore. The *Vital Spark* next day came into Campbeltown, and the intrepid swimmer, having quietly dropped over the side at not too great a distance, swam in the direction of the quay, at which he arrived with no demonstration of excitement on the part of the population.

" Swam aal the way from Skipness," Para Handy informed the curious; " we're raisin' a little money to encourage him; he's none of your Dover Frenchmen, but wan of Brutain's hardy sons. Whatever you think yoursel's in silver, chentlemen."

" Wass he in the watter aal the time? " asked a native fisherman, copiously perspiring under a couple of guernseys and an enormous woollen comforter.

" He wass that! " Para Handy assured him. " If you don't believe me, Dougie himsel' 'll tell you."

" Then he wass the lucky chap! " said the native enviously. " It must have been fine and cool. What's he goin' to stand? "

HOW TO BUY A BOAT

IT was shown in a former escapade of Para Handy's that he wasn't averse from a little sea-trout poaching. He justified this sport in Gaelic, always quoting a proverb that a switch from the forest, a bird from the hill, or a fish from the river were the natural right of every Highland gentleman. Sunny Jim approved the principle most heartily, and proposed to insert a clause including dogs, of which he confessed he had been a great admirer and collector in his Clutha days. Ostensibly the Captain never fished for anything but flounders, and his astonishment when he came on seatrout or grilse in his net after an hour's assiduous plashing with it at the mouth of a burn was charming to witness.

" Holy smoke! " he would exclaim, scratching his ears, " here's a wheen o' the white fellows, and us chust desperate for cod. It's likely they're the Duke's or Mr Younger's, and they lost their way to Bullingsgate. Stop you! Dougie, a meenute and hand me up a fut-spar. . . . I'm sure and I wassna wantin' them, but there they are, and what can you make of it? They might be saithe; it's desperate dark the night; what a peety we didna bring a lantern. Look and see if you divna think they're saithe, Dougie."

" Whatever you say yoursel'," was the mate's unvarying decision, and it could never be properly made out whether the fish were saithe or salmon till the crew had eaten them.

There was one favourite fishing bank of the Captain's inconveniently close to the county police station.

The constable was very apt to find a grilse on the inside handle of his coal-cellar door on mornings when the *Vital Spark* was in the harbour, and he, also, was much surprised, but never mentioned it, except in a roundabout way, to Para Handy.

" You must be makin' less noise oot in the bay at night," he would say to him. " By Chove! I could hear you mysel' last night quite plain; if you're not more caatious I'll have to display my activity and find a clue."

It was most unfortunate that the men of the *Vital Spark* should have come on a shoal of the " white fellows " one early morning when the river-watchers were in straits to justify their job. The lighter's punt, with an excellent net and its contents, had hurriedly to be abandoned, and before breakfast the Captain had lodged a charge of larceny against parties unknown at the police station. Some one had stolen his punt, he said, cutting the painter of her during the calm and virtuous sleep of self and mates. He identified the boat in the possession of the river-bailiffs; he was horrified to learn of the nefarious purpose to which it had been applied, but had to submit with curious equanimity to its confiscation. Local sympathy was aroused—fostered unostentatiously by the policeman; a subscription sheet was passed round the village philanthropists—also on the discreet suggestion of the policeman; and the sum of two pounds ten and ten-pence was collected—the tenpence being in ha'pence ingeniously abstracted by means of a table-knife from a tin bank in the possession of the policeman's only boy.

" You will go at wance to Tighnabruaich and buy yourself another boat, Peter," said the policeman, when informally handing over the money. "If you are circumspect and caautious you'll pick up a smert one chape that will serve for your requirements."

"I wouldna touch a penny," protested Para Handy, "if it wass not for my vessel's reputation; she needs a punt to give her an appearance."

A few days later the *Vital Spark* came into Tighnabruaich, and the Captain, by apparent accident, fell into converse with a hirer of rowing-boats.

"Man, you must be coinin' money," he said innocently; "you have a lot of boats."

"Coinin' money!" growled the boat-hirer; "no' wi' weather like this. I micht be makin' mair at hirin' umbrellas."

"Dear me!" said the Captain sympathetically, "that's a peety. A tidy lot o' boats, the most o' them; it's a wonder you would keep so many, and tred so bad."

"You werena thinkin' maybe o' buyin', were ye?" asked the boat-hirer suspiciously, with a look at the stern of the *Vital Spark*, where the absence of a punt was manifest.

"No," said the Captain blandly, "boats iss a luxury them days; they're lucky that doesna need them. Terrible weather! And it's goin' to be a dirty summer; there's a man yonder in America that prophesies we'll have rain even-on till Martinmas. Rowin'-boats iss goin' chape at Millport."

"If that's the look-out, they'll be goin' chape everywhere," incautiously remarked the boat-hirer.

"Chust that," said Para Handy, and made as if to move away. Then he stopped, and, with his hands in his pockets, pointed with a contemptuous foot at a

dinghy he had had an eye on from the start of the conversation. " There's wan I aalways wondered at you
keepin', Dan," said he; " she's a prutty old stager,
I'll be bound you."

" That! " exclaimed the boat-hirer. " That's the
tidiest boat on the shore; she 's a genuine Erchie
Smith."

" Iss she, iss she? " said the Captain. " I mind her
the year o' the Jubilee; it's wonderful the way they
hold thegither. A bad crack in her bottom strake;
you wouldna be askin' much for her if a buyer wass
here wi' ready money? "

" Are ye wantin' a boat? " asked the boat-hirer
curtly, coming to the point.

" Not what you would caal exactly," said the
Captain, " but if she's in the market I might maybe
hear aboot a customer. What did you say wass the
figure? "

" Three pound ten, and a thief's bargain," said the
boat-hirer promptly, and Para Handy dropped at his
feet the pipe he was filling.

" Excuse me startin'! " he remarked sarcastically,
" you gave me a fright. It wass not about a schooner
yat I was inquirin'."

" She's worth every penny o't, and a guid deal mair,"
said the boat-hirer, and Para Handy lit his pipe
deliberately and changed the subject.

" There's a great run on them motors," he remarked,
indicating one of the launches in the bay. " My friend
that iss wantin' a boat iss——"

" I thocht ye said ye werena wantin' ony kind o'
boat at a'," interjected the boat-hirer.

" Chust that; but there wass a chentleman that

spoke to me aboot a notion he had for a smaal boat;
he will likely take a motor wan; they're aal the go.
That swuft! They're tellin' me they're doin' aal the
hirin' tred in Ro'sa' and Dunoon; there'll soon no'
be a rowin'-boat left. If I wass you I would clear oot
aal the trash and start a wheen o' motors."

"A motor wad be nae use for the *Vital Spark*," said
the boat-hirer, who had no doubt now he had met a
buyer. " Hoo much are ye prepared to offer? "

" What for? " said Para Handy innocently, spitting
on the desirable dinghy, and then apologetically wiping
it with his hand.

" For this boat. Say three pounds. It's a bargain."

" Oh, for this wan! I wouldna hurt your feelings,
but if I wass wantin' a boat I wouldna take this wan
in a gift. Still and on, a boat iss a handy thing for
them that needs it; I'm not denyin' it. I'll mention it
to the other chentleman."

" Wha is he? " asked the boat-hirer, and Para Handy
screwed up his eyes, and was rapt in admiration of
the scenery of the Kyles.

" What you don't know you don't ken," he replied
mysteriously.

" Ye couldna get a better punt for the money if ye
searched the Clyde," said the boat-hirer.

" I'm no' in any hurry; I'll take a look aboot for
something aboot two pound ten," said Para Handy.
" Ye canna get a first-class boat a penny cheaper. I
got the offer of a topper for the forty shillings, and
I'm consuderin' it." He had now thrown off all disguise, and come out in the open frankly as a buyer.

" Ye shouldna consider ower lang, then," said the
boat-hirer; " there's a lot o' men in the market the

noo for handy boats o' this cless; I have an offer
mysel' o' two pounds fifteen for this very boat no later
gone than yesterday, and I'm hangin' oot for the three
pounds. I believe I'll get it; he's comin' back this
afternoon."

" Chust that! " said Para Handy, winking to himself. " I'm sure and I wish him weel wi' his bargain.
She looks as if she would be terrible cogly."

" Is Tighnabruaich quay cogly? " asked the boat-
hirer indignantly. " Ye couldna put her over if ye
tried."

"And they tell me she has a rowth," continued Para
Handy, meaning thereby a bias under oars.

" They're liars, then," said the boat-hirer; " I'll sell
ye her for two pound twelve to prove it."

The Captain buttoned up his jacket, and said it was
time he was back to business.

"A fine boat," pleaded the boat-hirer. " Two pairs
o' oars, a pair o' galvanised rowlocks, a bailin' dish,
and a painter—dirt chape! take it or leave it."

" Would you no' be chenerous and throw in the
plug? " said the Captain, with his finest irony.

" I'll dae better than that," said the boat-hirer. " I'll
fling in a nice bit hand-line."

" For two pound ten, I think you said."

"Twa pound twelve," corrected the boat-hirer.
" Come now, don't be stickin'."

"At two pounds twelve I'll have to consult my frien'
the chentleman I mentioned," said the Captain; " and
I'll no' be able to let you know for a week or two. At
two pounds ten I would risk it, and it's chust the money
I have on me."

" Done, then! " said the boat-hirer. " The boat's

yours," and they went to the hotel to seal the bargain.

The boat-hirer was going home with his money when he heard the Captain stumping hurriedly after. "Stop a meenute, Dan," he said; "I forgot to ask if you haven't a bit of a net you might throw in, chust for the sake o' frien'ship?"

.   .   .   .

The boat-hirer confessed to his wife that he had made ten shillings profit on the sale of a boat he had bought for forty shillings and had three seasons out of.

Para Handy swopped the dinghy a fortnight later in Tarbert for a punt that suited the *Vital Spark* much better, and thirty shillings cash. With part of the thirty shillings he has bought another net. For flounders.

THE STOWAWAY

" DID you ever, ever, in your born days, see such umpidence?" said the mate of the smartest boat in the coasting trade, looking up from his perusal of a scrap of newspaper in which the morning's kippers had been brought aboard by Sunny Jim.

"What iss't, Dougald?" asked the Captain, sitting down on a keg to put on his carpet slippers, a sign that the day of toil on deck officially was over. "You'll hurt your eyes, there, studyin' in the dark. You're gettin' chust ass bad ass the enchineer for readin'; we'll have to put in the electric light for you."

"Chermans!" said Dougie. "The country's crooded

K 2

wi' them. They're goin' aboot disguised ass towerists, drawin' plans o' forts and brudges."

" Now, issn't that most desperate! " said Para Handy, poking up the fo'c'sle stove, by whose light his mate had been reading this disquieting intelligence. " That's the way that British tred iss ruined. First it wass Cherman clocks, and then it wass jumpin'-jecks, and noo it's picture post-cairds."

" Criftens! " said Sunny Jim, who had come hurriedly down to put on a second waistcoat, for the night was cold: " Whit dae ye think they're makin' the drawin's for? "

" Iss't no' for post-cairds? " asked the Captain innocently, and the cook uproariously laughed.

" Post-cairds my auntie! " he vulgarly exclaimed. " It's for the German Airmy. As soon's they can get their bits o' things thegither, they're comin' ower here to fight us afore the Boy Scouts gets ony bigger. They hae spies a' ower Britain makin' maps; I'll lay ye there's no' a beer-shop in the country that they havena dotted doon."

" Holy smoke! " said Para Handy.

He watched the very deliberate toilet of Sunny Jim with some impatience. " Who's supposed to be at the wheel at this parteecular meenute? " he asked, with apparent unconcern.

" Me," said Sunny Jim. " There's naething in sicht, and I left it a meenute just to put on this waistcoat. Ye're gettin' awfu' pernicketty wi' your wheel; it's no' the *Lusitania*."

" I'm no' findin' faault at aal, at aal, Jum, but I'm chust considerin'," said the Captain meekly. " Take your time. Don't hurry, Jum. Would you no' give your hands a wash and put on a collar? It's always nice to have a collar on and be looking spruce if you're drooned in a collusion. Give a kind of a roar when you get up on deck if you see we're runnin' into anything."

"Collusion!" said Sunny Jim contemptuously. "Wi' a' the speed this boat can dae, she couldna run into a pend close if it started rainin'," and he swung himself on deck.

" He hasna the least respect for the vessel," said the Captain sadly. " She might be a common gaabert for aal the pride that Jum hass in her."

The *Vital Spark* had left Loch Ranza an hour ago, and was puffing across the Sound of Bute for the Garroch Head on her way to Glasgow. A pitch-black night, not even a star to be seen, and Sunny Jim at the wheel had occasionally a feeling that the Cumbrae Light for which he steered was floating about in space, detached from everything like a fire-balloon that winked every thirty seconds at the sheer delight of being free. He whistled softly to himself, and still very cold, in spite of his second waistcoat, envied Macphail the engineer, whom he could see in the grateful warmth of the furnace-door reading a penny novelette. Except for the wheeze and hammer of the engine, the propeller's churning, and the wash of the calm sea at the snub nose of the vessel, the night was absolutely still.

The silence was broken suddenly by sounds of vituperation from the fo'c'sle: the angry voices of the Captain and the mate, and a moment later they were on deck pushing a figure aft in front of them. " Sling us up a lamp, Macphail, to see what iss't we have a haad o' here," said the Captain hurriedly, with a grasp

on the stranger's coat-collar, and the engineer produced the light. It shone on a burly foreigner with
coal-black hair, a bronze complexion, and a sack of
onions to which he clung with desperate tenacity.

" Got him in Dougie's bunk, sound sleepin',"
explained the Captain breathlessly, with the tone of
an entomologist who has found a surprising moth.
" I saw him dandering aboot Loch Ranza in the
mornin'. A stowaway! He wants to steal a trip to
Gleska."

" I'll bate ye he's gaun to the Scottish Exhibeetion,"
said Sunny Jim. " We'll be there in time, but his
onions 'll gang wrang on him afore we get to Bowlin'.
Whit dae they ca' ye for your Christian name,
M'Callum? "

" Onions," replied the stranger. " Cheap onions.
No Ingles."

" Oh, come aff it! come aff it! We're no' such neds
as to think that ony man could hae a Christian name
like Onions," said Sunny Jim. " Try again, and tell
us it's Clarence."

"And what iss't your wantin' on my boat? " asked
Para Handy sternly.

The foreigner looked from one to the other of them
with large pathetic eyes from under a broad Basque
bonnet. " Onions. Cheap onions," he repeated,
extracting a bunch of them hastily from the bag.
" Two bob. Onions."

" Gie the chap a chance," said Sunny Jim ironically.
"Maybe he gie'd his ticket up to the purser comin' in."

" He hasna a word o' English in his heid," said
Dougie. " There's something at the bottom o't; stop
you, and you'll see! It's no' for his health he's traivel-

lin' aboot Arran wi' a bag o' onions, and hidin' himsel'
on board a Christian boat. I'll wudger that he's
Cherman."

" It's no a German kep he's wearin' onyway," said
Macphail, with the confidence of a man who has
travelled extensively and observed.

" That's a disguise," said Dougie, no less confidently. " You can see for yoursel' he hass even
washed himsel'. Try him wi' a bit of the Cherman
lingo, Macphail, and you'll see the start he'll get."

Macphail, whose boast had always been that he
could converse with fluency in any language used in
any port in either hemisphere, cleared his throat and
hesitatingly said, " Parly voo Francis? "

" Onions. Cheap onions," agreeably replied the
stranger.

" Francis! Francis! Parly voo? " repeated the
engineer, testily and loudly, as if the man were deaf.

" Maybe his name's no' Francis," suggested Sunny
Jim. " Try him wi' Will Helm, or Alphonso; there's
lots o' them no' called Francis."

" He understands me fine, I can see by his eye,"
said the engineer, determined to preserve his reputation
as a linguist. " But, man! he's cunnin'."

" It's the wrong shup he hass come to if he thinks
he iss cunnin' enough for us! " said the Captain firmly.
" It's the jyle in Greenock that we'll clap him in for
breakin' on board of a well-known steamboat and
spoilin' Dougald's bunk wi' onions."

The stowaway sat nonchalantly down on a bucket,
produced a knife and a hunk of bread, and proceeded
to make a meal of it with onions. Immediately the
crew was constituted into a court-martial, and treated

the presence of their captive as if he were a deaf-mute
or a harmless species of gorilla.

" What wass I tellin' you, Captain, at the very
meenute I saw his feet stickin' oot o' my bunk? "
inquired the mate. " The country's overrun wi'
Chermans. I wass readin' yonder that there's two
hunder and fifty thousand o' them in Brutain."

" What a lot! " said Para Handy. " I never set eyes
on wan o' them to my knowledge. What are they like,
the silly duvvles? "

" They're chust like men that would be sellin'
onions," said Dougie. " Lerge, big, heavy fellows like
oor frien' here; and they never say nothing to nobody.
You've seen hunders o' them though you maybe didna
ken. They're Chermans that plays the bands on the
river steamers."

" Are they? are they? " said Para Handy with surprise; " I always thought yon chaps wass riveters, or
brassfeenishers, that chust made a chump on board the
boat wi' their instruments when she wass passin' Yoker
and the purser's back wass turned."

" Germans to a man! " said Sunny Jim. " There's
no' a Scotchman among them; ye never saw yin o'
them yet the worse o' drink."

" Ye needna tell me yon chaps playin' awa' on the
steamers iss makin' maps," said Para Handy. " Their
eyes iss aalways glued on their cornucopias."

" They're goin' aboot ports and forts and battle-
ships drawin' plans," said the engineer. " Whit did
the Royal Horse Artillery find the ither day at Ports-
mouth? Yin o' them crawlin' up a gun to mak' a
drawin' o't, and they had to drag him oot by the feet."

" Chust that! " said Para Handy, regarding their

captive with greater interest. " I can see mysel' noo;
he looks desperate like a Cherman. Do you think he
wass makin' plans o' the *Vital Spark*? "

" That's whit I was askin' him in German! " said
Macphail, " and ye saw yersel's the suspicious way he
never answered."

" Jum," said the Captain, taking the wheel himself,
" away like a smert laad and make up a cup o' tea for
the chap; it's maybe the last he'll ever get if we put
him in the jyle in Greenock or in Gleska."

" Right-oh! " said Sunny Jim, gladly relinquishing
the wheel. " Will I set the table oot in the fore saloon?
Ye'll excuse us bein' short o' floral decorations,
Francis? Is there onything special ye would like in
the way o' black breid or horse-flesh, and I'll order't
frae the steward? "

" Onions," said the stranger.

The foreigner spent the night imprisoned in the hold
with the hatches down, and wakened with an excellent
appetite for breakfast, while the vessel lay at a wharf
on the upper river.

" There's money in't; it's like a salvage," Dougie
said to Para Handy, as they hurried ashore for a
policeman.

" I canna see't," said the Captain dubiously.
" What's the good o' a Cherman? If he wass a neegur
bleck, you could sell him to the shows for swallowin'
swords, but I doot that this chap hassna got the right
agility."

" Stop, you! " said the mate with confidence. " The
Government iss desperate keen to get a haad o' them,
and here's Mackay the polisman."

" We have a kind o' a Cherman spy on board,"

he informed the constable, who seemed quite uninterested.

"The Sanitary Depairtment iss up in John Street," said the constable. "It's not on my bate." But he consented to come to the *Vital Spark* and see her stowaway.

"Toots, man! he's no' a Cherman, and he's no' a spy," he informed them at a glance.

"And what iss he then?" asked the Captain.

"I don't ken what he iss, but he's duvvelish like a man that would be sellin' onions," said Mackay, and on his advice the suspect was released.

It was somewhat later in the day that Dougie missed his silver watch, which had been hanging in the fo'c'sle.

CONFIDENCE

THE Captain of the *Vital Spark* and his mate were solemnly drinking beer in a Greenock public-house, clad in their best shore-going togs, for it was Saturday. Another customer came in—a bluff, high-coloured, English-spoken individual with an enormous watch-chain made of what appeared to be mainly golden nuggets in their natural state, and a ring with a diamond bulging out so far in it that he could hardly get his hand into his trousers pocket. He produced a wad of bank-notes, peeled one off, put it down on the counter with a slap, and demanded gin and ginger.

"A perfect chentleman!" said Para Handy to his mate in a whisper; "you can aalways tell them! He'll likely have a business somewhere."

The opulent gentleman took his glass of gin and

ginger to a table and sat down, lit a cigar, and proceeded to make notes in a pocket-book.

" That's the worst of wealth," said Dougie philo-
sophically; " you have to be aalways tottin' it up in
case you forget you have it. Would you care for
chust another, Peter? I think I have a shullin'."

Another customer came in—apparently a seaman,
with a badge of a well-known shipping line on his cap.

" Hello, bully boys! " he said heartily. " Gather
around; there's a letter from home! What are we
going to have? In with your pannikins, lively now,
and give it a name," and he ordered glasses round,
excluding the auriferous gentleman who was taking
notes behind.

" Looks like a bloomin' Duke! " he remarked in an
undertone to Para Handy. " One of them ship-
owners, likely; cracker-hash and dandy-funk for Jack,
and chicken and champagne wine for Mister Bloomin'
Owner! Ours is a dog's life, sonnies, but I don't care
now, I'm home from Callao! "

" Had you a good trup? " asked Para Handy, with
polite anxiety.

" Rotten! " said the seaman tersely. " What's your
line? Longshore, eh? " and he scrutinised the crew of
the *Vital Spark*.

" Chust that! " said Para Handy mildly. " Perusin'
aboot the Clyde wi' coals and doin' the best we can."

" Then I hope the hooker's your own, my boy, for
there's not much bloomin' money in it otherwise,"
said the seaman; and Para Handy, not for the first
time, fell a victim to his vanity.

" Exactly," he said, with a pressure on the toe of
Dougie's boot; " I'm captain and owner too; the

smertest boat in the tred," and he jingled a little change he had in his pocket.

"My name's Tom Wilson," volunteered the seaman. "First mate of the *Wallaby*, with an extra master's papers, d——n your eyes! And I've got five-and-twenty bloomin' quids in my pocket this very moment; look at that!" He flourished a wad of notes that was almost as substantial as the one displayed a little before by the gentleman with the nugget watch-chain.

"It's a handy thing to have aboot ye," said Para Handy sagely, jingling his coppers eloquently. "But I aalways believe in gold mysel'; you're not so ready to lose it."

"I've noticed that mysel'," said Dougie solemnly.

Tom Wilson ordered another round, and produced a watch which he confidently assured them was the finest watch of its kind that money could buy. It had an alarm bell, and luminous paint on the hands and dial permitted you to see the time on the darkest night without a light.

"Well, well! issn't that cluver!" exclaimed Para Handy. "They'll be makin' them next to boil a cup o' tea. It would cost a lot o' money? I'm no' askin', mind you; I wass chust remarkin'."

"Look here!" cried Tom Wilson impulsively; "I'll give the bloomin' clock to the very first man who can guess what I paid for it."

"Excuse me, gentlemen," said the man with the nugget watch-chain, putting away his note-book and pencil. "I'd like to see that watch," and they joined him at the table, where he generously ordered another round. He gravely examined the watch, and guessed that it cost about twenty pounds.

" Yes, but you must mention the exact figure," said its owner.

" Well, I guess two-and-twenty sovereigns," said the other, and Tom Wilson hastily proceeded to divest himself of the chain to which it had been originally attached. " It's yours! " he said; " you've guessed it, and you may as well have the bloomin' chain as well. That's the sort of sunny boy I am! " and he beamed upon the company with the warmth of one whose chief delight in life was to go round distributing costly watches.

" Wass I not chust goin' to say twenty-two pounds! " said Para Handy with some chagrin.

" I knew it wass aboot that," said Dougie; " chenuine gold! "

The lucky winner of the watch laughed, put it into his pocket, and took out the wad of notes, from which he carefully counted out twenty-two pounds, which he thrust upon Tom Wilson.

" There you are! " he said; " I wouldn't take your watch for nothing, and it happens to be the very kind of watch I've been looking for."

" But you have only got my word for it, Mister, that it's worth that money," protested Mr Wilson.

The stranger smiled. " My name's Denovan," he remarked; " I'm up here from Woolwich on behalf of the Admiralty to arrange for housin' the torpedo workers in first-rate cottage homes with small back gardens. What does the Lords o' the Admiralty say to me? The Lords o' the Admiralty says to me, ' Mr Denovan, you go and fix up them cottage homes, and treat the people of Greenock with confidence.' I'm a judge of men, I am, bein' what I am, and the principle

I go on is to trust my fellow-men. If you say two-
and-twenty pounds is the value of this watch, I say
two-and-twenty it is, and there's an end of it!"

Mr Wilson reluctantly put the notes in his pocket,
with an expression of the highest admiration for Mr
Denovan's principles, and Para Handy experienced the
moral stimulation of being in an atmosphere of
exceptional integrity and unlimited wealth. "Any wan
could see you were the perfect chentleman," he confessed to Mr Denovan, ducking his head at him.
" What way are they aal keepin' in Woolwich?"

" I took you for a bloomin' ship-owner at first,"
said Mr Wilson. " I didn't think you had anything to
do with the Admiralty."

" I'm its right-hand man," replied Mr Denovan
modestly. " If you're thinkin' of a nice cottage home
round here with front plot and small back garden, I
can put you in, as a friend, for one at less than half
what anybody else would pay."

" I haven't any use for a bloomin' house unless there
was a licence to it," said Mr Wilson cheerfully.

Mr Denovan looked at him critically. " I like the
look of you," he remarked impressively. " I'm a judge
of men, and just to back my own opinion of you, I'll
put you down right off for the first of the Admiralty
houses. You needn't take it; you could sell it at a
profit of a hundred pounds to-morrow; I don't ask
you to give me a single penny till you have made your
profit," and Mr Denovan, producing his pocket-book,
made a careful note of the transaction lest he might
forget it. " ' Treat the people of Greenock with confidence,' says the Lords of the Admiralty to me; now,
just to show my confidence in you, I'll hand you back

your watch, and my own watch, and you can go away with them for twenty minutes."

"All right, then; just for a bloomin' lark," agreed Tom Wilson, and with both watches and the colossal nugget-chain, he disappeared out of the public-house.

"That's a fine, smart, honest-lookin', manly fellow!" remarked Mr Denovan admiringly.

" Do you think he'll come back wi' the watches? " said Dougie dubiously.

" Of course he will," replied Mr Denovan. "Trust men, and they'll trust you. I'll lay you a dollar he would come back if he had twenty watches and all my money as well."

This opinion was justified. Mr Wilson returned in less than five minutes, and restored the watches to their owner.

" Well, I'm jeegered! " said Para Handy, and ordered another round out of admiration for such astounding honesty.

" Would you trust me? " Mr Denovan now asked Tom Wilson.

" I would," said the seaman heartily. " Look here; I've five-and-twenty bloomin' quid, and I'll let you go out and walk the length of the railway station with them."

" Done! " said Mr Denovan, and possessed of Wilson's roll of notes, went out of the public-house.

" Peter," said Dougie to the Captain, " do you no' think one of us should go efter him chust in case there's a train for Gleska at the railway station? "

But Tom Wilson assured them he had the utmost confidence in Mr Denovan, who was plainly a tip-top gentleman of unlimited financial resources, and his confidence was justified, for Mr Denovan not only returned with the money, but insisted on adding a couple of pounds to it as a recognition of Mr Wilson's sporting spirit.

" I suppose you Scotch chaps don't have any confidence? " said Mr Denovan to the Captain.

"Any amount! " said Para Handy.

" Well, just to prove it," said Mr Denovan, " would you be willin' to let our friend Wilson here, or me, go out with a five-pound note of yours? "

" I havena the five pounds here, but I have it in the boat," said the Captain. " If Dougie'll wait here, I'll go down for it. Stop you, Dougie, with the chentlemen."

.   .   .   .

Some hours later Dougie turned up on the *Vital Spark* to find the Captain in his bunk, and sound asleep.

" I thocht you were comin' wi' a five-pound note? " he remarked on wakening him. " The chentlemen waited, and better waited, yonder on you, and they werena pleased at aal, at aal. They said you surely hadna confidence."

" Dougie," said the Captain, " I have the greatest confidence, but I have the five pounds, too. And if you had any money in your pocket it's no' with Mr Denovan I would leave you."

THE GOAT

PARA HANDY, having listened with amazement to the
story of the Stepney battle read by the engineer,
remarked, " If it wassna in print, Macphail, I wouldna
believe it! They must be desperate powerful men, them
Rooshian burgulars. Give us yon bit again aboot Sir
Wunston Churchill."

" ' The Right Honourable gentleman, at the close of
the engagement, went up a close and shook 127 bullets
out of his Astrakan coat,' " repeated Macphail, who
always added a few picturesque details of his own
invention to any newspaper narrative.

" It was 125 you said last time," Para Handy pointed
out suspiciously.

" My mistake! " said Macphail frankly; " I thocht
it was a five at first, but I see noo it's a seven. A couple
o' bullets more or less if it's anyway over the hundred
doesna make much odds on an Astrakan coat."

" Man, he must be a tough young fellow, Wunston! "
said the Captain, genuinely admiring. " Them bullets
give you an awfu' bang. But I think the London polisman iss greatly wantin' in agility; they would be none
the worse o' a lesson from Wully Crawford, him that
wass the polisman in Tarbert when I wass at the school.
Wully wouldna throw chuckies at the window to waken
up the Rooshians; he wass far too caautious. He
would pause and consuder. Wully wass never frightened for a bad man in a hoose: ' It's when they're goin'
lowse aboot the town they're dangerous,' he would say;
' they're chust ass safe in there ass in my lock-up, and
they're no' so weel attended.'

" Wully wass the first polisman ever they had in Tarbert. He wassna like the chob at aal, at aal, but they couldna get another man to take it. He wass a wee small man wi' a heid like a butter-firkin, full to the eyes wi' natural agility, and when he would put the snitchers on you, you would think it wass a shillin' he wass slippin' in your hand. If you were up to any muschief—poachin' a bit o' fish or makin' a demonstration—Wully would come up wi' his heid to the side and rubbing his hands thegither, and say a kindly word. I've seen great big massive fellows walkin' doon the street wi' Wully, thinkin' they were goin' to a Christmas pairty, and before they knew where they were they were lyin' on a plank in his lock-up. You never saw a man wi' nicer mainners; he wass the perfect chentleman!

" ' Stop you there, lads, and I'll be back in a meenute wi' a cup o' tea,' he would say when he wass lockin' the door of the cell on them. ' Iss there anything you would like to't?' The silly idiots sometimes thocht they were in a temperance hotel by Wully's mainners, and they got a terrible start in the mornin' when they found they had to pay a fine. You mind o' Wully Crawford, Dougie?"

" Fine!" said Dougie. " He was the duvvle's own!"

" ' Caaution and consuderation iss the chief planks in the armour of the Brutish constable,' Wully used to say, rubbin' his hands. ' There iss no need for anybody to be hurt.'

" It wass the time when Tarbert herrin'-trawlers wass at their best and money goin'. It wass then, my laads, there wass Life in Tarbert! The whole o' Scotland

Yaird and a regiment o' arteelery couldna have kept
the Tarbert fishermen in order, but Wully Crawford
held them in the hollow o' his hand——"

" It's a' very weel," said Macphail, " but they didna
go aboot wi' automatic pistols."

" No, they didna have aromatic pistols," admitted
Para Handy, " but they had aawfully aromatic fists.
And you never saw smerter chaps wi' a foot-spar or a
boat-hook. The wildest of the lot wass a lad M'Vicar,
that belonged to Tarbert and wass called The Goat for
his sagacity. He could punch his heid through a mill-
stone and wear it round his neck the rest o' the day
instead o' a collar. When The Goat wass extra lucky
at the trawlin' the Tarbert merchants didna take the
shutters off their shops and the steamboat agents had
to put a ton or two o' ballast in their shippin'-boxes.
Not a bad chap at aal, The Goat—only wicked, wicked!
The only wan that could stand up to him in Tarbert
wass three Macdougall brothers wi' a skiff from
Minard; him and them wass at variance.

" The Goat would be going through the toun wi' his
gallowses ootside his guernsey and his bonnet on three
hairs, spreading devastation, when the Free Church
munister would send for Wully Crawford.

" ' You must do your duty, Wullium,' he would say,
wi' his heid stickin' oot at a garret window and the
front door barred. ' There's M'Vicar lowse again, and
the whole o' Tarbert in commotion. Take care that
ye divna hurt him.'

" ' There's nobody needs to be hurt at aal, wi' a
little deeliberation,' Wully would say wi' his heid
to the side, and it most dreadful like a butter-firkin.
' I'll chust paause and consuder, Mr Cameron, and

M'Vicar 'll be in the cell in twenty meenutes. Terrible stormy weather, Mr Cameron. What way's the mustress keepin'?'

"Then Wully would put off his uniform coat and on wi' a wee pea-jecket, and go up to where The Goat wass roarin' like a bull in the streets of Tarbert, swingin' a top-boot full o' stones aboot his heid—clean daft wi' fair defiance.

"'John,' Wully would say to him, rubbin' his hands and lookin' kindly at him, 'it's a wonder to me you would be carryin' on here, and them Macdougalls up on the quay swearin' they'll knock the heid off you.'

"The Goat would start for the quay, but Wully wass there before him, and would say to the Macdougalls, 'In to your boat, my laads, and on wi' the hatch; M'Vicar's vowing vengeance on you. Here he comes!' He knew very well it wass the last thing they would do; five minutes later and the three Macdougalls and The Goat would be in grips.

"'Pick oot whatever bits belong to yoursel's, and I'll collect what's left of poor M'Vicar,' Wully would say to the Macdougalls when the fight wass done, and then he would hurl The Goat to the lock-up in a barrow.

"But that wass only wan of Wully's schemes; his agility was sublime! There wass wan time yonder when The Goat took a fancy for high jeenks, and carried a smaal-boat up from the shore at night and threw it into the banker's lobby. It wass a way they had in Tarbert at the time o' celebratin' Hallowe'en, for they were gettin' splendid fishin's, and were up to aal diversions.

"Wully went roond in the mornin' to M'Vicar's

house, and ass sure ass daith he hadna the weight or
body o' a string o' fish, but a heid on him like a firkin.
If The Goat had kent what he came for, he would have
heaved him through the window.

" ' You werena quarrellin' wi' Mackerracher last
night and threw him ower the quay?' asked Wully,
rubbin' his hands.

" I never set eyes on Mackerracher in the last fortnight!' said The Goat, puttin' doon a potato-beetle,
as you might say disappointed.

" ' Tuts! wassn't I sure of it!' said Wully, clappin'
him on the back. ' Mackerracher's missin', and there's
a man at the office yonder says he thocht he saw you
wi' him. It's chust a case of alibi; come awa' across
to the office for a meenute; he's waitin' there, and he'll
see his mistake at wance.'

" The Goat went over quite joco to the polis-office,
knowin' himsel' he wass innocent of any herm to poor
Mackerracher, and wass fined in thirty shullin's for
puttin' a boat in the banker's lobby. Oh, a cluver
fellow, Wullium! A heid like a butter-firkin!

" You would think The Goat would never be got
to the polis-office any more wi' such contrivances o'
Wully Crawford. ' If that wee duvvle wants me again,
he'll have to come for me wi' the Princess Louisa's
Own Argyll and Sutherland Highlanders and a timber-
junker,' he swore, and Wully only laughed when he
heard it. ' Us constables would be havin' a sorry
time wi' the like of John M'Vicar if we hadna the
Laaw o' the Land and oor wuts at the back o' us,' he
said, wi' his heid on the side, and his belt a couple o'
feet too big for him.

" Two or three weeks efter that, when the fishin'

wass splendid, and The Goat in finest trum, he wakened one morning in his boat and found that some one had taken away a couple o' barrels o' nets, a pair o' oars, and a good pump-handle on him.

" ' I'll have the Laaw on them, whoever it wass! ' he says. ' Tarbert will soon be a place where a dacent man canna leave his boat withoot a watch-dog; where's Wully Crawford, the polisman? '

" He went lookin' up and doon the toon for Wully, but Wully wasna to be seen at aal, at aal, and some wan said he wass over at the polis-office. The Goat went over to the polis-office and chapped like a chentlemen at the door withoot a meenute's prevarication.

" ' Some wan stole on me through the night, a couple o' barrel o' nets, a pair o' oars, and a good pump-handle, and I want you to do your duty! ' says The Goat to the polis-constable, and the head of him chust desperate like a butter-firkin!

" ' Did you lose them, John? ' said Wully, rubbin' his hands. ' Man! I think I have a clue to the depridaation; I have some of the very articles you're lookin' for in here,' and he opened the cell door, and sure enough there was a couple o' barrels o' nets in a corner. What did the silly idiot, John M'Vicar, no' do, but go into the cell to look at them, and the next meenute the door was locked on him!

" ' A couple o' barrel o' nets and a pair o' oars or the like o' that can be taken in charge withoot assistance from the Princess Louisa's Own Argyll and Sutherland Highlanders,' said bold Wully through the key-hole. ' Iss there anything I could get for your breakfast to-morrow, John? You'll need to keep up your strength. You're to be tried for yon assault last Saturday on the Rechabite Lodge.'

" The Goat lay in the cell aal day and roared like a bull, but it didna make any odds to Wully Crawford; he went aboot the toon wi' his heid more like a firkin than ever, and a kindly smile. But when The Goat begood at night to kick the door o' his cell for oors on end and shake the polis-office to its foundations, Wully couldna get his naitural sleep. He rose at last and went to the door o' the cell, and says, says he, ' John, ye didna leave oot your boots; if you'll hand them oot to me I'll gie them a brush for the mornin'.'

" M'Vicar put oot the boots like a lamb.

" ' There now,' said Wully, lockin' the door again, ' ye can kick away till you're black in the face. Would you like them oiled or bleckened?' And you never saw a man wi' a heid more like a firkin o' Irish butter!"

PARA HANDY'S VOTE

PARA HANDY had finished tea on Saturday night, and was ruefully contemplating the urgent need for his weekly shave, when Mary, his wife, was called to the outer door. She came back to the kitchen to inform her husband that a gentleman wished to see him.

"A chentleman!" said Para Handy, with surprise and even incredulity. " What in the world will he be wantin'? "

" He didna say," replied Mrs Macfarlane. " He said he wanted to see you most particular, and wouldna keep you a meenute. Whatever you do, don't go and buy another o' thae Histories of the Scottish Clans."

" Could you not tell him I'm away on the boat, or that I'm busy? " asked her husband, nervously putting on his jacket.

" I'm no' goin' to tell any lies aboot you," said Mrs Macfarlane. " It's nobody for money anyway, for we're no' in anybody's reverence a single penny."

" What the duvvle can the man be wantin'? What kind o' look did you get at him? Do you think he's angry? "

" Not a bit of him; he spoke quite civil to mysel', and he has a book wi' a 'lastic band on't, the same as if it was the meter he was comin' for."

"A book!" said Para Handy, alarmed. " Go you out, Mary, like a cluver gyurl, and tell him that I slipped away to my bed when you werena lookin'. Tell him to come back on Monday."

" But you'll be away wi' the boat on Monday."

" Chust that; but he'll be none the wiser. There's many a sailor caaled away in a hurry. Don't be a frightened coward, Mary. Man, but you're tumid, tumid! The chentleman's no' goin' to eat you."

" He's no' goin' to eat you either," said Mrs Macfarlane. " He's standin' there at the door, and you'll just have to go and see him."

" I wish I wass back on the boat," said Para Handy in despair. " There's no' much fun in a hoose o' your own if you'll no' get a meenute's peace in't. What in the mischief iss he wantin' wi' his book and his 'lastic bands? "

He went to the door and found an exceedingly suave young gentleman there, who said, " I'm delighted to find you at home, Captain Macfarlane; my business won't take five minutes."

" If it's a History o' the Clans, we have it already,"

said Para Handy, with his shoulder against the door.
" I ken the clans by he'rt."

" You have a vote in the College Division," said the
visitor briskly, paying no attention to the suggestion
that he was a book-canvasser. " I'm canvassing for
your old friend, tried and true, Harry Watt."

" Chust that! " said Para Handy. " What way iss
he keepin', Harry? I hope he's in good trum? "

" Never was better, or more confident, but he looks
to you to do your best for him on this occasion."

" That's nice," said Para Handy. " It's a blessin'
the health; and there's lots o' trouble goin' aboot.
Watch your feet on the stair goin' down; there's a
nesty dark bit at the bottom landin'."

" Mr Watt will be delighted to know that he can
depend on you," said the canvasser, opening up his
book and preparing to record one more adherent to
the glorious principles of Reform. " He'll be sure to
come round and give you a call himself."

"Any time on Monday," said Para Handy. " I'll
be prood to see him. What did you say again the
chentleman's name wass? "

" Mr Harry Watt," said the canvasser, no way surprised to find that the voter was in ignorance on this
point, an absolute indifference to the identity of its
M.P.s being not unusual in the College Division.

" Yes, yes, of course; I mind now, Harry Watt. A
fine chentleman. Tip-top! He wass aalways for the
workin' man. It's a fine open wunter we're havin'
this wunter, if it wassna for the fogs."

" What do you think of the House of Lords now? "
asked the canvasser, desirous to find exactly what his
victim's colour was, and Para Handy shifted his weight
on another leg and scratched his ear.

" It's still to the fore," he answered cautiously.
" There's a lot of fine big chentlemen in it. Me bein'
on the boat, I don't see much of them, except noo and
then their pictures in the papers. Iss there any Bills
goin' on the noo? "

" I think we're going to clip their wings this time,"
said the canvasser with emphasis; and the Captain
shifted hurriedly back to his former leg and scratched
his other ear.

" Capital! " he exclaimed, apparently with the
utmost sympathy. " Ye canna clup them quick
enough. They're playin' the very muschief ovei
yonder in Ireland. There's wan thing, certain sure—
I never could stand the Irish."

" Yes, yes; but you'll admit a safe measure of Home
Rule——" began the canvasser; and the Captain found
the other leg was the better one after all.

" I'll admit that! " he agreed hurriedly. " Whatever you say yoursel'."

" See and be round at the poll early," said the
canvasser. " It's on Thursday."

" I'm making aal arrangements," said the Captain
cordially. " Never mind aboot a motor-car; I can
walk the distance. Give my best respects to Mr
Harry; tell him I'll stand firm. A Macfarlane never
flinched! He's no' in the shippin' line, Mr Harry, iss
he? No? chust that! I wass only askin' for curiosity.
A brulliant chentleman! He hass the wonderful agility,
they tell me. Us workin' men must stand thegither
and aye be bringin' in a bill."

" Of course the question before the electors is the
Veto," said the canvasser.

" You never said a truer word! " said the Captain

heartily. " It's what I said mysel' years ago; if my mate Dougie wass here he would tell you. Everything's goin' up in price, even the very blecknin'."

" See and not be carried away by any of their Referendum arguments," counselled the canvasser, slipping the elastic band on his book. " It's only a red herring dragged across the track."

" I never could stand red herring," said the Captain.

"And remember Thursday, early—the earlier the better! " was the visitor's final word as he went downstairs.

" I'm chust goin' in this very meenute to make a note of it in case I should forget," said Para Handy, ducking his head reassuringly at him.

"A smert young fellow!" he told his wife when he got back to the kitchen. " He took my name doon yonder chust as nate's you like! " and he explained the object of the caller's visit.

" It's the like o' me that should have the vote," said Mrs Macfarlane humorously. " I have a better heid for politics than you."

" Mery," said her husband warmly, " you're taalkin' like wan of them unfidel Suffragettes. If I see you goin' oot wi' a flag and standin' on a lorry, there'll be trouble in the College Diveesion! "

The Captain had hardly started to his shaving when Mrs Macfarlane found herself called to the door again, and returned with the annoying intelligence that another gentleman desired a moment's interview.

" Holy smoke! " said Para Handy. " Do they think this hoose iss the Argyle Arcade? It must be an aawful wet night outside when they're aal crowdin' here for shelter. Could you no' tell him to leave his

L

name and address and say I would caal on him mysel'
on Monday? "

On going to the door he found an even more
insinuative canvasser than the first one—a gentleman
who shook him by the hand several times during the
interview, and even went the length of addressing him
like an old friend as Peter.

" I'm lucky to find you at home," he said.

" You are that! " said the Captain curtly, with his
shoulder against the door. " What iss't? "

" I'm canvassing for our friend——"

" It's no' ten meenutes since another wan wass here
afore," broke in the Captain. " You should take stair
aboot, the way they lift the tickets in the trains, and
no' be comin' twice to the same door. I made aal
arrangements for the Thursday wi' the other chap."

" Think it over again," said the canvasser, no way
crestfallen, with an affectionate hand on the Captain's
shoulder. " Don't be misled by plausible stories. I
have your name down here since last election as
a staunch upholder of the Constitution. You must
support Carr-Glyn."

" There's not a man in Gleska stauncher than
mysel'," said the Captain. " What did you say the
chentleman's name wass? "

" Mr Carr-Glyn," said the canvasser. " One of the
good old sort; one of ourselves, as you might say;
a nephew of the Duke of Argyll's."

" The very man for the job! I'll be there on Thursday; keep your mind easy on that. My mother wass
a Campbell. The Duke iss a splendid chentleman.
Tremendous agility! "

" The whole situation has changed in the last few

days. You see, the Referendum practically puts the final decision upon every new constitutional change in the hands of the individual elector, and the Lords are gone."

" Cot bless me! you don't say so? " said the Captain with genuine surprise. " Where are they away to? "

The canvasser rapidly sketched the decline and fall of the hereditary principle in the Upper House.

" Holy smoke! iss the Duke goin' to lose his job, then? " asked Para Handy with sincere alarm; and the visitor hastened to reassure him.

" If you like, I'll send round a motor-car on Thursday," said the canvasser, when he had satisfied himself that the vote of Para Handy was likely to go to the side which had his ear last.

" Don't put yoursel' to any bother aboot a car; I would sooner walk: it's the least a body could do for Mr Glyn," said the Captain. " Tell him that I'll stand firm, and that I'm terrible weel acquainted wi' his uncle."

" Thank you," said the canvasser. " Mr Carr-Glyn will be highly pleased."

" You'll not answer the door the night again if a hundred chentlemen comes to it," said Para Handy when he got back to his wife. "A man might ass weel be livin' in a restaurant."

" What day's the pollin' on? " said Mary.

" On Thursday," said her husband. " Thank Cot! I'll no' be within a hundred miles o't. I'll be on the *Fital Spark* in Tobermory."

HURRICANE JACK
OF THE *VITAL SPARK*

HURRICANE JACK
OF THE *VITAL SPARK*

I

HURRICANE JACK

" STOP you! " said Para Handy, looking at his watch, " and I will give you a trate; I will introduce you to the finest sailor ever sailed the seas. He's comin' aboard the vessel in a little to say good-bye to us before he joins a kind o' a boat that's bound for Valapariza. And I right or am I wrong, Dougie? "

" That's what he said himsel', at any rate," said Dougie dubiously. " But ye canna put your trust in Jeck. He meant it right enough at the time, but that wass yesterday, and Jeck hass wan o' them memories for mindin' things that's no' to be depended on—ass short and foggy ass a winter day! "

" You'll see he'll come! " said Para Handy confidently. " Jeck's a man o' his word, a perfect chentleman! Forbye, I have the lend o' his topcoat."

" Who is the consummate and accomplished mariner? " I asked, delaying my departure from the *Vital Spark*.

" There's only wan in all the cope and canopy o' British shippin'," said the Captain. " ' John Maclachlan ' in the books, but ' Hurricane Jeck ' in every port from here to Callao. You have heard me speak of him? An arm like a spar and the he'rt of a child! "

" I'll assure you there iss nothing wrong wi' his arm whatever," said the mate; " it's like a davit." But he offered no comment on the heart of the illustrious seaman.

" He'll be here in a chiffy," Para Handy assured me eagerly. " It's worth your while waitin' to meet him when you have the chance. You'll find him most agreeable; no pride nor palavers about him; chust like any common sailor. A full-rigged ship tattooed on his chest, and his hat wi' a list to starboard. A night wi' Jeck iss ass good ass a college education. You never saw such nerve! "

" I'll wait a little," I said; " life offers so few opportunities for seeing the really great."

Five minutes later, and a lanky weather-beaten person with a tightly buttoned blue serge suit, a brown-paper parcel in his hand, and a very low-crowned bowler hat at an angle of forty-five, dropped on to the deck of the *Vital Spark*.

" Peter," he said to the Captain anxiously, without preamble, " what did ye do wi' my portmanta? "

" I never saw it, Jeck," said Para Handy. " Iss it runnin' in your mind ye lost it? "

" Not exactly lost," said Hurricane Jack, " but it's been adrift in this old town since Friday, and I'm tackin' round my friends to see if any of them's wearin' a good Crimea shirt I had in it. No reflections upon anybody, mind—that was an A1 shirt," and he looked with some suspicion at the turned-up collar of my coat.

" Nobody here hass your shirt, Jeck, I'll assure you," protested the Captain. " What kind of a portmanta wass it? "

" It was a small tin canister," said Hurricane Jack

quite frankly, and, having said so, cheered up magically, unburdened his mind of his loss, and was quite affable when I was formally presented to his distinguished notice by the Captain. He had a hybrid accent, half Scotch and half American, and I flatter myself he seemed to take to me from the very first.

" Put it there! " he exclaimed fervently, thrusting out a hand in which, on my response to the invitation, he almost crushed my fingers into pulp. " I'm nothin' but an old sailor-man, but if I can do anything for anybody at any time between now and my ship sailin', say the word, sunny boys! "

I assured him there was nothing pressing that I wanted done at the moment.

" I told ye! " exclaimed the Captain triumphantly. "Always the perfect chentleman! He thinks of everything! " He beamed upon the visitor with a pride and gratification it was delightful to witness.

" We havena anything on the boat," remarked Dougie, with what, to stupid people, might seem irrelevance. Hurricane Jack, however, with marvellous intuition, knew exactly what was indicated, looked at me with some expectancy, and I had not the slightest difficulty in inducing them all to join me in a visit to the Ferry Inn.

The bright particular star of the British mercantile marine having given the toast, "A fair slant! " three minutes later, addressed himself to the disposal of the largest quantity of malt liquor I have ever seen consumed at one breath, put down the empty vessel with unnecessary ostentation, and informed all whom it might concern that it was the first to-day.

" The chentleman," said Para Handy, alluding to

L 2

me, " would take it ass a special trate, Jeck, to hear some specimens of your agility."

I did my best to assume an aspect of the most eager curiosity.

" In the old clipper tred," Para Handy informed me in a stage whisper. " Wan of the very best! Namely in all the shuppin' offices! Took a barque they called the *Port Jackson* from Sydney to San Francisco in nine-and-thirty days. Look at the shouthers o' him! "

" If a bit of a song, now—an old come-all-ye, or a short-pull shanty like ' Missouri River,'—would be any good to the gentleman," said Hurricane Jack agreeably, " I'll do my best endeavours as soon as I've scoffed this off. Here's salue! "

Para Handy looked a little apprehensive. " What wass runnin' in my mind," said he, " wass no' so mich a song, though there's none can touch you at the singin', Jeck, but some of your diversions in foreign parts. Take your time, Jeck; whatever you like your-sel'! " He turned again to me with a glance that challenged my closest and most admiring attention for the performance about to take place, and whispered, " Stop you, and you'll hear Mr Maclachlan! "

The gifted tar was apparently reluctant to abandon the idea of a song, and rather at a loss which of the stirring incidents of his life to begin with.

" Vino," he remarked, and then, lest there should be any mistake about the word, he spelled it. " V-i-n-o, that's wine in the Dago lingo. Wherever there's land there's liquor, and down away in the Dago countries you take a wide sheer in, see, to a place like Monte-vidio. Montevidio's like here, see——" and he drew some lines on the counter with spilt ale; " and down about here's Bahia, and round the Horn, say just right here, there's Valaparisa. Well, as I say, you tack in to any o' them odd places, it might be for a cargo o' beef, and you're right up against the vino. That's Dago for wine, sunny boys! V-i-n-o."

" Didn't I tell ye! " exclaimed Para Handy ecstatically, looking at me. " Jeck hass been everywhere. Speaks aal their languages like a native. Yes, Jeck; go on, Jeck; you're doin' capital, Jeck! "

" Extremely interesting! " I said to the fascinating child of the sea. " Valparaiso now; it's pretty liable to earthquake, isn't it? "

" Take your time, Jeck; don't be in a hurry," said Para Handy anxiously, as if I had been a K.C. trying to trap a witness.

" Never saw the bloomin' place but it was pitchin' like a Cardiff tramp," said Hurricane Jack. " It's the vino. V-i-n-o. Silly thing, the Dago lingo; I know it fine, all the knots and splices of it, but it's the silliest lingo between Hell and Honolulu. Good enough, I guess, for them Johnny Dagoes. What this country wants is genuine British sailormen, to sail genuine British ships, and where are they? A lot o' ruddy Dutchmen! None o' the old stuff that was in the Black Ball Line wi' me; it wasn't blood we had in our veins in them days, sunny boys, but Riga balsam and good Stockholm tar."

He suddenly put his hand into a pocket, dragged out a leather bag, and poured a considerable quantity of silver coinage on the counter.

" Set her up again, sunny boy! " he said to the barman; " and don't vast heavin' till this little pot o' money's earned."

"Always the perfect chentleman!" said Para Handy with emotion. "Money is nothing to Jeck; he will spend it like the wave of the sea." But he gathered it up and returned it, all but a shilling or two, to the leather bag, which was by force restored to its owner's pocket.

"What," I asked, "is the strangest port you have seen?"

Hurricane Jack reflected. "You wouldn't believe me, sunny boys," said he, "if I told you."

"Yes, yes, Jeck; the chentleman 'll believe anything," said Para Handy.

"The rummiest port I've struck," said Hurricane Jack, "is Glasgow. The hooker I was on came into the dock last week, the first time I've been home for three years, and I goes up the quay for a tot o' rum wi' a shipmate, Jerry Sloan, that comes out o' Sligo. It wasn't twelve o'clock——"

"At night?" asked Dougie.

"Certainly! Who wants rum in the middle o' the day? I'd been so long away, perusin' up and down the South America coasts and over to Australia, I'd clean forgot the Glasgow habits, and I tell you I got a start when I found the rum-shops battened down. There wasn't even a shebeen! They tell me shebeenin's against the law in Glasgow now. They'll soon be shuttin' up the churches!

"'This is the worst place ever I scoffed!' says Jerry, and he's a lad that's been a bit about the world. Next day Jerry and me takes a slant up-town to buy a knife, and blamed if there was a cutlery shop or an ironmonger's open in the whole village!

"'The man that makes the knives in Sheffield's dead,

and they're celebratin' his funeral, or this is the slowest town on the Western Hemisphere,' says Jerry.

" Next day we took another slant to buy boiled ham, and went into a shop that was full of ham, but the son-of-a-gun who kept it said he daren't sell us anything but oranges! So the both of us went back like billy-oh to the waterside and signed for Valaparisa. That's where the vino is, sunny boys, and don't you forget it! V-i-n-o."

" Capital! " said Para Handy, and, turning again to me, remarked: " It's wonderful the things you see in traivellin'. If you'll come over to the vessel now, we'll maybe get Jeck to give a stave o' ' Paddy came round.' "

But I tore myself away on the plea of urgent business.

II

THE MYSTERY SHIP

Up at the bar of the inn the crew of the *Vital Spark* mildly regaled themselves with munition ale which the Captain audibly surmised had been made on the premises after the last washing-day.

It seemed good enough, however, for a gang of young Glasgow Fair lads who were also in the bar, and made as much noise as if the liquor legislation of the past five years had been abandoned.

" They're only lettin' on," said Para Handy sadly. " Just play-actin'! It's no' on ale o' this dimensions that they're keepin' up the frolic. A barrel o' that wouldna rouse a song in a Templar lodge."

He cut himself a plug of thick black twist, and chewed it to remove as speedily as possible the flavour of Macalister's still undemobilised beer.

" I say, old chap," said the cheekiest of the Glasgow youths, " what do ye chew tobacco for? "

" Just to get oot the juice," said Para Handy. " Iss everybody weel aboot Barlinnie? "

The trippers came surging boisterously up to his end of the counter; there was about them an infectious jollity that slightly thawed even the saturnine Macphail.

" Is that your vessel at the quay? " said one of the strangers after a while. " She looks a bit battered. Needin' paintin' an' that——"

Para Handy sighed.

" Ye may weel say it! " he responded. " It would be droll if she wassna lookin' battered. Ye would read in the papers aboot the ' Mystery Ship '? "

" Often," said the Glasgow man.

" That's her," whispered Para Handy. " Q Boat 21 —the chenuine article! The cammyflage iss off her, and her cannons iss back at Beardmore's, but if ye had seen her a year ago ye would call her the gem o' the sea. Am I right or am I wrong, Dougie? "

" Ye chust took the word oot o' my mooth," responded the mate with impressive alacrity. " The gem o' the ocean."

Macphail merely snorted.

" What was she for? " asked one of the trippers, quite impressed.

" That's just the very words I asked the Admirality when they took her over," said Para Handy, " and they wouldna tell me. ' Ye'll fin' oot soon enough," says they; ' she's the very packet we're lookin' for to play a prank on Jerry. She looks like a boat that would have agility.'

" They painted her streakum-strokum like the batters o' a book I have at home called John Bunyan's ' Holy War,' so that ye couldna make her oot a hundred yerds off if ye shut your eyes; they put a wireless instrument doon her funnel, and a couple o' nice wee guns at her stern, wi' a crate on the top o' them the same ass they were chickens, and put on board her an old frien' o' my own by the name o' Hurricane Jeck that's weel acquent wi' the ocean tred, and another chap for a gunner. The hold was packed wi' ammunition."

" Where did ye a' sleep? " asked one of the Glasgow company.

" It wassna a place to sleep in that wass botherin' us," explained the Captain; " the trouble wass to find a place to put doon the pail in when Dougie and me and Macphail and Jeck was takin' oor baths in the morning."

" Oh, Jerusalem! " exclaimed Macphail to himself, with his face in another mug of munition ale. " Baths! "

" Had ye navy uniforms? " asked one of the intensely interested strangers.

" The very latest! " Para Handy assured him. " I'll assure you they did it handsome."

" ' Q 21 ' on the guernsey in red, red letters," added Dougie. " Tasty! "

" Every man a telescope and a heavily mounted blue pea-jacket," added Macphail, with an ironic humour that went over the heads of the audience.

" But whit was the mystery bit? " inquired an impatient listener. " Did ye sink onything? "

" Did we sink onything? " repeated Para Handy in

an impressive whisper, after looking round the bar, to assure himself no person of German sympathies might be present. "When I tell you, chentlemen, that Hurricane Jeck wass the Admirality's man on board my boat, there iss no need to go into the question aboot sinkin'."

"Perhaps the gentleman never heard o' Hurricane Jeck," suggested the engineer maliciously.

"Perhaps not by that name," said Para Handy briskly, "but they would hear o' John Maclachlan, V.C., and that's the same chentleman."

"I mind o' readin' the name o' a V.C. like that in the papers," said an intelligent Glasgow man.

"There iss no more namely sailor in the Western Ocean tred," said Para Handy, "and no man livin' that did more to win the war than my old friend Jeck. Yon old fellow Tirpitz had a great respect for Jeck; he gave orders to aal the German submarines to beware of Jeck in parteecular. But, mind ye—Jeck Maclachlan iss aalways the perfect chentleman! He would sink your boat on ye the way ye would think it wass a favour."

"What sort o' lookin' chap is he?" asked a Glasgow man.

"A great big copious kind o' fellow wi' fur in his ears and the he'rt of a child," said Para Handy with fervour. "He wass on the China clippers in his time; there's not a quirk of navigation that Jeck iss not acquent wi', nor a British sailor that hass seen more life. Am I no' right, Dougie?"

"Chust exactly what I would say myself," responded the mate. "Jeck's a clinker! I never met a more soothin' man—very soothin'!"

" Puts ye in mind o' Steedman's Powders," interpolated Macphail in a confidential whisper to Macalister, the publican. " Whit is it ye put in that beer? It has a queer effect."

" Where did ye sail to? " asked one of the strangers, eager to get on with what gave promise of being a most thrilling narrative.

Para Handy shook his head, and had another glass under pressure. " If I had a bit o' a map and two or three days wi' ye," he said, " I could show ye where we sailed. But it wouldna be fair to Jeck. Ye'll mind this was the Mystery Ship, and though I wass in command of her, Jeck wass for the Admirality. Would I dare put it any clearer, Dougie? "

" Ye'll have to be caautious, Captain," said the mate anxiously. " Keep mind o' the regulations! "

" Don't get into trouble, whitever you do! " advised the engineer with a sardonic air.

Para Handy paid no heed to the engineer. He had sized up the Glasgow visitors as a most agreeable and vivacious party of fine young gentlemen whose acquaintance was well worth cultivating in the absence of more exhilarating elements in John Macalister's bar.

" Where are ye bidin'? " he asked them abruptly, and was informed that the bell-tent round the point, on the shore, was to be their residence for another week.

" Capital! " said Para Handy. "A tent's the very place for speakin' your mind; ye never ken who's aboot ye in a bar. Dougie and me'll go roond to the tent at supper-time and tell ye things aboot the Mystery Ship that'll make your blood run cold."

" Right-ho! " said the Glasgow gentlemen with one accord.

" Mind ye! " warned the Captain, " strictly between oorsel's! If the Admirality thocht that we wass blabbin' the way we won the war, there would be trouble. We're no' a bit feared for oorsel's—Dougie and me—but we must consuder Jeck. It wass me that wass in command o' Q Boat 21, but it wass Jeck that had the agility. Just to let ye ken—we would be sailin' oot each trip wi' oor life in oor hands, and comin' back wi'——"

" Caautious, Captain! Caautious! " implored Dougie, with his eye on the clock.

" Half-past two; bar's closed, gentlemen! " announced Macalister, and his guests streamed out.

" Be round at the tent at six," said one of the Glasgow fellows.

" Ye can depend on it! " the Captain assured him. "And just to show ye the kind o' man he wass, I'll bring Hurricane Jeck's photygraf."

III

UNDER SEALED ORDERS

" THE first time the *Vital Spark* and us took up the line o' mystery shippin'," said Para Handy, settling down to his yarn, " she wasna cammyflaged at aal, but in her naitural colour. I wass thinkin' to spruce her up a bit for the occasion wi' a yellow bead aboot her, and the least wee touch o' red aboot her funnel, but Hurricane Jeck, wi' the Admirality's orders, made us sail the way we were.

" ' This boat, my sunny boys,' says he, ' iss to look

like any ordinar' packet that would be carryin' coals, or wud, or gravel,' and he wouldna let Dougie even wash his face for fear the enemy would have suspeecions she wass some vessel oot o' the usual. Indeed, I wass black affronted the way she took to sea—aal rust and tar, the deck reel-rall wi' buckets and boxes, a washin' o' clothes on the riggin', and everywhere Irish pennants. Am I right or am I wrong, Dougie? "

" Ye have it exact, Captain," promptly agreed the mate; " I have seen a bonnier boat on a valentine."

" ' The thing is to look naitural,' says Jeck, and his notion aboot lookin' naitural wass to have us like a boat in a pantomime, and a crew like a wheen o' showmen. He wouldna even let me put on my jecket! And, oh, but Macphail wass the angry man! Jeck's orders wass that we were to keep her at four or five knots, but make her funnel smoke like bleezes. Macphail had to burn up all his novelettes; if he wass here himsel' he would tell ye."

" Where did ye start frae? " asked one of the Glasgow men.

" I'll tell ye that withoot wan word o' devagation," said Para Handy. " We started from Bowling, under sealed orders that Jeck had at his finger-ends, and a lot o' impudent brats o' boys on the quay cryin' ' Three cheers for the *Aquitania*! ' "

" Oor lives in oor hands! " remarked Dougie solemnly. " We didna know but every minute would be oor next."

" There wass a lot o' talk at the time aboot submarines roond Arran, and we made oor course first for Loch Ranza," continued the Captain. " We never came on nothing—not a thing! Jeck and me and

Dougie put oot the punt at Loch Ranza, and went ashore to see the polisman. We took Jenkins wi' us —he wass the English chentleman in cherge of the guns, and he would aye be scoorin' them wi' soft soap —fair made pets o' them! The polisman assured us Kilbrannan Sound wass hotchin' wi' submarines the week before, and he wass of opeenion they were shifted up Loch Fyne, for a whale wass seen at Tarbert on the Friday.

"We carried on to Tarbert, and by good luck it wass Tarbert Fair. Jeck threw open the boat for visitors, considerin' the occasion. They came on board in droves to see a mystery ship, and Jeck put roond a hat in the aid of Brutain's hardy sons. He gaithered seventeen shillin's, and we stayed three days."

"Seventeen and ninepence ha'penny," said Dougie, apparently determined on absolute accuracy.

"I stand corrected, Dougald; it wass seventeen and ninepence ha'penny," admitted the Captain, on reflection.

"It wass a chentleman's life under Jeck; ye never saw a better hand for navigaation! Duvvle the place did we go into but there was sport—a displenishin' sale at Skipness that lasted a couple o' days; a marriage at Carradale wi' fifteen hens on the table, and everybody hearty——"

"Kind, kind people in Carradale!" enthusiastically testified the mate. "That homely! Ye had just to stretch your hand, and somebody would put something in it. It wass wi' us bein' in the Navy."

"But did ye no' see ony submarines?" impatiently inquired one of the Glasgow men.

The narrator refused to be hurried. "Jeck jaloosed,"

he proceeded, " that the Blackwaterfoot wass the kind
of a place where the Chermans might be lurkin'; we
went ashore and scoured aal roond the inn, ootside
and in, and up as far as Shisken, lookin' at night for
signals. We followed a light for an oor, and tracked
it to Shisken Inn; it wass only a man wi' a lantern.

" ' My goodness! aren't they cunnin'? ' said Jeck
at the end of the week, when there wassna ony sign o'
the Chermans. ' We'll have to go roond the Mull and
see if they're no' in Islay.' Ye'll mind o' him lookin'
the book, Dougie? "

" Fine! " said the mate, without a moment's hesitation, but with a questioning look in his eye for Para
Handy.

" It wass an almanac, and Jeck wass studyin' it like
a book o' Gaelic songs.

" ' What are ye studyin', Jeck? ' I asked him. ' Iss
it the tides ye're lookin'? '

" ' The tides iss aal right,' says Jeck; ' I'm lookin'
to see what day the wool market's on in Port Ellen.'
Man! ye couldna keep step to Jeck; he wass chokeful
o' naitural agility. We got into Port Ellen chust when
the market started, and they couldna trate us better
than they did. The English chentleman in charge o'
oor guns said he had traivelled the world, and never
seen the like o't. For a couple o' days his cannons
got little scourin', I'll assure you!

" Jeck looked the map on Monday, and gave a start.
' Holy sailors! ' says he, ' we forgot to caal on Campbeltown, and I have fifteen cousins there! '

" We were chust goin' roond by Sanda, and it wass
desperate dark, when a boat pops up and hails us. We
couldna mak' oot wan word they were sayin'!

" ' Now we're into the midst of it! ' said Jeck, quite cool, puttin' oot the light and takin' off his slippers. ' Heave oot the punt and start the panic party! ' "

" Whit was the panic party? " asked one of the Glasgow men.

" Chust me and Dougie and Macphail. I assure you we were well put through oor drills at Bowling! Whenever a U-boat hailed ye, ye understand, we were to get in the punt in a desperate confusion, and leave the English chentleman and Jeck on the vessel, below the crate where the guns wass.

" Macphail wass first in the punt, wi' his clock and a canister he kept his clothes in; Dougie fell into the water, and wass nearly drooned, and I wass chust goin' to jump in when I minded and went back to get my papers——"

" ' John Bull ' and the ' Oban Times,' " explained the mate with unnecessary and misunderstanding minuteness.

" When we put off in the punt, the gallant Jeck, wi' his gunner below the crate, was usin' terrible language, bawlin' oot to the Chermans to egg them to come on. A stiff bit breeze wass blowin' from the south'ard. We waited to hear the battle and pick up Jeck and the English chentleman when it wass feenished——"

" Ye mind we were driftin', Captain," remarked the mate.

"As dark ass the inside o' a coo," pursued Para Handy, " and, as Dougie tells ye, we were driftin'. Believe it or no', but in oor hurry wi' the panic, we clean forgot the oars! "

" Oor lives in oor hands! " said Dougie lugubriously. "And me at the bailin' dish. The chentlemen's gettin' tired listenin', Peter."

"Aal night we drifted in the punt, and it wass desperate dark, but a trawler towed us in to Campbeltown in the mornin'. There wass a demonstration when we landed, us bein' in the Navy, but it wass kind o' spoiled at first for me and Dougie, wonderin' aboot the vessel. And there she wass, lyin' at the quay!"

"Criftens!" said a Glasgow man, with an air of frank disappointment; "I thocht she would be sunk by that time!"

"Not under Hurricane Jeck!" said Para Handy. "Ye'll mind o' Jeck's agility. He had sunk the other fellow, him and Jenkins, and that's the way he got the Victoria Cross. And it wassna fifteen cousins he had in Campbeltown, when the story went aboot; the half o' aal the folk in Kintyre wass cousins to him."

"I have a bit here o' the Cherman boat," said Dougie, taking a fragment of a herring-box from below his guernsey. "Jeck picked it up for a sample. Any of you chentlemen that would like a souveneer——"

IV

A SEARCH FOR SALVAGE

"HURRICANE JECK got a great, great name wi' the Admirality for his cheneral agility, efter we sunk the Cherman submarine off Sanda," said Para Handy, "and they would be sendin' him letters every other day, but not an article in the way o' money, and Jeck got vexed. Ye never, never in your life saw a man in such a bad trum; I declare the sparks would fly

from him if ye rubbed his whiskers. He wass chust
wicked! Am I right or am I wrong, Dougie? "

" Ye have it chust exact, Captain," chimed in the
mate promptly. " His language wass deplorable for
a Christian vessel."

"And, indeed, I wassna in tremendous good trum
mysel' efter a fortnight or two o' danderin' roond the
islands in the search o' Mr Tirptiz, wi' my boat pented
in aal the colours o' a sixpenny kahouchy ball——"

" Chust makin' a bauchle o' the boat! " said Dougie,
with feeling.

" I had no money neither, and if it wass not that
Jeck had a fine brass-braided deep-sea kep in the bottom
o' his kist, we would be stervin'. Every noo and
then he would go ashore wi' a Western Ocean chart
rolled up under his oxter and the kep weel cocked,
and come back wi' a dozen o' eggs, a pound or two o'
poothered butter, and a hen. They're silly folk aboot
them islands—chust ass Hielan' ass Mull!—and when
Jeck would cock his deep-sea kep at them, and wave
the chart, and say he wass offeecial forger for the Navy,
they would give him the very blankets!

" We went one day for water to a creek o' a place
that was called Baghmohr, and spent the efternoon in
pausin' and consuderin'. There iss a trig wee cotter
hoose at Baghmohr, and a lot o' ducks aboot it; Jeck
went in to caal wi' his kep on, efter studying the ducks
to see which wass the fattest, and all that wass at home
wass a woman and a cat.

" Jeck is aye the chentleman; he took off his kep
and asked the woman in Gaelic where wass her
husband.

" ' I don't ken where in the world he iss,' said the

wife, ' but he left this mornin' wi' an empty keg on his shouther, and him singin'.'

" ' Chust that! ' said Jeck. ' It's a bonny place ye have here; iss there chust the two o' ye? '

" ' Bonny enough,' said the wife. ' There's only me and my man and the cat and the ducks, but it iss a terrible place for scandal! '

" When Jeck came back withoot a duck I was dumfoondered. ' Surely ye hadna the right cock on your bonnet? ' I says to him. ' I'm sure ye never saw finer ducks.'

" It wass then he told me aboot the keg. ' When a man goes away in them parts wi' an empty keg on his shouther, and him singin',' says Jeck, ' it's no' for holy water. We'll chust wait, Peter, till he comes back! ' Oh, man! Ye couldna be up to Jeck! He iss chust a perfect duvvle for contrivance! Am I right or am I wrong, Dougie? "

" Oh, he's smert enough wi' his heid," frankly admitted the mate.

" We watched for the man comin' back wi' the keg till it was nearly dark," continued Para Handy, " and when he came, he hadna a keg at aal wi' him, but wass singin' that lood it put the fear o' daith on the very ducks.

" ' Whatever he went away for, it wassna in the keg he put it,' says Hurricane Jeck, ' but I'll bate ye anything he'll go back in the mornin', and Jenkins and me 'll follow him up for fear that anything happens.'

" It wass hardly daylight when the man of Baghmohr wass out wi' a bowl at the well, and cold spring water didna please him, for before breakfast-time he wass leapin' like a hare across the island.

" ' Put by your polishin' paste and put on your Sunday garments," said Jeck to Jenkins, ' and the two o' us 'll find oot where that fellow goes for the hair o' the dog that bit him.'

" Jenkins stopped scourin' his cannon, and they started off in chase o' the Baghmohr man, for Jenkins had the greatest respect for Jeck and his agility.

" Ye'll maybe no' believe me, but they tramped six miles till they came to a clachan where everybody wass singin' like a Sunday School choir, and it a Tuesday mornin'! Every man in the place that had his wits aboot him wass doon on the shore aboot a cave wi' a great big puncheon o' rum in it. It had drifted ashore on the Sunday, but nobody put a hand on it till the Monday mornin'.

" They were singin' like hey-my-nanny when Jeck and Jenkins came in the midst o' them—Jeck wi' a terrible cock on his kep, and the North Sea chart as weel as the Western Ocean wan in his oxter, Jenkins wi' bell-moothed troosers and a white string wi' a whustle on't.

" ' Birl your whustle! ' commanded Jeck, and him throng buttonin' up his jecket.

" Jenkins birled his whustle the same's it wass for a British battle; Jeck cocked his kep on three hairs, turned up wan side o' his moustache, and steps in front o' the biggest man in the company. What wass it he said, Dougald? "

" Whatever ye say yoursel', Captain," replied the mate with deference.

" I canna mind the words exactly, but Jeck assured them it wass the jyle for them. ' You are fair pollutin' the island wi' the King's rum,' said Jeck, and him

sniffin'. ' Ye ken ass weel ass I do that every article
that drifts ashore belongs to the Admirality. Gie me
a tinny, and I'll see what will require for to be done.'

" They passed him a tinny—Jeck filled it at the
spigot-hole that they had made in the puncheon, took
a good sup, and said, ' Chust what I wass jalousin'—
Jamaica rum. Iss that not desperate, Jenkins? Chust
you taste it, to make sure.'

" Jenkins tasted near a pint, shut his eyes wan efter
the other, and said it wass rum, withoot a question.

" ' What ye'll do iss this,' says Jeck to the crofters,
' ye'll drive that spigot in again, put the puncheon on
a cairt, and hurl it over to Baghmohr, where ye'll find
oor gunboat lyin', and if ye're slippy aboot it I'll
maybe let the thing blow by.'

" Jeck and Jenkins wass back at the boat by dinner-
time, lookin' fine, and full o' capers, but the cairt wi'
the puncheon in it didn't come till late in the efternoon.
They said they had to travel seven miles to get a horse
and cairt.

" We slung the goods aboard wi' the winch, and the
men wass wantin' something for the salvage.

" ' I daurna do it,' said Jeck, ' it's against the regulations; forbye, ye didna bring your tinnies,' and in a
few meenutes we had up the anchor, and were off to
sea again.

" It would be near ten o'clock at night when Macphail the engineer took ill of a sudden, and nothin'
would do him but a drop o' spurits. Jeck took a
gimlet and bored a couple o' holes in the puncheon.
He filled a cup for Macphail, and the silly fool had it
swallowed before he found it wass nothing but a
sample o' the Sound o' Sleat. Weren't they the black-

guards! They had emptied the cask in their kegs and
filled it up again wi' plain sea water! Oh, my! but
Jeck wass angry! "

V

THE WONDERFUL CHEESE

" WE were, wan time yonder, perusin' up and doon
the Long Isle looking for mines," said Para Handy.
" We looked high, and we looked low, on sea and
land; many a droll thing we found drifting, but never
came on nothing more infernal than oorsel's. Hurricane Jeck had a terrible skill for mines. At night he
would take the punt, wi' a bit o' a net in her, and
splash the mooths o' the burns for oors on end in
search o' them. Not wan iota! The only thing he
would get in the net would be a grilse or two, or a
string o' troot; Uist is fair infested wi' them.

" But wan night yonder he came back wi' a whupper
o' a cheese; he got it on the high-water mark.

" ' Capital! ' I says to him; " that's something wise-
like! ' for I wass chust fair sick o' salmon—salmon—
salmon, even-on.

" Jeck rolled the cheese on board; sixty pounds wass
in it if there wass an ounce! I never saw a cheese that
better pleased the eye. Wi' a cheese like yon and a
poke o' meal, ye could trevel the world.

" But Jeck wass dubious. ' She looks aal right,' he
says, ' but ye canna be up to them Cherman blackguards. We'll be better to trate that cheese wi'
caaution. I didna put a hand on her mysel' till I

walked three times roond her lookin' for horns, and when I lifted her it wass wi' my he'rt in my mooth and a word o' prayer.'

" ' Hoots, man, but ye're tumid, tumid! ' I says to him. ' What harm's in a Cheddar cheese? Take her aft and put your knife in her.'

" He took oot his knife at that, and made to hand me't. ' Open her up yoursel', Peter,' says he, ' but first let me and the rest o' the crew get off a bit in the punt. I would be black affronted to be blown up wi' a Cherman cheese wi' a bomb inside o't.'

" I looked at the cheese, and, my goodness, it wass a whupper! Ye could feed an airmy on't! And I never wass as hungry in my life! There iss something aboot a cheese on board a ship that grows on ye! But I didna like the look o' Jeck, at aal, at aal, for he aye took care that the cheese wass on wan side o' the funnel, and he had a startled eye.

" ' I don't care a docken for cheese,' I says to him at last, ' but Dougie's fond o't. Gie the knife to Dougie.' By this time Dougie wass in the hold wi' a tarp'lain over his heid, but he heard me fine.

" ' Take it away and sink it,' he bawls; ' cheese never agreed wi' me; I promised my wife I would never taste it.'

" Jeck looked roond for Macphail, but he was off like a moose among his engines, and meh'in' like a sheep.

" The only man on the ship that wass quite cool and composed wass Jenkins, and he wass under the crate where his gun wass, and him sound sleepin'.

" ' Mind ye, I'm no' sayin' there is anything wrong wi' the cheese,' says Jeck. ' She may be a topper o' a cheese for aal I ken, but chust you put your ear doon close to her, Peter, and tell me if you don't hear something tickin'.'

" I made wan jump for the punt, and rowed away like fury!

" ' Heave that cursed cheese o' Satan over the side this instant, or there'll be the duvvle's own devastation!' I roared to Hurricane Jeck. 'Ye were surely oot o' yer mind to meddle w'it.'

" I came back in twenty meenutes, and found Jeck and the gunner Jenkins had the cheese below a barrel.

" ' It's all right,' said Jeck; ' it wass my mistake aboot the tickin'; Jenkins couldna hear it. But aal the same, we'll better keep her at a distance till we come to some place where there's folk that is keener on cheese than we are.'

" For near a month—ay, more than a month—we pursued oor devagations roond the islands seekin' mines, and aye the cheese was in below the barrel. Nobody would touch it. Dougie had his Book oot every night, and indeed I wasna in the best o' trum mysel', wi' my ear aye cocked for clockwork and the boots never on my feet.

" Every other day Jeck would tilt the barrel up, and we could see that cursed cheese ass like a cheese ass anything, but lookin' duvelish glum. I couldna have worse nightmares if I ate it. We gave it, between us, the name o' Jerry.

" It wass the time o' the plewin' matches. The night before a plewin' match we came into Portree, and a wheen o' chentlemen were gatherin' prizes. Ye ken yoursel' the kind o' prizes they have at a plewin' match—a smoked ham for the best start-and-finish;

a trooser-length o' tweed cloth from J. & A. Mackay, the merchants, for the best oots-and-ins; a gigot o' black-faced mutton for the best-groomed horse; a silver chain and pendulum for the largest faimily plewman; and a pair o' gallowses for the best-dressed senior plewman at his own expense.

" The chentleman at the store had a fine collection o' prizes when Jeck and me went in to look at them, and Jeck's eye lighted up when he saw the gallowses. For months his breeks wass hingin' on him wi' a lump o' string.

" ' What ye're needin' to complete them prizes,' says he, ' iss a fine big sonsy Cheddar cheese. I'll make a bargain wi' ye. If ye'll let me into the plewin' competition, I'll gie ye a prize o' the bonniest biggest keppuck between Barra Heid and the Butt o' Lewis.'

" The man in charge o' the prizes looked hard at Jeck, who had a gless in him, but not wan drop more than he could cairry like a chentleman, and he says quite sharp, ' What's wrong wi' the cheese? '

" ' There's nothing wrong wi' the cheese,' says Jeck; ' she's a chenuine Thomas Lipton, but my mates and me iss desperate keen on the agricultooral tred, and we'll gie the cheese to promote the cheneral hilarity.'

" 'Are ye sure ye can plew?' asks the other one, dubious.

" ' I've been plewin' all my days,' says Jeck, quite smert; ' chust look at the boots o' me! '

" They agreed that Jeck would get into the competition, and sent doon to the vessel to fetch the cheese, and all the time they were away for 't I wass in the nerves, for fear they might jolt it. ' God help the harbour o' Portree this night,' says I to Jeck, ' if they start to sample Jerry! '

" The plewin' match wass a great success. Jeck dressed himsel' in his Sunday clothes, and his Navy kep, and his hair was oiled magnificent. Ye never saw a more becomin' man between the stilts. He had got the lend o' a horse and plew from a cousin o' his on the ootskirts o' Portree.

" His plewin' wass lamentable, but he got the gallowses for bein' the best-dressed senior plewman at his own expense.

"A young man by the name o' Patrick Sinclair won the cheese, and Jeck and me helped him to hurl it in a barrow to his hoose. The whole time we were helpin' him home wi 't my he'rt wass in my mooth for fear it would go off, and we laid it on the kitchen bed the same's it wass a baby!

" We got two good drams apiece from Sinclair's wife, and were no sooner oot o' the hoose than Jeck began to run for the ship ass fast as he could shift his legs, me efter him.

" ' It's time we were oot o' Portree,' says he, when we got on board; ' there's likely to be trouble.'

" ' Do ye think that cheese 'll burst before we're started? ' I asked him, busy lowsing the ropes.

" ' It's no' the cheese I'm frightened for,' says Jeck, ' but it's Patrick Sinclair. I'm no' a bit vexed for him: a fine strong young man like that should be in the Navy when the land's at war, and no' idlin' his time away at plewin'. But when he opens up that cheese there'll be a desperate explosion.'

" ' What do ye think 'll be in it, Jeck? Will it be dunnymite? '

" ' Duvvle the dunnymite! ' says Jeck; ' chust chucky-stones! Jenkins an' me scooped oot the inside o' the cheese between us in the last four weeks. We sliced the top off first, and used it for a lid. Three days ago, when you and the rest wass sleepin', we filled her up to the proper weight wi' stones and tacked the top on.' "

VI

THE PHANTOM HORSE AND CART

THE *Vital Spark*, with the labours of the day completed, dozed in her berth inside the harbour, enveloped in an atmosphere of peace and frying mackerel. From the stove-pipe rose the pale blue smoke of pine-wood: she had been loading timber. A couple of shirts were drying on a string; the Captain felt them. " Duvvle a drop o' drouth iss in it, Dougie," he remarked to the mate impatiently; " they'll no' be dry till Monday! "

" My goodness! " said the mate. " I wish I wass a shirt! I'm that dry you could use me for a blot-sheet! And there iss Jum again wi' his mackerel for the tea; the fellow has no contrivance at the cookin'—mackerel even-on since we came roond Ardlamont! Ye would think he was stockin' an aquarium. Fried mackerel iss the thirstiest fish that ever swam the sea! "

"All right, chaps! " Sunny Jim cried from the stove; " to-morrow ye'll get boiled yins! "

Dougie cast a pathetic look at the engineer.

" Issn't that the ruffian? " said he. " Many a man

M

that caals himself a cook would put his mind into the
business noo and then and think o' something else
than mackerel. It iss my opinion Jum goes doon to
the slips wi' a pail at night and picks them up where
the fishermen threw them over the quay in the mornin'.
Man, I never, never, never wass so thirsty! "

Macphail, the engineer, who was rather bored with
mackerel himself, was in a nasty humour. " It's my
opeenion," he remarked, " that that's no' a mackerel
thirst at a', but the thirst ye started wi' last Setturday
when ye got yer pay. There's naething 'll cure it for
ye, Dougie; it would tak' far mair money than ye
earn, and it's worse noo that tratin's no permitted on
the Clyde."

The mate was so indignant at the suggestion that
trouble seemed impending, when Para Handy hurried
to the restoration of a more peaceful humour with a
defence of Dougie which, to subtler instincts, would
have rather appeared an added insult.

" Never you mind him, Dougie! " said he; " Macphail iss aalways jibing. And he's aal wrong aalthegither; the worst man in the world can be turned from
drink if his friends go aboot the thing wi' kindness.
It's aal in the kindly word! That puts me in mind o'
wan time yonder my old frien', Hurricane Jeck, made
a Rechabite for life o' a man in Campbeltown that up
till then wass keepin' the distilleries goin' till his wife,
poor body, wass near demented. It wass aal in the
kindly word, and Jeck's agility.

" It wass long afore Jeck sailed on the clippers and
made his reputation. Me and him and a bit o' a boy
wass on the *Margaret Ann*, a gaabert that made money
for a man in Tarbert. At that time, even, Jeck wass a

perfect chentleman; his manners wass complete. To
see him stavin' up the quay ye would think he wass off
a steamboat, and 'twas him, I'll assure you, had the
gallant eye! 'Peter,' he would say to me, and his
bonnet cocked, 'I'm goin' for a perusal up the village,
chust to show them the kind o' men we breed in Kinlochaline.' My Chove! he had the step!

"There wass wan time yonder, we were puttin' oot
coals in Campbeltown, and a cairter wi' the bye-name
o' the Twister wass a perfect he'rtbreak to us wi'
drink. He couped ower the side o' the cairt the best
part o' the coals we slung to him, and came back from
every rake wi' another gill in him. The cargo was
nearly oot, and him no' over the side o' the quay yet
wi' his horse and cairt, when his wife came doon and
yoked on us for leadin' her man astray.

"'Mrs MacCallum,' Jeck said to her, calm and
gentle, 'there iss not a man on board this boat the day
hass drunk ass much ass would wet the inside o' a
flute; when wass the good-man sober last?'

"'The year they took the lifeboat over the Machri-
hanish; he was at the cairtin' o't,' says she, and her
near greetin'.

"'It iss high time he wass comin' to a conclusion
wi't!' said Hurricane Jeck. 'Away you home, and I'll
send your husband back to ye a dufferent character.
For the next three months have in a good supply of
buttermilk!'

"The woman went away. Her man came back to the
boat ten meenutes efter, worse than ever. 'No more
the night,' said Hurricane Jeck; 'we'll put the rest oot
in the mornin',' and the Twister made a course at wance
wi' his horse and cairt for the nearest public-hoose.

" Jeck and me and the boy went efter him, and found the horse tied to a ring at the mooth o' a close. The Twister wass in the next door in the public-hoose, and so wass the rest o' Campbeltown, perhaps, for the street was like a Sunday mornin'.

" ' There's goin' to be a cairt amissin' here,' said Jeck, quite blithe wi' us, and made a proposeetion. We took the horse oot o' the trams and led it through the close to a washin'-green that wass at the back. We then took off the wheels o' the cairt and rolled them in beside the horse. Between us we lifted the body o' the cairt on its side and through the close wi't, too, like hey-ma-nanny, and back on the green we put on the wheels again and yoked the horse.

" ' There you are! ' said Jeck. ' The first time ever a cairt wass here since they built the tenement! Stop ye till ye hear what the Twister says when he finds it!'

" Oh, man! man! I tell you it wass Jeck had the agility! He wass chust sublime!

" It took nearly half an oor for the Twister to find where his cairt wass, and we gave him twenty meenutes to himsel' before we went up to the close to see what he wass doin'.

" He had a bit o' string. First he would measure the width o' the close and then the cairt, and he was greetin' sore, sore!

" ' What iss't? ' says Hurricane Jeck, quite kindly.

" ' Issn't this the fearful calamity that's happened? ' said the cairter. ' I canna get my cairt oot.'

" ' What cairt? ' said Hurricane Jeck, quite cool— oh, man, he was a genius!

" ' What cairt but this wan,' said the Twister. ' The horse in some way that I canna fathom broucht it in, and noo I canna get it oot! '

" ' Willyum,' said Jeck, and clapped his shouther, ' that's no' a horse and cairt at all; it's just imaginaation! Hoo on earth could a cairt get in here? Chust you go home like a decent lad, and stop the drinkin' or ye'll see far worse than cairts! '

" We got him home. ' Mind what I said aboot the buttermilk! ' said Jeck to the Twister's wife; ' he's fairly in the horrors! ' And then we went back, took doon the cairt again and through the close, and to the yaird where it belonged, and stabled the horse as nate as ninepence.

" From that day on the Twister never tasted drink. I can tell you he got the start! It wass ten years efter that before he found oot it wass railly his cairt wass up the close, and no' a hallucinaation. And by that time it wass hardly worth while to start drinkin' again."

<h2 style="text-align:center">VII</h2>

HURRICANE JACK'S LUCK-BIRD

PARA HANDY, with his arms plunged elbow-deep inside the waist-band of his trousers, and his back against a stanchion, conveniently for scratching, touched the animal misgivingly with the toe of his boot, and expressed an opinion that any kind of pet was unnecessary on the *Vital Spark* so long as they had Macphail. " Forbye," said he, " you would have to pay a licence for the beast, and the thing's no' worth it."

" Your aunty! " retorted Sunny Jim, lifting the hedgehog in his cap; " it's no' a dug. Ye divna need a licence for a hedgehog ony mair nor for a mangle.

There's no' a better thing for killin' clocks; a' the foreign-goin' boats hae hedgehogs. Forbye, they're lucky."

But the Captain still looked with disapproval on the animal which Sunny Jim had picked up in a ditch along the shore that morning and brought aboard in a handkerchief.

"There wass never a beast on board this boat," said he, "but brought bad luck. I once had desperate trouble with a cockatoo; Dougie himsel' 'll tell you; and you mind yoursel' yon dog caaled Biler that you brought, that kept me ashore till the break o' day because it didna know me in my Sunday clothes? You never can tell the meenute you would get an aawful start from a hedgehog; you don't know when you might be sittin' doon on't suddenly. It might be worse than Col Macdougall's tortoise."

"What happened wi' it?" asked Sunny Jim.

"It wass the time o' the big Tarbert fishin's," said Para Handy, "and Hurricane Jeck wass home from sea and workin' a net wi' cousins that had a skiff caaled the *Welcome Back*. There never wass another boat that season had the luck o' the *Welcome Back*—she wass coinin' fortunes. She had only to dander over in the cool o' the evening to the Skate or Ealan Buie, and pick up an eye o' fish that would load her to the gunnel, and the others would be slashin' at it on the other side o' Otter and not a bloomin' tail.

"The other Tarbert boats wass desperate. They were sure there wass something in't, and one Sunday night they asked at Hurricane Jeck for an explanation. Jeck was a man that never took a mean advantage; he wass ass open ass the day.

" ' I'll not deceive you, sunny boys,' says he. ' If the *Welcome Back* iss gettin' fishin's, it's because she carries a luck-bird,' and he took a tortoise oot o' his top-coat pocket.

" ' She's no' a bird at aal! ' said one o' the Mac-Callums.

" ' Perhaps you'll tell me what she iss, then,' said Hurricane Jeck, quite patient, and withoot a word o' divagaation. ' You can see for yoursel' she's no' an animal.'

" ' I would say she was an insect,' says MacCallum, and Jeck put the tortoise back in his top-coat pocket.

" ' If it wassna the Sabbath evenin',' says he, ' and me wi' my reputation to consider, I would give you a lesson in naitural history that would keep you studyin' in your bed for a day or two.'

" There wass no doubt efter that in Tarbert that the *Welcome Back* got her luck from Jeck's tortoise, and many a crew in Tarbert tried to buy her. But Jeck was terribly attached to her, and money wouldna tempt him. The beast had wonderful agility—not nimble, if you understand, but terrible sagacity. When Jeck would whustle to her she would come and put her heid oot to be scratched, and she knew his very step when he wass comin' doon the quay. My own he'rt never warmed to them tortoises; for aal the sport that's in them you would be better wi' a partan, but Jeck aye said she grew on you. There's beasts in nature I never could see the use o'—lollipin' about wi' neither meat nor music in them, chust like polismen; and of aal the pets a man could make a hobby of, I think the tortoise iss the most rideeculus. You might ass well be friendly wi' a floo'er-pot.

" Jeck caaled her Sarah efter an aunt he had in Stirling. He wass never very sure aboot her sect, but he said he had a feelin' in his mind that the name o' Sarah suited. When he would be chirpin' to her and caalin' her Sarah, it made my blood run cold; he couldna be more respectful if she had a sowl, and still-and-on he only bought her off a barrow in Stockwell. I think mysel' it wass the great big he'rt o' him; Jeck must aye have something to be kindly to. Isn't that so, Dougie? "

" The very man," said Dougie. " If he wassna puttin' the fear o' daith on his fellow-bein's, he wass lookin' aboot for people to give money to."

" He wass ass chentle ass a child. He would be clappin' Sarah on the back, and her wi' no more sense o' kindness than a blecknin' bottle. He could feed her from the hand. They said she would trot roond the deck behind him, cheepin' like an English curate, and when he went ashore he aalways had her in his pocket, feared the Tarbert men would steal her.

" Many a time I heard him comin' doon the quay at night, and him throng taalkin' away to Sarah in his pocket. If she had lived I don't believe he ever would have mairried. ' The best o' a tortoise,' he would say, ' iss that she never gives you any back chat.'

" There wass never a man more downed than Jeck when Sarah went and died on him. It wass the start o' the winter-time, and he said she took a chill. The *Welcome Back* wass at the long-line fishin', and from the day that Sarah slipped away the luck wass clean against them.

" Col Macdougall, a fisherman in Kilfinnan, wass a gentleman that offered a bonny penny for the luck-bird when she wass in life, and her eye was hardly closed in daith when Jeck wass over at Macdougall's boat wi' her remains in a pocket-naipkin.

" ' If ye're on,' says he, ' for Sarah noo, you can have her at a bargain,' says Jeck, and he clapped her doon on a thwart.

" ' She doesna seem to have much vivacity. What's wrong wi' her? ' said Col, and he wass a man that played the bagpipes.

" ' Not one article iss the matter wi' the poor wee cratur, except that she's kind o' deid,' said Hurricane Jeck. He wass, in all respects, the perfect chentleman and would never take advantage.

" ' Dear me,' said Col, ' isn't that a peety! She wass worth her weight in gold when she wass livin'.'

" ' And she's worth her weight in silver noo she's deid,' said Jeck. He proved to Col that the luck-bird wass ass good ass ever, and went away wi' seven-and-sixpence in his pocket, leavin' Sarah's mortal elements behind him.

" ' I wouldna part wi' her,' said he, ' unless to a comfortable home.' There wass nothing wrong wi' Jeck; he had the finest feelin's.

" Col put the late lamented in behind the stove o' his skiff, and started out for splendid fishin's. They werna in't. There didna seem to be a single cod or whitin' left in aal Loch Fyne. He would go doon to the den o' his skiff and turn poor Sarah over on her back, and give her the worst abuse because she didna came to his assistance, but Sarah was no more concerned than a smoothin'-iron.

" He used her for breakin' coal, and he used her for a toaster, and the winter slipped away. It wass a

M 2

period namely still in Tarbert ass the Big New Year, money bein' rife, and Col wass oot wi' his bagpipes every evening till the month o' March. He wass over wi' his boat one night at Tarbert at a horo-yally, and came back on board, himsel', wi' his bagpipes aal reel-rall below his oxter, greatly put aboot because o' the barren fishin's.

" Doon to the den o' the boat he went, and struck a match, and turned up Sarah, who wass lyin' on her back.

" ' You're there,' said he, ' and the name to you of bein' lucky, but duvvle the tail iss Col Macdougall in your reverence. Paid good money for you, and there you are like a lump of stick, and the white fish laughin' at you! '

" The next meenute and Sarah put oot her heid and started walkin'!

" He wass the valiant laad, wass Col, like aal the folk he came off, but at that he started squealin', for to see a deid tortoise wi' such agility, and took his feet from the skiff the same ass if the duvvle wass efter him. He fell and staved his arm on the quay, but still had the sense to throw his bagpipes into the middle o' Loch Tarbert.

" The parish munister, Macrae, wass gettin' ready for his bed wi' a drop o' toddy, when a ring came to the door, and a meenute efter Col Macdougall grabbed him by the elbow in the lobby.

" ' Oh, Mr Macrae,' said he, ' isn't this the visitaa-tion? Yonder's Sarah skippin' aboot the boat, and her a corpse since Martinmas. I'll assure you this'll be the bonny lesson for me! '

" ' Whatna Sarah? ' said the munister.

" ' Hurricane Jeck's tortoise,' said Col Macdougall, trumblin' aal over. 'Her ghost iss crawlin' through my boat, so I want to lead a better life, and I've drooned my bagpipes.'

"A tortoise,' said the munister, lookin' droll at Col Macdougall, who wass lamentably known to him for a musician. 'Are you sure it wass an actual tortoise?'

" ' If you heard her bark! ' said Col. ' She wass bitin' at the heels o' me, and her, as you might say, poor Jeck's relict since last Martinmas. I'll never touch the pipes again. Excuse me caalin', but I came to give a pound for the Foreign Missions.'

" ' What you want,' said the munister, ' iss to take the temperance pledge. You have been keepin' the New Year too long.'

" ' It's no' so bad as that,' said Col. ' I only saw but one o' them.'

" But Macrae took him into his study-room, and told him there wass nothing that would keep away tortoises but the temperance pledge. Col must keep teetotal for a twelvemonth, and put his promise doon in black and white.

" ' And what aboot yoursel'?' said Col Macdougall, wi' his eye on the gless o' toddy.

" ' I'll sign it too if you want,' said the munister with much acceptance; and Col agreed. The munister wrote out a line and said, ' I, Col Macdougall, promise to abstain from all intoxicatin' liquors for a twelve-month,' and Col put his name to it.

" ' That's aal richt,' said the munister. ' Now for me,' and he signed at the bottom, ' George Macrae, M.A., witness.'

" ' That shows you,' said Para Handy, " that it's no'

aalways lucky to have any kind of beast aboot the boat. Col staved his arm, and lost his pipes, and a pound for the Foreign Missions, and his liberty for a twelvemonth."

" He must have been an awful idiot that didna ken a tortoise sleeps a' winter," said Macphail, the engineer.

VIII

A ROWDY VISITOR

THE only man of the crew who dared to go ashore at Bunessan was Hurricane Jack. He had joined the *Vital Spark* again for a season, fed up with " going foreign." It was subsequent to the deplorable incident of the minister's hens, when Para Handy and his men had to fight their way to their vessel through an infuriated populace, and the *Vital Spark*, for the Ross of Mull, got the unpleasant reputation of being nothing better than a buccaneer.

It was nightfall when she came grunting into Loch Lathaich, and lay-to, while Jack went ashore in the punt on an urgent search for milk and butter.

The Captain gave him money to pay for these provisions. "Take a good big can wi' ye, and don't bring less than two or three prints o' butter," he instructed Jack. " Don't let on what boat ye're off, or they'll twist the neck off ye. And for God's sake, never let your eye light on a hen! "

"Anything at aal but hens! " implored Dougie. " They watch their hens like hawks. A body might lift a horse in Bunessan, and no' much said aboot it, but the loss o' a hen makes them fair demented."

" Right-oh! sunny boys," said Hurricane Jack, and rowed off into the darkness.

He was gone for hours, and in the absence of the punt nobody could get ashore to look for him.

" I doot Jeck's in trouble," said Para Handy about midnight. " He has too flippant a style wi' him aaltogether! After yon calamity we had wi' the Bunessan folk last Candlemas they're no' to be trifled wi'. We'll chust need to go roond to Tobermory and look for him in the polis-office. Wassn't I stupid to gie him the half-croon? "

. . . . . .

It was the early hours of the morning, and the crew were sound asleep on the *Vital Spark* when Jack came aboard again with a clatter to wake the dead, and apparently with some companion who required assistance.

" Bless my sowl! " said the Captain, sitting up on the edge of his bunk. " Who on aal the earth hass he wi' him here? He's far too flippant, Jeck, for a coastin' sailor! "

" No consideration! Not the least! " said Macphail, the engineer, bitterly. " There's my sleep sp'iled for the night! "

" Perhaps it's a chentleman he hass wi' him," said Dougie hopefully, listening to some terrific banging up on deck. " It sounds like a chentleman from the hotel, that would have a gless or two in him. Jeck wouldna bring him unless he had something wi' him in his pocket. Light you the lamp, Peter.

The Captain was fumbling at the lamp when a shout of " Stand from under! " came from Hurricane Jack on deck, and some frantic object, kicking wildly, landed between the bunks.

" Holy smoke! " exclaimed Para Handy, and the next moment he was doubled up on the floor from a violent impact in the pit of the stomach.

For ten minutes pandemonium reigned in the sailors' narrow quarters, without its occupants being able to form any idea of the nature of this alarming visitation. The wooden sides of the bunks resounded with blows; a galvanised pail and a box of potatoes were flung back and forward with the wildest racketing; sea-boots were flying; it looked as if the visitor meant to batter the *Vital Spark* to pieces.

Para Handy had gathered himself together and gone under the blankets again. " I'm done for! " he proclaimed, gasping. " Whoever Jeck's friend iss, he iss no chentleman."

" It's an Englishman," said Dougie, sniffing, his nose the only part of him uncovered as he cowered in his bunk. " Ye can feel the smell o' him, he's in the horrors. Light you the lamp, Peter. Man! don't be tumid! "

There was an interval of silence, broken only by the Captain's groans and the visitor's noisy breathing. Macphail cautiously put out a leg, with the idea of rising to light the lamp himself, slipped on the potatoes with which the floor was strewn, and fell on the top of the Captain, who, putting up his hands to clear himself, seized an unmistakable frantic pair of horns!

" It's no' an Englishman at aal! " he yelled in

terror; " it's the duvvle! He has on a wincey shirt, and I have him by the horns! "

Dougie's instant and vociferous praying was interrupted by the descent of Hurricane Jack with a lantern he had lit on deck, which revealed the mysterious and turbulent visitor as a shaggy yellow goat.

" What iss all the commotion? " angrily demanded the Captain, skipping briskly out of his bunk. " Ye're far too flippant, Jeck! Did ye get my butter and my milk? "

" I had the milk, right enough," said Hurricane Jack, " but I put the can down at my feet till I would talk wi' the fellow that had the goats, and this one emptied it before I noticed. It was milk I went for, and milk I was bound to bring, and the only way I could do it was to bring her ladyship here, the goat. Isn't she a topper? "

The goat, as if calmed by the presence of light on the subject, was lying down, peaceably chewing the top of a sea-boot with the utmost gusto.

" But did ye bring the butter? " pursued the Captain.

" There's no' an ounce of butter in Bunessan," said Hurricane Jack. " That's another reason for me bringin' ye the goat. If we're wantin' butter we must make it oorsel's. A coo's oot o' the question on the *Vital Spark*, for we havena the accommodation, but a goat can pick up its livin' anywhere, and it's far more hyginkic than a coo."

" I'm warnin' ye it's no' me that'll milk it, I wou'dna lower mysel'! " loudly declared Dougie. " I'll leave the vessel first! "

" Where's my half-croon? " inquired the Captain,

having rescued half a boot from the still unsatiated
visitor.

"It's cost me more than half-a-croon to get that
valuable goat," said Hurricane Jack. "There's a swab
o' an Irishman yonder on the roadside wi' a herd o'
thirty goats he's takin' aboot the country, but I couldna
go away wi' wan as long as he could coont them. It
took me more than half-a-croon, but I left him yonder
thinkin' he had a herd o' fifty."

"It's no' me that'll milk that brute!" again protested Dougie. "I wadna be in the same boat wi't.
Look at its eye! Fierce! Fair wicked! Forbye, ye
canna make butter wi' a goat's milk."

"Ye can!" said the Captain; "it's ass easy ass anything. The best o' butter!" He was looking now
with more friendly eyes on the visitor, who was finishing off supper with a sock of the engineer's. The odd
thing was that the engineer seemed in no way worried
about his sock; he was in a helpless paroxysm of
laughter, lying in his bunk.

A violent altercation rose between the Captain,
Jack, and Dougie—first, as to whether goat's milk
would make butter, and second, as to which of the
crew should be what the Captain called the "dairy-
maid." It came to wrestling. Pandemonium prevailed again, and the goat, apparently much refreshed
by its meal, leapt into the fray with strict impartiality,
butting at anything soft or hard that lay in the way
of its lowered horns. Though seriously handicapped
by the narrowness of the fo'c'sle limits, it had all the
honours of the battle, and the three men ignominiously
rushed on deck.

Macphail was still convulsed in his bunk, safe out

of the conflict, and the goat turned joyfully to a change of diet in the form of raw potatoes.

Para Handy's head appeared in the companion.

" Macphail," he said coaxingly, " we forgot to bring her ladyship up wi' us. Slip you that piece o' marlin' roond her neck, and take her up on deck till we'll consuder who iss to be the master of this vessel."

" Come doon and get the beast yoursel'," retorted the engineer. " The dairy's no' in my depairtment."

"At least ye'll put up oor clothes," implored the Captain; " Dougie and me'll get oor daith o' cold."

And now the mate's head appeared at the top of the companion. " Don't be stickin', Macphail," he pleaded piteously. " It's a cold east wind, and I want my garments. The Captain and me hass compromised the situation. I'm willing to do the milkin' and Jeck'll churn."

" Good luck to the churnin' then! " shouted the engineer. " The whole lot o' ye's a lot o' Hielan' stots. Your goat's a billy! "

IX

THE FENIAN GOAT

A WHITE elephant would have been no more awkward a gift to the *Vital Spark* than the yellow goat which Hurricane Jack purloined from the Irish goat-herd in Bunessan. It had apparently been nurtured in the principles of Sinn Fein, and was utterly unamenable to restraint, law, order, or the chastening influence of a stiff rope's end. From dawn to dark it was up to mischief, and gave as much trouble as a cargo of rattlesnakes.

On account of its incorrigible bad character and its presumable origin, they called it Michael, and Hurricane Jack professed to have great expectations of the luck that would go with it as a mascot. But this consideration weighed less with the rest of the crew than the possibility of selling it at a pleasing price at some port of call remote from Mull.

"A capital goat!" said Para Handy. "Everything's complete! There's money in him! A fine big strappin' goat like that would be worth a pound."

"Ay, and more nor a pound!" calculated Dougie. "We would get far more than that even if we were selling his remains for venison."

"Naebody in their senses wants a billy-goat," said Macphail, the engineer, unfeelingly. "But perhaps ye could pass him off for a she if ye shaved him."

Michael really might have been shaved on the strength of the ironical suggestion; but already it was manifest that he was a goat to take no liberties with. He had broken away through the night from the stanchion to which they had tethered him, and roamed about the vessel, haughty and truculent, his eye for ever cocked for anything to butt at, and his appetite unappeasable.

The Captain had put his trousers over the stove to dry the night before; in the morning all that was left of them was the blade of a pocket-knife, and Michael chewed his cud with an air of magnificent detachment.

Dougie was sent ashore on Oronsay for a bag of grass, and came back with withered bog hay, which Michael refused to put a tooth to, and strewed about

the deck until it looked like the Moor of Rannoch in
a droughty spring.

Two or three turnips that were in the bag seemed
more to the passenger's fancy: they quickly disappeared, with the most stimulating effect on the con-
sumer, who caught the Captain bending twice to tap
his pipe on his boot, and on each occasion butted him
clean across the hatches.

" I'll have his he'rt's blood! " roared Para Handy,
dancing with rage. " It iss not a Fenian goat will be
the master of my boat, and affront me behind my back!
Get me a coal-slice or a shovel, Macphail, and I'll give
him a bit o' Boyne Water! "

But Macphail, discretion itself, refused to involve
himself in any way in a vulgar brawl, and retired
among his engines.

For the rest of the day Michael was content to keep
the ship's company interned abaft the funnel. Even
Hurricane Jack, with a wonderful reputation for
encounters with all sorts of wild forest animals in his
voyages with the China clippers and the Black Ball
Line, showed the utmost respect for Michael's lowered
horns.

They threw lumps of coal at him till Macphail
rebelled, finding himself in danger of being left with
insufficient fuel to keep up a head of steam: the goat
was no more affected than if it had been hailstones.

It was Dougie who had at last discovered that even
an Irish goat has some human susceptibilities.

" There's no use o' batterin' away at that duvvle o'
a beast," he said, " we should try kindness. I wonder
would he take a lozenger? " Since he had stopped
smoking a month before, the mate incessantly devoured

pan drops of a highly peppermint nature; he never
sailed from the Clyde without a half-stone of them.

Pan drops appeared to be a passion with Michael;
he devoured them readily from Dougie's hand, and
became the most friendly goat in Britain, following the
mate about the ship continually with his nose in the
pocket where the sweets were.

In the Sound of Islay, Dougie's store of imperial
pan drops went done, and Michael became more
wicked than ever. He would tolerate no sound or
movement of any kind on board his vessel. If timbers
creaked—and creaking was a feature of the *Vital
Spark*—he laid out with horns and hoofs at the nearest
part of the bulkwark; if the man at the helm altered
the course, the goat swept down on him at fifty
knots.

The Captain positively wept! " I don't believe that's
a human goat at aal! " he declared. " It's something
super-canny. Iss it the will o' Providence that we're
to be gybin' and yawin' aboot the Atlantic Ocean aal
the rest o' oor days because a brute like that'll no' let
us steer for harbour? "

" We could trap him," suggested Hurricane Jack.
" I've seen them trappin' the elephants in India."

" What way would ye trap him? " inquired the
Captain eagerly.

" We would need a pit, but the hold would do if
we could get the hatches off—and then—and then we
would need some cable, and a lot o' trees," explained
Jack weakly.

" And whar the bleezes are ye gaun to get the trees?"
asked the engineer indignantly. "Are ye gaun to grow
them? I'll be clean oot o' coal to-morrow mornin',
and ye daurna touch the sails."

" There iss nothing for it but abandon the ship and take to the punt," said Dougie lugubriously. " We're no far from Port Askaig."

" We'll do better than that! " said the Captain, with an inspiration; " ye'll row ashore yoursel' and bring back a poke o' sweeties. That'll maybe keep that cratur in trim till we reach Port Ellen."

Dougie succeeded in getting into the punt with difficulty, for Michael objected to having the only source of pan drops desert him. Half an hour later, a further supply of his favourite provender quite restored him to amiability, and they were able, at Port Ellen, to lead him ashore on a string.

" If we'll no' sell him we can wander him," was the Captain's idea. " Many a wan would be gled to have him."

" He would look fine in a great big park," remarked Hurricane Jack. " I've seen goats just like that one on the River Plate. They make wineskins o' them. Exactly the same in Bilbao."

" Watch you his eye. I don't like the look o't," said Macphail, as they went up the quay.

At that very moment Dougie's second supply of sweets was finished, and Michael, with the old Fenian ferocity aroused again, escaped from his halter, and proceeded to give animation to the scenery and populace of Port Ellen.

The first thing he altered was the structure of a shipping-box, whose vivid red colour apparently displeased him. A man who emerged from it was instantly butted back among its debris. The goat put its head through a large framed map of the Royal Route, and, thus embellished, swept up the town with the proud and lofty gait of a stag.

" I'm gaun to clear oot o' this for wan thing! " cried Macphail, and bolted back to the vessel.

The others would have liked to follow him, but were irresistibly compelled to follow their property as he strewed terror and havoc in his track. Port Ellen shops hastily put up their shutters, unable to rescue barrels and boxes of goods displayed at their doors; into the only one too late of closing its door the goat went bounding furiously, but calmed down instantly at the odour of peppermint.

Dougie went immediately after him.

"A pound of imperial pan drops!" he gasped to the shopkeeper, who proceeded to weigh them out, all unsuspicious of the commotion in the street.

There was a woman customer at the counter.

" Do ye care for lozengers? " Dougie asked her, calmly patting Michael.

" I whiles take them," she admitted.

" Then here's a present for ye," said Dougie, hurriedly thrusting the sweets in her hand. " Give wan or two to the goat; he's desperate fond o' them."

" Come away oot o' this! " he commanded his shipmates, as he hurriedly quitted the shop. " I have Michael planted on a wife, and he'll bide wi' her ass lang ass her poke holds oot."

" Whatna cairry on! It iss chust lamentable! " panted Para Handy, as they sped for their vessel.

The *Vital Spark* was leaving the quay when an infuriated carter ran up and bawled, " Stop you a meenute till I talk to ye! "

" What are ye wantin'? " asked the Captain.

" I'm wantin' a word wi' a bowly-legged man ye have there wi' whiskers on him, that tried to come roond my wife wi' a poke o' lozengers," roared the jealous carter.

" No offence at aal, at aal! " cried Dougie, answering for himself. " I wassna flirtin' wi' her; tell her to keep the sweeties for the goat. He's quite a good goat, and answers to the name of Michael."

" Take oot the chart and score oot Port Ellen," said the Captain a little later; " that's another place we daurna enter in the Western Isles! "

X

LAND GIRLS

ON the morning of Hallowe'en the *Vital Spark* puffed into the little creek where the cargo of timber was already waiting for her. The Land Girls who had felled, and snedded, and sawn the trees in the forest two miles off, and driven the logs down to the water's edge, completed their job by waiding knee-deep in Loch Fyne, leading the horses that dragged the logs from the beach right out to the vessel's quarter, where the steam-winch picked them up and lowered them into the hold.

Amazing young women! It was the first time Para Handy and his crew had seen their kind. Those girls, in their corduroy breeches, leggings, strong boots and smocks, with their bobbed hair, and Englified accent, made as much sensation as if they had been pantomime princesses.

They were not unconscious of the impression they created. They put, accordingly, a lot of sheer swank

into their handling and hauling of the timber; one or
two boldly smoked cigarettes; a little plump one,
apparently known as Podger, who had come from a
Midlothian Manse, actually stammered out a timid
" d-d-damn! " in the hearing of the crew, and blushed
furiously as she did so.

" My goodness! chust look at them! Aren't they
smert? " said Para Handy. " If they were in Gleska
they would make money at the dancin'."

Dougie could not keep his gaze off them.

" I wish my wife could see them! " he remarked
regretfully. " She never gets over the door to see anything. I'll wudger ye it would open her eyes. Chust
fancy them wi' troosers! "

" That's the latest style, sunny boys," intimated
Hurricane Jack, with all the assurance of a man of the
world, up to date in all new movements. " First the
vote and then the breeches. Ye can see them's no
common carteresses—born ladies! "

Jack's natural gallantry, even at the age of fifty-five,
had made him oil his hair, put on his best pea-jacket,
and borrow a pair of misfit boots which Dougie had
bought a week or two before in Greenock, found far
too small for him, and intended to take back to the
vendor. They fitted Hurricane Jack like a glove.

" If my wife wass to go aboot in troosers wi' her
hair cowed, I would bring her before the Session,"
said the Captain. " It's not naiture! There is not
wan word aboot women wearin' breeches between the
two boards o' the Bible."

" You look the Book o' Hezekiah! " said Hurricane
Jack. " In the fifteenth chapter ye'll see there that a
time would come, accordin' to the prophets, when

women would arise in Babylon and put their husband's garments on, and the men go forth in frocks."

The Captain was plainly staggered. He had over-looked that bit. " Go you doon, Dougie," he said, " and look your Bible to see if Jeck iss right. I thocht I knew every word o' Hezekiah by he'rt."

Twenty minutes later the mate came back with the Bible and his specs on. " I canna put my hand on Hezekiah at aal, at aal," he admitted. " What way do ye spell it? "

Hurricane Jack took the Bible from him and hur-riedly flicked through its pages; then he turned to the dedication to " The Most High and Mighty Prince James by the Grace of God, King of Britain, France, Ireland, Defender of the Faith."

" Tach! " he said; " no wonder ye canna find it! You might as well look a last year's almanac for the Battle o' Waterloo, as look in a Bible that's oot o' date completely for the Prophet Hezekiah."

"Anyway," said Dougie fervently, "ye'll never in aal your life see me in a frock. I never thocht much o' Hezekiah. He wass a waverer."

" I'll bate ye a pound to your pair o' boots ye'll wear a frock this winter," challenged Hurricane Jack.

" Done wi' ye! " said Dougie. " Ye may as weel hand over the money."

By the time the vessel was loaded, her crew and the surprising ladies were on terms of the utmost cordiality. Old Macphail stood off—reserved and cynical. He knew about women, all they were up to, all they were capable of: for twenty years he had been studying them in novelettes. The profound impression created on his shipmates by these bob-haired, be-breeched huzzies merely amused him.

That was why he was not invited to the Hallowe'en party.

It was to take place that night at the forest huts, two miles off, where the girls lived and worked. The Captain and Hurricane Jack were to come in their Sunday clothes; Dougie's despair was that his Sunday clothes were in Glasgow.

" That's all right! " said the girls, languishing round him till his shyness made his very whiskers tickle him. " The wood manager is from home; he's just your build of a man—with a suit in his wardrobe to fit you like a halo. We'll parcel it up and send it down to you in an hour."

" Nothing fancy, I hope? " said Dougie nervously. " I canna stand knickerbockers. I never had them on my person."

" It's quite all right! " Podger assured him. " Mr Taylor's taste is chaste. You can turn up the foot of the legs a little—that will be more convenient for the dancing."

" But I'm no' goin' to dance! " protested Dougie in alarm. " The only dance I ken iss Paddy O'Rafferty."

" Then we'll have it every now and then," said Podger, beaming on him. " But you needn't join in anything else. You can sit out on the doorstep and hold our hands."

" My gracious! " said the mate to himself, " we're seein' life! "

In Mr Taylor's morning coat and a pair of shepherd-tartan trousers, Dougie was unmistakably the most conspicuous guest at the Land Girls' party. The garments were obviously made for an ampler person, but by the time the borrower had worked his way through several plates of mashed potatoes, which, he was assured, were full of threepenny-bits, but found loaded with nothing but buttons, and had consumed apples, nuts, cold ham, and tea till he perspired, there was not a single crease in the waistcoat.

" Mind, I'm no' goin' to dance wan step! " he confided to Hurricane Jack and the Captain. " It iss twenty years since I shook a foot at a pairty, and the only dance I ken iss Paddy O'Rafferty."

" I doot it's oot o' date; I'm no' goin' to dance mysel'," said Para Handy.

" Wi' a splendid pair o' shepherd-tartan troosers like that," said Hurricane Jack, " the thing for you to do, Dougie, is to drape yoursel' over the stern o' the piano and turn the music. Be up an' doin', man! Cairry yoursel' like a sailor! "

To Dougie's horror Podger came up at this stage with a partner for him.

" Here's a lady who is dying to dance with you," she announced. " Her Sunday name is Miss Mathilde Vavasour MacKinlay, but you can call her 'Tilda. In the Greek that means ' very choice.' "

" I can see that," said Dougie gallantly, " but if it's dancin' she wants, she'll better take the Captain. Wi' aal them buttons I swallowed, I'm no' in trum at aal, and the Captain's a fine strong dancer."

" Me! " cried Para Handy, horrified. " I daurna dance a step for palpitation! Jeck's the chentleman for 'Tulda! He hass great experience in Australia, and the boots for't. There's no a man on the roarin' deep more flippant on his feet."

Hurricane Jack's performance for the rest of the evening justified this testimony; he went through the country dances like a full-rigged ship among the lug-sail young lads who were in the party, and refrained from the waltzes and fox-trots only on the grounds of moral disapproval.

It was shortly after midnight when Podger, all in a tremble, pale with apparent alarm, though really from more application of powder than usual, came in to intimate that Mr Taylor had unexpectedly returned, and was to join the party as soon as he had had supper.

"And he'll want to wear these very clothes!" she said to Dougie; "what on earth are we to do?"

"I'll go back to the boat and shift," said Dougie agreeably; he had discovered a very obvious defect in the trousers. The pockets had been sewn up by Podger, and he had nowhere to put his hands.

"There's no time for that. He'll want them in fifteen minutes," said Podger. "We could loan you quite a good waterproof. He'd bring down the house if he found we had meddled with his wardrobe."

"'Dalmighty! What am I to do?" bleated Dougie. "This iss a bonny habble! And there iss not a pair of breeches in the company will fit me."

"Ye'll no' get mine, whatever!" firmly declared Para Handy.

"Ye havena, by any chance, a kind o' kilt?" inquired Hurricane Jack, who took contretemps of this sort with amazing calmness and resource.

"The very thing!" cried Podger. "There's 'Tilda's tartan skirt! It's good enough for a kilt. Go out to the hut at the back and we'll throw it in to you."

Twenty minutes later, attired, with the aid of Jack and the Captain, in a tartan skirt and a knitted jumper of a vivid yellow, Dougie was coaxed back to the ballroom.

A roar of uncontrollable laughter greeted his appearance. He stood for a moment, blinking and confused, in the middle of the room, in a nether garment much too short for a skirt and yet too long for a kilt, to which in other respects it bore no earthly resemblance.

" Dougie will now oblige wi' the Reel o' Hullichan for the sake of the cheneral hilarity," announced the Captain.

" I'll see you aal to the duvvle first! " cried the mate; ' I didna come here for guisin'."

He bolted from the company, and an hour or two later, when Para Handy and Jack got back to their ship, they found him in bed still painfully conscious that he had been made to look ridiculous.

" Hoots, man! " said Hurricane Jack, " what for did ye run away? It wass chenerally admitted that ye were the belle o' the ball. Didn't I tell ye frocks wass goin' to be aal the go for men this winter, accordin' to the Prophet Hezekiah? I never, never, in aal my life got a better bargain in a pair o' boots! "

XI

LEAP YEAR ON THE *VITAL SPARK*

THE last cart of coals was no sooner out of the *Vital Spark* than the crew were up at the Ferry Inn with a bright new tin can Para Handy had bought three days before from a tinker in Ardrishaig. It would hold a

gallon. To carry a gallon of ale from the Ferry Inn
to the quay obviously did not require two sturdy
sailormen and an engineer, but it was thought best
that all of them should accompany the can to obviate
any chance of accident.

" I have seen a can couped before noo," the Captain
had remarked, with his eye on the engineer, who had
offered to go alone; " it takes a steady hand and a
good conscience to cairry a gallon o' ale withoot
spillin'."

" Wha are ye yappin' at noo? " asked the engineer
truculently.

" I am not yappin' at nobody," replied the Captain
calmly. " I wass chust mindin' some droll things that
happened in the way o' short measure wi' the last can
that we had. Keep you calm, Macphail, and don't
put on a bonnet that your heid doesna fit! "

They went into the back room of the public-house,
and, sitting down, carefully sampled a schooner each
before presenting the wholesale order for a canful.

" What way did Jeck no' come? " inquired Dougie.
" I thocht he wass at oor back."

" Ye'll no' see Jeck for an oor or two," replied Para
Handy. " He's away gallivantin'. I'm sure ye saw
him washin' his face? If ye were to go over twenty
minutes efter this to Mary Maclachlan's delf and
sweetie-shop, I'll wudger ye'll get Hurricane Jeck
languishin' on the lady wi' his hench on the coonter,
and smellin' like a valenteen wi' hair-oil. The last
time we were here she made a great impression on
Jeck wi' her conversation lozenges. He's no much o'
a hand at flirtin' by word o' mooth, but he's desperate
darin' when it comes to swappin' sweeties."

" I havena seen a conversation lozenger since the war," said Dougie. " They'll no' be printin' them."

" If they're no'," said Para Handy, " it's a blue look-oot the night for Jeck! There wass never a gallanter man in oilskins, but he's tumid, tumid among women. It's my belief that Jeck would make a match of it wi' his namesake Mary Maclachlan if only he could summons up his nerve to ask her."

Macphail gave a sardonic laugh. " If bounce would dae, Jeck would be the champion lady-killer," he remarked unkindly. " The man's no' thinkin' o' merrage, in my belief; he has nerve enough to sample, every noo and then, the sweetie boxes on the coonter."

There was genuine indignation in the Captain's reception of a remark so unflattering to the absent shipmate. He had to call in another schooner for himself and Dougie; Macphail this time he overlooked.

"Amn't I the forlorn poor skipper o' a boat to have an enchineer like you, Macphail, that's aalways makin' light o' other people! " he retorted. " Ye have chust been sailin' dubs aal your days, when Jeck wass makin' his name in the Black Ball Line and the China clippers. He wass sailin' roond the Horn before ye learned your tred in the gasfitter's shop in Paisley—that's where ye came from, and all ye ever learned aboot engines, or I'm mistaken! "

" I'm no' sayin' onything against the chap," said the engineer, " except that I don't think ony wise-like woman would ever mairry him. The man's fifty if he's a day! "

" He iss not a brat o' a boy, I admit," said the Captain, " but he's in the prime o' life and cheneral agility."

"It's time he wass married, anyway," chimed in Dougie. "It's a poor life, ludgin's. Are ye sure, Peter, he has a chenuine fancy for Miss Maclachlan?"

"She has him that tame he would eat oot o' her hand and jump through girrs," said the Captain. "Did he no' tell me himsel'? It's costin' him half his wages for hair-oil, pan drops, and 'Present-for-a-good-Boy' mugs every time he's in Lochfyne and goes to see her, but he canna, for his life, screw up his nerve to ask her."

"It's Leap Year; maybe she'll ask hersel'," suggested the engineer.

Para Handy's visage glowed at the suggestion. He banged the table.

"For a low-country man," he exclaimed, "ye have sometimes a wonderful sagacity, Macphail. If Mary Maclachlan would only put the word to Jeck and save him from confusion, it would be capital!"

"We could give her a bit o' a hint," proposed Dougie. "Break it to her gently that Jeck is bashful."

"I have a wonderful lot o' nerve mysel'," said the Captain, "but I'm no' wan' o' them gladiators to risk my life in a delf shop. Perhaps Macphail would venture to put the position to Miss Maclachlan."

"Seein' it wass his idea——" said Dougie.

"I'll dae better than that," said the engineer; "if ye ring the bell for ink and a pen and paper, I'll write a nice wee letter for Jeck frae Miss Maclachlan that'll bring things to a heid and show if he's in earnest."

Macphail's forged Leap Year letter was a masterpiece of tact. It indicated that the ostensible writer was fully aware of the difficulty a sensitive gentleman might have in expressing his feelings to a young lady as sensitive as himself, and pointed out that as this was

Leap Year, she was justified in making the first overtures. She remarked that Jack was no longer a youth, and was arriving at that period of life when he required some one to look after him. It was a position she felt thoroughly qualified to occupy. Though he might be of the impression that she was happy in her present position, it was far from being the case, and she was willing to change her condition on the slightest encouragement from him.

" Capital! " exclaimed the Captain when the note was finished. " Chust the way a girl like Miss Maclachlan would put it. If I wass not a married man and got a letter like that I would merry the girl, even if she was a bleck from South Australia."

" It should save a desperate lot o' hair-oil, that! " was Dougie's view. " I wonder where they'll get a hoose? "

A discreet boy, with instructions to say the letter was given him by a girl, was sent with it to the vessel, and the can and its convoy an hour or two later got on board.

Hurricane Jack was invisible. More remarkable was the fact that his dunnage bag and all his belongings were gone too. Inquiries on the quay brought out the information that he had left with the *Minard Castle* an hour ago, having got, as he explained to one informant, an unexpected letter which made his instant departure imperative.

" Holy sailors! " exclaimed Para Handy, " isn't this the bonny caper? Do ye think we scared him? "

Para Handy and Macphail went down to the delf and sweetie-shop to make inquiries, and found it in charge of Miss Maclachlan's sister.

N

" Did ye see any word o' Hurricane Jeck the night? "
he inquired.

" He was here two hours or more ago, and only
stopped a minute," said the girl.

" Did he see your sister Mary? " asked the Captain.

" Hoo could he see Mary? " replied the girl. " She
was married a week ago to Peter Campbell, and she's
left the shop."

XII

BONNIE ANN

IT was Macphail the engineer who first discovered the
fame of Bonnie Ann, and the little shop, half dairy,
half greengrocery, where that gifted lady had far more
young customers for her occult powers than for her
excellent potted-head and home-made soda scones.
The occult department of her thriving business was
carried on behind the shop, in a room where she read
tea-cups, disclosed the future vicissitudes of any love
affair with the aid of a pack of cards, or—for a somewhat larger fee—took cataleptic fits, in the course of
which she held communication with the dead.

Nor even then was Bonnie Ann's versatility exhausted; she called this chamber of hers a " Beauty
Parlour and Séance Saloon," and could guarantee the
most ravishing complexions, busts of an agreeable
contour, lustrous long hair, fascinating eyelashes,
finger-nails to do credit to any lady, and an infallible
cure for chilblains, corns, and cuticular blotches.

The notorious Madame Blavatsky was a bungling

amateur in the magic arts compared with the shy, almost morbidly unostentatious Ann, who never advertised.

Macphail, having gone to Bonnie Ann for treatment of an ingrowing toe-nail, had been privileged to witness a trance performance, in which she conversed fluently with Mary Queen of Scots, and he returned to the *Vital Spark* immensely impressed.

" I'm tellin' ye, there's something in't! " he declared to his shipmates. " She had Bloody Mary to the life, and I ken, for I've read history. Ye can get it a' in ' The Scottish Chiefs.' "

" Did she read the palm o' your hand? " inquired Para Handy, his interest wakened.

" There's nane o' that hanky-panky about Bonnie Ann," replied the engineer. " Pure science! She throws hersel' into a trance till ye only see the whites o' her eyes, and then ye hear the depairted jist the same's they were in the room. She's weel in wi' the Duke o' Wellington; he tell't her three years ago we would win the war."

Dougie, the mate, was not surprised to hear of these wonderful manifestations. " The papers iss full o' them," he said. " It's aal the go wi' the titled gentry and Epuscopalian munisters. I heard mysel', wan night, a noise I couldna understand inside a kitchen dresser."

" I'm no' sayin' whether I believe in the spirits or no'," remarked Para Handy cautiously. " There iss spirits in the Scruptures, though they were different in the Holy Land, and no' up to capers—shiftin' side-boards, spillin' oil on the ceilin', rappin' in coal scuttles. But if Bonnie Ann hass the gift, we should give her a trial to see what she can make o' Hurricane Jeck."

Three weeks before, Hurricane Jack, alarmed at the apparent intentions of a lady who wished to take advantage of her Leap Year privilege and propose to him, had disappeared. He had left the *Vital Spark* without warning, and never been heard of since. Convinced—or almost convinced—that Jack had drowned himself—for they knew the lady—his three shipmates proceeded to Bonnie Ann's shop at night, and began negotiations diplomatically with an order for turnips and cabbages.

" Could we hae a word wi' ye at the back? " inquired Macphail in a husky whisper over the counter. " I wass tellin' my mates aboot Bloody Mary."

Bonnie Ann, who apparently had got the adjective to her name from an ironic customer, looked at her watch, and intimated that it was shutting-up time.

" Forbye," she added, " if it's Mary Queen o' Scots ye're wantin', it's no her nicht oot; I couldna get her. A lot o' you sailor chaps thinks a beauty parlour and séance saloon is jist like a shebeen that ye can come intae ony oor o' the day or nicht and ring for the depairted the same's it was a schooner o' beer."

" It's no' Bloody Mary we're wantin'," explained Para Handy soothingly. " We'll no' put ye to the slightest bother. To let ye ken—a shipmate o' oors, Jeck Maclachlan, went missin' three weeks ago. He's no' in the polis-office, he's no' in his uncle's hoose in Polmadie, and he must be deid, fair play or foul. Could ye help us, Ann, to find oot something aboot Jeck? "

He bent upon Bonnie Ann a gaze of compelling languishment.

"Awa' into the back," she said, " and I'll put up the shutters and jine ye in a meenute."

They were seated in the beauty parlour and séance saloon when she joined them.

She lit the gas and turned it down to a peep, after first having lowered the blind. Picking up, and gazing intently at, a crystal ball, the size of a satisfactory Seville orange, she muttered, " There's a man missin'. He has a tattoo mark on his airm—it's blue. He's been missin' three weeks; his friends is anxious to hear aboot him."

"And that's the God's truth," exclaimed Dougie, awestruck by this swift, unerring comprehension of the situation. " He had a lend o' my pocket-naipkin."

" He's a sailor," continued Bonnie Ann. " The initials o' his name is J. M'L., and he's a Scotchman. He traivelled a lot on boats. He wasna a teetotaller and whiles his language was coorse——"

" Holy Frost! Jeck to the life! " exclaimed Para Handy. " I doot he iss done for; he never even came for his pay. Iss he on deck or under hatches, Annie? "

" Did I no' tell ye! " cried Macphail triumphantly. " Never mind the glessy, Annie; throw us a trance, and get in touch wi' somebody that was in the sea tred when he was in the body. There's nae use botherin' Bonnie Mary o' Argyll to ask for Jeck: if he's in the Better Land, he'll be doon aboot the quay, or in a beershop whaur she wouldna care to venture."

" I could try the Duke o' Wellington," suggested Bonnie Ann. " Mind, I'm no' guaranteein' ony communication; the Duke, whiles, tak's a lot o' humourin'."

Para Handy looked dubious. " Is there no' a wee chape skipper chap could do the job? His Grace would be an expensive pairty. If Jeck iss there at aal, I'll wudger he's weel kent."

" In life he wass a toppin' singer, and he could play the trump," remarked Dougie helpfully.

Bonnie Ann put the crystal ball back on the chimney-piece, and pulled out a little table to the middle of the room.

" Ye'll hae to help yoursel's," she intimated, having placed chairs for them round the table. " Draw in."

" Don't put yoursel' to any bother, Annie," huskily implored the Captain, under a misapprehension. " We're chust efter a splendid tea."

" I wasna gaun to offer ye onything," said Bonnie Ann. " Ye needna be sae smert! A' put your baith hands flet on the table wi' me and concentrate your minds on—what did ye say the chap's name was— Maclachlan? "

" Better kent as Hurricane Jeck," explained Macphail, who entered into the ceremony with absolute enthusiasm. " If ye put some tumblers on the table he'll be wi' us in a jiffy."

This suggestion that the spirit of their departed shipmate was to join the company alarmed Para Handy, who hastily withdrew his hands.

" Bless my sowl! " he exclaimed, " are ye thinkin' to bring Jeck here in the spirit? "

" I thocht that was whit ye wanted," answered Bonnie Ann peevishly. " It's shairly no' to play catch-the-ten we're gaithered here! "

"And it's no' to see the ghost o' Jeck Maclachlan, I'll assure ye! " exclaimed Para Handy. " Take my advice, and don't you bother him, Annie. He wass a tricky lad in life, and dear knows what he would be up to in the spirit! Am I no' right, Dougie?"

"Ye're quite right, Captain," agreed the mate emphatically. "We're no' wantin' to see himsel' at aal, but chust to get the news o' him. Let him keep his distance! Could ye no' get him, Annie, to do something in the air wi' a tambourine?"

"As shair's daith I canna come the tambourine the nicht," pleaded Bonnie Ann; "I'm deid tired—bakin' a' the aifternoon. There's naething for't but to ask the Duke o' Wellington for your frien'."

"I don't believe the Duke's a bit o' good; he'll go on haverin' aboot the battle o' Waterloo, and that's the wan battle Jeck wass never in," declared the Captain.

Macphail looked at the skipper with disgust. "Ye're makin' a fair cod o' the thing," he exclaimed. "Gie the woman a chance! Fling us a trance, Annie, and see whit the Duke says."

Bonnie Ann sat back in her chair, shut her eyes, and in a minute or two was in wireless communication with the Iron Duke, who, in a falsetto baritone through her lips, conveyed the information that he had seen John Maclachlan in the last two days.

"What happened to Jeck?" inquired Para Handy, in an awestruck whisper.

The unfortunate seaman, it appeared, had fallen over the side of a ship in a storm, swam three days, and perished within sight of land.

"That's Jeck, sure enough!" exclaimed Dougie. "He was a capital sweemer!"

"Iss he happy, Annie?" whispered Para Handy. "Ask His Grace what sort o' trum he's in."

" The life and soul o' the place! " replied the Duke
of Wellington. "As happy's the day's long. He sends
his best respects to all concerned."

Having recovered from her trance, Bonnie Ann
briskly collected a fee of five shillings which the crew
of the *Vital Spark* made up with difficulty between
them; saw her clients off the premises as quickly as
possible, shut up her shop, and retired to the beauty
parlour to make herself some supper.

The crew made for the quay in a state of considerable mental excitement, solemnised by the knowledge
of their shipmate's fate, and were staggered to find
Hurricane Jack himself on board the *Vital Spark*! He
had arrived by the *Minard Castle*.

" 'Dalmighty! where were ye, Jeck? " inquired Para
Handy, who was first to recover himself.

" Oh, jist perusin' about the docks o' Gleska," said
Jack airily. " I fell in wi' a lot o' fellows."

" Of aal the liars ever I heard," said the Captain
viciously, " the worst iss the Duke o' Wellington! "

XIII

THE LEAP-YEAR BALL

SUNNY JIM, back again on one of his periodical short
spells of long-shore sailoring, went ashore on Friday
morning with a can for milk, and an old potato-sack
for bread, and, such is the morning charm of Appin,
that he made no attempt to get either of them filled
until he reached the inn at Duror. He wasn't a fellow
who drank at any time excessively, but, Glasgow-born,

he felt always homesick in foreign parts unless he could be, as Para Handy said, " convenient and adjaacent to a licensed premise." In a shop beside the inn he got his bread, and he might have got the milk a mile or two nearer Kintallen quay, from which he had come, but a sailor never goes to a farm for milk so long as he can get it at an inn.

"A quart," he said to the girl at the bar, and pushed the can across the counter. As she measured out and filled his can with ale, he sternly kept an averted eye on a bill on the wall which spoke in the highest terms of Robertson's Sheep Dips.

" What in the world do ye ca' this? " he exclaimed, regarding the can's contents with what to an unsophisticated child would look like genuine surprise. " Michty! what thick cream! If the Gleska coos gave milk like that, the dairies would mak' their fortunes."

" Was it not beer you wanted? " asked the girl, with sleeves rolled up on a pair of arms worth all the rest of the Venus de Medici, and a roguish eye.

" Nut at all! " said he emphatically. " Milk. What ye sometimes put in tea."

" Then it's the back of the house you should go to," said the girl. " This is not the milk department," and she was about to empty the can again, but not with unreasonable celerity, lest the customer should maybe change his mind.

" Hold on! " said Sunny Jim, with a grasp at it. " Seein' it's there, I'll maybe can make use o't. See's a tumbler, Flora."

For twenty minutes he leaned upon the counter and fleeted the time delightfully as in the golden world. He said he was off a yacht, and, if not officially, in

N 2

every other sense the skipper. True, it was not exactly
what might be called the yachting season, but the
owners of the yacht were whimsical. Incidentally, he
referred to his melodeon, and at that the girl declared
he was the very man she had been looking for.

"Oh, come aff it, come aff it!" said Sunny Jim,
with proper modesty, but yet with an approving glance
at his reflection which was in the mirror behind her.
"I'm naething patent, but I'll admit there's no' a
cheerier wee chap from here to Ballachulish."

"Ye would be an awful handy man at a ball," said
the girl, "with your melodeon. We're having a leap-
year dance to-night, and only a pair of pipers. What's
a pair of pipers?"

"Two," said Sunny Jim promptly.

"You're quite mistaken," replied the girl with equal
promptness; "it's only two till the first reel's by, and
then it's a pair o' bauchles no' able to keep their feet.
You come with your melodeon, and I'll be your
partner."

He went back to the *Vital Spark* delighted, looked
out his Sunday clothes and his melodeon, and chagrined
his shipmates hugely by the narrative of his good
fortune.

"What's a leap-year baal?" asked Para Handy.
"Iss there a night or two extra in it? No Chrustian
baal should last over the week-end."

"It's a baal where the women hae a' the say,"
explained Macphail, the engineer, whose knowledge
was encyclopædic.

"Iss that it?" said Para Handy. "It's chust like
bein' at home! It's me that's gled I'm not invited.
Take you something wise-like wi' ye in your pocket,
Jum; I wouldna be in their reverence."

" I would like to see it," said Dougie. " Does the lady come in a kind of a cab for you? "

" It's only young chaps that's invited," explained Sunny Jim, with brutal candour.

The Captain looked at him reproachfully. " You shouldna say the like o' that to Dougie," he remonstrated. " Dougie's no' that terrible old."

" I was sayin' it to baith o' you," said Sunny Jim. " It's no' a mothers' meetin' this, it's dancin'."

" There's no man in the shippin' tred wi' more agility than mysel'," declared the indignant skipper. " I can stot through the middle o' a dance like a tuppenny kahoochy ball. Dougie himsel' 'll tell you! "

" Yes, I've often seen you stottin'," agreed the mate, with great solemnity. Para Handy looked at him with some suspicion, but he presented every appearance of a man with no intention to say anything offensive.

" You havena an extra collar and a bit o' a stud on you? " was the astonishing inquiry made by Dougie less than twenty minutes after Sunny Jim had departed for the Duror ball. " I wass thinkin' to mysel' we might take a turn along the road to look at the life and gaiety."

" Dougie, you're beyond redemption! " said Para Handy. "A married man and nine or ten o' a family, and there you're up to all diversions like a young one!"

" I wassna going by the door o' the ball," the mate exclaimed indignantly. " You aye take me up wrong."

" Oh, ye should baith gang," suggested the engineer, with malicious irony. "A couple o' fine young chaps! Gie the girls o' Appin a treat. Never let on you're mairried. They'll never suspect as lang's ye keep on your bonnets."

" I think mysel' we should go, Dougie, and we might

be able to buy a penny novelle for Macphail to read on Sunday," said the Captain. "Anything fresh about Lady Audley, Macphail?"

Macphail ignored the innuendo. "Noo's your chance," he proceeded. "Everything's done for ye by the fair sect: a lady M.C. to find ye pairtners; the women themsel's comin' up to see if your programme's full, and askin' every noo and then if ye care for a gless o' clairet-cup on draught. I wouldna say but ye would be better to hae a fan and a Shetland shawl to put ower your heids when you're comin' hame; everything's reversed at a leap-year ball."

He would simply have goaded the Captain into going if the Captain had not made up his mind as soon as Dougie himself that he was going in any case.

"Two-and-six apiece for the tickets," said the man at the door when Para Handy and his mate came drifting out of the bar and made a tentative attempt at slipping in unostentatiously.

"Not for a leap-year dance, Johnny," said the Captain mildly. "Everything is left to the ladies."

"Except the payin'; that's ass usual," said the doorkeeper, and the Captain and his mate regretfully paid for entrance. The room was crowded, and the masculine predominated to the extent that it looked as if every lady had provided herself with half-a-dozen partners that she might be assured of sufficient dancing. One of the pipers had already lapsed into the state so picturesquely anticipated by the girl whom Sunny Jim called Flora; the other leant on a window-sill, and looked with Celtic ferocity and disdain upon Sunny Jim, who was playing his melodeon for the Flowers of Edinburgh.

" You're playin' tip-top, Jum. I never heard you better," said the Captain to him at the first interval; and the musician was so pleased that he introduced his shipmates to Flora.

" We're no' here for the baal at aal, at aal, but chust to put bye the time," the Captain explained to her. " I see you're no' slack for pairtners."

" Not at present," she replied; " but just you wait till the supper's bye and you'll see a bonny difference."

She was right, too. The masculine did certainly not predominate after midnight, being otherwise engaged. The fact that Flora was a wallflower seemed to distress Sunny Jim, who would gladly now relinquish his office of musician to the piper.

" That's a charmin' gyurl, and a desperate sober piper," said the Captain to his mate, who spent most of the time looking for what he called the "commytee," and had finally discovered, if not the thing itself, at all events what was as good. " Jum's doin' capital at the melodeon, and it would be a peety if the piper took his job."

They took out the piper, and by half an hour's intelligent administration of the committee's refreshments rendered him quite incapable of contributing any further music to the dancers.

" Now that's aal right," said the Captain cheerfully, returning to the hall. "A piper's aal right if ye take him the proper way, but I never saw one wi' a more durable heid than yon fellow. Man, Jum's doin capital! Hasn't he got the touch! It's a peety he's such a strong musician, for, noo that the pipers hass lost their reeds, he's likely to be kept at it till the feenish."

" Lost their reeds! " said Dougie.

" Chust that! " replied the Captain calmly. " I took them oot o' their drones, and I have them in my pocket. It's every man for himsel' in Duror of Appin. You and me'll dance with Flora."

Nothing could exceed the obvious annoyance of Sunny Jim when he saw his shipmates dance with Flora to the music of his own providing. Again and again he glanced with impatient expectancy towards the door for the relieving piper.

" The piper 'll be back in a jiffy, Jum," said Para Handy to him, sweeping past with Flora in a polka or a schottische. " He's chust oot at the back takin' a drop of lemonade, and said he would be in immediately."

" You're doing magnificent," he said, coming round to the musician again as Dougie took the floor with Flora for the Haymakers. " Ye put me awful in mind of yon chap, Paddy Roosky, him that's namely for the fiddle. Man, if ye chust had a velvet jecket! Flora says she never danced to more becomin' music."

" That's a' richt," said the disgusted musician; " but I'm gettin' fed up wi' playin' awa' here. I cam' here for dancin', and I wish the piper would look slippy."

" He'll be in in wan meenute," said Para Handy, with the utmost confidence, turning over the pipe reeds in his trousers pocket. " It's a reel next time, Jum; you might have given us ' Monymusk ' and 'Alister wears a cock't bonnet '; I'm engaged for it to Flora."

Dance after dance went on, and, of course, there was no relieving piper. The melodeonist was sustained by the flattering comments of his shipmates on his playing and an occasional smile from Flora, who was that kind of girl who didn't care whom she danced with so long as she got dancing.

"Special request from Flora—would ye give us 'The Full-Rigged Ship' the next one? That's a topper," said the Captain to him. Or, "Compliments of Flora, and would you mind the Garaka Waltz and Circassian Circle for the next, Jum? She says she likes my style o' dancin'."

"I wish to goodness I'd never learned to play a bloomin' note," said Sunny Jim.

But he played without cessation till the ball was ended, the fickle Flora dancing more often with his shipmates than with anybody else.

As they took the road to Kintallen quay at six o'clock in the morning, Para Handy took some chanter reeds from his pocket and handed them to Sunny Jim.

"You should learn the pipes, Jum," he remarked. "They're no' so sore on you ass a melodeon. Man, but she wass a lovely dancer, Flora! Chust sublime! Am I no' right, Dougie?"

"A fair gazelle! The steps o' her!" said the mate poetically.

"And we were pretty smert on oor feet oorsel's," said Para Handy. "It doesna do to have aal your agility in your fingers."

XIV

THE BOTTLE KING

THE *Vital Spark* at nightfall put into the little bay where her cargo of timber was assembled. On an ingenuous excuse of " takin' the air," Hurricane Jack, who had not been there before, went ashore at the earliest possible moment in the dark, and, trusting to an instinct usually unerring, searched for some place of cheer.

He came on the inn through a back yard, where were several vans and dogcarts, and a curious sort of chariot, highly ornamental to the feel, that puzzled him considerably, till he struck a match, and found it was a hearse.

The hearse, however, engaged his attention less intently than the enormous array of empty bottles which were piled up all round the yard. Crates were full of them, barrels were brimming over with them; they were in layers ten deep under the stable eaves, and tinkling with the water that fell through them from a broken rhone.

" Whatever they are in this place," said Jack to himself, " they're no' nerrow-minded. They must have a fine cheery winter of it! If they drank all that, there must have been great tred wi' the hearse."

He opened that solemn vehicle, looked inside, and found it too was filled with the relics of conviviality, mostly wine-bottles.

" English gentlemen. Towerists. Shooters. The money them folk waste! "

He shook some of the bottles, to make certain they were empty. " No fears o' them! " he reflected cynically. " It makes me sad. Puttin' bottles in a hearse—it's no respectable; I wonder what the ministers would say! "

There was no access to the inn from the yard that he could find, so to save time he climbed a wall, and found himself on the other side of it, by that marvellous intuition of his, exactly at the door of the bar where all the winter business of the inn was done.

Nobody was inside but the innkeeper, who was washing tumblers in the light of a hanging paraffin-lamp, and was suspiciously flushed.

" A wet night," said Hurricane Jack, taking off his soaking cap and slapping it against the skirt of his oilskin coat to get rid of part of its moisture. " I'll take a small sensation."

The landlord looked surprised. " I thought you were from Balliemeanach," said he, " to order the hearse. Where in the world did ye come from? "

" From the boundin' deep," said Hurricane Jack. " My ship's outside there, as ye might say, on the doorstep."

The landlord looked immensely relieved.

" As sure as death," said he, " I thought ye were from Balliemeanach. Maclean the wudman had a couple o' glesses o' Cream de Mong here yesterday, and I havena slept a wink since, wonderin' would he get over it."

" Cream de Mong," said Hurricane Jack, with genuine interest; " if it's anything like that, I'll try it."

The landlord produced a bottle of green liqueur from below the counter. " Mind ye," he said, " it's at your own risk. I don't fancy the look o't mysel'. It was in the cellar when I came here three years ago, and I hadna the nerve to offer it to any one till Maclean was here in desperation yesterday, and me withoot a drop o' spirits in the hoose."

Hurricane Jack picked up the bottle, looked at it, and put it down again. " Starboard Light," he remarked. " I've seen it. They take it in cabins. I wouldn't use it to oil my hair. What I'm wantin's something to drink."

A bottle of beer was promptly uncorked and put before him. " Ninepence," said the landlord.

" Holy sailors! " exclaimed Hurricane Jack. " I could buy wine for that on the Rio Grande."

" There's a penny for the bottle," said the landlord. " Eightpence if ye bring back the bottle."

Jack, two seconds after, handed him back the empty bottle and eightpence.

" Ye're surely keen on empty bottles," he remarked.

" A penny apiece, and glad to get as many as I can; they call me the Bottle King," said the landlord. " But someway, this while back, my mind's a' reel-rall."

Para Handy and Dougie were going to bed, and Macphail was there already, when Hurricane Jack got back to the ship and excitedly demanded a large spale basket.

" What on earth are ye goin' to do wi' a spale basket, Jeck? " inquired the Captain. " Were ye fishin'? "

" No, nor fishin'! " retorted Jack; " but there's a man up yonder at the inn that calls himsel' the Bottle King, and payin' a penny apiece for them. I think I can put a lot o' tred in his way." He had already found a basket.

Para Handy looked at him uneasily. " Iss it Peter Grant? " he asked. " Ye'll no' get roond Peter wi' aal your agility. If it's buyin' bottles he is, ye'll no' put him off wi' jeely jars. Where in the name o' fortune are ye goin' to get the bottles? There iss not wan bottle in this boat, unless it's under Macphail's pillow."

" Hoots, man! " said Dougie, remonstrative; " give

Jeck a chance! Jeck never yet put oot his hand farther than he could streetch his arm."

" Come on the pair o' ye, and see a pant! " said Hurricane Jack. " We'll have to look slippy afore Grant shuts his shop."

" I hope it's nothing that'll be found oot," said Para Handy, still uneasy. " Ye're a duvvle for quirks, Jeck, and I wouldna like the ship to get into trouble."

Ten minutes later they all trailed up to the inn with the empty basket.

The innkeeper was still washing tumblers when the Captain and Dougie, carrying a spale basket of empty bottles between them, came into his bar, and Hurricane Jack behind them.

" Three pints o' ale," said Jack, with the utmost confidence, " and here's two dozen bottles. We're glad to get rid o' them."

The Bottle King was frankly surprised at such a consignment from such a quarter.

" Wherever ye got them bottles, it wasna here," he said. "At least, as far as I can mind. My heid's a' reel-rall, but it doesna maitter. I'm willin' to tak' them," and, having emptied the basket, he produced the beer for his customers.

"Are ye sure they're no' worth more than a penny the piece? " inquired Para Handy. " We were gettin' tuppence for them in Port Askaig. Am I right, Dougie, or am I wrong? "

" It wass tuppence in Port Askaig, and tuppence ha'penny in Port Ellen," replied the mate, with unhesitating assurance. " Bottles is scarce. They're no' makin' them. And ye never in your life saw bonnier bottles than them; they're the chenuine gless."

" Pure plate-gless," said Hurricane Jack. " Look at the labels—' Sherry Wine '—I'll wager there's a lot o' money in them."

" We have a ship-load yonder o' them," said the Captain. " Could ye be doin' wi' a gross or two? Chust for the turnover. We must aal put oor hand to the plew to help the government, Mr Grant."

The Bottle King for a moment suspended his washing of tumblers, with tremulous hands put on a pair of spectacles, and looked more closely at his purchase.

" God bless me! " he exclaimed; " them's my own wine bottles! Where did ye get them? "

" We got them in a hearse behind the hoose here," frankly admitted Hurricane Jack. " There's a thoosand deid men yonder, if there's wan."

" My Chove! aren't you the ruffians? " cried Peter Grant. " Sellin' me my own bottles! I never could mind where I put them, and me lookin' for them high and low since the Old New Year. But tach! it doesna maitter; they caal me the Bottle King."

XV

" MUDGES "

" By Chove! but they're bad the night! " said Dougie, running a grimy paw across his forehead.

" Perfectly ferocious! " said Para Handy, slapping his neck. " This fair beats Bowmore, and Bowmore iss namely for its mudges. I never saw the brutes more desperate! You would actually think they were whustlin' on wan another, cryin', 'Here's a clean sailor, and he hasna a collar on; gather about, boys!'"

"Oh, criftens!" whimpered Sunny Jim, in agony, dabbing his face incessantly with what looked suspiciously like a dish-cloth; "I've see'd midges afore this, but they never had spurs on their feet afore. Yah-h-h! I wish I was back in Gleska! They can say what they like aboot the Clyde, but anywhere above Bowlin' I'll guarantee ye'll no' be eaten alive. If they found a midge in Gleska, they would put it in the Kelvingrove Museum."

Macphail, his face well lubricated, came up from among the engines, and jeered. "Midges never bothered me," said he contemptuously. "If ye had been wi' me on the West Coast o' Africa, and felt the mosquitoes, it wouldna be aboot a wheen o' gnats ye would mak' a sang. It's a' a hallucination aboot midges; I can only speak aboot them the way I find them, and they never did me ony harm. Perhaps it's no midges that's botherin' ye efter a'."

"Perhaps no'," said Para Handy, with great acidity. "Perhaps it's hummin'-birds, but the effect iss chust the same. Ye'll read in the Scruptures yonder aboot the ant goin' for the sluggard, but the ant iss a perfect chentleman compared wi' the mudge. And from aal I ever heard o' the mosquito, it'll no' stab ye behind your back withoot a word o' warnin'. Look at them on Dougie's face—quite black! Ye would never think it wass the Sunday."

It was certainly pretty bad at the quay of Arrochar. With the evening air had come out, as it seemed, the midges of all the Highlands. They hung in clouds above the *Vital Spark*, and battened gluttonously on her distracted crew.

" When I was at the mooth o' the Congo River—" began the engineer; but Para Handy throttled the reminiscence.

" The Congo's no' to be compared wi' the West o' Scotland when ye come to insects," said Para Handy. " There's places here that's chust deplorable whenever the weather's the least bit warm. Look at Tighna-bruaich!—they're that bad there, they'll bite their way through corrugated iron roofs to get at ye! Take Clynder, again, or any other place in the Gareloch, and ye'll see the old ones leadin' roond the young ones, learnin' them the proper grips. There iss a spachial kind of mudge in Dervaig, in the Isle of Mull, that hass aal the points o' a Poltalloch terrier, even to the black nose and the cocked lugs, and sits up and barks at you. I wass once gatherin' cockles in Colonsay——"

" I could be daein' wi' some cockles," said Sunny Jim. " I aye feel like a cockle when it comes near the Gleska Fair."

" The best cockles in the country iss in Colonsay," said the Captain. " But the people in Colonsay iss that slow they canna catch them. I wass wance gatherin' cockles there, and the mudges were that large and bold, I had to throw stones at them."

" It was a pity ye hadna a gun," remarked Macphail, with sarcasm.

"A gun would be no' much use wi' the mudges of Colonsay," replied the Captain; " nothing would dis-courage yon fellows but a blast o' dynamite. What wass there on the island at the time but a chenuine English towerist, wi' a capital red kilt, and, man! but he wass green! He was that green, the coos of Colonsay would go mooin' along the road efter him, thinkin' he wass gress. He wass wan of them English chentlemen that'll be drinkin' chinger-beer on aal occasions, even when they're dry, and him bein' English, he had seen next to nothing aal his days till he took the boat from West Loch Tarbert. The first night on the island he went oot in his kilt, and came back in half an oor to the inns wi' his legs fair peetiful! There iss nothing that the mudges likes to see among them better than an English towerist with a kilt: the very tops wass eaten off his stockin's."

" That's a fair streetcher, Peter! " exclaimed the incredulous engineer.

" It's ass true ass I'm tellin' you," said Para Handy. " Any one in Colonsay will tell you. He had wan of them names shed in the middle like Fitz-Gerald or Seton-Kerr; that'll prove it to ye. When he came in to the inns wi' his legs chust fair beyond redemption, he didna even know the cause of it.

" ' It's the chinger-beer that's comin' oot on you,' says John Macdermott, that had the inns at the time. ' There iss not a thing you can drink that iss more deliteerious in Colonsay. Nobody takes it here.'

" 'And what in all the world do they take? ' said the English chentleman.

" ' The water o' the mountain well,' said John, ' and whiles a drop of wholesome Brutish spirits. There's some that doesna care for water.'

" But the English chentleman was eccentric, and nothing would do for him to drink but chinger, an' they took him doon to a shed where the fishermen were barkin' nets, and they got him to bark his legs wi' catechu. If it's green he wass before, he wass now ass brown's a trammel net. But it never made a bit o' odds to the mudges oot in Colonsay! I tell you they're no' slack! "

" They're no' slack here neithers! " wailed Sunny Jim, whose face was fairly wealed by the assailants. " Oh, michty! I think we would be faur better ashore."

" Not a bit! " said Dougie, furiously puffing a pipe of the strongest tobacco, in whose fumes the midges appeared to take the most exquisite pleasure. " There's no' a place ashore where ye could take shelter from them—it being Sunday," he significantly added.

" I'm gaun ashore anyway," said Macphail, removing all superfluous lubricant from his countenance with a piece of waste. " It wouldna be midges that would keep me lollin' aboot this auld hooker on a fine nicht. If ye had some experience o' mosquitoes! Them's the chaps for ye. It's mosquitoes that spreads the malaria fever."

They watched him go jauntily up the quay, accompanied by a cloud of insects which seemed to be of the impression that he was leading them to an even better feeding-ground than the *Vital Spark*. He had hardly gone a hundred yards when he turned and came hurriedly back, beating the air.

" Holy frost! " he exclaimed, jumping on deck, " I never felt midges like that in a' my days afore; they're in billions o' billions! "

" Tut, tut! " said Para Handy. " Ye're surely getting awfu' tumid, Macphail. You that's so weel acquent wi' them mosquitoes! If I wass a trevelled man like you, I wouldna be bate wi' a wheen o' Hielan' mudges.

They're no' in't anyway. Chust imagination! Chust a hallucination! Ye mind ye told us?"

"There's no hallucination aboot them chaps," said Macphail, smacking himself viciously.

"Nut at all!" said Sunny Jim. "Nut at all! If there's ony hallucination aboot them, they have it sherpened. G-r-r-r! It's cruel; that's whit it is; fair cruel!"

"I promised I would go and see Macrae the nicht," said the engineer. "But it's no' safe to gang up that quay. This is yin o' the times I wish I was a smoker; that tobacco o' yours, Dougie, would shairly fricht awa' the midges."

"Not wan bit of it!" said Dougie peevishly, rubbing the back of his neck, on which his tormentors were thickly clustered. "I'm beginning to think mysel' they're partial to tobacco; it maybe stimulates the appetite. My! aren't they the brutes! Look at them on Jim!"

With a howl of anguish Sunny Jim dashed down the fo'c's'le hatch, the back of his coat pulled over his ears.

"Is there naething at a' a chap could dae to his face to keep them aff?" asked the engineer, still solicitous about his promised visit to Macrae.

"Some people 'll be sayin' paraffine-oil iss a good thing," suggested the Captain. "But that's only for Ro'sa' mudges; I'm thinkin' the Arrochar mudges would maybe consuder paraffine a trate. And I've heard o' others tryin' whusky—I mean rubbed on ootside. I never had enough to experiment wi't mysel'. Forbye, there's none."

"I wadna care to gang up to Macrae's on a Sunday

smellin' o' either paraffine - oil or whisky," said Macphail.

"Of course not!" said Para Handy. "What was I thinkin' of? Macrae's sister wouldna like it," and he winked broadly at Dougie. "Ye'll be takin' a bit of a daunder wi' her efter the church goes in. Give her my best respects, will ye? A fine, big, bouncin' gyurl! A splendid form!"

"You shut up!" said Macphail to his commander, blushing. "I think I'll gie my face anither syne wi' plenty o' saft soap for it, and mak' a breenge across to Macrae's afore the effect wears aff."

He dragged a pail over to the water-beaker, half filled it with water, added a generous proportion of soft soap from a tin can, and proceeded to wash himself without taking off his coat.

"Ye needna mind to keep on your kep," said the Captain, grimacing to Dougie. "Mima 'll no' see ye. He's been callin' on Macrae a score o' times, Dougie, and the sister hasna found oot yet he's bald. Mercy on us! Did ye ever in your life see such mudges!"

"I'm past speakin' aboot them!" said the mate, with hopeless resignation. "What iss he keepin' on his bonnet for?"

"He's that bald that unless he keeps it on when he's washin' his face he doesna know where to stop," said Para Handy. "The want o' the hair's an aawful depredaation!"

But even these drastic measures failed to render Macphail inviolate from the attack of the insects, whose prowess he had underestimated. For the second time he came running back from the head of the quay pursued by them, to be greeted afresh by the irony of his Captain.

" There's a solid wall o' them up there," he declared, rubbing his eyes.

" Isn't it annoyin'? " said the Captain, with fallacious sympathy. " Mima will be weary waitin' on ye. If there wass a druggist's open, ye might get something in a bottle to rub on. Or if it wassna the Sabbath, ye might get a can o' syrup in the grocer's."

" Syrup? " said the engineer inquiringly, and Para Handy slyly kicked Dougie on the shin.

"There's nothin' better for keepin' awa' the mudges," he explained. " Ye rub it on your face and leave it on. It's a peety we havena any syrup on the boat."

" Sunny Jim had a tin o' syrup last night at his tea," said the engineer hopefully.

" But it must be the chenuine golden syrup," said Para Handy. " No other kind 'll do."

Sunny Jim was routed out from under the blankets in his bunk to produce syrup, which proved to be of the requisite golden character, as Para Handy knew very well it was, and five minutes later Macphail, with a shining countenance, went up the quay a third time attended by midges in greater myriads than ever. This time he beat no retreat.

" Stop you! " said Para Handy. " When Mima Macrae comes to the door, she'll think it's no' an enchineer she has to caal on her, but a fly cemetery."

XVI

AN OCEAN TRAGEDY

GEORGE IV., being a sovereign of imagination, was so much impressed by stories of Waterloo that he began to say he had been there himself, and had taken part in it. He brought so much imagination to the narrative that he ended by believing it—an interesting example of the strange psychology of the liar. Quite as remarkable is the case of Para Handy, whose singular delusion of Sunday fortnight last is the subject of much hilarity now among seamen of the minor coasting-trade.

The first of the storm on Saturday night found the *Vital Spark* off Toward on her way up-channel, timber-laden, and without a single light, for Sunny Jim, who had been sent ashore for oil at Tarbert, had brought back a jar of beer instead by an error that might naturally occur with any honest seaman.

When the lights of other ships were showing dangerously close the mate stood at the bow and lit matches, which, of course, were blown out instantly.

" It's not what might be called a cheneral illumination," he remarked, " but it's an imitataation of the Gantock Light, and it no' workin' proper, and you'll see them big fellows will give us plenty o' elbow-room."

Thanks to the matches and a bar of iron which Macphail had hung on the lever of the steam-whistle, so that it lamented ceaselessly through the tempest like a soul in pain, the *Vital Spark* escaped collision, and some time after midnight got into Cardwell Bay with nothing lost except the jar, a bucket, and the mate's sou'-wester.

"A dirty night! It's us that iss weel out of it," said Para Handy gratefully, when he had got his anchor down.

The storm was at its worst when the Captain went ashore on Sunday to get the train for Glasgow on a visit to his wife, the farther progress of his vessel up the river for another day at least being obviously impossible. It was only then he realised that he had weathered one of the great gales that make history. At Gourock pierhead shellbacks of experience swore they had never seen the like of it; there were solemn bodings about the fate of vessels that had to face it. Para Handy, as a ship's commander who had struggled through it, found himself regarded as a hero, and was plied with the most flattering inquiries. On any other day the homage of the shellbacks might have aroused suspicion, but its disinterested nature could not be called in question, seeing all the public-houses were shut.

" Never saw anything like it in aal my born days," he said. " I wass the length wan time of puttin' off my sluppers and windin' up my watch for the Day of Chudgment. Wan moment the boat wass up in the air like a flyin'-machine, and the next she wass scrapin' the cockles off the bottom o' the deep. Mountains high—chust mountains high! And no' wee mountains neither, but the very bens of Skye! The seas was wearin' through us fore and aft like yon mysterious river rides that used to be at the Scenic Exhibeetion, and the noise o' the cups and saucers clatterin' doon

below wass terrible, terrible! If Dougie wass here he
could tell you."

"A dog's life, boys!" said the shellbacks. "He
would be ill-advised that would sell a farm and go to
sea. Anything carried away, Captain?"

A jar, a bucket, and a sou'-wester seemed too trivial
a loss for such a great occasion. Para Handy hurriedly
sketched a vision of bursting hatches, shattered bul-
warks, a mate with a broken leg, and himself for hours
lashed to the wheel.

It was annoying to find that these experiences were
not regarded by the shellbacks as impressive. They
seemed to think that nothing short of tragedy would
do justice to a storm of such unusual magnitude.

Para Handy got into the train, and found himself in
the company of some Paisley people, who seemed as
proud of the superior nature of the storm as if they
had themselves arranged it.

"Nothing like it in history, chentlemen," said Para
Handy, after borrowing a match. "It's me that should
ken, for I wass in it, ten mortal hours, battlin' wi' the
tempest. A small boat carried away and a cargo o'
feather bonnets on the deck we were carryin' for the
Territorials. My boat was shaved clean doon to the
water-line till she looked like wan o' them timber-
ponds at the Port—not an article left standin'! A
crank-shaft smashed on us, and the helm wass jammed.
The enchineer—a man Macphail belongin' to Mother-
well—had a couple of ribs stove in, and the mate got
a pair o' broken legs; at least there's wan o' them
broken and the other's a nesty stave. I kept her on
her coorse mysel' for five hours, and the watter up to
my very muddle. Every sea was smashin' on me, but

I never mudged. My George, no! Macfarlane never mudged! "

The Paisley passengers were intensely moved, and produced a consoling bottle.

" Best respects, chentlemen! " said Para Handy. " It's me that would give a lot for the like o' that at three o'clock this mornin'. I'm sittin' here withoot a rag but what I have on me. A fine sea-kist, split new, wi' fancy grommets, all my clothes, my whole month's wages, and presents for the wife in't—it's lyin' yonder somewhere off Innellan. . . . It's a terrible thing the sea."

At Greenock two other passengers came into the compartment, brimful of admiration for a storm they seemed to think peculiarly British in its devastating character—a kind of vindication of the island's imperial pride.

" They've naething like it on the Continent," said one of them. " They're a' richt there wi' their volcanic eruptions and earthquakes and the like, but when it comes to the naitural elements——" He was incapable of expressing exactly what he thought of British dominance in respect of the natural elements.

" Here's a poor chap that was oot in his ship in the worst o't," said the Paisley passengers. Para Handy ducked his head in polite acknowledgment of the new-comers' flattering scrutiny, and was induced to repeat his story, to which he added some fresh sensational details.

He gave a vivid picture of the *Vital Spark* wallowing helplessly on the very edge of the Gantock rocks; of the fallen mast beating against the vessel's side and driving holes in her; of the funnel flying through the air, with cases of feather bonnets (" cost ten pounds apiece, chentlemen, to the War Office "); of Sunny Jim incessantly toiling at the pump; the engineer unconscious and delirious; himself, tenacious and unconquered, at the wheel, lashed to it with innumerable strands of the best Manila cordage.

" I have seen storms in every part of the world," he said; " I have even seen yon terrible monsoons that's namely oot about Australia, but never in my born life did I come through what I came through last night."

Another application of the consolatory bottle seemed to brighten his recollection of details.

" I had a lot o' sky-rockets," he explained. " We always have them on the best ships, and I fired them off wi' the wan hand, holdin' the wheel wi' the other. Signals o' distress, chentlemen. Some use cannons, but I aye believe in the sky-rockets: you can both hear and see them. It makes a dufference."

" I kent a chap that did that for a day and a nicht aff the Mull o' Kintyre, and it never brung oot a single lifeboat," said one of the Paisley men.

It was obvious to Para Handy that his tragedy of the sea was pitched on too low a key to stir some people; he breathed deeply and shook a melancholy head.

" You'll never get lifeboats when you want them, chentlemen," he remarked. " They keep them aal laid up in Gleska for them Lifeboat Setturday processions. But it was too late for the lifeboat anyway for the *Vital Spark*. The smertest boat in the tred, too."

" Good Lord! She didna sink? " said the Paisley men, unprepared for such a *dénouement*.

" Nothing above the water at three o'clock this mornin' but the winch," said the Captain. " We managed to make our way ashore on a couple o' herrin'-boxes. . . . Poor Macphail! A great man for perusin' them novelles, but still-and-on a fellow of much agility. The very last words he said when he heaved his breath—and him, poor sowl, withoot a word o' Gaelic in his heid—wass, 'There's nobody can say but what you did your duty, Peter.' That wass me."

" Do ye mean to say he was drooned? " asked the Paisley men with genuine emotion.

" Not drooned," said Para Handy; " he simply passed away."

" Isn't that deplorable! And whit came over the mate? "

" His name wass Dougald," said the Captain sadly, " a native of Lochaline, and ass cheery a man ass ever you met across a dram. Chust that very mornin' he said to me, ' The 5th of November, Peter; this hass been a terrible New Year, and the next wan will be on us in a chiffy.' "

By the time the consolatory bottle was finished the loss of the *Vital Spark* had assumed the importance of the loss of the *Royal George*, and the Paisley men suggested that the obvious thing to do was to start a small subscription for the sole survivor.

For a moment the conscience-stricken Captain hesitated. He had scarcely thought his story quite so moving, but a moment of reflection found him quite incapable of recalling what was true and what imaginary of the tale he told them. With seven-and-sixpence in his pocket, wrung by the charm of pure imagination

o

from his fellow-passengers, he arrived in Glasgow and
went home.

He went in with a haggard countenance.

" What's the matter wi' ye, Peter? " asked his wife.

" Desperate news for you, Mery. Desperate news!
The *Vital Spark* is sunk."

"As long's the crew o' her are right that doesna
matter," said the plucky little woman.

" Every mortal man o' them drooned except mysel',"
said Para Handy, and the tears streaming down his
cheeks. " Nothing but her winch above the water.
They died like Brutain's hardy sons."

"And what are you doing here? " said his indignant
wife. " As lang as the winch is standin' there ye should
be on her. Call yoursel' a sailor and a Hielan'man! "

For a moment he was staggered.

" Perhaps there's no' a word o' truth in it," he
suggested. " Maybe the thing's exaggerated. Anything could happen in such a desperate storm."

" Whether it's exaggerated or no' ye'll go back the
night and stick beside the boat. I'll make a cup o' tea
and boil an egg for ye. A bonny-like thing for me to
go up and tell Dougie's wife her husband's deid and
my man snug at home at a tousy tea! . . . Forbye,
they'll maybe salve the boat, and she'll be needin' a
captain."

With a train that left the Central some hours later
Para Handy returned in great anxiety to Gourock.
The tragedy of his imagination was now exceedingly
real to him. He took a boat and rowed out to the
Vital Spark, which he was astonished to see intact at
anchor, not a feature of her changed.

Dougie was on deck to receive him.

" Holy smoke, Dougie, iss that yoursel'? " the Captain asked incredulously. " What way are you keepin'? "

" Fine," said Dougie. " What way's the mistress? "

The Captain seized him by the arm and felt it carefully.

" Chust yoursel', Dougie, and nobody else. It's me that's prood to see you. I hope there's nothing wrong wi' your legs? "

" Not a drop," said Dougie.

"And what way's Macphail? " inquired the Captain anxiously.

" He's in his bed wi' 'Lady Audley,' " said the mate.

" Still deleerious? " said the Captain with apprehension.

" The duvvle was never anything else," said Dougie.

" Did we lose anything in the storm last night? " asked Para Handy.

"A jar, and a bucket, and your own sou'-wester," answered Dougie.

" My Chove! " said Para Handy, much relieved. " Things iss terribly exaggerated up in Gleska."

XVII

FREIGHTS OF FANCY

DURING several days on which the *Vital Spark* lay idle at Lochgoilhead, the crew spring-cleaned her. " My goodness! ye wouldna think she would take such a desperate lot o' tar! " said Para Handy, watching the final strokes of Dougie's brush on the vessel's quarter.

There seemed, however, to be as much of the tar on the person and clothing of himself and his shipmates as on the boat.

" Ye're a bonny-lookin' lot! " said Macphail, the engineer, who never took any part in the painting operations. " If ye just had a tambourine apiece, and could sing ' The Swanee River,' ye would do for Christy Minstrels."

But all the same, in spite of such tar as missed her when they slung it on, the *Vital Spark* looked beautiful and shiny, and the air for half a mile round had the odour of Archangel, where the Russians come from.

With his own good hand, and at his own expense, her proud commander had freshened up her yellow bead and given her funnel a coat of red as gorgeous as a Gourock sunset. He stood on one leg, in a favourite attitude of his when anything appealed to his emotions, and scratched his shin with the heel of his other boot.

" Man! it's chust a trate to see her lookin' so smert! " he said with admiration. " The sauciest boat in the coastin' tred! If ye shut wan eye and glance end-on, ye would think she wass the *Grenadier*. Chust you look at the lines of her—that sweet! I'm tellin' you he wassna slack the man that made her."

Sunny Jim wiped his brow with the cuff of his jacket, and made a new smear on his countenance which left him with a striking resemblance to the White-Eyed Kaffir. His comparatively clean eye twinkled mischievously at Macphail.

" What I say is this," said he; " there's no' much sense in bein' so fancy wi' a boat that's only gaun to cairry coals and timber inside the Cumbraes. Noo that we're blockaded, do ye no' think, Macphail, she should be cairryin' passengers? "

" Holy smoke! " ejaculated Dougie, with genuine surprise. " Ye might chust ass well say that the Admirality should put some guns on her and send her to the Dardanelles."

Sunny Jim, with his back to the Captain, winked.

" There's maybe something in't," added Dougie hurriedly. " There's boats no' better carryin' passengers aal winter, and I'll warrant ye there's money in't."

" It's the chance o' a lifetime! " broke in the engineer, warming up to the play. " Half the regular steamers will be aff the Clyde for months takin' Gleska breid and the sodgers' washin's to the Bosphorus and thereabouts; if you have ony say at a' wi' the owners, Peter, you advise them to let oot the *Vital Spark* for trips."

" Trups! " said Para Handy, beaming. " Man, Jum, ye hit the very thing! It wass aalways my ambeetion to get oot o' the common cairryin' tred and be a chentleman. I aalways said a boat like this wass thrown away on coal, and wud, and herrin'; if she had chust a caibin and a place for sellin' tickets, I wouldna feel ashamed to sail her on the Royal Rowt."

Again his eye swept fondly over her bulging hull, with the tar still wet and glistening on it; the bright new yellow stripe which made her so coquettish; the crimson funnel.

" Of course, ye would need a band if ye went in for trips," suggested Macphail in a ruminating way. " Yin o' thae bands that can feenish a' thegither even if they're playin' different tunes, or drap the piccolo oot every noo and then to go roond and lift the pennies."

"Ach! I wouldna bother wi' a band," said Para Handy. " A band's no use unless ye want to chase the passengers below to take refreshments, and we havena the accommodation. We maybe might get haud o' a kind o' fiddler. I mind when the tippiest boats on the Clyde had chust wan decent fiddler or a poor man wantin' the eysight, wi' a concerteena. Tip-top! "

He took a piece of twine from his trousers pocket and measured the standing room between the wheel and the engines; Sunny Jim was in a transport of delight at a joke which went so smoothly.

" Two and a half," said Para Handy firmly, like a land surveyor. " I think there would be room for a no' too broad-built fiddler, if he didna bate the time wi' his feet. Stop you till we make a calculaation for the passenger accommodation. We'll need to make it cubic."

" There's only forty cubic feet allo'ed for every lodger in the Garscube Road," said Sunny Jim. " That's the Act o' Parliament. Ye can easy get the cubic space if ye coont it longways up in the air, and there's naething to prevent it."

Para Handy stood on one leg again and scratched a shin, with a look of the profoundest calculation.

" Ye couldna have cabin passengers," suggested Dougie, snatching up an oil-can of Macphail's and pouring some of its contents into his hands to clean the tar off.

" There's no' goin' to be no caibin in this boat," said the Captain quickly. " Short runs and ready money! Gourock and Dunoon, maybe, and perhaps a Setturday to Ardentinny. I could get a dozen or two o' nice wee herrin' firkins doon at Tarbert for passengers to sit on roond the hatch."

" Do ye no' think it would look droll? " asked Dougie, a little remorseful to have awakened such ecstatic visions.

" What way would it be droll? " retorted his Captain sharply. " I'm thinkin' ye havena much o' a heid for business, Dougie. If you would just consider—a shillin' a heid to Hunter's Quay——"

" Ye would need a purser," suggested Sunny Jim.

"Allooin' I did! " replied the Captain. " Aal a purser needs is a pocket-naipkin, a fancy tie, a flooer in his jaicket, and a pleasant smile. There iss not a man on the Clyde would make a better purser than yoursel' if ye showed the right agility. I'm tellin' you there's money in't! The people 'll chust come in and pay their tickets. Look at the way they crood doon at the Gleska Fair! We could put their wee tin boxes in the howld."

" Of course, we would have moonlight cruises," said Macphail. " It's just found money—no extra cost for the engineer and crew."

On the prospect of moonlight cruises the Captain pondered for a moment. " No," he said. " I'm aal for daylight sailin'; they slip in past ye in the dark withoot a ticket, or give ye a Golden Text from the Sunday School that looks like the chenuine article, and then where are ye? Forbye, it's no' that easy to watch a purser on the moonlight cruises; he would make his fortune."

He looked at his bright new funnel; imaginatively peopled the narrow deck with summer trippers; smelled the pervading odour of paint and tar, and

glowed all over at the thocht of his beloved vessel
taking the quay at Dunoon on a Saturday afternoon
with a crowd of the genteelest passengers seated on
herring firkins, and a fiddle aft.

" I'll speak my mind aboot it to the owners whenever I get to Gleska! " he declared emphatically. " It's
no' a chance they should let slip. They might could
put up a bit o' a deck-house where a body could get
a cup o' tea and a penny thing at tuppence."

"And wha would serve the tea, like? " asked Sunny
Jim.

" There's nobody could do it cluverer than yoursel',
Jum," said Para Handy. " You would wash your hands
and put on a brattie, and every noo and then a chentleman would slup a penny in below his plate for a
testimonial."

" That puts the feenish on it then! " said Sunny
Jim, with emphasis. " I jined this ship for a sailorman,
and no' to hand roond cookies and lift the tickets."

"And the mate would need to wear a collar," said
Dougie. " It's no' a thing I fancy at aal, at aal."

"A bonny-like skipper ye would look withoot a
bridge to stand on," wound up the engineer. " Besides,
ye would need a Board o' Tred certificate."

The Captain's visage fell. His dream dispelled.
" Perhaps ye're right," said he. " It would look a
little droll. But, man, I aalways had the notion that
the *Vital Spark* wass meant for something better than
for cairryin' coals."

SUMMER-TIME ON THE *VITAL SPARK*

PARA HANDY, on Saturday night, wound up the ship's Kew-tested 2s. 11½d. tin alarm chronometer with more than usual solemnity. It stopped as usual in the process, and he had to restore it to animation, after the customary fashion, by tapping it vigorously on the toe of his boot.

" If it wassna the law o' the land," he remarked, " I would see them at the muschief afore I would be tamperin' wi' the time o' day the way God made it. We'll have to come up the quay to our beds next Setturday in broad daylight; there's no consuderation for the sailor's reputaation."

" Science! " said the mate, with bitterness. " Goodness knows what prank them fellows 'll be up to next! There wass nothing wrong wi' the time the way it wass, except that it wass aalways slippin' past when ye werena thinkin'."

" There's the nock for ye, Jim," said Para Handy. " Ye'll stay up till two o'clock, and do the needful."

" What'll I stay up for? " asked Sunny Jim indignantly. " Ye can shift the handles noo; it's a' the same."

" But it's no' aal the same! If you would read the papers instead o' wastin' your time gallivanting, ye would see the Daylight Ack says two o'clock's the oor for shifting nocks. Ye daurna do it a meenute sooner."

Sunny Jim laughed. " Right-oh, Captain! " he agreed. " I'll sit up and dae the shiftin' for ye. You

o 2

and Dougie better leave me your watches, too; it'll be a' the yin operation."

"Can ye see the nock, Dougie? What time iss't by the Daylight Ack?" the Captain sleepily asked next morning without turning out of his bunk.

The mate unhooked the clock, and incredulously surveyed its face. "Stop you till I get my watch," he said, crawling out of his bunk. "Them German nocks iss not dependable; ye couldna boil an egg wi' them."

A rich resonant snore came from the bunk of Sunny Jim.

"Holy sailor!" exclaimed Dougie, having consulted his watch; "it's half-past ten o'clock! No wonder I wass hungry! That's your science for you!"

"Half-past ten o'clock!" said the Captain. "And chust you listen at the way that fellow iss snorin'! Up this meenute, Jum, and make the breakfast!"

It was with difficulty Sunny Jim was wakened, and then he proved of the most mutinous temper. "Ye can mak' your breakfast for yoursel's!" he protested. "If I'm to sit up till twa o'clock in the mornin' to shift the time, I'm no' gaun to rise till my sleep's made up."

Two seconds later he was snoring more resonantly than ever, in syncopated time with MacPhail, the engineer, who had volunteered to sit up till two o'clock with him, and who had a snore of an intermittent gurgling character like one of his own steam pipes.

Between them the Captain and the mate made breakfast.

A blissful Sabbath calm was on loch and land when Para Handy put his head up through the hatch. The *Vital Spark* was bumping softly against her fenders at a deserted quay; the smoke of morning fires was rising in the village. The tide was ebbing, but not yet far from full.

" I didna think they could do't," said the Captain.

" Do what? " asked Dougie, finishing off the last of the marmalade.

" The tide," said Para Handy; " it's no' near where it wass at this time yesterday. It's shifted too."

" Chust what I told ye—science! The ruffians'll do anything! Do you no' think, Peter, we'll get punished some day for all this schemin' and contrivance? Chust the work of unfidels! What way iss a man to ken noo whether it's Setturday night or Sunday morning? Many a wan 'll go wrong at twelve o'clock on the Setturday night and start whistling. Noo that they're startin' takin' liberties wi' clocks and tides, ye'll see they'll cairry it further and play havoc wi' the almanacs. If they can rob us o' an oor they can steal a fortnight."

" Chust that! " agreed the Captain. " I could spare them a day or two at the Whitsunday term; that's the sort o' thing they should abolish." He sighed. " Indeed, it's a solemn thing, Dougie, to see the way they're flyin' aal round to new human devices; do ye no' think me and you should go to the church this mornin'? "

" Whatever you say yoursel'," said Dougie.

The bell was ringing as they went up the street, and had ceased when they reached the church. No other worshippers were visible.

" This place needs a great upliftin'," said Para Handy piously. " On a day like this, with the things of time upset and shifted, ye would think they would be croodin' in to hear Mr M'Queen. Have ye any losengers? "

" Not wan! " said Dougie, " but maybe he'll no' be long."

The beadle was shutting the door of the church as they approached to enter. " Where are ye goin'? " he asked, with a curious look at them.

" Where would we be goin' but to hear my good frien', John M'Queen," said the Captain fervently.

" Then ye'll better come back at half-past eleven," said the beadle dryly. " This is no' the place for you at all; it's the Sunday School."

" Holy sailors! " exclaimed the Captain; " what o'clock iss't? "

" Exactly half-past nine by the summer time," said the beadle, " but it's only half-past eight by naiture."

The Captain looked at Dougie. " Aren't we," said he, " the fools to be leavin' nocks and watches to fellows like Sunny Jim and Macphail! The tricky duvvles! There's no' an inch o' a chentleman between them. It's no' wan oor but three they put us forrit, and they're still snore-snorin' yonder! "

XIX

EGGS UNCONTROLLED

SUNNY JIM, with his sleeves rolled up, a sweat-rag stuck in the waistband of his trousers, and his face much streaked with soot, clapped down a bowl of eggs before the Captain, rinsed his hands in a pail of water, dried them on his waistcoat, and sat down on the edge of his bunk to enjoy his breakfast.

A gloomy silence fell upon the crew when they saw

the eggs. They were just plain ordinary eggs of oval shape, and no more soiled on the shells than usual, but their presence seemed momentous. Para Handy looked at them like one entranced; Dougie put a finger out and touched them gingerly; Macphail withdrew his incredulous gaze from them with a muttered exclamation, and starting furiously spreading bread with marmalade.

" Iss that eggs? " said the Captain, like one who was uncertain whether they were eggs or curling-stones.

" Oh no! Not at all! " cried Macphail, with bitter irony; " it's the best Devonshire bacon, fried kidneys, kippered herring, finnan haddies, omelets, pork sausages. Jim would never shove us off wi' eggs! "

" They're duvvelish like eggs! " said Dougie lugubriously. " I never saw a better imitation. The look o' them fairly makes me grue."

" What way's the wind, Jum? " said Para Handy mildly. " I don't feel the smell o' ham. Hurry you up, like a good laad, and bring us doon a wise-like breakfast."

" That's a' the breakfast that's gaun," said Sunny Jim. " There's no a bit o' ham in Tarbert."

" But, bless my he'rt! there's many another thing than ham a body could enjoy! " said Para Handy. " There's things like—fush, and—sausages, and—fush, that a man could eat wi' some diversion. You're awfu' nerrow, Jum! You havena no variety. Even-on it's eggs wi' you; you havena had a thing but eggs since we left Bowling."

" Tak' them or leave them! " said the cook; " the day 'll come ye'll be gled to get them. I'm no' a Grand Hotel nor an Italian Warehouse; I can only gie ye what I can get, and there's dashed all left to eat in Tarbert since the Fair, unless it's rhubarb."

The Captain chipped an egg with no enthusiasm. "Goodness knows," said he, "what this country would come to withoot the hens! Everybody in the land is eatin' eggs—eggs—eggs! Half the year there's nothing in the morning for ye but an egg. What, in aal the world, iss in an egg?"

"That's what I'm aye wonderin' when I start yin," said the engineer.

"There's nothing patent in an egg; it's chust a thing ye would expect from hens. If it wassna for the salt, ye might ass weel be eatin' blot-sheet. Did ye ever see any dufference between wan egg and another?"

"Some o' them's bigger," suggested Dougie, scooping out his own, apparently without much interest in the contents.

"That's the thing that angers me aboot an egg!" continued the Captain. "It never makes ye gled to see it on the table; ye know at wance the thing's a mere put-by because your wife or Jum could not be bothered makin' something tasty."

"We'll hae to get the hens to put their heids the-gither, and invent a new kind o' fancy egg for sailors," said Sunny Jim, consuming his with ostentatious relish. "Ye can say whit ye like—there's naething bates a country egg; and I can tell ye this, the lot o' ye, it's eggs ye're gaun to get for dinner tae; there's no' a bit o' butcher meat in Tarbert!"

"Holy smoke!" exclaimed the Captain. "Eggs for dinner! Not a morsel more will I be eating; you have spoiled my breakfast on me!"

The *Vital Spark* had her coals discharged by noon, and the Captain went ashore to a public-house for a change of diet. The very idea of eggs again for dinner was repugnant to him, and several schooners of beer intensified his inward feelings of revolt against monotony of cuisine. There came into the bar a man he thought he knew; he said, " Hallo, Macdougall! " to him; " hoo's the fishin'? " and they had a glass together.

" What way's hersel'—the mustress keepin'? " Para Handy asked. " I hope she's splendid? "

" She's no bad at aal," said the other, with a little hesitation.

" Tell her I was askin' kindly for her health. I'm fine mysel'. Yon's a nice bit hoose ye have, Johnny; it's very creditable to aal concerned."

" It's no' that bad at aal! " replied the other, thinking for a moment. " What way do ye no' come up some night and see us? "

" Nobody would be better pleased! " said Para Handy. " Iss your mother-in-law still wi' ye? "

"Aye, she's yonder yet, but ach! ye needna mind for her; come up some night, and have your supper. . . . Bring the boys! " Macdougall added with effusive hospitality. So far, he had not suggested another drink.

" If I go up, I'll better go mysel'; there's four of us on board," said Para Handy.

" Bring them all! This very night at seven o'clock, and, I assure you, you'll have supper."

" Hoots! That would be puttin' the wife to bother," said the Captain, with polite solicitude. " We would chust be goin' to have a crack."

" Ye'll have a crack, and ye'll have your supper too! " said Macdougall firmly. " Mind and bring the boys! Sharp at seven, mind, and take your music."

. . . . . .

The Captain hurried on board his vessel, watched his crew disgustedly eat eggs, which he professed disdain for, and when they had finished, told them of his invitation.

" Ye micht hae tell't us sooner! " said Macphail, with genuine vexation. " There's a supper spoiled! "

" A capital cook, Mrs Macdougall!—namely, in the place for cooking," callously said Para Handy. " I'm chust in trum mysel' for something else than eggs."

They dressed in their Sunday clothes, and went up at night to the house of John Macdougall.

" He's not at home, he's at the fishin'! " said a lady whom the Captain shook warmly by the hand, and addressed as Katrin.

" I met him in the toon at twelve the day, and he asked us to be sure and come to supper," said the Captain, much surprised.

" What was he like? " said she, with some amusement.

" A burly wise-like man, wi' a tartan kep; I ken him fine! "

She laughed; she was a cheerful body. " That's no' my man at all, Captain," said she; " but I'll tell ye who it was—his brother Peter; they're as like as peas! "

" Isn't this the bonny caper! " said Dougie, with distress. They stood like sheep.

" It's no' the first time Peter played that trick," said

the woman; "he's a rascal! If he had a house and a wife of his own, I would just advise ye to go up, and take him at his word, but seein' ye're here, ye'll just come in and have your supper."

They went in, with mingled hope and diffidence, and she boiled them eggs!

XX

COMMANDEERED

"STOP you! We'll have a fine pant oot of Dougie; he's ass timid ass a mountain hare," said Para Handy in the absence of his mate, who was ashore on one of the missions the crew of the *Vital Spark* entirely disapproved of—to buy some special and exclusive "kitchen" for his tea. He had an unpleasantly ostentatious way of eating ham or kippered herrings when the rest had nothing more piquant or interesting than jam.

As a consequence of some deliberation and rehearsal, when Dougie came back to the boat with his parcel he found an unusual bustle at an hour when, waiting for the tide to get her off at flood, the crew of the *Vital Spark* were apt to be yawning their heads off. The Captain was peeling his guernsey off, preparatory to washing himself—a proceeding in itself unusual enough to be surprising. Macphail, the engineer, was studying a map of the North Sea cut from some recent newspaper, and flourishing a one-legged compass. Sunny Jim was oiling the parts of a telescope he had won once in a raffle.

Such signs of unaccustomed activity could not but impress Dougie. " What's wrong wi' ye? " he asked; " ye're duvvelish busy! "

" We'll be busier yet before we're done! " said the Captain, gravely and mysteriously, and turned his back to look over the shoulder of Macphail at the North Sea map. " Did ye find the place, Macphail? " he asked anxiously.

"Ay! " said the engineer. " It's just aboot whaur I said it was—a dangerous place, fair hotchin' full o' mines."

" Chust that! " said Para Handy. " It's chust what I wass thinkin' to myself. Well, well; we canna help it when the King and country caals. I'm only vexed aboot the boat." He stifled a sigh, bent over the enamelled basin, and hurriedly damped himself: it must be admitted the afternoon was cold.

" There's no' even the chance o' a medal on the job," said Sunny Jim. " That's what gives me the needle! "

They behaved as if Dougie with his irritating groceries had no existence. He determined to show no curiosity.

" It might be sweepin' mines they mean," said Para Handy in a little, drying his face. " Whatever it iss, it iss goin' to be a time of trial."

" It's me that's gled I can swim," said Sunny Jim. " The very first bang, and aff goes my galoshes! It's no' sae bad for me, as if I had a wife and family."

Dougie pricked his ears.

" It's no' sweepin' mines," said the engineer emphatically. " If it was to sweep mines they wanted us they would put steel plates roond the bows and leave her light; there wouldna be any sense in stuffin' her hold

wi' cement and stones. Tak' you my word for it—
she's gaun to jam the Kiel Canal. It's a risky job we're
on, I'll warrant ye! "

" I wouldna care so much if it wasna for my aunty,"
said Sunny Jim in a doleful accent, with a wink to the
engineer. " I aye made up her rent. Perhaps it's to
cairry troops we're needed."

" Not at aal! " said Para Handy. " Where would
ye put troops on the *Vital Spark*, and her hold filled
up wi' causey and cement? "

Dougie's curiosity could no further be restrained.
" What in aal the earth are ye palaverin' at? " he asked
impatiently, and with some forebodings.

" I'm sorry to tell ye that, Dougald," said the Captain feelingly, " for it's a serious, serious business for
us aal; the boat is commandeered. I have a kind o'
letter here from the Admirality "—he produced it with
a flourish from his trousers pocket. " Chust a line in
their usual way:—' Report at Renfrew; get an extra
dummy funnel and some wuden guns; fill up wi'
causey and cement, and take the North Sea for it. To
Captain Peter C. Macfarlane.' "

" ' Peter C. Macfarlane,' " Dougie said, surprised.
" I never heard o' the ' C ' before; where did ye get
the title? "

" They must have kent my mother was a Cameron,"
said Para Handy; " and they're always for the stylish
thing in the Admirality. Never you mind aboot the
title, Dougald; have ye an extra shirt or two and a
pair o' mittens? Ye'll need them yonder."

" Where? " asked the mate, alarmed.

" In the North Sea. Amn't I tellin' ye we're
commandeered! "

" I'll see them to the muschief first! " said Dougie

warmly. " If I'm to do the British Navy's work, it's no' in a cockle-shell! " But his heart was in his boots.

For once his meal had no attractions for him, and the others, for the first time, shared his private ham with surprising appetite and relish, considering the tragic possibilities they discussed. So perfectly did they sustain their parts as previously arranged among them that it never occurred to him to doubt the story.

" Of course, ye'll break the news to your mustress the best way that ye can," said the Captain, spreading jam on the bread with a soup spoon; " ye needna put the worst face on the job; chust say it's an East Coast cargo, and ye'll send a postcaird home. I hope and trust ye kept up your insurance! "

" Of course, there's aye a chance they micht take us prisoners," said Sunny Jim. " That wouldna be sae bad."

" I ken a man that's no' goin'," said Dougie with profound conviction.

" There's nane o' us can get oot o't," said the engineer, finishing the last of the ham in an absent-minded way. " I think your letter makes that quite plain, Peter? "

" It does that," said Para Handy, having scrutinised the document again, and shoved it under his plate for further reference if necessary. Dougie eyed it slyly, unobserved.

" The dashed thing is there's no' a uniform," said Sunny Jim. " I wouldna mind sae much if we wore a blue pea-jaicket wi' brass buttons, and the name o' the boat on oor keps; if I'm to be drooned for my country I would like to be a wee bit tasty."

"There's a man I ken, and he's no' goin', whatever o't!" again said Dougie firmly.

The Captain had another inspiration. " Of course," said he, " they're goin' to change the name o' the boat. There's a cruiser caaled the *Vital Spark*, and if we were sunk it would make confusion. The Chermans would be sayin' we were the big one."

" There's one thing I can tell ye, and it's this—the man that iss not goin' on this ploy iss me!" said Dougie, and slapped his knee.

"Toots, man! ye shouldna be so tumid!" said Para Handy; " Brutain's hardy sons!"

The rule of the vessel was that a man who indulged in extras to his tea had to wash the dishes, and Dougie was left behind when the others went on deck. He lost no time in reading the document the Captain had forgetfully left below his plate, and a great illumination came to him when he found it was nothing more than a second and final notice demanding the Captain's poor-rates.

" My goodness! wass there ever such a lot o' liars? " said their victim. " Spoiled my tea on me! Stop you! "

By and by he went up on deck, and found his ship-mates solemnly discussing the purpose of the dummy funnel and the wooden guns.

" It's to draw their torpedo fire," the engineer suggested. " When they're bangin' awa' at us the cruiser 'll slip by."

"And then it's domino wi' us! " said Sunny Jim lugubriously.

" There's wan thing I can say," said Para Handy unctuously, " and it's this—that my affairs is aal in

the best condeetion; quite complete. There's no' a
penny that I'm owin'."

" Except your poor-rates," broke in Dougie wither-
ingly. " There's your letter from the Admirality. It's
in Berlin the whole o' ye should be, and writin' Cherman telegrams."

XXI

SUNNY JIM REJECTED

WHEN tea was finished, Sunny Jim put on his Sunday
clothes, turned up the foot of his trousers, oiled his
boots, put his cap on carefully, with a saucy tilt to it,
and then spent several minutes violently brushing what
was left below it of his hair. Thus only could his curl
be coaxed into that tasty wave above the forehead,
and complete his fatal beauty for the girls.

" Capital! " said Para Handy. " Never saw ye
nicer, Jum; chust a regular Napoleon! Don't you
shift another hair, or ye'll spoil yersel'! "

" The only other thing I could recommend," said
Macphail, " is to put some soap and water on a brush
and gie a flourish aboot the ears."

Sunny Jim paid no attention. From the small tin
box that held his dunnage he produced his mouth
harmonium and a tin of Glasgow toffee, which he
stowed in his jacket pockets.

" My goodness! " said Dougie, the mate, " it's a
desperate thing this love; there's such expense in it!
There's a sixpence away on sweeties for another
fellow's dochter! "

" Of course, we'll have a bite o' something ready for ye, Jum, when ye come back," remarked the Captain with magnificent sarcasm. " Dougie 'll sit up. Will a bit of cold roast chucken do, or would ye like an omelet? "

" Best respects to Liza," said the engineer rudely. " I think it's specs she's needin' if you're her fancy."

Sunny Jim calmly lighted a cigarette and buttoned up his jacket. " So long, chaps! " he said. " It's a pity ye're a' that old! Just a lot o' bloomin' fossils from the Fossil Grove, Whiteinch. Mak' yoursel's some gruel in a while, and awa' to your beds."

He was back to the *Vital Spark* in less than an hour in an obviously agitated state of mind.

" Bless me! " said Para Handy, starting up; " iss it that time o' night? The way time has o' slippin' past when ye're a fossil! Set you the table, Dougie, and put oot a chucken for his lordship. Maybe ye would like a drop o' something, Jum? To start wi', like. What way iss Liza keepin' in her health! My Chove! But yon's the beautious gyurl! "

" Shut up! " said Sunny Jim disgustedly. " I'm done wi' her, onywey! I wouldna trust a woman like yon the length that I could throw her! "

" That's no far," said Macphail reflectively. " Sixteen stone, if she's an ounce. Tell me this—is she wearin' specs at last? "

" It would need to be some sort o' specs she was wearin' to see onything in yon chap o' Mackay's she's awa' for a walk wi'," said Sunny Jim with feeling. " Naething at a' to recommend him but a kilt and a hack on his heel! "

Dougie, who never lost his head even in the most

exciting circumstances, asked the despondent lover abruptly if he had brought the tin of toffee back. In a moment of aberration Sunny Jim produced it, and put it down on the top of a barrel, and it sped so quickly round them several times that when his turn came there were only two sticky bits left in the bottom. He sucked them like one for whom toffee had no greater taste than gas-work cinders. Such is the effect of unrequited love.

He was too profoundly grieved to be reticent. " I had a tryst wi' her, right enough, chaps. Eight o'clock, she said, at the factor's corner, and just at that very meenute she went sailin' past wi' Dan Mackay, that's hame frae the Territorials at Dunoon, lettin' on he's wounded, and a' the time, I'll bate ye, it's only a hack on his heel.

" ' It's eight o'clock, Liza,' says I, and gied her the wink.

" ' Fancy that! ' says she, as nippy 's onything. ' But ye've loads o' time; they're signin' on recruits in the armoury up till ten. Did ye hear aboot the war? ' says she afore I could get my breath. ' It's fairly ragin' Corporal Mackay's gaun oot to the front as soon as his feet get better.'

"And aff she went wi' Mackay, and left me standin' like a dummy! Yon's no gentleman! He hadna a word to say for himsel'. Naething to tak' the eye aboot him but a kilt and a hack on his heel! "

" Holy smoke! " said Para Handy sympathetically. " Isn't that the desperate pity? There's nothing noo in the heids o' the gyurls but sodgers. But ye canna blame the craturs! There's something smert aboot the kilt and the cockit bonnet."

" If I wassna one o' them old fossils from White-inch," remarked Dougie, with rancorous deliberation, " it wouldna be the like o' Liza Cameron, the tyler's dochter, could cast up to me a war wass ragin' and go off wi' another man—aye, even if he had a hack on every heel inside his boots."

Sunny Jim was distressed almost to the verge of tears. " I'm fair sick o' this! " said he. " I'm gaun to 'list! Every quay this boat comes in to somebody's shair to chip in something aboot my age and me no' bein' married, and whitna regiment I'm gaun to. The last trip we cam' up Loch Fyne I got as mony feathers as would stuff a bolster."

"I wass aye wonderin' what for so many feathers got into the porridge," said Dougie. " Did I no' say to the Captain yesterday, ' I'm fond o' porridge and I'm fond o' chicken, but I never cared to get them both mixed'? "

" Mind ye, it's no' that I'm feared to 'list," said Sunny Jim. " I never seen a German yet I couldna knock the napper aff, and it couldna be worse in the trenches than in the howld o' this old vessel shovellin' coal. But I'm feared they wouldna tak' me for a recruit——"

" If it's the bowly legs ye're thinkin' o'," said Macphail, " that's no ony obstacle; ye're just the very make o' a horse marine."

Para Handy measured the disconsolate lover with a calculating eye. " I doot," says he, " Jum hassna got the length for a horse marine unless they put him through a mangle first. The regiment for you, Jum, is the Bantams."

" I doot they wouldna pass me," said Sunny Jim.

" But to show that woman I'm game enough, although I'm no' bloodthirsty, I'll go up this very meenute and put in my name."

" You be fly and stand on your tiptoes! " Macphail cried after him as he climbed up on the quay from the vessel's rail.

He came back in half an hour a little more disconsolate than ever. " I tell't ye! " said he, " they wouldna sign me on," and stood with his back close to a glowing stove.

" No wonder," said the engineer. " Warpin' your legs still worse wi' standin' against the fire! Did I no' tell ye to get on the tips o' your taes? "

" You're a disgrace to the boat," said Para Handy, with genuine vexation. " I'm black affronted! If Dougald and me wass a trifle younger, it's no' wi' troosers on we would be puttin' past the time. Just bringin' a bad name on the boat—that's what ye are! What way would they no' take ye? "

" Just look at the legs o' him! " said the engineer, as if they made the question quite ridiculous.

" It would likely be his character," suggested Dougie sadly. "They're duvvelish parteecular noo aboot the character; it's no like the old Milishia."

" It's no' my legs at a'; there's naething wrang wi' my legs," said the disappointed candidate. "And they never asked aboot my character. But I kent fine a' alang they wouldna tak' me."

" What for? " asked Para Handy. " Ye have all your faculties aboot ye, and ye're in your prime."

" It was this e'e o' mine," explained Sunny Jim, and indicated his dexter optic, which had always a singularly stern expression even in his amorous hours.

" That wan? " exclaimed the Captain. " That's the best o' the pair, to my opeenion, it's aye that steady. What's wrong wi't? "

" It's gless," said Sunny Jim, blushing; " they found it oot at the first go-aff."

" Holy frost! " said Para Handy. " Five years in this boat wi' us, and we never kent it. Did I no' think ye were chust plain skeely! "

XXII

HOW JIM JOINED THE ARMY

" JUMPIN' Jehosophat! " said Para Handy. " Here's Macphail. I doot they havena lifted him."

Dougie's visage fell. He had been confident that the want of an engineer would keep them idle in Tarbert for at least a week. " Isn't that the trash! " he said lugubriously. " Ye never could put dependence on him. Look you, has he any badge in his coat lapel? He iss chust the man would let on a enchineer on the *Vital Spark* was a special tred. Ye canna be up to the quirks o' him."

" There is nothing on his coat lapel that I can see but a patch o' egg," said Para Handy, " and he had that when he started to go to Stirling. Ye'll see we'll no' get rid o' Macphail so easy; they're gettin' gey parteecular in the airmy, and he never could keep the step."

" Oh, man! if I had jist the ither eye! " said Sunny Jim in a passionate outburst of yearning.

Macphail came down to the quay with the biscuit
tin which fulfilled the function of a suitcase when he
travelled. His gait was most dejected, and his general
air of infestivity was accentuated by the fact that he
wore his Sunday clothes and a hat that, having been
picked up casually some years before at the close of a
ball in Crarae, had never fitted.

" See's your canister in case ye break the bottle,"
suggested the Captain politely as his engineer stood
on the edge of the quay and prepared to jump on
board.

" We werena expectin' to see ye again withoot your
kilt," said Dougie maliciously. Macphail's anatomical
defects had been considered to render kilts so absurdly
out of the question that his shipmates always insisted
General Haig would instantly pick him for the Gordons.

Without a word the engineer sat down on his biscuit
tin and burst into tears.

" Man, Macphail, I'm wonderin' at ye! " exclaimed
the Captain. " Your system's chust run doon wi'
travellin'; a little drop o' Brutish spurrits—have ye
much left in the canister? "

" Stand back and gie the chap breath! " implored
Sunny Jim. " I'll bate a pound they found there was
something wrang wi' him internal. I wouldna bother,
Mac, if it's checked in time ye'll maybe linger on for
years."

" Tach! " said Para Handy sympathetically. " I
wouldna heed them doctors, Mac; it's only guess-
work wi' them. But to tell ye the truth I didna like
yon chrechlin' cough ye had since ye went afore the
Tribunal. The only hope I had wass ye were puttin' 't
on. If I had chust a wee small drop of spurrits wi'

some sugar in't—will ye no' sit on this bucket?—a canister iss cold."

" Ye may be glad they wouldna take ye! " said Dougie consolingly. " Even if it wass only for the sake o' yer wife and pickle children."

" That's the dashed thing! " sobbed Macphail shamelessly; " they're takin' me richt enough. I've passed the doctors at Stirling, and I have a ticket here to jine a regiment to-morrow at Fort Matilda."

" Oh, michty! " exclaimed Sunny Jim with envy. " Whit regiment? "

" I canna mind its name," said the engineer, drying his eyes with a piece of waste; " but it starts wi' an F, and I'm to be a private. And me!—I don't ken the least wee thing aboot the way to be a private! I was bred an engineer."

In proof of these lamentable tidings he produced an official document which declared he was physically fit in every respect, and a card with which to present himself to the office for recruits.

" Man alive! Did ye no' cough at them? " asked Para Handy. " Yon chrechlin' cough wass chust a masterpiece."

" Cough! " exclaimed Macphail. " I coughed till ye would think it was the Cloch on a foggy night, but yon chaps never heeded. They put a tape aboot my chest, and chapped me between the shoulders, and listened could they hear my circulation. I was stripped stark naked——"

" My Chove! issn't that chust desperate! " said the Captain, horrified.

" I don't care! " cried Macphail in an excess of indignation. "I'm no' gaun to go, and that's a' aboot it!" He incautiously rose from his seat and stamped the deck.

"Wi' a little wee drop sugar in't, there's nothing better for a cough," said the Captain, hurriedly opening the biscuit tin. He looked disappointed. "Tach!" he said. "There's only an empty gill bottle and wan other garment. That iss not the way a chentleman would be travellin' from Stirling."

"See here!" said Sunny Jim with some eagerness. "Did they tak' your photograph?"

"No," said the melancholy engineer.

"Then gie me your tickets and I'll go to Fort Matilda in the name o' Dan Macphail. They'll never ken the difference. If it wasna this e'e o' mine was gless, I would hae 'listed a year ago. I've tried, and I've better tried to jine, but they'll no' let ye jine wi' a glessy yin unless ye have lots o' influence."

"Ye canna hide that eye on them; it looks that flippant!" said the Captain incredulously.

Macphail hurriedly handed over his documents lest any debate should diminish the young man's ardour.

"They canna go back on the doctor's line!" said Sunny Jim. "It says here Dan Macphail is medically fit—that's me, and I'm faur better value for the British Airmy wi' my glessy than Macphail would be wi' a full set o' een and his Sunday specs and his he'rt no' in it. It's the chance o' my life!"

"I wash my hands of it!" said Dougie, who had not yet recovered from his disappointment at the engineer's return. "It is against the Defence o' the Realm to pass gless eyes on the British Airmy, and ye'll get this boat in trouble."

" I jist have time to catch the boat for Greenock,"
said Sunny Jim. He put the documents in his pocket,
buttoned his jacket, and climbed ashore.

XXIII

THE FUSILIER

THREE weeks after Sunny Jim stole into the Scottish
Fusiliers under false pretences with the name and
papers of Macphail, the engineer, and a glass eye he
had previously made a dozen vain attempts to foist on
recruiting officers as the natural article, he turned up
in his uniform on the *Vital Spark*. He carried himself
so erect that he had a rake aft like a steamer's funnel,
his chest preceding him by about nine inches, and his
glengarry bonnet cocked on three hairs. Every button
glinted.

" Jumpin' Jehosophat! " exclaimed the Captain.
" It's on you they've made the dufference! Wi' a step
like that ye would make a toppin' piper. Ye're far
more copious aboot the body than ye were."

" Broader in every direction! " said Dougie, with
genuine admiration. " By the time they're done wi'
ye, ye'll be a fair Goliath."

Macphail looked sourly on his substitute, but even
he could not restrain surprise. " I take the credit,"
said he, " for the makin' o' ye; if it wasna for my
testimonials ye wouldna be in the airmy yet."

Sunny Jim saluted his old shipmates with a rapid
movement that threw his bonnet on to two hairs and
an eyebrow, then cut away the right hand smartly.

" Cheer up, chaps! " he said; " the war's near by; I'm gaun oot wi' the very next draft to put the feenisher on it."

" Did they no' say nothin' aboot your eye? " asked Para Handy, intently regarding that notorious organ.

" Oh, they just passed the remark that it was a fair bummer for the shootin'-ranges, seein' I wouldna need to shut it," said Sunny Jim. " But we had a kind o' a pant wi' the first day I was on parade. I was daein' the Swedish exercise, and sweatin' that much the glessy yin near slipped oot. I put up my hand to kep it, and the sergeant-major says, ' Whit's wrang wi' your eye, Macphail? '

" ' There's something in it,' says I.

" ' Then fall to the rear three paces and tak' it oot,' says he, ' and no' mak' a bloomin' demonstration o' the squad; the folk that's lookin' on'll think ye're greetin'.'

" I took it oot and slips it into my pocket, and when I steps into the ranks again the sergeant-major nearly fainted.

" ' Gless! ' said he, when I explained it was a fancy yin. ' Man, it's no' a sodger you should be, but a war correspondent; ye have half the full equipment for the job! ' "

"And whit kind o' a situation hae ye? " asked Macphail.

" Oh, I'm a cook," said Sunny Jim. " It's really a chef's job, for ye hae to be parteecular."

" Oh, my goodness! " cried Macphail. " The Scottish Fusiliers is gaun to suffer."

" No fears! " said Sunny Jim; " cookin' in a camp is no' like cookin' in a coal-boat; it's no' a pound o' boiled beef ham and a quarter loaf that's yonder; the place is fair infested wi' the best o' butcher meat."

" Still-and-on it must be a hard life, James," suggested Para Handy. " Everything by word o' command, and no time for to pause and to consuder."

" It's a gentleman's life," declared the young recruit. " Naething hard aboot it, except that ye have to keep your teeth brushed. I don't think I could think o' goin' back to follow the sea when the war's past; sodgerin' puts ye aff the notion o' a sedimentary life. I'm thinkin' o' gaun in for bein' a major; the best yins does it, and ye get a horse."

They gave the ambitious son of Mars a cup of tea, and two boiled eggs to it; he politely disposed of them, though it was evident such fare was rather homely for a chef. His new fastidiousness only came out when he asked for a saucer; he forgot that the only one on board was used for the engineer's black soap.

" The only thing that's wrang wi' the Fusiliers is that they spoil ye," he explained apologetically. " Every other day there's a duff."

" Whit like iss the other chentlemen in the business wi' ye? " inquired Dougie.

" The very best! " said Sunny Jim, with enthusiasm. " It's yonder ye meet wi' genteel society; regular gentlemen, tip-top toffs right enough. The chap that's lyin' next to me in the hut's in a capital business o' his ain aboot Dalry; I think it's linen drapery, for every sleeve he has is filled to the brim wi' hankies."

" Jehosophat! " said Para Handy. " Dougie will boil another egg for ye this meenute."

" I hope," said Macphail, " that ye'll no' mak' a Ned o' yoursel' in ony way in the airmy, seein' ye're

P

there in the name o' Dan Macphail. The Macphails was aye respectable, and I wouldna care to have my reputation spiled."

Dougie laughed derisively. " The Macphails! " he exclaimed. " Everybody kens they came from Ireland —Fenians and Sinn Feiners."

" Your reputation," said Sunny Jim indignantly. " Ye're aye takin' oot your reputation and polishin' it up the same's it was a trombone or a cornet; no' much o' a reputation, and ye needna bother. To tell ye the truth, I found your reputation was the worst thing I could tak' wi' me to the Fusiliers. By George, they had your history in their books! "

" It's a lie! " shouted the engineer, reddening.

" It's as true as I'm tellin' ye! I wasna jined a week when I went to my officer and tellt him straight I wasna Macphail at a'; and wasna gaun to stand the brunt o' bein' Dan Macphail. For the recruitin' officer had Dan Macphail doon in his books for a married man wi' five o' a family, and they were gaun to tak' so much aff my pay every week for your wife's allooance! "

XXIV

PARA HANDY, M.D.

THE rain came down on Tarbert in a torrent. Dougie, while the cards were being shuffled and dealt again, put his head out by the scuttle, and looked up the deserted quay at the blurred lights of the village.

" What in the wide world are ye doin' there? " querulously demanded Para Handy. " If ye keep that scuttle open any longer we'll be swamped! Come in and take your hand; it's no' ke-hoi we're playin'."

" It's a desperate night," said Dougie, shivering in an atmosphere that, now the hatch was closed, was stuffier than that of an oven. " Rain even-on; ass black ass the Earl o' Mansfield's waistcoat, and nothin' stirrin' in the place but the smell o' frying herrin'."

" Herrin'! " exclaimed the Captain, starting to his feet, and slamming down his cards. " That puts me in mind I wass to caal the night on Eddie Macvean, the carter. I clean forgot! I'm sorry to leave ye, laads, but ye'll get your revenge to-morrow, maybe."

A minute later, and he was off the *Vital Spark*, with two-and-ninepence in his pocket, the total amount of gambling currency on the boat, not counting Dougie's lucky sixpence.

It was discovered by his shipmates, left behind, that the cards he had abandoned were " rags " without exception.

.   .   .   .

Macvean was apparently alone in his house when the Captain entered, sitting quite disconsolately by his fire, smoking.

" I wass up the toon for a message, Eddie," explained the visitor, " and I thocht I would gie ye a roar in the passin'. What way are ye keepin', this weather? "

" I canna compleen," replied the carter in a doleful tone, as if he bitterly regretted his obviously robust condition of health. " Are ye fine yoursel'? "

" What way iss the mustress? " politely continued the Captain. " I hope she's keepin' muddlin' weel."

Eddie Macvean sighed profoundly. " That's the
P 2

trouble in this hoose," he remarked; "there's no come and go in her. She's that dour! I got the finest offer o' a wee coal business in Lochgilphead, but she's that taken up wi' Tarbert for gaiety and the like, she'll no' hear tell o' flittin'."

"Chust that!" commented Para Handy sympathetically. "Did ye no' try coaxin' her?"

"It's no' the poker I would try wi' Liza Walker, you may be sure, Peter! I have been throng coaxin' her aal this week wi' that much patience ye would think I wass coortin', but she'll no budge! She says if I'm goin' to take her to Lochgilphead, it'll be in her coffin. Nothin' for her but gaiety! It's them Young Women's Guilds that's leadin' them off their feet!"

"Iss she oot at the Guild the night?" inquired the Captain, with a well-simulated air of regret at the lady's absence.

"No," said the husband sadly, "she's away to her bed wi' a tirravee of a temper."

There was a loud banging on the wall which divided the room of Macvean's house from the kitchen; he darted next door with significant alacrity, and was gone ten minutes.

"I canna make her oot at aal, at aal!" he remarked on returning. "She's tellin' me where I'll get clean stockin's for mysel', and to send oot a pair o' sheets she has in the bottom of the kist for manglin'."

"Iss she angry?" inquired Para Handy.

"That's the duvvelish thing aboot her noo," replied the distracted husband. "She's quite composed, and caalin' me Edward. She says I wass a good man to her nearly aal the time we were togither."

"God bless me!" exclaimed Para Handy, staggered.

" Ye should get the doctor. Never let the like o' that go too far! It might be something inward! "

There was another banging on the wall; Macvean went out again, and came back more confounded than ever.

" I never saw Liza in my life like that before! " he said. " She says she's quite resigned, and the only account against her iss a gallon of paraffin oil she got last Tuesday in the merchant's. I think she's kind o' dazed. She's wantin' a drink o' water."

" If I was you, Eddie, I would get the doctor," advised the Captain firmly. " Ye would be vexed if anything happened to her, and she died on ye in weather like this."

The carter returned from his wife's bedside with the empty cup and a look of greater anxiety.

" She says there's nothing wrong wi' her; no pain nor nothing, except that when she dovers over she dreams she's in Lochgilphead poorhouse, and wakens wi' a start. Her voice is aal away to a whisper. When I spoke aboot the doctor she said I wassna to let him in the door ass long ass she had aal her faculties. I'm to gie ye her best respects, and tell ye her faith wass aye in the Protestant releegion. ' Tell Captain Macfarlane,' she says, ' to be a sober man, and be good to his family.' "

" It's the munister she's needin', Eddie, or a drop o' spirits," said the Captain gravely, though a little annoyed at the imputation. " Slip you oot and rouse the munister; he'll be in his bed. Or, do ye think yoursel' ye would try the spirits first? "

But another knocking summoned the carter, who returned to the kitchen, weeping.

" There's something desperate wrong wi' Liza!" he blubbered; " she wants me to go round to the baker's shop and order a seed-cake."

" What for? " asked Para Handy, astonished.

" Goodness knows! " said Macvean; " the only seed-cake ever I saw wass at New Year or a funeral. I'm vexed I ever spoke about Lochgilphead! Do ye think yoursel' there is any danger, Peter? "

The Captain had no time to answer, for another knocking had called away his host, who returned in a little wringing his hands.

" There iss nothing for it but to go for the doctor," he said. " She's ramblin'; she says I'm to try and keep the hoose together, and no' pairt wi' her mother's sofa."

" I'll go ben and see her," said Para Handy.

An oil-lamp on the chimney-piece lit up the room where Mrs Macvean was lying. The Captain was surprised to find her looking remarkably well, with the hue of health on her face, though a little embarrassed by his unexpected appearance. She whipped off her nightcap.

" What way are ye keepin', Mrs Macvean? " he asked, in sympathetic tones.

The patient paid no heed to him, beyond putting up her hands to feel if her hair was tidy. In a feeble voice she remarked to her husband, " Edward, ye'll give my Sunday frock to Aunty Jennet, and my rings to Mary MacMillan; she wass kind, kind to me! "

" 'Dalmighty! " said the Captain, scratching his ear. " Do ye no' think the least wee drop o' spirits would lift ye, Liza? "

" Nothing 'll lift me noo but John Mackay, the

joiner," sobbed the patient. " Tell him to keep my heid away from them M'Callums when he's carryin' me doon the stairs. . . . And oh, Edward! " she continued, " I hope ye'll be happy in Lochgilphead, though it's a place I never cared for."

Her husband by now was prostrate with emotion, incapable of speech.

" Did ye order the seed-cake? " she asked.

" It's aal right aboot the seed-cake," broke in Para Handy. " Mrs Cleghorn, the baker's widow, iss takin' it in hand. I wudger ye she'll make a topper! She's terrible vexed to hear ye're poorly, and says ye're no' to bother. She's comin' in in the mornin' to make Eddie's breakfast."

Mrs Macvean at this sat up in bed with an amazing recovery of strength and speech, her visage purple with indignation.

" Comin' here! " she cried. " She'll no' put a leg inside this door if I can help it! I can see, noo, Edward, what ye're plottin'—to get me oot o' the road and mairry the bakehoose, but I'm no deid yet! It's only you and your Lochgilphead——"

" It's aal right aboot Lochgilphead, Liza," said the Captain soothingly. " Edward's changed his mind; he's goin' to cairry on in Tarbert."

" Cairry on! " exclaimed the wife. " He'll no' cairry on wi' Susan Cleghorn anyway, and I'm goin' wi' him to Lochgilphead. If he had chust asked me the right way, I would be quite agreeable from the start. Away oot o' this, the pair o' ye, till I get on my garments! "

XXV

A DOUBLE LIFE

" PHILANDERIN'; what in the world's philanderin'? " inquired Dougie, honestly eager for the definition of a word which Macphail the engineer had recently learned from a Blue Bell novelette, and was apt to drag into every conversation about the female sex.

" It's the same as flirtin', but fancier, if ye follow me," replied Macphail. " Many a chap starts flirtin' jist to pass the time and get the name o' being a regular teaser, and finds himsel' married withoot knowin' hoo the devil it happened to him. A philanderer's different. He has a' his wits aboot him and doesna mak' a pet o' any woman in particular. He'll have half a dozen o' them knittin' socks for him at the same time in different localities, but the last thing he would think o' wastin' money on would be a bride's-cake. There's no philanderers in lodgin's; they're all supportin' poor old mothers."

" The best philanderer I ever kent," said Para Handy, " wass Hurricane Jeck. He wass a don at it when he wass younger. He would cairry on wi' a whole Dorcas meetin' if they didna crood roond him aal at wance. Ye never saw a more nimble fellow, and there he iss—no' married yet, nor showin' any signs o't."

" Hurricane Jeck's no' my notion o' a proper philanderer," commented the engineer with some acidity. " He hasna the knowledge for't—a chap that never opens a book! "

" There's no books needed," retorted the Captain.

" Jeck had the gift by nature. I'm speakin' o' the time before he went sailin' foreign, when he had his whuskers. We were on the *Mary Jane* thegither, and faith I wasna slack mysel', though I never had his agility. He wass ass smert ass salt on a sore finger. There wassna a port inside o' Paddy's Milestone where Jeck wass not ass welcome wi' the girls ass Royal Cherlie! But I can tell ye it took some management!

" I mind that wan time Jeck got into a nesty habble wi' a couple o' girls in Gleska.

" He wass very chief at the time wi' a young weedow wife in Oban that had a pickle money o' her own. If Jeck wass not a rover he would have merried her, for she was a fine big bouncin' woman quite suitable for a sailor, but he couldna make up his mind between her and a girl called Lucy Cameron he wass walkin' oot wi' any time the vessel wass in Gleska.

" Wan time yonder when the *Mary Jane* wass in Oban the weedow trysted Jeck to take her to the Mull and Iona Soirée, Concert, and Ball in the Waterloo Rooms in Gleska. Jeck wass always the perfect chentleman; he would promise anything if it wassna that week.

" The night o' the Mull and Iona Gaitherin' came on, and Jeck clean forgot his engagement wi' Mrs Maclachlan. That very night he was booked for Hengler's Circus wi' Lucy Cameron. It wassna till the weedow came to his lodgin's in a cab, wi' a fine new pair o' white kid gloves for him and a flooer for his button-hole, that the poor chap minded o' his promise.

" A lad less nimble in his wits would have thocht the poseetion hopeless, but Jeck wassna so easy daunted. Though he wass dressed aal ready for the Circus, he went to the Mull and Iona, clapped Mrs Maclachlan doon among a wheen o' freen's o' hers from Tobermory chust before the soirée started; took a bloodin' nose, by his way of it, and wass oot in the street again in a jeffy, skelpin' it for Lucy Cameron's."

" Wasn't that the rogue? " exclaimed Dougie admiringly.

" When the Mull and Iona wass singin' the chorus o' Farewell to Fuinary, or maybe aboot the time the orangers wass passin' roond in the Waterloo Rooms, Jeck wass sittin' across the street in Hengler's wi' Lucy Cameron, clappin' his hands at my namesake, Handy Andy the clown.

" Every noo and then he would take oot his watch when Lucy wassna lookin', and calculate hoo far the Mull and Iona folk would be in their programme, and in twenty meenutes his nose began to blood again.

" ' Beg pardon! ' says Jeck—for he was aalways the perfect chentleman—' but I'll have to go oot a meenute for a key to put doon my back.' And away he went like the wind across the street to the Waterloo Rooms.

" He was chust in time for the start o' the Grand March.

" ' Are ye better? ' asked the weedow, quite anxious, never jalousin' Jeck wass a fair deceiver.

" ' Tip-top! ' says Jeck, and into the Grand March wi' her like a trumpeter. It wass chenerally allooed there wassna a handsomer couple on the floor. He feenished Triumph wi' the weedow, saw her settled wi' another pairtner for Petronella, and then skipped like a goat across to Hengler's. Little did Lucy Cameron ken her lad wass at the dancin'!

" Every twenty meenutes Jeck wass oot o' the circus

HURRICANE JACK OF THE *VITAL SPARK*   449

on some excuse or other, and puttin' in a dance wi' the Oban weedow, then back again to Lucy. He wass so busy between the two o' them he couldna even get a drink, and at the Mull and Iona his condeetion was noticed. At the circus Lucy wass wonderin' too, for he aye came back wi' an oranger, or a poke o' sweeties from the baal, and a smell o' lavender, but as right as a Rechabite.

" For four mortal oors Jeck ran the ferry this way; when the circus wass feenished he took Miss Cameron home, and then back to the Waterloo Rooms, where he made a night o't.

" He told me aal aboot it himsel' next day. ' If I hadna my health, Peter,' he said, ' I couldna do it. And the dash thing iss they're both fine girls! I wass nearly poppin' the question to Lucy, and Mrs Maclachlan wass most attractive.'

" The thing would have passed aal right if it wassna that the ' Oban Times ' next week gave an account o' the Mull and Iona, wi' Jeck's name among the chentlemen that wass present, and Lucy saw it. She wass desperate angry!

" Jeck denied it; said it wass aalthegither a mistake; that somebody must have been tradin' on his reputation; but Lucy's mother had a lodger in the polis force that made an investigation, and it wass all up wi' poor Jeck and the Cameron family.

"And it didna stop there neither, for the polisman informed the Oban weedow the way Jeck had been cairryin' on, and the next time Jeck made a caal on her in Oban to clinch things for a merrage, Mrs Maclachlan wouldna speak to him."

" That shows ye," said the engineer, " that he wasna a rale philanderer; a philanderer's never found oot."

XXVI

THE WET MAN OF MUSCADALE

" Talkin' aboot the health," said Para Handy, " the drollest man I ever saw that made a hobby o' his health wass a pairty in Muscadale caaled the Wet Man."

" What in the name o' goodness did they caal him that for? " asked the mate.

" Chust because he wass never dry," replied the Captain. " He went aboot damp for forty years, and would be livin' yet if it wassna for the doctors. They took him to a cottage hospital in Campbeltoon, dried his clo'es on him, and packed him in a bed wi' hot-water bottles. He drank every drop that wass in the bottles before the mornin', and efter that they wouldna gie him any more, so he withered like the rose o' Sharon in the Scruptures. Died o' drooth, like a geranium in a flooer-pot! He wass over ninety years o' age, wi' aal his faculties aboot him till the end, and never used a towel."

" My goodness! " exclaimed the mate.

" Many a time I'll be thinkin'," said Para Handy, " that the man in Muscadale wass born a bit before his time. If he wass spared another fifty years the world would see there iss a lot o' nonsense aboot science and the droggists' shops, and that long life iss aal a maitter o' moisture."

" If bein' wet would keep us healthy," interjected Macphail the engineer, " we would never dee at a' in the West Coast shippin' tred."

" There iss a lot o' rubbidge talked regairdin' damp,"
continued the Captain. " Colin MacClure in Muscadale proved it. He wass fifty years o' age when he
took a desperate cold that he couldna get rid o' till he
fell wan day in the watter in the Sound o' Jura, and
when they fished him oot he hadna a vestige. A
chrechlin' cough he had wass gone completely.

" From that day he wass a changed man, and pinned
his faith in watter, ootside and in. He couldna pass a
pump-well withoot a swig at it, and when any other
fisherman would be takin' a Chrustian dram in
moderation wi' his frien's, nothin' but a barrel and a
bailin'-dish would serve the Wet Man o' Muscadale."

" Issn't that chust duvvelish! " exclaimed Dougie.
" I would say there iss nothing worse for a man's inside
than watter; look at the way it rots your boots! "

" He got heavy, heavy on the watter; aye nip-nippin'
at it when he thocht that nobody wass lookin'. Many
a time his wife—poor body!—had to go and look for
him at the river-side and bring him home."

" I can take a little watter in moderation," said the
mate; " a drop o't in your tea does herm to nobody,
but it's ruinaation to be always tipplin' at it."

" It would be diabetes," suggested the engineer.

" There wassna a diabete in Colin's composeetion,"
said the Captain. " His constitution wass grand. He
could eat tackets and sleep like a babe on a slab o'
granite. A big bold healthy fisherman wi' a noble
whusker on him!—wan o' the chenuine old MacClures
that's in the ' History o' the Clans.' If there wass any
germs o' any kind in the Wet Man o' Muscadale they
would need to wear life-belts. The only time that
Colin wass in danger for his health was in frosty

weather; he would get ass hard then ass a curlin'-stone, and the least bit jar against the corner o' a hoose would knock a chip off him.

" ' Be wet and ye'll be weel! ' wass Colin's motto; he could prove it wi' the Bible. ' Noah,' he would say, ' made a fair hash o' the business in landin' on Ben Ararat; if it wassna for that, we would be sweemin' aboot the deep the day like fishes, in the best o' health and trum, and no need for your panel doctors. Ye never heard o' a herrin' yet that had lumbago.'

" From the day that he wass picked oot o' the Sound o' Jura, he never let his clo'es dry on his back for fear o' trouble, and the very sight o' a dry shirt on a washin'-green would make him shiver. He wass the wan man in Scotland ye would find lamentin' if it wassna rainin'. Colin's notion o' comfort wass a good big hole in the roof o' the hoose, a dub on the hearth, a thin alpaca jecket stickin' to his ribs, all plashin', and his sea-boots full o' watter."

" Did he no' get rheumatism? " inquired the mate, astounded.

" Not him! He wass ass flippant on his feet ass an Irish ragman, and never spent a penny on his health till the day they buried him. He cairried his notion to a redeeculous degree, for he was staunch teetotal."

" If he was livin' the day he would get a' the watter he needed in half a mutchkin," suggested the engineer cynically.

" That wouldna do for the Wet Man o' Muscadale," said the Captain. " Ye see, he had to be wet ootside ass well ass in. Many a sore trauchle his wife had wettin' him wi' a watterin'-can in the summer, the same's he wass a bed o' syboes. She wass a poor wee cricket o' a low-country woman, and darena even dry the blankets efter washin' them for fear that Colin would get a cold. On their golden weddin' day she said to a neebour, ' Bonny on the golden weddin'! My man's yonder sittin' on the ebb and steepin' like a lump o' dulse.'

" The Wet Man thrived so weel on the watter treatment that a lot o' the folk in the countryside aboot began to follow his example, and then nothin' would do for Colin but to start a new releegion. At first he thocht, himsel', o' joinin' the Baptists, thinkin' that the Baptist churches had a pond in them the same ass the Greenheid Baths in Gleska, but when he heard that the Baptists only got a splash in a kind o' boyne and then came oot and dried themsel's, he wass fair disgusted.

" ' They're chust a lot o' back-sliders," he says; ' they havena the fundamentals o' releegion in them! ' So he started a body o' his own they caaled the Mac-Clurites. The other denominations gave them the by-name o' the Muscadale Dookers, and they suffered a lot o' persecution, them bein' so close on Campbeltoon. The MacClurites never used oilskins nor umberellas; they're tellin' me the second cheneration o' them had web feet and feathers on them chust like jucks.

" The MacClurites quarrelled among themsel's aboot the doctrine; some sayin' salt watter wasna the naitural element o' salvaation, and others that ye werena proper wet unless ye fell in the Sound o' Jura. It clean broke up the MacClurites, and they aal went back to the Wee Free Church ass dry ass anything, and died in the prime o' life at seventy or eighty.

" But Colin MacClure never flinched nor bowed the

knee to Ramoth-Gilead. When the laird put rhones and a galvanised roof on his dwellin', he took his abode below high-water mark in a skiff turned upside doon that wass aalways flooded at every tide."

" He would be a' mildew," said the engineer.

" Fair blue-moulded!" said the Captain. " For fifty years the clo'es wass never dry on him; ye would think it wass gress wass growin' in his back, but he went aboot to the very last wi' wonderful agility. It is from scenes like them that Scotia's grandeur springs."

XXVII

INITIATION

THERE was absolutely nothing to do to pass the time till six o'clock, and Hurricane Jack, whose capacity for sleep under any circumstances and at any hour of the day or night was the envy of his shipmates, stretched himself out on the hatches with a fragment of tarpaulin over him. In about two seconds he was apparently dreaming of old days in the China clipper trade, and giving a most realistic imitation of a regular snorter of a gale off the Ramariz.

" There's some people iss born lucky," remarked the Captain pathetically. " Jeck could go to sleep inside a pair o' bagpipes and a man playin' on them. It's the innocent mind o' him."

" It's no' the innocent mind o' him, whatever it iss," retorted Dougie with some acidity. " It's chust fair laziness; he canna be bothered standin' up and keepin' his eyes open. Ye're chust spoilin' him. That's what I'm tellin' ye! "

Para Handy flushed with annoyance. " Ye think I'm slack," he remarked; " but I'm firm enough wi' Jeck when there's any occasion. I sent him pretty smert for the milk this mornin', and him wantin' me to go mysel'. I let him see who wass skipper on this boat. A body would think you wass brocht up on a man-o'-war; ye would like to see me aye bullyin' the fellow. There's no herm in Jeck Maclachlan, and there iss not a nimbler sailor under the cope and canopy, in any shape or form! "

Dougie made no reply. He sat on an upturned bucket sewing a patch on the salient part of a pair of trousers with a sail-maker's needle.

" There ye are! " resumed the Captain. " Darnin' away at your clothes and them beyond redemption! Ye're losin' aal taste o' yoursel'; what ye're needin's new garments aalthegither. Could ye no', for goodness sake, buy a web o' homespun somewhere in the islands and make a bargain wi' a tyler? "

" Tylers! " exclaimed Dougie. " I might as weel put mysel' in the hands o' Rob Roy Macgregor! They're askin' £6, 10s. the suit, and it's extra for the trooser linin'."

Para Handy was staggered. He had bought no clothes himself since his marriage, and had failed to observe the extraordinary elevation in the cost of men's apparel.

" Holy Frost! " he cried. " That's a rent in itsel'! If that's the way o't, keep you on plyin' the needle, Dougie. It's terrible the price o' everything nooadays. I think, mysel', it's a sign o' something goin' to happen.

It runs in my mind there wass something aboot that in the Book o' Revelations. I only paid £2, 10s. for a capital pilot suit the year I joined the Rechabites."

The mate suspended his sewing, and looked up suspiciously at the skipper.

" It's the first time ever I heard ye were in the Rechabites," he remarked significantly. " Hoo long were ye in them? "

" Nearly a week," replied Para Handy, " and I came oot o' them wi' flyin' colours at the start o' the Tarbert Fair. It wass aal a mistake, Dougie; the tyler at the time in Tarbert took advantage o' me. A fisherman by the name o' Colin Macleod from Minard and me wass very chief at that time, and he wass a Freemason. He would aye be givin' grips and makin' signs to ye. By his way o't a sailor that had the grip could trevel the world and find good company wherever he went, even if he didna ken the language.

" Colin wass high up in the Freemasons; when he had all his medals and brooches on he looked like a champion Hielan' dancer.

" He wass keen, keen for me to join the craft and be a reg'lar chentleman, and at last I thocht to mysel' it would be a great advantage.

" ' Where will I join? ' I asked him.

" ' Ye'll join in Tarbert; there's no' a Lodge in the realm o' Scotland more complete,' says Colin. 'And the first thing ye'll do, ye'll go up and see my cousin the tyler; he'll gie ye a lot o' preluminary instruction.'

" The very next time I wass in Tarbert I went to the tyler right enough for the preluminaries.

" ' I wass thinkin' o' joinin' the Lodge,' I says to him, ' and Colin Macleod iss tellin' me ye're in a poseetion to gie me a lot o' tips to start wi'. What clothes will I need the night o' the meetin'? '

" He was a big soft-lookin' lump o' a man, the tyler, wi' a smell o' singed cloth aboot him, and the front o' his jecket aal stuck over wi' pins; and I'll assure ye he gave me the he'rty welcome.

" ' Ye couldna come to a better quarter! ' he says to me, ' and it'll no' take me long to put ye through your facin's. There's a Lodge on Friday, and by that time ye'll be perfect. Of course, ye'll have the proper garments? '

" ' What kind o' garments? ' says I. ' I have nothing at aal but what I'm wearin'; my Sabbath clothes iss all in Gleska.'

" ' Tut! tut! ' says he, quite vexed. ' Ye couldna get into a Lodge wi' clothes like that; ye'll need a wise-like suit if ye're to join the brethren in Tarbert. But I can put ye right in half a jiffy.'

" He jumped the counter like a hare, made a grab at a pile o' cloth that wass behind me, hauled oot a web o' blue-pilot stuff, and slapped it on a chair.

" ' There's the very ticket for ye! ' he says, triumphant. ' Wi' a suit o' that ye'll be the perfect chentleman! '

" I wassna needin' clothes at aal, but before I could open my mouth to say Jeck Robe'son he had the tape on me. Noo there's something aboot a tyler's tape that aye puts me in a commotion, and I lose my wits.

" He had the measure o' my chest in the time ye wud gut a herrin', and wass roond at my back before I could turn mysel' to see what he wass up to. ' Forty-two; twenty-three,' he bawls, and puts it in a ledger.

" He wass on to me again wi' his tape, like a flash

o' lightnin'; pulled the jecket nearly off my back and took the length o' my waistcoat, and oh! my goodness, but he smelt o' Harris tweed, and it damp, singein'!

" ' Hold up your arm! ' says he, and he took the sleeve-length wi' a flourish, and aal the time he wass tellin' me what a capital Lodge was the Tarbert one, and aboot the staunchness o' the brethren.

" ' Ye'll find us a lot o' cheery chaps,' he says; ' there's often singin'. But ye'll have to come at first deid sober, for they're duvvelish particular.'

" By this time he wass doon aboot my legs, and the tape wass whippin' aal aboot me like an Irish halyard. I wass that vexed I had entered his shop withoot a dram, for if I had a dram it wasna a tyler's tape that Peter Macfarlane would flinch for.

" By the time he had aal my dimensions, fore and aft, in his wee bit ledger, I wass in a perspiration, and I didna care if he measured me for a lady's dolman.

" ' Do ye need to do this every time? ' I asked him, put aboot tremendous.

" ' Do what? ' says the tyler.

" ' Go over me wi' a tape,' says I.

" ' Not at aal,' he says, quite he'rty, laughin'. ' It's only for the first initiation that ye need consider your appearance. Later on, no doot, ye'll need regalia, and I can put ye richt there too.'

" ' It's only the first degree I'm wantin' to start wi','
I says to him; ' I want to see if my health 'll stand it.'

" ' Tach! ' says the tyler; ' ye'll get aal that's goin' at the wan go-off. There's no shilly-shallyin' about oor Lodge in Tarbert. Come up to the shop to-morrow, and I'll gie the first fit on.'

" I went to him next day in the afternoon, and ye

never in aal your life saw such a performance! The tape wass nothin' to't! He put on me bits o' jeckets and weskits tacked thegither, withoot any sign o' sleeves or buttons on them; filled his mooth to the brim wi' pins, and started jaggin' them into me.

" ' Mind it's only the first degree! ' I cries to him. ' Ye maybe think I'm strong, but I'm no' that strong! '

" Him bein' full o' pins, I couldna make oot wan word he wass mumblin', but I gaithered he wass tellin' me something aboot the grips and password. And then he fair lost his heid! He took a lump of chalk and began to make a regular cod o' my jecket and weskit.

" ' Stop! Stop! ' I cries to him. ' I wass aye kind o' dubious aboot Freemasons, and if I'm to wear a parapharnalia o' this kind, all made up o' patches pinned thegither, and chalked aal o'er like the start o' a game o' peever, I'm no' goin' to join! '

" The tyler gave a start. ' My goodness! ' he says, ' it's no' the Freemasons ye were wantin' to join? '

" ' That wass my intention,' I told him. ' And Colin said his cousin the tyler in Tarbert wass the very man to help me. That's the way I'm here.'

" ' Isn't that chust deplorable! ' says the tyler, scratchin' his heid. ' Ye're in the wrong shop aal-thegither! The tyler o' the Mason's Lodge in Tarbert's another man aalthegither, that stands at the door o' his Lodge to get the password. I'm no' a Mason at aal; I'm the treasurer o' the Rechabites.'

" ' The Rechabites! ' says I, horror-struck. ' Aren't they teetotal? '

" ' Strict! ' he says. ' Ye canna get over that—to start wi'. And ye're chust ass good ass a full-blown

Rechabite noo, for I've given ye aal I ken in the way
o' secrets.'

" So that's the way I wass a Rechabite, Dougie. I
wass staunch to the brethren for seven days, and then
I fair put an end to't. I never went near their Lodge,
but the suit o' clothes came doon to the vessel for me,
wi' a wee boy for the money. It wass £2, 10s., and I
have the weskit yet."

" £2, 10s. and aal that sport! " said Dougie ruefully.
" Them wass the happy days! "

XXVIII

THE END OF THE WORLD

" WHEN men gets up in years—say aboot eighty or
ninety—there should be something done wi' them,"
said Para Handy.

" What in the world would ye do wi' them? " asked
Dougie. " Ye darena wander them."

" Ye canna wander them nooadays; the Government iss watchin' them like hawks, and, anyway,
they'll never venture half a mile from the Post Office
where they get their Old Age Pensions. I would put
them aal oot on the island o' St Kilda, wi' a man in
cherge. Any old man of ninety that wass dour and
dismal I would ship him yonder wi' aal his parapharnalia. I'm no sayin' but here and there ye'll find
an old chap worth his keep—chust as jolly and full o'
mischief as if he wass a young man, but most o' them's
a tribulation to their frien's, and always interferin'.
Hurricane Jeck could tell ye."

The Captain's startling scheme for dealing with nonagenarians originated in a conversation on longevity among the people of Arran.

" Jeck," he continued, " had his life fair spoiled on him wi' an uncle he had in Govan. He wass ninety-two if he wass a day, but wasna pleased wi' that; he would aye be braggin' that he wass a hundred. He lived by himsel' in a but-and-ben, and he made poor Hurricane's life a torment.

" Jeck at the time wass in his prime, and sailin' back and forrit, skipper o' a nice wee boat they caaled the *Jenet*. It wass years before he started goin' foreign. A more becomin' man on a quay ye never clapped an eye on—ass trig's a shippin'-box, and always wi' a nate wee roond broon hat.

" His Uncle Wilyum wass a tyrant. In his time he wass a landscape gairdner——"

" What iss a landscape gairdner? " asked Dougie.

" A landscape gairnder iss a man that scapes gairdens. . . . But for twenty years old Wilyum lived on his money and spent his time contrivin' what way he would make his nephew Jeck a credit to the Second Comin' and the family o' Maclachlan.

" He had every failin' that a man could have, Uncle Wilyum—he wass lame wi' rheumatism, as deaf's a post, teetotal to the worst degree, and never went to church but made a patent kind o' releegion o' his own oot o' the ' Christian Herald ' and the ' Gospel Trumpet.' Chust an old pagan! Ye would be sick listenin' to him on the prophet Jeremiah and the Second Comin' and the opening o' Baxter's Seven Phials."

" Whatna man was Baxter? " inquired the mate.

" Chust Baxter! " replied Para Handy petulantly. " The man that wass a prophet and wrote the ' Christian Herald.'

" Nobody could be nicer to an uncle up in years than Jeck. Many a firkin o' herrin' and scores o' eggs he brocht from the Hielan's for the old chap. He wass his only livin' relative except a sister o' his that lived in Colonsay, and any money that the old man left wass likely to be Jeck's.

" Money wass the last thing Jeck at the time had his mind on; he wass a born rover that asked for nothing better than to dodge aboot the Western Hielan's in his own dacent boat, or go percolatin' roond the Broomielaw wi' a cheery frien' or two when his vessel wass in Clyde.

" There wass no more harm in Jeck than in a goldfish, but the silly old body thocht he was a limb o' Satan, and never missed a chance to board him wi' a bundle o' tracts. Jeck had no sooner his foot on shore in Gleska than Uncle Wilyum, wi' his sticks, would hirple up and follow him every place he went to keep him oot o' temptation.

" He put the peter on't at last wan time he went efter Jeck to the Oban and Lorn Soirée and Ball in the Waterloo Rooms, and found him wi' a clove hitch round the waist o' a bouncin' girl and them throng waltzin'.

" I can tell you Jeck got Jeremiah from his Uncle Wilyum that night!

" ' The like o' you dancin' there wi' a wanton woman, and us on the verge! ' says the old chap, groanin'.

" ' What verge? ' says Jeck.

" ' Did ye no' hear? ' says his uncle, lookin' fearful unsatisfactory.

" ' No,' says Jeck,

" ' That's what I wass thinkin',' says his uncle, whippin' oot a ' Christian Herald,' and showin' him a bit o' Baxter that said the end o' the world wass fixed for that day fortnight.

" ' Chust that! ' says Jeck. ' I heard a kind o' rumour aboot it doon at Greenock; but I'm no' botherin', for I'm goin' to take the boat for't when the time comes.'

" My goodness, but the old man wass staggered! It had never entered his head to take to the sea for't when the end o' the world came, and he cocked his ears when he heard that Jeck wass goin' to get the better o' the Prophet Baxter wi' the *Jenet*.

" ' Will ye take me wi' ye? ' he says to his nephew.

" ' Wi' aal the pleesure in the world,' says Jeck, who wass aye the perfect chentleman. ' Get you your bits o' sticks collected; we'll put them in the hold for broken stowage, and ye'll come wi' me on Wednesday. We'll be roond the Mull before the trouble breaks oot.'

" Jeck wass only in fun, and you can imagine his consternation when a lorry came doon to his boat next day wi' aal Uncle Wilyum's plenishin', and the old man on the top o' a chest o' drawers wi' a bundle o' Baxter's prophecies!

" There's one thing aboot Jeck—he's never bate!

" He took the old man on board wi' all his dunnage, and started oot for Colonsay, where he wass takin' coals.

" It was the dreariest trip he ever made in aal his life; for when the old man wassna takin' his meat or sleepin', he wass greetin' aboot the end o' aal things and swabbin' his heid-lights even-on wi' a red bandana hanky, or groanin' over the ' Christian Herald.'

" ' Tach! I wouldna bother aboot the Prophet Baxter,' says Jeck to him at last. ' Perhaps he wass workin' wi' a last year's almanack, and fairly oot o't wi' his calculations.'

" But Uncle Wilyum said that wass blasphemy, and kept on reelin' oot fathoms o' Jeremiah, till poor Jeck wass near demented.

" ' What place iss this? ' says Uncle Wilyum when they came to Colonsay, and Jeck began dischairgin' coal.

" ' It's the end o' the world,' says Jeck, quite blithe. ' Away you ashore and see your sister Mary, and I'll send up your furniture ass soon ass the coals iss done.'

" ' For aal the time we have thegither,' wailed his Uncle Wilyum, ' is it worth my while? '

" ' Worth your while! ' cried Jeck. ' Of course it's worth your while! I'll bate ye Baxter never heard o' the Isle o' Colonsay. It's forty years since ye saw your sister. Away and spend your money on her like a chentleman.'

" Uncle Wilyum went ashore wi' his bundle o' the prophets, and settled down wi' his sister, waitin' for the day o' tribulation. He lingered seven years, and shaved himsel' every mornin', so as to be ready; but Baxter failed him at the last, and he died o' influenza, leavin' his pickle money to his sister."

" That wass a pity for Jeck," said Dougie.

" Tach! Jeck didna care a docken! He wass enjoyin' life."

XXIX

THE CAPTURED CANNON

As soon as it grew dark, when the quay was quite deserted and the village seemed wholly asleep, the crew of the *Vital Spark* set briskly about getting the gun ashore.

They passed two unrailed gang-planks between the vessel and the slip, took the tarpaulins off the mysterious mass of inert material at the bow and revealed a German 18-pounder, without its breech-block, exceedingly battered and rusty. Hurricane Jack fastened a stout rope to the gun itself, and going behind lifted up the trail of the carriage with an effort.

" Tail you on to the rope and pull like bleezes," he cried to Dougie; " Macphail and Peter 'll shove roond the wheels o' her, and I'll hold up this cursed contrivance. . . . Aalthegither, boys; heave! "

Para Handy took up the task allotted to him, almost weeping. " Holy Frost! " he wailed; " isn't this the bonny habble we're in? I wish we had never seen the blasted thing; it's aal your fault, Jeck."

" There'll be trouble aboot this, you'll see! " said Macphail, putting all his propulsive vigour into a wheel spoke. " I knew from the beginnin'. But ye wouldna listen to me! "

" Shut up, and haul like Horse Artillery! " growled Hurricane Jack. " Ye're no' in the Milishy."

By almost superhuman efforts they got the gun on to the slip, and up to the level of the wharf.

" What are we to do noo? " panted the Captain.
" We canna leave it here; mind you, it's no' Crarae;
there's a polisman in the place."

" We'll hurl it doon the quay and oot on the ebb,"
said Hurricane Jack with confidence and alacrity. " Ye
can put anything ye like under high-water-mark,
there's no law against it. If we get it oot on the ebb
noo it'll be covered wi' the tide afore the mornin',"
and he picked up the trail again.

They trundled the piece noisily over the granite pier,
perspiring at the task; the weapon had never heard
such lurid language in the process since it left the
Hindenburg Line.

" If anybody catches us at this! " moaned Dougie
apprehensively, blowing like a whale.

They were just on the verge of the sand when
Macnaughton appeared in his official glazed tippet, but
without his helmet. He had just been making his last
round for the night.

" What in the name o' goodness are ye doin' here? "
he inquired sternly. " Whose cairt have ye there? "

" It's no' a cairt," said Hurricane Jack, letting down
the trail. " It's a quite good cannon the War Office
sent for a War Memorial for the place. We're jist
dischargin' it."

" Dischargin' it! " exclaimed the constable, horrified; " ye'll waken the whole community! " He came
closer, peered in the dark at the weapon, and had a
sudden inspiration.

" I know your capers fine! " he exclaimed, throwing
back his tippet to show his metal buttons. " We're
no' that far behind in this place but we ken aboot
that gun; it's the hue and cry o' the county."

" What did ye hear aboot it? " asked Hurricane Jack, coolly taking a seat on the carriage.

" I have it aal here in my book," said the constable, slapping his tail-pocket. " I might have ken't when I saw your boat come in this efternoon wi' a tarp'lin over the bows o' her, that you were up to some o' your dydoes. Ye got the gun from a hawker in Lochgilphead."

" Right enough! " acknowledged the Captain soothingly. " But it wass his own gun; the burgh that got it from the War Office for a souvineer got sick o't, and gave him't for old metal."

" We took it for a speculation," added Hurricane Jack. " Ye would think there's many a place in Loch Fyne would like a chenuine German cannon."

" We were goin' to make oor fortune wi't," said Macphail, with bitter sarcasm. " Jeck assured us there was money in't."

" I ken aal aboot it," said the constable, with an air of profound omniscience. " Ye've been cairryin' that lumber up and doon the loch for the last three weeks tryin' to palm it off on His Majesty's lieges. It's aal in my book! Ye offered it for a pound in Cairndow; the price wass down to ten shillin's at Strachur; ye couldna sell't for a shillin' in Crarae, and ye left it on the quay there, but they made ye shift it."

" It's the God's truth—every word o't," confessed Hurricane Jack. " A German cannon's worse than a drunken reputation; ye canna get rid o't."

The crew of the *Vital Spark* stood in the rain and dark round the degraded and rejected relic of Imperial power, and violently abused Jack.

" A bloomin' eediot! I told him it would be left

on oor hands!" cried Macphail. "Whit could ony-body dae wi' a cannon?"

"There might be another war at any time," suggested Hurricane Jack defensively.

"I never wass ass black affronted in my life," bleated Para Handy. "The whole loch-side iss laughin' at us. The very turbine steamers blows their whistles when they pass and cry '*Hood*, ahoy!' It's no' like a thing ye could break in bits and burn in Macphail's furnace; it's solid iron in every pairt. Nobody hass a kind word for it; we tried to get a minister to put it in his glebe, or fornent the door o' his manse, and he put his dog on us."

"Ye'll take it oot o' here anyway," said the constable firmly. "We have plenty o' trash o' oor own. It's a mercy I came on ye tryin' to leave it here and spoil the navigation!"

"I never dreamt that a gun wass so ill to manœuvre," remarked the imperturbable Jack. "Do ye no' think, sergeant, there's anybody in the place would care for it for an ornament? Anybody wi' a bit o' a gairden: they could cover it wi' fuchsias."

"No expense at aal!" added Para Handy eagerly. "We would put it in poseetion. Many a wan would be gled to have it if it wass in London or in Gleska. It's a splendid cannon! Captured by the Australian Airmy. Cost the British Government £50 to take to Loch Fyne."

"I don't care if it cost £100," said the constable fiercely; "it's no' goin' to be palmed off on this community that suffered plenty wi' the war. Get it back on board your ship at wance, like dacent lads, and don't make any trouble."

" 'Dalmighty! " cried the Captain, wringing his hands, " are we goin' to have this Cherman abomination on oor decks the rest o' oor naitural lifes? . . . It's all your fault, Jeck, ye said there wass a fortune in it."

" My mistake! " admitted Hurricane Jack, most handsomely. " I wash my hands noo o' the whole concern."

" I would wash my hands too, if they werena aal blistered," said Dougie piteously. " What are we to do wi' the cursed thing? There iss no place we dare leave it."

" Could ye no' put it over the side o' the boat somewhere doon about Kilbrannan? " suggested the constable.

They stared at one another, utterly astounded.

" My Chove! " said Para Handy. " We never thocht o' that! Aren't you the born eediot, Jeck, that would have us cairtin' it up and doon the ocean for the last three weeks! "

" I didna want to see a good gun wasted," explained Hurricane Jack, rather lamely, and he picked up the trail again. " But maybe that's the best way oot o' the difficulty; get a ha'd o' the rope again, and pull, Dougie."

XXX

AN IDEAL JOB

As the *Vital Spark*, outrageously belching sparks and cinders from fuel eked out by wood purloined some days before from a cargo of pit-props, swept round the point of Row, Para Handy gazed with wonder and admiration at the Gareloch, full of idle ships.

" My word! " he exclaimed, " isn't that the splendid sight! Puts ye in mind o' a Royal Review! "

" I don't see onything Royal aboot it," growled the misanthropic engineer, Macphail. " It's a sign o' the terrible times we're livin' in. If there was freights for them boats, they wouldna be there, but dashin' roond the Horn and makin' work for people."

" Of course! Of course! You must aye be contrairy," said the Captain peevishly. " Nothing on earth 'll please you; ye're that parteecular. It's the way they chenerally make work for people that spoils ships for me. I like them best when they're at their moorin's. What more could ye want in the way o' a bonny spectacle than the sight o' aal them gallant vessels and them no' sailin'? "

Macphail snorted as he ducked his head and withdrew among his engines. " There's enough bonny spectacles on board this boat to do me for my lifetime," he said in a parting shot before he disappeared.

Para Handy turned sadly to the mate. " Macphail must aye have the last word," he said. " The man's no' worth payin' heed to. Greasin' bits o' enchines every day o' your life makes ye awfu' coorse. I'm sure that's a fine sight, them ships, Dougie? There must be nearly half a hundred there, and no' a lum reekin'."

" They're no bad," answered Dougie cautiously. " But some o' them's terrible in need o' a stroke o' paint. Will there be anybody stayin' on them? "

" Ye may depend on that! " the Captain assured him. " There iss a man or two in cherge o' every vessel, and maybe a wife and femily. The British Mercantile Marine iss no' leavin' ocean liners lyin' aboot Garelochheid wi' nobody watchin' them. A chentleman's life! It would suit me fine, instead o' plowterin' up and doon Loch Fyne wi' coals and timber. Did I no' tell ye the way Hurricane Jeck spent a twelvemonth on a boat laid up in the Gareloch when tred was dull aboot twenty years ago?"

" Ye did not!" said Dougie.

" She wass a great big whupper o' a barquenteen caaled the *Jean and Mary*, wi' a caibin the size o' a Wee Free Church, and fitted up like a pleesure yacht. She had even a pianna."

" God bless me!" gasped the mate, half incredulous.

" Jeck had the influence in them days, and he got the job to look efter her in the Gareloch till the times got better. The times wass good enough the way they were for Jeck, wance he had his dunnage on board. ' Never had a job to bate it! ' he says; ' I wouldna swap wi' the polisman in the Kelvingrove Museum.' "

" I would think he would be lonely," said Dougie dubiously. " A great big boat wi' nobody but yersel' in it at night would be awfu' eerie."

The Captain laughed uproariously. " Eerie!" he repeated. " There iss nothin' eerie any place where Hurricane Jeck iss; he had the time o' his life in the *Jean and Mary*.

" Wance they got their boat clapped doon in the Gareloch and Jeck in charge o' her, the chentlemen in Cardiff she belonged to forgot aal aboot her. At least they never bothered Jeck except wi' a postal-order every now and then for wages.

" The wages wassna desperate big, and Jeck put his

brains in steep to think oot some contrivance for makin'
a wee bit extra money.

" It came near the Gleska Fair, and there wassna a
but-and-ben in Garelochheid that wassna packed wi'
ludgers like a herrin'-firkin. When Jeck would be
ashore for paraffin-oil or anything, he would aye be
comin' on poor craturs wantin' ludgin's, so he filled the
Jean and Mary wi' a fine selection. For three or four
weeks the barquenteen wass like an hotel, or wan
o' them hydropathics. Jeck swithered aboot puttin'
up a sign to save him from goin' ashore to look for
customers.

" Ye never saw a ship like it in aal your life! It wass
hung from end to end wi' washin's aal July, and Jeck
gave ludgin's free to a man wi' a cornacopia that he
played on the deck from mornin' till night."

" Wass it no' a terrible risk? " asked Dougie.

" No risk o' any kind, at aal, at aal. The owners
wass in Cardiff spendin' their money, and they never
saw the Gareloch in their lifes but in the map. Jeck
kent he wass doin' a noble work for the health o' the
community—far better than the Fresh Air Fortnight!

" When the Fair wass feenished, and his ludgers went
away, I'll assure ye they left a bonny penny wi' the
landlord o' the *Jean and Mary*. He thocht the season
wass done, but it wasna a week till he wass throng again
wi' a lot o' genteel young divinity students that came
from Edinburgh wi' a banjo.

" ' Gie me a bottle o' beer and a banjo playin', and
it's wonderful the way the time slips by,' says Jeck.
He learned them a lot o' sailor songs like ' Ranza,
Boys! ' and ' Rollin' doon to Rio,' and the folk in
Garelochheid that couldna get their night's sleep came

oot at last in a fury to the ship and asked him who she belonged to.

" ' Ye can look Lloyd's List,' says Jeck to them, quite the chentleman, ' and ye'll see the name o' the owners. But she's under charter wi' a man that's aal for high jinks and the cheneral hilarity—and his name iss John Maclachlan. If there iss any o' ye needin' ludgin's, say the word and I'll put past a fine wee caibin for ye, wi' a southern exposure.'

" They went away wi' their heids in the air. ' I ken what's wrong wi' them,' says Jeck. ' Oh, man! if I chust had the spirit licence! '

" That wass his only tribulation: he had ass good an hotel below his feet as any in the country, but he daurna open a bar.

" The summer slipped by like a night at a weddin'; the cornacopia man went back to his work, but Jeck fell in wi' an old pianna-tuner that could play the pianna like a minister's wife, and aal the autumn Jeck gave smokin' concerts on the *Jean and Mary*, where all the folk in cherge o' the other vessels paid sixpence apiece and got a lot o' pleesure.

" ' If I had chust a brass band! ' says Jeck, ' and a wise-like man I could trust for a purser, I would run moonlight trips. But it would be an awful bother liftin' the anchor; perhaps I'm better the way I am; there's no' the responsibility wi' a boat at moorin's.'

" But the time he showed the best agility wass when he had a weddin' on the ship. The mate o' another vessel was gettin' spliced in his good-mother's hoose in Clynder, where there wasna room for dancin'.

" Jeck hired the *Jean and Mary* to them; the company came oot in boats from aal ends o' the Gareloch, wi' a couple o' pipers and that many roasted hens ye couldna get eggs in the shire for months efter it. They kept it up till the followin' efternoon, wi' the anchor lamp still burnin' and aal the buntin' in the vessel flyin'.

"A well-put-on young Englishman from Cardiff came alongside in a motor-lench in an awfu' fury, and bawled at Jeck what aal this carry-on meant. There wass sixty people on board if there wass a dozen.

"'Some frien's o' my own,' says Jeck, quite nimble, and aye the chentleman. 'I have chust come into a lot o' money, and I'm givin' them a trate.'

"But that was the last o' Jeck's command in the *Jean and Mary*; the poor duvvle had to go back and work at sailorin'."

Printed in Great Britain by
WILLIAM BLACKWOOD & SONS LTD.